HOU
Houston, James A.,
1921-

Running west

$19.95

DATE			

DO NOT REMOVE THIS CARD FROM POCKET

© THE BAKER & TAYLOR CO.

RUNNING WEST

Books by James Houston

RUNNING WEST
JAMES HOUSTON

CROWN PUBLISHERS, INC.
NEW YORK

Published by Crown Publishers, Inc.,
201 East 50th Street, New York, New York 10022
Originally published in Canada by McClelland & Stewart, Inc., in 1989.
CROWN is a trademark of Crown Publishers, Inc.
Manufactured in the United States of America
Library of Congress Cataloging-in-Publication Data
Houston, James A., 1921–
Running west: a novel/by James Houston.
p.   cm.
I. Title.
PR9199.3.H598R8   1989
813'.54—dc20
89-25156
CIP
ISBN 0-517-57732-1
10 9 8 7 6 5 4 3 2 1
First American Edition

TO THESE FRIENDS WITH GRATITUDE:

Norman Ross, a Hudson's Bay Company factor,
Ralph & Frederica Knight, Hudson's Bay Company,
Shirlee Smith, HBC-Manitoba Archives,
John Parker, Commissioner Northwest Territories,
Jimmy Cheechoo, Swampy Cree, James Bay,
Dr. Hamish W. McIntosh, Royal College of Physicians & Surgeons,
Douglas M. Gibson, Robert Emmett Ginna, Jr.,
Julian P. Muller, Rebecca Moniz.

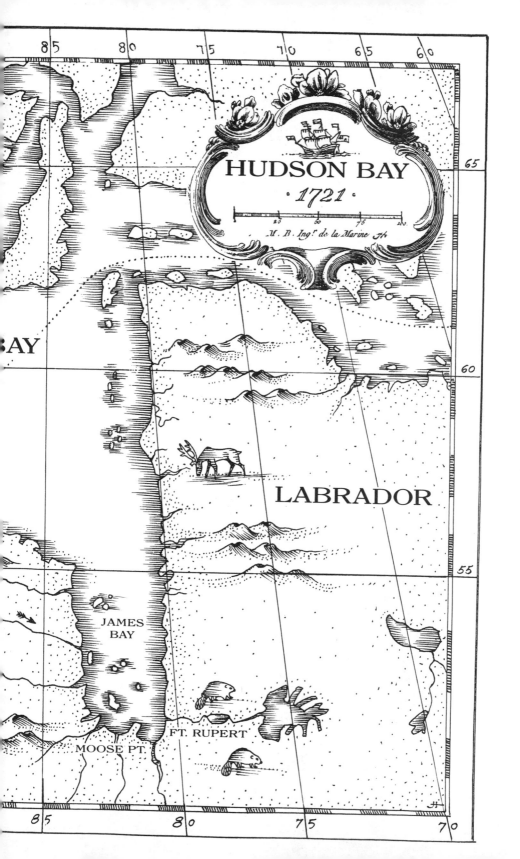

RUNNING WEST

WILLIAM

1

I, William Stewart, or you might spell that Stuart, if you wish, lay dreaming in the heather. In my mind's eye, I could see a naked lass with skin as smooth and white as cow's milk. She was kneeling in the flowering spring grasses, smiling and beckoning to me.

Just then, the guard's bullhide slipper nudged me and my cousin, Hamish. "Wake up, Willie, and help wee Angus catch the horses," he said in Gaelic.

I raised my head and in a panic searched the bracken. My milk-skinned lass was gone. In her stead, our laird James Stewart of Appin lay stretched out beside my friend, his son, Jamie. Near them sat the other guard, awake, and twenty-seven of our clansmen wrapped in their plaids, sleeping soundly. We returned with the two horses and squatted by the morning fire, as its smoke drifted slowly down the glen toward the massive granite shoulder of the mountain.

One by one our party rose, stretched, and stepped away to water the thistles. Each man returned and gnawed cold bannock with chunks of last night's mutton from the black iron pots, washing it down with icy water from the stream. Then we all set out together, only two ahorse and the rest of us walking in a clannie manner, not all clumped in close together like a clutch of English redcoats, but spread out loosely like well-seasoned fighting men. I walked beside the laird and Jamie. It was Wednesday, the 6th of June, 1714, and we were inspecting the borders of the Stewart Appin lands, establishing our clan territories by parading around the boundary in force. It was dangerous, mountainous country which was known to shelter Campbells and raggle-taggle bands of ruffians and broken men who had, for serious reasons, been driven from their clans.

Our laird James Stewart of Appin had planned to have his uncle, Douglas Stewart, escort his wife Lady Islay and her women on their journey north from Stalker's Keep. The plan was that our boatmen would row or sail up Loch Linnhe, bringing them to meet us at their hunting lodge. This had been a custom in the clan, whenever possible. After we finished our traditional feasting, the laird assured us that we would complete our beating of the Stewart borders before returning south.

As I and my fellow clansmen walked along the misty glens, I felt the spring sun warm my back. I thought of the two very different lives that I had lived, without having any say in either. My family came from a proud but penny-hungry branch of the Stewart clan. When I was very young, my father had hired me out as a shepherd boy, to help tend the laird's flocks. Three springs and summers I had spent wandering with sheep and dog on the grazing hills below Ben Vair. That loneliness had taught me independence from my family and the gentle ways of animals, as well as the awesome power of God's mountain storms.

Men in our family had always been tall and had for generations been recognized for their curious minds, strong backs, and sturdy climber's thighs. But by some miracle, it was said, my iron-rimmed mind was left ajar.

I had been given the gift of easily remembering almost every word or song I ever heard. For this reason, I was chosen by the laird to come and live at Stalker's Keep, where he had hired tutors from the continent to instruct his children. Jamie, his eldest son, was opposed to almost any kind of learning. The Stewart family hoped that my quick ways would challenge the young laird to pursue his studies much more vigorously. In fact, my sitting side by side with Jamie seemed to have just the opposite effect. The laird's son's true interests lay in more sensuous pleasures –

riding, dancing, perhaps a wee bit of fishing, gambling, and playing cock lane with young serving wenches, whenever he could catch one.

Herr Captain Hans von Cranach was our German swordmaster. He more than earned his pay, as did Monsieur Claude LeMoine, our language tutor. They both instructed me and Jamie, when they could. But he most often slipped away from them in hot pursuit of upstairs chambermaids, or, if that failed, he would go fishing trout or salmon in the loch. Mind you, I, myself, was very fond of fishing and of lassies, too. But I also much enjoyed the pleasures of learning. I was grateful to our French tutor, who was a highly skilled calligrapher. He taught me also the geography and history of the world and how to cut and wield a goose quill artfully, using graceful curlicues that would widen into manly strokes.

The laird had engaged the captain from Bavaria to teach his son and me the manly arts: horsemanship, physical exercise, swordplay, and the proper skills and use of other weapons. Monsieur LeMoine, a scholar from the university at Bordeaux, had been engaged to teach us French, Greek, Latin, logic, drawing, penmanship, and calculus.

During those rewarding students days, I studied, ate, and slept at Stalker's Keep. It was a somewhat small, steep-walled stone fortress that some said looked far more like a prison than a lordly dwelling. For its defense, it had been built upon a rocky isle just off the Appin coast in the west, north of the port of Oban. Alas, my place at the high end of the table with the laird, Lady Islay, and their family, demanded that I, too, affect the habits of my wealthy clan chief. I returned home to my family less and less. Once when I did, my grandfather heard me trying to teach my sister a few Latin phrases. He cursed me in the Gaelic tongue, accusing me of aping lordly ways. But he allowed me to return among those high-born Stewarts, so that I might improve my fortune.

In the glen I was jolted from my thoughts when Jamie's voice called back to me, "Willie, we can see the lodge."

When I reached the rise, I looked down toward the loch and I could see it and, as well, the laird's blue and yellow standards

---

blowing gently in the wind above the two slender long boats that had brought Lady Islay's party here.

As we rode down toward the hunting lodge, and we observed a piper marching to and fro, playing a favorite Stewart air. The doors of the lodge burst open and we saw Lady Islay and her four daughters, all as brightly clothed as bantam roosters, come running on the path toward us. They were surrounded by her staff of seamstresses, cooks, and housemaids, who were garbed as modestly as wrens.

We gave them all a great halloo, as our men hurried past them to their quarters to rest a while, then clean up to join the feast. I stayed with Jamie, and we two followed his father upstairs to dress.

Entering the main hall, we heard the Irish harper strumming in that joyful way of his that makes you tremble, makes you thrilled to be at such a feast. The laird and Lady Islay stepped to the high end of the table, where he spoke a prayer. Then we sat down in the soft glow of a hundred candles and devoured fresh-caught salmon and oysters from the sea, and hearty racks of mutton washed down with Scottish beers and foreign wines. I sat enchanted by the harper's magic and the sight of us all gathered at this grand table loaded with such plenty.

When the laird rose and held his crystal goblet high, the harping ended. He stood upon his chair and placed his right foot on the table. He toasted the Lord in Heaven, then our Scottish king in exile. He drank once more to all his gallant clansmen, and to his son, Jamie Stewart, who would one day, he prayed, become the laird of Appin. He drank a whiskey again to all the clan fold, weavers, crofters, shepherds, servants, and lastly to the health of all our Stewart sheep and cattle that grazed upon the Appin Hills.

Our laird, after so many toasts, became more excited than I'd ever seen him. He sent his piper marching around the table, skirling our famous Stewart challenge with his pibroch: "*Gabhaidh sin an rat had mor* – we will take the highway." When that was done, the laird ordered more strong beer for every one of those below the salt, while we few seated at the upper table shared the rich red wines and cognac brought from France. It was such a glorious evening that I could scarce remember going to bed.

When I did rise and go down for breakfast, I was surprised to see young Jamie and his father still sitting at the long table, sharing a mumbled conversation. The decanters were empty and the drinking goblets tipped asunder. Their piper, with his head upon the table, was still fast asleep.

When the laird's uncle, Douglas Stewart, came into the hall, he tried to speak to the two of them, but when they did not answer, he beckoned me to follow him.

"I fear the laird and Jamie will not sit ahorse today," he said, "so we must finish the beating of these borders for them. I'll have the groom saddle my horse and Jamie's horse for you. I'll send the gillies now to rouse the men. God willing, we'll only have to sleep out one more night before we're done. Get yourself ready, Willie. I don't like this shilly-shallying when there's work left to be done."

When we set out a wee bit later, the laird's uncle urged me up to ride beside him, for he wished to talk. He grumbled away to me as usual, as though we two were Stewarts of an equal rank. That had always been his style.

About midday, my head began clearing from the feast. We were leading our men through the narrowing end of the glen, when suddenly we surprised a marauding band of Campbells. They, like us, had only two men ahorse. Though I had never laid my eyes on either one of them before, I knew, by mere description, they must be Mad Duncan Campbell and his son.

Like the laird's uncle, I pretended to be steadying my horse, but in truth, like all our clansmen, I was craning my neck while trying to judge the Campbells' strength and numbers. They seemed to have only a dozen men afoot, and it was unlikely others would be trailing out of sight. That meant we had them outnumbered, more that two to one. Their laird, Mad Duncan Campbell, rode a big-boned chestnut stallion; his son, Ian, sat astride a bay mare. I studied both of them with care. As I had heard, Mad Duncan was indeed a huge and fearful-looking sight with his bushy mutton chops, blazing green eyes, and bristling mustache. His son, Ian, was a heavy-gutted, pig-eyed lad I judged to be a year or so my elder.

Our laird's uncle signaled to our men to spread out cautiously, each seeking his own advantage, easing up the hillside through the gorse. Dear God, it was exciting! Every Highlander, ours or theirs, had his hand clasped upon his sword. Our men waited eagerly to hear the uncle's battle cry that would send them screaming down upon the Campbells.

Mad Duncan stood high in his stirrups. I watched his fingers moving, tallying up our numbers, frowning as he saw that we outnumbered them and had gained the higher ground.

"We're not here for trouble," he called out to Douglas Stewart. "So stand well back, and we shall pass."

"Sheep stealer," the uncle growled at him. "Ye've no right to be here on our lands."

Duncan Campbell eyed him fiercely. "We are marching peaceably along this road to Loch Linnhe, and we'll not suffer any slurs or interference."

"Then turn yourself about," Douglas Stewart barked, "and get yer thieving arses back from whence ye came. We'll not have Campbells snatching sheep from off our pastures." Mad Duncan's face flared red.

I spurred my horse forward. "We know well why ye have come round about this way," I added in a voice high with excitement, "because you Campbells fear the ghosts of all those MacDonalds you so cruelly murdered at Glencoe."

Young Ian Campbell stood up in his stirrups, snatched off his leather gauntlet, and flung it on the ground in front of the horse that I was riding. Both our animals shied in fright as he yelled, "Whelp of a Stewart chief, I challenge you to fight, if you've the stomach for a duel."

I looked at Douglas Stewart. He stared at me, then shook his head.

But I was so carried away that I shouted, "Be damned to you! I accept your challenge!"

Mad Duncan looked at his son, his eyes brimming with pride, for he knew well that a duel would save them all from an out-numbered battle.

I would never have had the nerve to fight Mad Duncan. He seemed to have skin so leathery thick that I doubted any ball or broadsword blade would pierce his hide. He wore a Scot's bonnet on his head, a loose shirt of monkish gray with his dark green hunting plaid gathered helter-skelter round his ample belly and pinned high upon his shoulder. He had his trews tied battle-tight, with scarlet ribbons fluttering at his knees.

Mad Duncan Campbell had gained his frightful reputation during a bitter duel with broadswords and dirks against Donald MacDonald, a fiery-tempered Glencoe chief. At first, the watchers said, Mad Duncan held the upper hand, and it had seemed that he would surely win, when suddenly the MacDonald chieftain had the luck to strike the blade off Campbell's sword, then knocked away his dirk. Mad Duncan managed to twist and dodge until he saw the chance, then lunging forward, he grasped MacDonald by both wrists. Because he dared not release his enemy's hands, both of which still held weapons, Mad Duncan used the only weapon left to him – his teeth. With the fierceness of a Highland wildcat, he bit open his adversary's throat, tearing out his windpipe and his jugular vein, savaging his opponent, until Donald MacDonald breathed his last. Is it any wonder that we Stewarts and our neighbors, the MacDonalds, are wary of the Campbells in a fight?

Now Mad Duncan threw a murderous glance at me, while young Ian Campbell shifted his bulk in the saddle and sneered, "They say you're a clever one at dancing fancy minuets, but do ye understand the manly art of pistol dueling?" It was not the first time I had been mistaken for our laird's son, Jamie.

"Aye, I do," I answered, though in truth I was only a raw beginner with the pistol.

"Then those shall be our weapons."

Douglas Stewart looked askance at me, for had I not been drawn into a foolish fight? Broadswords would have so much better

---

served me. Anyone could see that this gross lad, Ian Campbell, would have been very quickly winded in swordplay. Herr Captain von Cranach had told me that my strong arms, legs, and quickness would be to my great advantage in a feat of strength.

From his saddle pouch, Ian Campbell removed two green velvet bags, which he opened, revealing a handsome pair of dueling pistols. Long-barreled they were and of the modern flintlock type, with bright silver mountings marvelously engraved. Just the loving way he looked at them and the disdainful way he took my measure convinced me that he was a marksman.

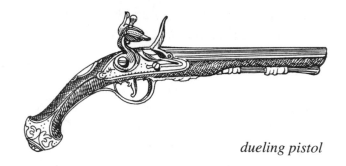

dueling pistol

"Who shall act as your second?" he asked me.

I nodded toward Jamie's great uncle, and Ian pointed at his father.

"Does this ground look well enough for us to settle this affair?" the young Campbell called to me.

"Oh, yes," I answered. "Well enough indeed."

Douglas Stewart got off his horse and studied the ground. "It looks fair enough to me," he declared, after kicking away a stone or two that lay along the path. "Come, drive a peg for us," he called to Roy, the Stewart standing nearest him.

When a wood peg had been cut and well set in the center of the path, the Stewarts and the Campbells gathered near, then stood or squatted, waiting, with an unfriendly gap between them. I could hear some coarse talk and unguarded laughing, for we true Highlanders like nothing better than to watch a cock fight or a duel between opposing clanmen, even if it had to be with prissy gentleman's pistols instead of slashing broadswords and dirks.

We two duelists walked away, as was the custom, and held quiet counsel with our seconds.

"Willie, I fear you've made a grave mistake," whispered Douglas Stewart. "This is not the fight for you. Why did you not call for blades? Or the right to draw a straw or flip a coin? You'd have been far better off with blades. I do not like the fact that he was carrying a pair of dueling pistols in his saddlebag."

"Well, it's settled, and cannot now be changed," I told him. "Captain von Cranach has taught me some marksmanship. Enough to strike a Campbell down."

While I was speaking in this nervous boastful manner, the old man withdrew a small thick book from his saddlebag. "Now, bow your head and pray for your success today, or ask our Saviour for deliverance into heaven. Step this way." He called to Roy, "Protect us from the Campbells' spying eyes. It is not seemly," he whispered to me, "for a duelist to wear chain mail or armor underneath his shirt. But surely it cannot be wrong for any man to stand protected by the sacred teachings of our highest Holy Lord. Look up, Willie Stewart. This is the very day, God willing, that ye are about to cut the Campbells' breeding stock."

He handed me his own King James Bible. It was not much larger than my hand but it was thick with well-laid paper, strongly bound with tanned bull's hide, and held with a silver clasp. "Willie," he said, "I trust that these sacred words will protect you from all harm."

I took the Bible and held it to my lips.

"Not that way, you simple booby," he exclaimed. Then cautiously raising my shirt, he opened the Holy Book beneath my right armpit, and bound its thickness snug in place, using my own neckerchief. "Now, Willie," he whispered, tucking in my shirt again, "you fling your plaid about your shoulder in plain sight. Young Ian Campbell tricked you into giving him his choice of weapons, so he deserves a sly one in return."

"Pay strict attention," the uncle said. "When the moment comes, I want ye to stand sideways to him, right arm full extended, aiming straight at your opponent's middle. Do not expose your brave heart, or too many of your vital organs, to his pistol ball.''

"It's damned unfair," Roy whispered to me, knowing the laird's uncle was a little deaf, "him allowing ye to take a ball in the place of Jamie Stewart."

"Remember," said the old man, "suck in your gut and your two wee groin stones. I want you to hold yourself up straight and slender as a willow wand. You'll make a slim mark, very difficult to hit."

I practiced drawing in my belly until it seemed to touch my backbone and as for my wee stones, they, too, poor dears, were hanging just beneath my heart. I watched young Ian Campbell as he strode out full of confidence, his belly thrust forward, carefully gauging the dueling range. I watched him put the heels of his cowhide slippers neatly to the peg, then take seven measured strides, testing the unevenness of the ground. With his left fist upon his hip, he whirled, pointing his trigger finger straight.

"Jamie Stewart," he called, "I've heard that you're a great carouser with the housemaids in your father's keep. This may be the bitter end of all that for you."

I could think of no clever answer to his remark, so we marched back with our seconds to the starting peg in the path. Roy and their loading man, using the same horn, carefully measured equal powder into the muzzles of both weapons, then firmly wadded each leaden ball in place. They checked the flints and primed the flash pans. Ian and I looked each other in the eye as they shuffled the pistols back and forth, then offered us our choice. Each taking a weapon, we cocked it and turned, standing rigid back to back.

"As agreed, each man shall take seven measured paces, then turn and discharge his piece," said our laird's uncle.

Young Ian Campbell must have been sweating, for he gave off the strong musky smell of a Highland bull. I stood staring down the purple glen, with my pistol pointed reverently to heaven.

"I shall call, 'Mark!' " Mad Duncan Campbell told us in a steady voice. "Then I shall count out each pace in an even manner. Only when the numbers have grown to seven will each man be free to halt, turn, and fire." He paused, then called loudly, "May God have mercy on your youthful souls."

I sensed the grandest feeling of elation.

"Mark!" he said, and I filled my lungs with sweet air.

My pistol hand was steady as a rock.

"One!"

I took a long pace forward, then felt my knees begin to quiver and prayed they would not let me down.

"Two!"

Another pace. I felt my nerves clutch in fear.

"Three!"

I shortened my pace, fearing I might carry myself too far away to hit my target squarely.

"Four!"

I lengthened my pace again, to draw myself further from Ian Campbell's deadly line of fire.

"Five!"

My pistol barrel began to shake. "Steady, fool," I whispered to myself, "you'll not be firing at a harmless figure painted on a board."

"Six!"

My mouth turned sour and my heart was pounding in my breast.

"Seven!"

I took that last pace quickly, then, sucking in my belly, I whirled on heel and toe. I aimed at him and pulled the trigger.

At that same moment, I saw smoke belch from Ian's pistol. I heard no sound, but felt a monstrous blow strike me fair beneath the armpit. My breath was knocked out of my body, as I went stumbling backwards, but I flung my shoulders forward and I did not fall.

Ducking my head below the sulfurous smoke, I saw Ian Campbell staggering sideways. He stared down at his bulging shirt. There I could see two dark round holes turning red. His knees sagged as his legs gave out, and he sat down heavily in the path. "I am a killed man," Ian called out to his father, as Mad Duncan and their other attendant ran forward to his aid.

Douglas Stewart came and took me by the arm. "That was a poor shot, passing mostly through his belly fat. What a pity, when you had that one grand chance to lay young Campbell low. Still, you have won the duel, lad. Yes, you have won the duel!"

Our men sent up a shout of triumph. Together we watched the Campbell chief remove his long scarf and swaddle it twice round the belly of his son before they eased him on his bay mare. Then without a word to us, they turned around and started back toward the Campbell lands. As they went, Mad Duncan turned and gave me and Douglas Stewart a withering scowl.

Douglas Stewart remounted, as did I, before he bid our men go forward through the glen. When the Campbells were out of sight, he told me to withdraw the King James Bible from beneath my arm. He opened it with care and caught the heavy pistol ball that fell from it.

"What a lovely shot that young Ian Campbell made. This ball was speeding straight toward your heart. Look! It traveled through the bull's-hide cover and half the books of the Old Testament, through Psalms. Then easily pierced Daniel, and dug deep into the Book of Zechariah, stopping perilously close to entering your chest. You are well blessed, Willie. The Lord's Book has surely saved your life!"

He handed me the ball. " 'Tis said that if you cut a cross in this and wear it around your neck, it will protect you from all future harm."

I thrust it in my pocket and felt my heart begin to sing, for had not I, the son of a poor sheep drover, fought honorably for the Stewart clan by knocking Mad Duncan Campbell's son onto the ground?

We continued to beat our borders, and many of our men afoot called out to me, "Well done, Willie. And ye've won yourself a bonnie pistol," for it was sticking out my waistband.

I was seated in my saddle straight and proud when we all returned to the hunting lodge. As the old uncle had predicted, our laird and his son had recovered from their long night of carousing. Both were eager, now that our border march was ended, to leave the lodge and return to Stalker's Keep.

Douglas Stewart had me wait out in the hall, while he went into the laird's sporting room and told him all that had befallen us. I just stood there, trying to guess what reward they would give me. Some large gift for my part in upholding the honor of the clan? It was some time before Douglas Stewart opened the door and beckoned me inside.

The laird rose, glaring at me with a look not much less fierce than that of Mad Duncan Campbell. "A devil of a pile of problems you have caused us now," he said in a flinty voice. "Who gave you the right to impersonate my son?" Saying that, he threw a dirty look at his own uncle.

"We were pressed in such a way," the uncle tried to explain, "that as time passed, it would have seemed cowardly to do otherwise. Our only other choice would have been for all of us to come down on them," he told the laird. "We Stewarts outmanned them more than two to one and held the higher ground. They would have called that a foul sheep slaughter!"

"What will the Campbells call it when they learn that we Stewarts secretly put up a drover's son to fight a duel, to try and save Jamie and kill that highborn Campbell?"

"I was mindful," said his uncle, "that you, yourself, announced after the slaughter at Glencoe that you wanted peacefulness to reign again throughout the western Highlands."

"There'll be no peace now, once this deceit is out," yelled James Stewart. He paced a bit, then pondered thoughtfully. "The Campbells will want revenge when they hear of it. The only thing for us to do is send this lad out of the country and bring his family close in to the protection of Stalker's Keep."

I could feel the blood rise in my face as I thought of this injustice. Imagine him, sending me out of my own country.

"Do you agree with me?" the laird demanded of his uncle.

"Yes, I agree."

"Willie, you take a wee piece of my damned good advice," the laird demanded, frowning at me. "Sign an apprenticeship with the East India Company or the Africa Trading Company. Either one will take you sailing to a distant part of the world."

13

"Careful of the Africa Trading Company," warned Douglas Stewart. "They say officers and clerks alike take the fevers and die out there like flies."

"Make whatever choice you wish," shouted the laird, "but from this day forward your presence in these western Highlands will cause bloodshed between ourselves and the Campbells. I order you, William Stewart, to depart from all the Highlands and seek your fortune in some different region of the world. Do you have my order to you straight?"

Even as I left that hunting lodge, I knew that I was the one true loser in that duel, for now I was forced to leave Scotland or remain a broken man, a thief hiding in the hills, beyond the law. Some Stewarts, hearing of the laird's harsh words, sympathized with me. Others jeered in Gaelic, saying, "Willie, you've nothing but your fancy ways to blame. Take your damned pistol and your French and Latin and be gone."

That evening, when I was departing, Jamie stood above me in a window. He waved farewell but did not speak. Captain Hans von Cranach had given me a broadsword and dirk, and he and Monsieur LeMoine both embraced me and wished me well.

Lady Islay and the laird's uncle accompanied me down to the boat landing. Lady Islay's servant carried a small hamper filled with journey cakes, mutton, a jar of jam, and a jug of whiskey along with a pewter plate and spoon and cup. They both agreed it would probably be safe for me to return to the Highlands in a dozen years or so.

"I suggest you make your passage on the packet boat that sails from Oban down to northern Ireland," said the uncle. "You'll not be the first to take that road. Many folk have had to run there because of the religious troubles or blood feuds."

As her parting gift, Lady Islay gave me a handsome cairngorm stone set in a heavy silver circlet to shoulder-pin my plaid. "Willie, this is a small gift for all you've done within this family. Take this wee letter. It's to an uncle of mine who lives now in the south of England. He is said to have high connections with wealthy families living there. Perhaps he could find you a situation where you could help tutor some other boy like Jamie."

Not to be outdone, the laird's uncle unstrapped his own badger-headed sporan and buckled it round my waist. I felt a weight of coins inside. "Go where you wish," said he. "But stay clear of Scotland and be wary of the Campbells."

"What a pity, Willie," said Lady Islay sadly, "that sorry business of the duel has spoiled all your opportunities, your student life with us."

"Och, well," I tried to cheer her. "The pity is I spent too much time with languages and penmanship and did far too little practice with the pistols."

Lady Islay kissed me lightly on the cheek. "Ye may well have saved my dear son's life."

Old Douglas Stewart shook my hand before we parted. I thanked them both before I pushed off in the small dinghy and sailed south in the rising moonlight along Loch Linnhe until dawn, when I could see my father's croft.

I woke the family and explained the fate that had befallen me. I warned them they must take their meager flock and seek safety close to Stalker's Keep. They were much upset when I told them and deemed it to be all my fault.

I slept past midday, had a bowl of salted porridge, then gathered the few items I possessed, packing them carelessly in a cowhide-covered box. My parents readily agreed that they in no way blamed the laird for being in a rage with me. My favorite sister, Sheila, was the only one to weep when I was leaving. She gave me, as her farewell gift, a wee brass locket holding a curl of her fair auburn hair.

I made my way afoot along the road until I reached the local docks at Oban, where I saw two packet boats tied side by side. The posted notices stated that the *Skye Bird* was bound for Donegal in Ireland, and the *Thistle Head* was leaving for the city of London. I went aboard the vessel bound for Ireland. But just before I paid my passage, I thought of life there and decided to travel even farther south and take my chances among the bloody Englishmen.

I ran up the gangplank of the packet *Thistle Head* just as they were raising it to set sail around the southeast side of the Isle of

Mull. From there, past Jura and Colonsay, we had a fair wind and smooth passage. After days of coasting off the English shores, eventually, at sunset, we entered the Strait of Dover. Next morning, we sailed up the Thames, past Gravesend Beach, past Limehouse Reach, and took our docking. I leaned against the rail like most of the other voyagers, gawking at the sprawling sights of London town as we tried to count her squat clock towers and all the tall church spires half lost in fog.

We disembarked and climbed the worn steps and stared at Tyburn in the very shadow of the Tower of London. A mustard-colored gloom had come to wrap the city. I looked up and saw that fearful warning from the queen to all her enemies, cutpurses, highwaymen, and thieves. A dozen human corpses hung in iron cages, and near them the heads of nine men and one long-haired woman were displayed on sharp pike poles.

My nostrils pinched themselves at the awful stenches that came wafting from the city. London did not enjoy that clean white sea fog that purifies the Highlands and makes our heather bloom. London's fog was caused by reeking coal smoke and soot from a thousand chimney pots, and the noise of the city was like ten thousand overturned beehives.

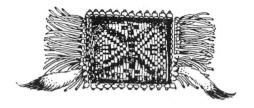

THANA

2

I, Thanadelthur, pulled off my mitts and, kneeling on the snow-covered ice, started to pull in our gill net very carefully. The air was stinging cold, but still. The sky above the frozen lake arched like a great blue cap above our heads. I tried to think of nothing but kind thoughts toward the fishes that swam beneath my feet. Without moving my lips, I sang inside myself a woman's song to those dear watery creatures, trying to woo the very biggest trout into our net.

I looked up and saw my cousin, Dingee, release the line that held the other end of our sinew net. She hurried back to me, rolling her hips as she ran lightly on her snowshoes, packing down the newly fallen snow. Together we moved back from the ice hole, carefully drawing up our net.

It was not long before the first silver-sided fish appeared, its gills well caught in the sinew mesh. That trout was alive but gave only one flip in the cold, then froze to death, its body thinly glazed with ice. Dingee knelt and with her bare hands respectfully removed it from our spider's web. We moved back again, drawing up the entire length of the net, one by one discovering four more fish, the last one being an old male with an upjutting jaw twice as large as all the others.

"In the end, he did come to our singing," I told Dingee as I retied the sinew strands the heavy fish had broken.

She laughed and eased the wide carrying strap beneath her infant son. "Isn't that just like a hunter?"

We bound the five fish into one large frozen bundle and carefully reset our net, redrawing it beneath the ice and anchoring it at each end to upright stakes. We filled our two bark buckets with fresh water from the fish hole and paused to look along the clear white flatness of the frozen lake. It was not much past midday, but already the sun man's evening fire was glowing red as he went sliding down beyond the west edge of the world.

Dingee took off her snowshoes and climbed atop a rock. Shielding her eyes, she stared into the south across the long blue shadows cast by a grove of dwarfed spruce trees. "They should be back by now," she said, for her young husband, like my brother, Keewatan, and five other hunters had set out in search of caribou. They had been gone for more than half a moon. I turned my head and looked instead at the four thin white plumes of smoke rising arrow-straight above our winter camp.

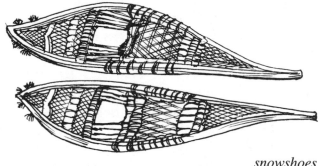

snowshoes

Seeing nothing, we two followed our own trail back. I kept close behind her until we could see our winter dwellings, four low caribou skin tents, each smoke-darkened at the top, with snow heaped halfway up their hairy sides for warmth. Before we neared the tents, I shifted my before-marrying veil around until it covered my whole face, fearing that at any moment some young man or boy might suddenly jump out and see me. My cousin, Dingee, being newly married, no longer had to wear a veil. Oh, how I envied her! "These veils made of long quill and beaded strands are troublesome and useless except in fly time," I said, "or on poor-looking girls whose parents wish to hide their ugliness."

"Being married is not all good," said Dingee. "You get used to sleeping warmly with a young man. Then when he's gone you wake up cold and worry if he's ever coming back."

That wasn't my trouble. I had studied my face in the dark reflecting pools and knew I would never be as beautiful as Dingee. She had a small nose, wide clear cheeks, large deerlike eyes, and a forehead smoothly rounded as a brown owl's egg. Dingee did not look strong, but she was. Both of us believed that we could carry as much as almost any man we knew.

The delay in my marriage had been caused because the young Chipewyan I was to marry had died, and now my father wanted to offer me to an old hunting companion whose wife had frozen while they were journeying south two years ago. I was grateful that in the last two years of hunting, we had not met that ancient widower, though my father eagerly asked all those we knew where to find him. It was not surprising that we did not cross his path, for our Da-Dene lands are very wide, and we human wanderers are all too few.

"Come with me inside our tent," I said to Dingee, "while the children run and tell the others we have fish."

You would be surprised how quickly our neighbors gathered. It was not long before the fire and the heat from all of our bodies made the tent hot and filled it with good smells and feelings. My father sang a respectful song to all the lovely swimmers, while we tried to withhold our hunger and sniffed the rich perfume of the boiling stew. When it turned rich fat yellow in the cooking basket, we dipped in with our wooden ladles and we drank, then ate our fill of the delicious trout before we cast the leavings to our dogs.

When the feast was over and the neighbors went away, I lay down in my place on our wide family bed and sniffed the fresh aroma of crushed spruce boughs. In the darkness broken only by the glow from our dying fire, I laid aside my veil and drew off my pointed leather shirt. In the winter's silence, I could hear

Dingee softly singing a magic song which would bring her husband safely home to her.

I drew the thick warm caribou skins up to my neck and, closing my eyes, I let my thoughts drift just above my head, trying to recapture a secret dream that I had had last autumn. In that dream a narrow-hipped young man came to our camp and asked my father for me. Straight and strong he was, with a bold nose and a sparkle in his eyes. He gave grand gifts and hunted for my parents, which caused them to agree to our marriage. I was allowed to sit near that young dream man and feast with him. When it was dark, my grandmother allowed him to remove my veil and I was about to begin a joyful life with him. I drifted off to sleep imagining I could feel that young man lying hot and naked in the bed beside me.

Just at dawn we were awakened by the excited barking of our dogs and the huff-huff-huff of snowshoes beneath men's running feet.

"Attack! Attack!" my father bellowed, but his words came far too late.

I tried to scramble out of bed as I saw men's bodies come hurtling against our tent sides, bending the support poles, breaking them, forcing the tent skins down on top of us. I lay pinned flat on our bed beneath a writhing human weight. Our air vent was gone and the smoke from our fires spread everywhere beneath the tent. The fumes were choking us to death. Men and women were coughing violently, and the children were screaming in fright. Outside I could hear the high yelps of our camp dogs, as they were being tied or driven off. Above us I could hear the guttural sounds of foreign voices snarling, grunting, calling out words I did not understand.

My aunt, who lay beside me, let out a sudden gasp when she saw a sharp iron knife come ripping through our tent skin. A strange man's face appeared above her. He grabbed my aunt by the hair and looked into her face. Too old. I saw his knife stab deep into her chest. I tried with all my strength to slither toward the back edge of the tent. As I moved away from the gasping sounds of my aunt dying, I grasped my shirt and with only the slightest movement eased my veil across my face. In the darkness, I could not see my mother or my two younger sisters. The smoke grew worse as our enemies came crawling over us like heavy beasts in rut. Their searching, stabbing, killing went on and on, until finally a dreadful silence lay over our whole camp. They've missed me, I thought. I am going to slip out into the dark and run.

At that moment, I felt a strong pair of hands begin to feel my body through the tent skin and a knife ripped open the skins beside my head. The coarse face of a man appeared above me. On his head he wore a lynx mask with tufted ears. He was a raider from the south, a Wood Cat greatly feared by us. His rough hands ripped away my veil, and when he saw that I was young and nearly naked, he let out a grunt of pleasure. With his knife, he warned away another man, then grabbed me by the hair and dragged me from the choking smoke.

I moaned in horror when I saw that all four of our tents were down, and the snow was spattered red with blood. I could see the lifeless human shapes of my relatives, who now lay beneath the long knife slashes in the gore-soaked tents. Our dogs, the ones that had been caught, were lashed together like dead fish. All our stretched caribou and beaver skins had been snatched down from the lower branches of the spruce trees. Our fish cache had been broken open. The raiders were making a big fire, using the fuel that we had gathered. I did not even try to keep myself from shuddering and sobbing.

The big man who held me from behind had his left arm clamped around my neck. He hooted as he forced my body tight against him. Suddenly another attacker lunged at me, clutching me around the waist, trying to tear me away from the man who held me. My captor bellowed at this second killer, slashing at him with his knife. I was hoping they would kill each other. Instead of that, their sharp eyes fell on my cousin, Dingee, as she crawled out from beneath her family tent and, clutching her child, stumbled toward the shelter of the nearest tree. Dingee had no snowshoes and was waist-deep in the drifts. My second attacker let out a gleeful shout as he let go of me and bounded after Dingee.

21

I saw him spring on her like a lynx taking a rabbit. He pinned her in the snow. She twisted frantically, trying to bite and scratch him, trying to drive her knee into his groin. When her strength finally failed, he flung her baby away, then took her by the throat and struck her three times brutally. I closed my eyes and turned my head.

The dawn was spreading bleak yellow in the east, but our camp still lay in shadow. Bloody footprints were everywhere upon the snow. A dozen of the Wood Cats walked around, inspecting nine young captive women and three older female children. I hung my head, trying to let my hair conceal my unveiled face. I could hear the others weeping, for there was not a single Dene hunter left alive to save us, no mothers, no old men or women to tell us young ones what to do. I thought of my eldest brother, with our hunters far away. Had they, too, been slaughtered? I could not keep from sobbing.

The big man who held me tightened his armhold around my neck, cutting off my cries so violently I could not breathe. He did not release his grip until he felt my body sag against him. I hung there gasping for breath, shuddering from fear and cold, for I wore only waist-high leggings and my moccasins. I was terrified of what I knew would surely happen to us.

Those murderous Wood Cats forced us to drag away our ruined tents for them so they could search among the bodies for any useful loot. The man who held me reached down and ripped the necklace of eagle claws and yellow beads from my dead father's throat. I wept. I saw my pointed shirt and, as I bent to pick it up, I recognized my mother, my aunt, and two younger brothers – all sprawled beyond my father, dead. Looking sideways, I could see two Wood Cat hunters, each with one of my younger sisters in his grasp. I called out to them, "Survive! Have courage. Survive!" My captor did not understand my words, but he grabbed my throat to silence me.

Our attackers, who were now our masters, forced us to help them set up a long crude lodge, using some of our poles and tent skins mixed with theirs. Inside, we younger women spread out spruce boughs and built three fires. Some Wood Cats raped their

---

22

captives, while others started gambling. I watched the big man who had caught me wagering for Dingee, too. At each throw of the handful of painted sticks upon a skin, they argued savagely. The big man was always at the center of any violent disagreements. Instead of losing me to the other Wood Cat, the big man won Dingee on the seventh cast of sticks. Grunting with pleasure, that boastful brute made a great show of hobbling Dingee's leg to mine, using complicated rawhide knots, so that we could not run away from him. After that he tied a thong to each of us, binding them to his left arm, to show all the others that we two were now his slaves. He threatened any who came near him or us, and we soon discovered that the other raiders hated him.

My cousin, Dingee, was still racked with trembling and sobbing and, like me, she refused to raise her head. I tried to comfort Dingee, for I knew that she had seen her only child murdered before her eyes.

On the following day, our new master hauled Dingee and me away from our blood-stained lodges. I cried out, "Good-bye, good-bye," to my two younger sisters and my brother's weeping wife, believing that it was the last time I would ever see them.

Our new master was a tall, cruel, half-crazed brute who, we soon discovered, lived alone, hating his own people as much as they detested him. He hitched Dingee and me into his dog team and ordered us to drag him as he rested comfortably on his toboggan, puffing blue smoke from his short trade pipe.

Kunn was the first Dene word that our new master learned from us. *Kunn* means fire. Oh, how he loved that word. When we and the dogs were exhausted, he would make camp, then lash out at us shouting, "*Kunn, kunn, kunn!*" demanding that we immediately find wood and start a fire to heat his tent.

We did not know that Wood Cat's proper name, so we called him Kunn. It was a good name for him, and when he heard us using it, he did not mind. Perhaps he thought we spoke of his well-being.

Kunn always wore his lynx mask as a hood above his caribou hunting shirt. His moccasins and leggings were of the same skins but with the hair turned in. Around his neck he wore my father's

23

necklace of sharp eagle claws. His pointed shirt, like ours, was cut high, well above his hips for easy running. Kunn's leggings were fringed along his outer thigh, down to his moccasins. He had decorated his shirt and leggings with ocher, red, and black stripes that all ran sideways, instead of up and down like ours.

A few times, that prideful brute tried to impress us with his beauty by rubbing his face and hands with the bright red ocher which he carried in a bag and by blackening around his eyes with charcoal from the fire. We had to smile and blow out our breaths, pretending that he looked very fine or risk a beating.

What caused us to rub our eyes in disbelief was when, one evening, he unpacked his dancing coat and his best moccasins and knife case. He put these on, to show us his great wealth. We had never seen anything like that. His dance coat had a wide beaded collar sewn in a band across his chest, over his shoulders, and along his hood. Even his knife case and the vamps on his moccasins were encrusted with blue beads, red beads, and white beads, each one twinkling like a small bird's eye as he did his dance for us. Dingee's veil had had seventeen beads: eleven red, six blue, spread among her quills. My veil had had only fourteen beads – all of them blue. This Wood Cat from the south had beads beyond our counting sewn in clever patterns on his dance shirt and even his leggings.

"Where did all those beads come from?" I asked Dingee.

"I don't know," she answered. "Could he have met the Ballahooly, the sunrise men who have floated from across the world?"

We had never seen such strangers, but we did know that Kunn's proudest possession was a long weapon he kept carefully wrapped in sealskin. This we were never allowed to see or touch.

We traveled endlessly for the remainder of that winter, pulling our dreadful Wood Cat master in his search for game along the edge between the dwarf trees and the open barren lands. Whenever one of us dared to glance back, we could see him staring at our moving haunches, as he waited for nightfall, planning some insane new ways to impose himself on us. Oh, how we came to hate him at night, and yet, in spite of his cruelty, I must admit that he was a wily tracker and a cunning hunter. He always found enough food for himself, his dogs, and we two slaves to eat. The worst part was that we were forced to share his bed with him.

Except for my snowshoes and the clothing that I wore, the only things I had kept from my family's camp were my mother's scratcher and small yellow flensing knife. It was a blunt skin scraper made of soft stone that had been pounded into shape. It could not be keenly sharpened like Kunn's Ballahooly knife of iron. One did not want it sharp, when scraping hides. I had always carefully tied these to my hip string, so that they dangled down inside my legging. Of course, our Wood Cat master found them the first night he stripped us down. He examined the flenser and snorted in disgust, for he could see that it was small and dull, almost useless as a weapon. Still, he would not allow me to keep it. He only lent it to us for flensing the animals he killed.

After hunting with this Wood Cat for more than two whole moons, we finally smelled smoke from another camp. These were our dreaded enemy, the Cree, and when they recognized our master, they threatened him and taunted him. Their women screamed insults, and the men shouted curses across the snow and threw frozen dog turds at him. "Thieving wolverine!" they yelled. "Bitch lover!" their women laughed.

scraper

So angry did our master become when he heard their words that he flung two of his caribou spears toward them, using all his might. That evening he strode crazily back and forth before their

25

camp. Finally, he became so enraged with one of the Cree hunters, who ran out beyond the others, cursing him most foully, that our master unwrapped his long sealskin package. Snatching the small stone fire box from his toboggan, he blew into it until it glowed. Then he held its wormlike fuse until it started burning. He aimed this strange weapon and touched the fuse to it. There was a puff of smoke and fire, followed by a tremendous roar!

When Dingee and I saw that magic, we held our hands against our ears and fell down in awful fright, for though we two had been warned of the dreadfulness of guns, we had never seen one, watched it spit out lightning, nor heard its thunder.

When I opened my eyes, Dingee was pointing in amazement at blood that was running down the legs of the hunter who had cursed our master. Though he was still some distance away, the Cree taunter staggered sideways. He looked down and rubbed his hands against his red-soaked groin, then he knelt down moaning and fell face forward on the snow.

Other Cree hunters continued to shout threats at our half-crazed Wood Cat, as women came out and carried the bloody man inside a tent. We could see that they, too, were afraid of our master's gun. He laughed and patted the thunder-maker as he pointed it at each of them.

It grew dark, but our master was not afraid to pitch his tent near the Cree camp. Suddenly, a Cree woman started screaming, then others joined in her lament. We guessed from the sound of them that the lightning and the thunder must have killed the man. Our master grew nervous when he heard the wailing. Like Dingee and me, he was frightened of the dead man's vengeful spirit and his relatives who might come seeking their revenge. He ordered us to take his tent down quietly and to harness ourselves among the dogs. As we left that place of wailing women, Kunn snowshoed close beside us, for he, too, greatly feared the blackness and the mournful spirit that might grab him in the night.

That winter seemed to cling endlessly. Some days were cold and others damp. Our master was a restless man and kept us always on the move. Dingee and I grew lean and sinewy from overwork. Kunn thought nothing of forcing us to pull until we fell onto our knees among his exhausted dogs. At night he would often take his long musket from its skin wrappings and caress it and show it off to us. He would rub carefully all along its length with bear grease. Certainly he admired that thunderous weapon more than any human. He did not use it on the animals. Those he could get with spear or snare. Sometimes he would point the gun's black eye at us and hold the braided fuse into the fire and, when it was smoldering, place it against the little iron pan and shout, "Kunnn!" to frighten us. But because of our usefulness to him, he never sent the lightning at our faces.

We came to know that Kunn slept as lightly as a fox. If the slightest sound occurred outside his tent, he would leap up and clutch his gun while peering out the entrance. We three knew that the relatives of the bloody Cree man would be eager to avenge his death. When he had such a night of wakefulness, our tormentor would sleep fitfully far into the morning. This weakness must have worried him, for he would surely guess that when good weather came, we two would try to run away from him. For this reason, he once more took to tying a short rawhide line between our thighs and his so that no matter how long he slept, we could not rise and creep away. He always lay with his iron knife hidden in his clothing and the gun beyond our reach.

Dingee grew desperate when the spring moon came to us. "I can't stand him anymore," she whispered. "I believe his gun will only kill one person at a time. At least the other one might get away."

Unfortunately, the big man was listening and guessed the meaning of her words.

Our master was furious with Dingee and beat her harshly. Stripping her and forcing her down on her back, he knelt on her hair and whipped her cruelly on the insides of her thighs. I knew how much that hurt. I held my hands over my ears, but still I could hear Dingee screaming out in pain. I clenched my teeth and hid the worst thoughts of revenge deep inside me.

During our enslavement, our master had slyly learned many of our Dene words. We, too, had been forced to learn his curious southern way of speaking Cree, so that we might survive. Yes, the Wood Cats were different from most Cree, despised by them, and yet they roughly understood each other's language.

On the second morning after Dingee had insulted the Wood Cat's gun, we all three woke to the excited calling of the first big flocks of snow geese heading north. It was the surest sign of spring.

Dingee clenched her teeth and whispered, "We can't go on like this – afraid of him forever."

With the waxing of the goose moon, we had one more heavy storm, then winter lost its strength. The spring sun shone down on the land, and the snow turned soft, then melted, exposing the higher gravel ridges. We traveled at night in the valleys, where the snow remained. Even then its wetness clogged our snowshoe webbing and piled against the front curve of the toboggan. At night the sky did not grow fully dark. Pairs of eagles wheeled and screamed above us in the air as they prepared to mate, then to search together for their nesting places.

One day we crossed a rise of ground and saw smoke rising from five fires. This far south and east we knew it could not be Dene, but must be a Cree encampment. Kunn shoed ahead of us toward that camp and when they saw him, many Cree appeared. Kunn lay down on the snow, which they knew was a sign that he had not come for fighting. These hunters seemed to know our Wood Cat master and called to him. Their head man also lay down on the snow, showing Kunn that it was safe for him to walk into their camp.

After our long winter's isolation, Dingee and I were too over-whelmed to speak. Suddenly, we found ourselves surrounded by these strangers. But that was nothing compared to our amazement when we saw Dene girls whom we had known. They, too, had been stolen from our northern camps. When we had the chance, Dingee and I asked every one of them about Dingee's husband, my two younger sisters, and my older brother. But none of them had seen them. Like myself, these young unmarried Dene women wore no veils. They all seemed plump beside the two of us. They worked hard, they said, but two of them had been adopted as daughters. They had suffered none of the awful miseries we had known.

Our Wood Cat master and these Cree seemed to get on quite well together. During the early part of that summer, our lives, too, became more tolerable, for in that camp Kunn went away hunting with the men almost every day. That gave us the chance to speak to the other Dene captives. Just hearing our own language and remembering with them how joyful life had been brought strength to us.

One day in the dying summer moon, I was lying on the smooth sun-warmed rocks with Dingee and the others, waving off mosquitoes and thinking summer thoughts, when suddenly we heard a roar. It was our vile master, Kunn. He was chasing another man whose arm was red with blood. The Cree hunters came running after Kunn, reviling him and ordering us to collapse his tent and go.

We wept when we had to leave those Dene and Cree women whom we had come to like. We began once more to live alone again with that half-crazed woman beater. This time it was endless walking, with Dingee and me loaded down with tent, poles, baskets – and meat, if we were fortunate. Each day when it was windless, stinging pests rose from the shallow muskeg ponds and followed us, seeking blood with such determination that one night they sucked and killed the youngest dog. We were grateful when autumn came and the morning frosts destroyed those pests.

We moved eastward along the forest line toward the rising sun. Each day Kunn forced us further from our Dene country. The weather began to change, the sky was most often clouded, and the wind blew cold. Using scraps left over from the new clothing he forced us to make for him, we each made ourselves a pair of mittens.

Again and again, Dingee asked me, "How can we suffer another winter with this brute?"

"Be patient," I told her. "We will find a way to go."

One gray day when we saw fresh caribou tracks, the Wood Cat called a halt. He ordered us to lie down among the dogs and quiet them while he climbed a low rise to observe the animals.

"I had a dream last night," I whispered to Dingee, knowing Kunn was out of earshot. "In the dream I could see my brother,

Keewatan, and your husband come snowshoeing into this camp, trying to save us. We two fought Kunn, trying to stop him from lighting the thunder gun against them. When our two men got a grip on him, they hauled him out and drowned him, right there," I pointed, "in that bend of the river."

"I wish they'd come," said Dingee. "This morning, did you see what he was doing?"

"Yes, I watched him. When the icy fog was turning into rain, he thought of nothing except to keep the cover on the gun."

"Why does he worry about it in wet weather, always wrapping that trout skin around its middle as though it was a sickly child?"

"He is afraid to let that gun get wet," I told her. "Remember, rain drives off thunder."

"Oh, how I detest him," Dingee moaned. "If we were not afraid of that thunder, we would run away from him. I cannot live through another winter doing every filthy thing that brute demands of us."

"I am no longer afraid of him," I lied. "When we get the chance, let's run."

When Kunn returned, he was carrying a young male caribou slung across his shoulders. It had been killed by wolves and only partly eaten. With his sharp iron knife, he slit the skin from its belly to its throat and along its inner thighs, then tossed me my mother's yellow flensing knife. We two removed the soft wet skin, careful to keep hairs off the meat. On a nearby gravel ridge we found a level place to set the tent, then pegged out the bluish skin, stretching it carefully, so we could scrape and dry it in the evening wind and morning sun.

"Give me back that little flenser," Kunn shouted at me.

It was dark when we blew on the embers from the fire box and set a bit of dried tundra and some willow roots ablaze. I dug a pit and into it I sank our birch-bark basket full of water, while Dingee built the fire and heated up the stones. We dropped them in until we had the water boiling in the basket, then quickly prepared a haunch of caribou in the way the Wood Cats like it best. While he ate, we were forced to squat among the dogs and watch Kunn as he gnawed the half-raw meat, wolfing down as much as his lean belly would allow. When he finished, he fed the dogs. Then, wiping off his greasy mouth, he leered at both of us. In a suspicious burst of generosity, he severed the joint and tossed two good-sized pieces at our feet. Whenever he showed such kindness, it marked the moment we most feared. It meant that he intended to indulge in what he called a two-woman feast. We knew he was about to force himself upon us – hard.

First he lay back in the tent and demanded that we two pull off his moccasins and leggings. As usual, he ordered Dingee to be first with him. That was how it usually started. I made an excuse to go outside. The tent's flap was open, and I stayed carefully in his view. I squatted on the gravel, staring out across the endless rolling plain of muskeg and wind-dwarfed scattering of trees. The bright half-face of the goose-leaving moon was rising above the far edge of the plain and laid its shimmering path across the rivers and the ponds. I wanted to scream to Dingee, to come and flee with me along that moonlit path toward our own dear country. I tried to think of some way to kill Kunn, but I was too upset.

I heard poor Dingee shriek in sudden pain. I place my hands over my ears and made a sad face at the moon, for I knew that it was going to be a dreadful night for both of us. I whistled upward softly to the ghostly dancers in the sky as their lights flowed northward to the Dene lands.

Kunn heard me, for he shouted, "Get in here, you whistling bitch. Help me finish this one off before I start on you."

I rose and went inside the tent, only to see poor Dingee crouching naked on her hands and knees. I closed my eyes and did not watch, hoping that Dingee would somehow wear down that monstrous beast. Poor thing, she tried but could not do it.

At last I could feel him weakening. He rolled onto his back between us, a sheen of sweat across his face and chest. His lean belly was heaving, as at last we saw him close his eyes. His heavy jaw sagged down as he fell asleep. Or was he tricking us again?

I waited for some time before cautiously easing myself up onto one elbow and in the fire's still-glowing embers studied his face. The pupils of his eyes shifted slowly back and forth beneath his closed eyelids. Yes, I believed he was asleep. I watched his chest to check the rhythm of his breathing. It was then that I saw the handle of his knife protruding from beneath his back. Right then I knew that I was going to try to take it. When he shifted slightly, slowly I reached out and touched the rawhide on its handle, wondering if I could draw it. I eased it just a bit, then stopped. I watched his eyes and listened to his breathing, then, holding my own breath, I dared to draw the whole blade from its sheath. Kunn sighed and muttered, but he did not wake.

My left hand that held the knife was trembling. I eased the sharp point down to the level between his naked loins and mine and held the blade ready if he moved. Then with a cautious downward slice, I severed the rawhide cord that bound us both to him. Still holding the knife point so it almost touched his groin, I reached across his chest with my right hand and touched Dingee lightly on the cheek. She opened her eyes and gently raised her head. We both feared that he might be awake by now, listening, tensing his muscles to lunge out, grabbing us by the hair.

I was afraid to stab him, because I had once seen a young Dene hunter try to kill a crazy man and though he knifed his victim many times, the wounded man survived long enough to throttle his attacker.

Silently we rose and gathered up our moccasins, our leggings, and our pointed shirts. I was trembling as I picked up his long gun. Then, crouching, I slipped outside the tent. The naked Dingee followed close behind me, picking up Kunn's knife. Outside I took up the birch-rind cooking basket and fire flints.

Mindful of the crunching sounds the gravel made beneath our feet, we both stood still, shivering with excitement, our breaths pumping white steam into the freezing night air. Cautiously, I unwrapped the protective sealskin and the fish skin from his thunder iron and laid it on the gravel. Then squatting, I urinated on his musket from one end to the other. Dingee, with a look of triumph, did the same. Only then did we draw on our moccasins, our leggings, and our caribou-skin shirts.

So excited were we with our feelings of freedom that instead of walking quietly, we began to run. That was our worst mistake, for we had forgotten about our friends and teammates, the sleeping dogs. They leapt up excitedly and came yelping after us. Of course, their barking woke up Kunn. We heard him let out a roar when he felt the bed deserted.

I looked back as he flung the tent flap open. He held a glowing club of wood snatched from the fire, as he came leaping after us. He paused when he saw the fish skin stripped from his musket and, bending, felt that it was wet. He came bellowing after us.

Fearing the moonlight, we two ran crouching, trying to hide from him in the sharp black shadows of the stunted tamaracks. When we reached the stony bank, we plunged straight down and splashed across the shallows of the icy river. Of course, we had no fear of Kunn's dogs that gamboled beside us as we fled along the moon's path.

I could hear Kunn's long strides scattering gravel as he drew closer and closer to me. Dingee was ahead, for she had always been the fastest runner. Kunn was just behind me, swinging the burning club above his head. I ducked down as I ran.

"Faster!" Dingee screamed at me. "Faster!"

I was running zigzag, holding my head so he would not hit me. Together we went splashing through the waters of another shallow stream. I could feel the heat of his flaming club, for he now was just behind me. I knew that he could grab me and set my hair afire.

I stumbled over a running dog and fell. I scrambled to my feet as I felt flying gravel strike my back. Kunn's full weight came lunging onto me. The light from his torch was blinding as his hard hand raked across my face, seeking a firm grip in my hair.

WILLIAM

3

I, William Stewart, visualized the towns of London in my studies, imagining them like little separate silver clouds that floated just above the River Thames. I was not at all prepared for the rumbling din of iron-shod carts across its cobblestones, nor the shrieking of its hawkers, nor the boldness of its townfolk rudely pushing through its narrow, twisty streets. Pungent piles of horse dung and dank yellow pools of urine stank in every gutter. Mottled flocks of pigeons cooed and strutted boldly almost underneath one's feet. Pale-faced young fishmongers with bleary eyes and raw red noses scratched themselves in front of open shops, shouting, with only a tooth or two left in their heads. Thin chimney sweeps begrimed with soot trotted past me with their tall hats and hazel brooms. Whorish young sluts stood winking and goosing prospects as they called out their prices. Tall Dragoons from some Duke's regiment strode along in pairs, dressed as bright as fighting cocks, forcing those they thought beneath them to lurch into the gutter or get knocked against the wall. I saw poor wretched begggars, some with parrots or monkeys on a string, others with crippled children, eyes bandaged or legs and arms twisted up behind them, whining, holding out their hands and begging for a coin or crust of bread. Then cutting through this jumble of the hawkers and the poor came rich folk, lords and ladies grandly dressed in powdered wigs and silk and lace and ribbons, carried by two flunkies in half-closed sedan chairs preceded by a great brute who stode before them, threatening with his heavy oaken staff any who might try to shower them with the contents of a chamber pot. Usually behind the sedan chair came at least one blackamoor dressed in feathered turban and brilliant livery. I pushed my way past men with minced-pie stands hung round their waists and noisy apple girls and cheap apple brandy sellers. Once I saw a skinny bobtailed cat pounce out of an alleyway and catch a rat. The two of them fought bitterly. It was the rat that won.

While still aboard the packet boat, I had been warned never to wear my proper Highland dress in London, where bare male knees were thought to be a joke. Urchins as well as whores were forever pulling up my kilt to see if anything was worn beneath. To guard myself against such city crudities, I tied my trews with ribbons neatly round my knees and wore my Stewart hunting plaid pinned over my left shoulder. Of course, I carried my new sword and dirk, as did all men of means, for the city was awash with thieves, cutpurses, and boisterous gangs of ne'er-do-wells who waited in the alleys to accost an unarmed gentleman.

Aboard the packet, a kindly fellow traveler had given me a safe address in Eastcheap. An errand boy, for a farthing, led me there. The man I met was a Mactaggart from the Highlands. When I asked him where I should take up lodgings, he leaned across his doorframe and eyed the ancient cairngorm that I wore, then wrote an address on a slip of paper.

When I reached that place, the doorkeeper saluted as he led me through the shabby graystone entrance. Inside I was surprised to see that it was at least as grand as the feasting hall in Stalker's Keep. The owner, Richard Flender, knew Sandy Mactaggart and asked me only for a single guinea in advance. He led me to a small but well-appointed room with a handsome, white-walled fireplace and a nicely cushioned seat beneath a pair of narrow leaded windows that gave one a view of the quiet mews below. Each morning and late afternoon, an old servant woman brought me tea and scones or cakes and laid my fire and brushed my shoes and shined the silver on my shoulder brooch and sporan and all the buttons on my coat. Even young Jamie Stewart had never known more lordly treatment. That old woman curtsied to me, calling me Young Master Stewart. She begged me never to go alone into the London streets at night, and what she said proved right.

Indeed, I, myself, was set upon, the second evening after she had warned me, by four young ruffians carrying clubs. Just in time I turned on them and got my back against a wall, as I unsheathed my sword and dirk. Then I commenced to curse them in a voice that was loud enough to draw a crowd that jammed in tight behind the thugs and started cheering for me, yelling, ''Thieves, cutpurses! Fight 'em, Scotty, cut 'em dead!''

When the boldest lout rushed in at me, I slit him from his elbow to his wrist, using a classic thrust and slash I had been taught by Captain von Cranach. The thieving brute turned with the blood spurting from his arm and ran, as did the other three. I could not help myself from letting out the Stewart battle cry as I went after them. Using the broad side of my sword, I struck the trailing thief across the back with such vigor that it sent him sprawling in the gutter.

In that very instant, the trailing crowd of Londoners turned against me, shrieking, ''Armed man bullying poor lads!'' And several picked up fresh horse balls and hurled them at me. In the end, it was the crowd I feared as I withdrew, walking backwards in a hurry, still with my sword and dirk unsheathed. Let me tell you, Londoners can be as hard-headed as outcast Highlanders, when aroused.

Cautious and thrifty as I tried to be, the pennies, shillings, then the guineas seemed to fly like magic from my sporan. Through windows, I could see pale-faced clerks slaving over ledgers, and fearing such drudgery, I wondered if I dared sneak back to Scotland. Some nights I dreamed of my sister, Sheila, playing on the harp, and I could see our flocks of sheep grazing peacefully on the moonlit pastures right above our loch.

One day, when my homesickness became almost more than I could bear, I hurried from my room, for I had decided to leave the city to seek the help that Lady Islay had offered me.

———

I was striding down the street, looking for some respectable person who might guide me to this country seat, when I noticed a young Englishman walking my way, carefully observing me.

"You look somewhat confused," he said. "My name is Tobin Peeks." He shook hands heartily. "May I help you?"

"I'm seeking the whereabouts of this address," I said, showing him the envelope of Lady Islay's letter.

"I'll have to think on that a bit," he said. "Would you care to join me for a bite to eat? Later I'll put you on the right coach where you wish to go."

I jumped at the chance, for it was a rare thing to find a Londoner so friendly. Peeks took me to the entrance of a coffee house that led into a high-ceilinged room full of good food smells and prosperous-looking merchants. We sat at a small table where Tobin ordered each of us roast beef and batter pudding and a tankard of ale. But first, the serving girl brought us each a bowl of oxtail soup. She smiled at me and pressed her thighs in close to mine, then bent so low she made me want to lay my cheek between her two plump breasts.

I enjoyed being advised by Tobin and telling him all the troubles I had suffered since my duel with Ian Campbell. He swore I was absolutely right and that both lairds sounded like a pair of muddle-headed arses.

When the proprietor sent the bill, Tobin calculated swiftly and complained, "Damned pricey buggers – they ought to be ashamed." Fishing into his waistcoat, he drew out one shilling sixpence and slapped it on the table, then kindly handed me a bright new Queen Anne penny with which to tip our serving wench.

She giggled when I handed it down her bodice, then rubbed her hip against me, saying, "Thank you, sir. Come back when the clock strikes ten and ask for Alice."

I felt my heart jump, for she looked and spoke like a country girl with an accent from the Border Country.

"Be careful of such willing trulls," said Tobin. "Come with me, Stewart. I'm going to see a play," he said, glancing up at Clockmaker's Tower. "The curtain's going up just now. We'll have to hurry."

I dodged along the narrow, crowded street with him until we reached the theater. He gave fourpence to the money taker, and we two were led into our seats.

It was the first time I had been inside a playhouse. It was dark and smelled of sweat and gin and stale perfume and English apple brandy. I was amazed when they drew up the heavy velvet curtain and revealed a bevy of actors in bright costumes with high white wigs, their powdered faces so bright with rouge they looked like masks above the candle footlights.

"I know the prettiest girl," Tobin whispered, pointing at a slim young lass in a butter yellow dress, who had just skipped and curtsied onto stage. "She's a very dear friend of mine; her name is Pamela."

All Pamela managed to say during that whole play was 'No, M'Lord,' once and 'Yes, M'Lord,' twice. But Tobin was right. She was the most beautiful girl I had ever seen.

After the performance, we two went around by a dark passage to the back door of the theater and waited. It was not long until Pamela came tripping out with several others.

"Oh, dear Tobin," she cried, "I'm so glad to see you. Who's your handsome friend?"

Tobin kissed her hand and introduced me very courteously. I was overwhelmed, for she was as graceful as a cat from Persia, with one tiny beauty patch on skin as pale and white as Dresden porcelain. She wore a high powdered wig made beautiful with rosebuds, fluttering ribbons, and a small bluebird. She held her silk skirts high and skipped along between us chatting gaily, not minding the filthy streets at all.

We did not return to our lunching room but went instead to a far grander place with costly paintings on the walls and many gilt-edged mirrors. The English servants bowed to us with a groveling servility that I'm pleased to say we scarcely know in Scotland, as they led us to a table set with crystal goblets, fine pewter plates, and a clean white linen cover. Tobin immediately ordered a punch bowl of cinnamon-mulled brandy, a mountain of raw oysters, three boiled-red lobsters, and a deep-crusted pigeon pie, to be followed by sweet cakes and port. Our servant

---

lit two costly beeswax candles and leered and winked his eye at me before he drew the heavy velvet draperies, making a small and very private room for just the three of us.

When we had finished eating, Tobin rose and left me alone to share the long settee beside the lovely Pamela. I felt so thrilled but shy of her that I could barely speak or answer, and when I did, she scarcely seemed to understand my words, for I could think of little else to say but 'Aye,' or 'Nooo,' or 'Is that truly true.' We two drank another cup or so of brandy, then that bonny lassie took my hand as she admired the well-cut stone in Lady Islay's heavy silver brooch. She asked me why I wore a badger's head upon my lap. I told her it was an ancient custom of some highborn Stewarts in our clan. She slipped her hand from mine and with a giggle fondled my sporan's clever silver clasp. Ooooh! I cannot well describe my feelings of excitement as she left her warm hand quivering like a small bird in my lap. She laid her perfumed cheek against my neck and gently nipped my ear. I peeked down between her lovely dovelike breasts and thought, what fool would ever return to those rude hills of Scotland when London has such girls as these.

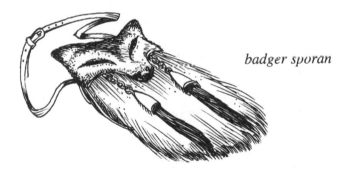

badger sporan

My head went reeling as the fumes from the hot mulled brandy took effect. Perhaps I closed my eyes just for one wee moment until I felt Pamela ease her hand from underneath my sporan. I sat up with a start.

"Sweet William, what a pity that I woke you," Pamela whispered as she stood up, wriggling prettily. "Truth is I've got to go and find a potty." With parted lips she kissed me on the mouth in a way that made me reach and grasp her round the waist. "Patience, dear boy, I'll come back straight-away." Smiling, she slipped between the velvet draperies and was gone.

I drank another cup of brandy and practiced the words of a Gaelic love song I planned to sing to her. Pamela took forever to return. Finally, the servant came and laid before me a gold-crested leather folder that contained a slip of paper. On it read: Guin.2-12-6. He stood there waiting.

"Two guineas, twelve shillings, and sixpence for dinner!" I gasped. "That is more than four seasons' wages for a Highland drover. You must wait for Mr. Tobin to return. He will settle up with you."

"Not bloody likely," said the waiter, losing his servile tone. "I saw him and that saucy bit of baggage go galloping out of here together. You sit right there. Don't move," he said in a threatening voice. "You must settle with the owner."

A dark-eyed, foreign-looking man appeared, angrily pulling the draperies apart. "Two guineas twelve and six, I'll thank you for." He held a little silver plate beneath my nose and pointed sternly at his written calculations.

What could I do but pay? I reached inside my sporan and found its little silver clasp was open, and my leather money purse was gone. How could it be gone? I searched my lap. Then I stood up and searched the cracks of the settee, and the waiter held the candle while I searched the floor beneath the table. All my money was gone.

"I have no doubt that you've been diddled by that fancy pair." The owner nodded his massive head of coal-black ringlets toward the door. "That's no affair of mine. I demand every farthing that you owe me. Now."

I showed him my empty sporan.

His eyes narrowed as he stared at me. "Take off that shoulder brooch of yours and let me see it."

When I did not move, the servant stepped up menacingly. "Come on, be quick, or do we have to rip it off you?"

Reluctantly, I unclasped Lady Islay's heavy silver cairngorm pin. The proprietor snatched it from my hand and held it near the candle flame. "It's probably not worth two guineas," he lied, "but I'll take it to save the cost and fuss of hiring in the soldiers. Now you be off, you nasty lump of Highland trash.

I challenged him to fight a duel, but he scarcely seemed to understand. He and the waiter together drove me into the street and slammed the heavy door. The sun was glowing red behind St. Paul's Cathedral as I hurried to my rooming house, truly feeling for the first time like a broken man with not a friend in all the world.

"You've been robbed!" said the doorkeeper as he let me in. "Now aren't that God's truth, young master? You've lost your feather bonnet and your silver shoulder piece, and I would guess you've lost your monies as well."

"That is the truth," I said, biting my lips to keep my chin from trembling.

"Mr. Flender! Mr. Flender!" the doorkeeper called, drumming his knuckles on the landlord's door.

Mr. Flender came out and heard my troubles. "Tell me, Stewart, exactly how much have you left?"

I answered, "Not a single penny."

He pursed his lips and scowled at me. "How long will it take you to obtain the monies that you owe me from your family?"

"They have no money," I told him. "They are Stewarts, but not the ones with wealth. I had a letter explaining, but it was stolen, too."

"Well, I'm not going to be the man that suffers because of your damned foolishness," he shouted. "You'll stay in that room that you've not paid for until I decide what I am going to do with you."

I heard the key turn in the lock.

When I woke next morning, the door was hanging open and I could see Mr. Flender with the doorkeeper close behind him, carrying a thick brass-headed cane. Both men had a treacherous look upon their faces. I leapt naked from the bed as they rushed in and stood between my weapons and myself. Seizing my sword and dirk and pistol, the landlord flung them clattering out the door.

"Now you get dressed right quick," he said as the two of them stood and watched. When that was done, they seized me by the wrists. "Walk quietly with us," warned Mr. Flender, "or my man will give you a frigging awful crack across your noggin."

We three marched together through the London drizzle down Ludgate Hill, then straight toward St. Paul's Cathedral until we turned left up Old Bailey Street and came in sight of the court and Newgate Prison. A pair of blue-chinned soldiers in busbies and tall varnished boots stood guard as we mounted the wide stone steps and passed down a grim hallway to enter a high-windowed room.

The old doorkeeper looked nervously about himself and wiped his nose against his sleeve. "Now you're in for it," he whispered. "I'd be wetting in my shoes if I were you. Look over there," he said, pointing into the stone courtyard where some twenty shabbily dressed prisoners stood shivering in the rain. "Those unlucky bastards are just out the debtor's door at Newgate. Guards are going to brand them now and crop their ears," he said, "and march them to the transports that will ship them to the Virginian and Georgian colonies in America, to be sold as servants. More like slaves, I'd say. No pay, mind you. They'll live on cattle fodder. Good riddance to them." He chuckled. "We've no room for the likes of them in London. They'll learn to work from dawn to dark, or feel the whip. That's what's going to happen to you, Mr. Stewart, for cheating decent folk."

I was forced to go and stand in line with a gaggle of London whores and cutpurses whilst the magistrate dealt out that swift brand of English justice that is so greatly feared in Scotland. When my turn came, he asked my name, my home, and how I'd come into the city. I told him I'd arrived by packet and taken lodgings, then been robbed of every farthing and had my hat, my shoulder pin, and my pistol, sword, and dirk all stolen. He hunched his shoulders and the corners of his mouth turned down.

"Can you read and write?" he asked.

"Yes, sir," I answered brightly. "I have studied calculus and can speak proper English and Gaelic and some Latin and French as well."

"Describe in Latin this courtroom," he demanded, and when I had done so, he whispered for a moment to his court clerk. "Well done, lad," he said. "Now you wait right over there with Landlord Flender."

I listened as he dealt out three more sentences, released a sickly-looking man, and sent two hardened strumpets into prison. Finally, the court runner returned, accompanied by a short, plump-bellied man who wore a puce-colored coat and an expensive-looking vest with an irregular design of food and wine spots spattered down its front. He had faint snuff smudges underneath his nose and wore a wig that was so badly shaped that it looked like an Orkney man's fur hat.

"Step back here, Stewart," the magistrate called to me. "This gentleman, Mr. Goodwin, represents the Honourable Company of Gentlemen Trading into Hudson Bay. Have you heard of them?"

"Yes, I have, sir. They trade furs in North America."

"That's right," he said, "and they are offering full bond for indentured clerks and servants they see fit to hire in their employment."

The Company man looked me up and down, turned me around. "You're a brawny sort," he said. Then he, too, tested my education. "How much is five and three?" he asked, watching to see if I counted on my fingers.

"Eight," I told him.

"What is nineteen minus eleven?"

"Eight," I said.

"That's good enough," he said. "Now spell 'beaver peltry.'"

I easily did it for him.

"Explain the French meaning of *Honi soit qui mal y pense*, which is on the royal coat of arms."

When I told him, he said next in French, "Venez ici." I took a step toward him and he said to the magistrate, "Yes, he'll do as a clerk. How much does he rightfully owe this landlord?"

Mr. Flender calculated very slowly for the judge, then answered honestly enough, "Three guineas, one shilling, sixpence, and another two shillings for all the troubles he has caused."

"The Company shall make payment for him here and now," the puce-coated man assured the magistrate, "if your Honor will be kind enough to co-sign this indenture placing this same William Stewart fully in the Company's charge."

"What is the length of his indenture?" the magistrate asked suspiciously.

"Only seven years," replied the Company man, "with one more year for transport to and from America."

"That sounds reasonable enough, if it also warrants that you'll feed and clothe him and give him a stout new pair of boots each year."

"That is quite clearly spelled out here," the Company man assured him, pointing at the longest paragraph in my letter of indenture.

"That's only eight shillings per annum," I complained.

The magistrate looked at me admiringly. "Stewart, you are admirably quick at calculations. Take him along with you, Mr. Goodwin," he said as he boldly made his seal and scrawled his signature. "A few years in the Company will make a proper Englishman of you. Go along now with this gentleman," he said, "and thank the good Lord that the press gangs didn't catch you for the army. Keep your eyes open and your mouth shut. Learn to be a steady, useful servant." He frowned at Landlord Flender and said sternly, "Sign here that you have received full payment for your grievance."

The landlord swiftly pocketed the Company money.

"Sir, what about the pistol, sword, and dirk they stole from me?" I asked the magistrate.

"You'll not be needing those," he shook his head. "Where you're going, lad, you shall more likely want an axe to chop the ice."

The landlord and his watchman laughed, then quickly turned away. We followed them along the courthouse corridor. Landlord Flender looked back at me and shouted, "Good riddance

---

to you, Jacobite. America's the proper place for all the likes of you.''

''You bloody Sassenach!'' I wanted to cry, though I had no choice but to walk quietly beside the heavy-bellied Mr. Goodwin, for he kept a tight grip on my doublet's sleeve.

''What do those two know of America?'' Mr. Goodwin snorted. ''The Company is going to make a trader out of you. Remember that, William Stewart. It's an honor for a man to serve with the Gentlemen Adventurers Trading Into Hudson's Bay.''

His words sounded grand, but my heart sank low as we made our way through the long, dark shadows of Fenchurch Street to the northeast corner, where stood Hudson's Bay House. I marched with Mr. Goodwin up the wide steps of that somber graystone building. He hurried me along the central hall past many oak doors, all shut. Near the end, we saw a tall, bent Company pensioner, whose right arm ended abruptly at his elbow. In his left hand, he held a large American eagle-feather duster.

''You there, McGillivary,'' Mr. Goodwin called to him. ''Take this lad, Stewart, to the stable with you. Show him where to fill his palliase with nice fresh-smellin' straw.'' The plump man released his hold upon my sleeve, when he saw that Mr. McGillivary had me by the collar.

''He'll sleep sound here,'' said Mr. McGillivary. ''He won't let the weepin', the snorin', and the fartin' of these young London street apprentices trouble him.'' He chuckled. ''Tomorrow I'll show you what's expected. Oh, don't worry. We don't believe in leaving our young lads idle. The Company will find useful work for you to do whilst awaiting transport to America.''

Mr. McGillivary marched me into an ill-lit livery stable. Its dusty, cobwebbed, iron-barred windows made it secure as any prison. Sitting listlessly in the shadows, I could see the pale faces of hungry-looking bonded boys. The wooden stalls had that ancient stench of urine that would never air away. Inside the horse stalls were dozens of narrow wooden bunks.

The first bonded person I spoke with was a Scot about my age, a stutterer, who said his name was Kinnon McNulty. He slept in

45

the bunk above me. I woke when he let out a howl, because a pigeon in the rafters had done the dirty on him.

I watched old McGillivary come and shake two of the youngest boys from their bunks to poke the dying embers, then throw some soft coal on the fire. Slowly the stable turned gray with smoke, while they took turns stirring up a black iron pot of lumpy oatmeal porridge. We others stood impatiently in a line, clutching our pewter spoons and bowls. My porridge, when I got it, was only slightly warm.

"What's your name?" I asked one of the youngsters who was dishing out the grub.

"Dinwiddie. Angus Dinwiddie," he answered shyly.

"How old are you?"

"I'm nearly twelve," he said, and shuddered.

"Don't worry, lads," old McGillivary said, to cheer us. "You'll get issued woolly clothing when the company sends you thither on the transport. God knows, you'll need it," he said, looking sadly at the younger ones. "Courage, lads, you'll be just fine, if you survive the crossing."

McGillivary was a retired Company pensioner and our first adviser, eking out his last days in London because of his infirmities.

Mr. Goodwin reappeared and called out nine names from a list. I'm proud to say that mine was first. We bonded lads were then marched upstairs into a musty office lined with half a dozen high stools and slant-topped desks. I was assigned to Mr. Alexander Althorp, a Company accountant. Oh, what a woeful day that was for me. Mr. Althorp had been forewarned by Mr. Goodwin that I had studied French and Latin. Mr. Althorp possessed not a single word of either. I could see he hated me for that and also, perhaps, because I had more strength in my forefingers than he had in all his limbs.

Mr. Althorp sternly set three of us to the task of copying formal entries in the Company's daily journals. Out of the corner of my eye, I watched him sneak up and strike the Welsh boy across the knuckles with a heavy ruler. "Shoddy penmanship will get each of you the same," he warned us, with his mouth turned down.

Accountant Althorp was a lean, pale, mean-faced man without the slightest wit or touch of humor. I soon discovered that his passion was for poking into others' private affairs. Mr. Althorp invariably dressed like a country clergyman, with a musty tricorn hat, black wool coat, long gray vest and somber britches, dull brown wool stockings, and a gray scarf bound around his neck in winter. In cold weather, he wore a knitted half glove on his right hand that warmed his long, pale, sweaty palms, while freeing his bony fingers for the quill. Mr. Althorp enjoyed demanding that I bring his tea when it was hot enough to scald a pig. He used to tilt back his head and stare at me disapprovingly through his narrow oval spectacles. "I cannot abide you Scottish Jacobites," he hissed through his crooked teeth. Before the new year came around, I hated Mr. Althorp.

One night I had a dreadful dream wherein I saw myself struggling for my life against Mad Duncan Campbell. I must have called aloud.

"Calm yourself," said old McGillivary. "You must be suffering a nightmare."

I greatly respected Mr. McGillivary, who always used the Gaelic when he spoke to me. Though stooped with age, he was a tall man with a fierce, beaklike nose in the middle of a proud, craggy face. He had a crablike way of walking. His cheeks and nose were rosy purple with a hundred tiny burst blood vessels. He confided to me that not only his right arm had been frozen off, but most of his toes as well. Mr. McGillivary had served the Company in two fur-trading posts on James Bay, first at Moose Factory, and then Fort Albany. He had remained in America for almost twenty years, and he told me that whilst there he had shared his bed with an exciting variety of young Cree women. From them, he had learned to speak that tongue and to cherish their thoughtful, loving ways.

Slowly, within his Gaelic sentences, Mr. McGillivary started sprinkling Indian words, then phrases, as he began to introduce me to the language of the Cree. From those first expressions that I heard him utter, I thrilled to the soft sound of that lilting language. I began to make lists of the more complex words he taught me. But for the most part, I just stored those exotic Cree phrases deep inside my mind and let them play like piper's tunes through both my sleeping and my waking dreams.

The London winter days, the weeks, the months passed in exciting ways. I will say for the Honourable Company that on Boxing Day they stuffed us with goose and ale and rich plum pudding and did not give us any chores to do.

During the foggy, rain-soaked weeks of March, Captain James Knight, who was to be our governor when we reached America, came through the offices and shook the hand of every bonded clerk. James Knight was a shortish man, but still he was impressive. Thickset through the neck and jowls like a pugilist, with barrel-like chest, he had short, stocky English legs with bulging calves. He had powerful, square hands and wide-splayed feet that marked him as a man familiar with hard work. His eyes possessed a steel-gray twinkle, and his rosy cheeks were plump and of a color that Althorp said comes from mixing port with Holland gin. His nose had been twice broken and retained a this-way, that-way twist. The cut of his jaw convinced me that James Knight was a most determined man. He rarely smiled, but when he did, his whole face lit up in a way that I, for one, would never quite forget.

Because of Mr. McGillivary's gentle urging, Captain Knight spoke some words to me in Cree and seemed delighted that I not only understood him but could respond in that lyrical, almost unknown language.

"Imagine hearing that from him," gasped Captain Knight, "when William Stewart has yet to see a Cree!"

McGillivary assured James Knight that I had a remarkable gift for languages and that all I needed to master fully the Cree tongue was to lay beneath a blanket for a bit with any lass of good Cree family, and I would instantly become a valuable linguist for the Company.

Alexander Althorp scowled at both of them, took a heavy pinch of snuff, and sneezed into his brown-stained handkerchief. "You and your men stay clear of all native women," he warned Governor Knight, "or be prepared to suffer the penalties."

48

James Knight clasped his thick, muscled hands behind his back. "We are grateful to you, McGillivary, for helping young William Stewart learn the rudiments of Cree. When he has mastered that language, the Company will be able to speak for itself instead of relying on some local Indian interpreter. This could make our trade more profitable, not only with the Cree, but perhaps with other unknown tribes."

Mr. McGillivary nodded in agreement with James Knight, then turned on Accountant Althorp. "If I had known that I was teaching Willie Stewart here to speak the Cree so he could go into the country and help you spy and ruin the fairest pleasures left to traders, I would not have taught him one damned word. You there, money counter, you can kiss my *yeak*! I'm going out of here," the old trader said, "and drink a dram or two of whiskey to wash away my thoughts of you."

"Will you allow that one-armed floor sweeper to speak like that to me?" Mr. Althorp demanded of James Knight.

"Since you seem to have mysterious connections with the high authorities here in London," Captain Knight replied, "you can ask them to restore your dignity for you."

Accountant Althorp eyed me slyly, then whispered in a confidential tone, "Tell me, Stewart, what is the meaning of that word *yeak*?"

"I don't know, sir," I said. "My Cree lessons haven't taken me that far. But it sounds to me, sir, like a thing that dangles doon."

Kinnon McNulty was the first to see the news as it was chalked upon the Company's shipping slate. "It-it-it says the frigate *Union* has been chartered by the Company, to set sail for Hudson Bay on Tuesday, June the fifth, A.D. 1714. Both our names are listed for Yor-Yor-York Factory. I hate to tell you this – but, so is Mr. Althorp. Are you still going to go," he whispered, "or shall we both jump bond and ru-ru-run home to our clansmen?"

"I can't do that. I have no clan to go to. I am a broken man," I said. "But Mr. Althorp, is he going with us – are you sure of that?"

"Yes. And who is Mr. Kelsey? Have you seen him?"

"No," I answered.

We went together to the slate, and I noticed something there that Kinnon had not told me. First the names of the Company's officers to Fort York were posted:

James Knight, Governor

Henry Kelsey, Deputy Governor

Jonathan Carruthers, Surgeon

Alexander Althorp, Accountant

I was greatly surprised to see my name listed separately: William Stewart, Head Clerk. It was followed by the names of the twenty-five men and bonded boys who would accompany us.

Just before we were to set sail for America, I wrote a letter to my sister and my family, bidding them farewell. On the day of our departure, the weather was soft and lovely. England was at its very finest, with shrubs and flowers blooming in every square. We moved toward the river in double file, with six red-coated guards on either side of us. Accountant Althorp wore a face as sour as that roundhead Cromwell as he marched at our rear to see that none of us escaped.

At the loading dock we halted near a nervous group of ordinary family folk, most waiting to see their sons or brothers depart

the Union

from them – perhaps forever. I could easily recognize Angus Din-widdie's fair-headed sister, for she looked exactly like him. She was standing with his mother, both of them weeping quietly. I could feel my heart begin to pound when I realized that I would not be seeing girls like these for seven endless years. Those were the desperate thoughts I carried with me as we boarded the waiting hoy, then moved down the Thames to the anchored *Union*.

I had never set my foot aboard an ocean-going vessel. This one, they said, had been built by Dutchmen. She seemed huge to me and black with age, riding low in the water, for she was overloaded with trade goods and with cannon. Later we discovered that she leaked in every seam. Her fo'c's'le, where we clerks and tradesmen were ordered to hang our hammocks, had a smell like rotting fish and cheese.

The ship's first officer was a hard-looking man who proved meaner than a pit bull. "You bonded lads are crew," he warned us. "Shape up square, or our captain will have you given twenty of the best with this." He let the leather cat out of the bag. The first one I had ever seen. It had nine yard-long lashes, which dangled from the whip's short oaken handle; each lash was knotted and tipped with a cutting shard of lead.

James Knight arrived at shipside, accompanied by a group of Company gentlemen. The one in the silk waistcoat with the fanciest wig, we clerks were told, was the highest governor of all the Company. These grand officers shook hands with James Knight and nodded to the rest of us, saying, "Good health and God's speed to you, lads," and "Do please send us every precious pelt that you can find." They gave James Knight hamper after hamper full of cognac, wines, cheeses, and sugar puddings and had an extra barrel of English apple brandy rolled aboard for us. "By the by," one asked James Knight, "wherever is your deputy governor?"

"He's a shy one," James Knight said, "hates any kind of ceremony, but I expect he'll find his way aboard before we sail."

I was later told Deputy Governor Kelsey came aboard at midnight, as stealthy as a cat. He was seen by no one, save the man on watch. Surgeon Carruthers did not appear until just before we

---

51

sailed. It was not yet dawn, but we could hear him shouting and singing along the river as his hoy approached the *Union*. I watched him from the fo'c's'le.

Jonathan Carruthers was a soft, plumpish man, wigless, with a high domed head surrounded by a feathery fringe of pale gray hair. Four of the hoy's crew were ordered to boost our doctor onto the *Union*'s deck and take his personal effects aboard. He had two large, soft leather bags of clothing and countless wicker hampers filled with bottles, meats and pies, and cakes and cheeses. Oh yes, as well, he had a little medicine box and bag.

Below us on the deck of the hoy, I could see in the lantern light a tall elegant lady, no longer young, but still graceful. She, too, had high color in her cheeks and wore a fashionable silk cape and gown and a tall white wig. A liveried male servant stood beside her.

"Farewell, my dear," she called out in a piercing voice. "Bon voyage, good doctor. Don't sit about in nasty drafts at sea."

"Get that damned hoy clear!" the *Union*'s captain shouted rudely, as he ordered us to haul up anchors and prepare to set our sails.

On that first night out, more than half we Company men were sick because of the swaying of the ship and our unfamiliar hammocks. But on the second day the clouds broke and we had a light following sea. In the evening we were carried out into the Atlantic Ocean beyond the southmost coast of Ireland. The sea blazed like a mirror of reflecting gold, and for the first time I saw Mr. Kelsey. He was leaning on the windward rail with his back to all of us.

Almost from the beginning of this lengthy sea voyage, I had the luck to befriend the ship's third officer, a young Englishman of my own age named Charles Davol. He had attended the Royal Naval School at Greenwich and had been well trained in astronomical navigation. It was he who first allowed me to take a sun shot and introduced me to the thrilling problems of longitude and latitude and the creation of useful panoramic maps and drawings. Charles Davol patiently allowed me to practice with his sextant and showed me how to make accurate observations of our ship's position, navigating by the stars. Using, too, an azimuth compass by day, I correctly learned to sight the sun at noon and calculate our latitude. As if that were not enough, he lent me a fascinating book in French that speculated on a northwest passage to China and the Indies. How exciting! Almost every one of the northern charts he showed me had wide spaces marked *Terra Incognita.* I tried to imagine those unknown lands. Charles Davol looked seriously at me and said, "You've got sturdy legs for walking and a head for navigation. I'll tell Captain Knight that you should be the one to go and map those places."

I liked the sound of that.

Our voyage, which I believed would be far worse than the tortures of the damned, turned out to be quite smooth for the first few weeks. Our worst problem was that the ship's cook and our Company cook detested one another and between them served us food not fit for dogs. But a month later, when we were sailing off south Greenland, the devil turned the tables, battering us with violent northern winds that sent towering icebergs looming down on us through freezing fog. Finally, we edged past Resolution Island and entered the Hudson Strait off Baffinland and encountered mighty tides that turned us in their whirlpools, and icebergs that sailed at us like ghostly castles as we entered the fog-bound vastness of Hudson Bay.

I woke one morning early and went up on deck. There I saw Captain Hurley pacing back and forth across the poop deck, staring glumly at a moving field of ice. He was careful to stay well away from James Knight, who stood midships, feet planted wide apart, swaying against the rolling of the *Union*, keeping his distance from both the captain and his long lean deputy, Mr. Kelsey, who was leaning against the bow. I guessed it was the nature of these three lonely northern veterans not to speak to or trust each other.

Henry Kelsey was a tall solitary man, raw-boned and sinewy, with pale gray eyes, a determined jaw, and a quick nervousness about him. He was a silent man, withdrawn from all of us. He had the reputation of being a great walker who preferred the company of Indians and their untamed dogs over any Europeans he had ever known. James Knight knew Kelsey all too well. He swore that restless Scot had a gnawing in his belly to be the first white man to stride across America, climb the western mountains, and discover any passage over land or sea that would lead him to those distant Mongol lands of China.

On our eleventh day in Hudson Bay, I for the first time saw a score of sea horses, walrus, or walri, as Jamie's tutor would have had me pluralize them. Half a hundred of those great brown beasts lay crowded together, basking on a wide flat field of ice. When our frigate neared them, two of the largest stallions, roaring and shaking their magnificent ivory tusks, flung themselves into the water. Their two harems of sea mares separated and went lunging after them. To my amazement, the two males swam straight toward our frigate *Union* and, gallantly rearing like a pair of cavalry chargers, attacked our ship's prow with warlike ferocity. Two crewmen attempted to harpoon these sea beasts, but they failed, leaving them grunting and bellowing as they disappeared in fog.

"You've got useless bloody sailors on this rotting hulk," our governor shouted up to Captain Hurley. "Fresh sea-horse flesh would have helped to fortify the lot of us against the seaman's sickness."

It was true. By this time our heads ached, our gums bled, and our teeth were coming loose – all well-known signs to deep sea sailors suffering from scurvy.

"I have something secret to tell you," whispered Charles Davol. "During this disastrously slow sea voyage, a piece of treachery has been carried out on all you Bay men. Its purpose has been robbery and personal gain."

"I don't understand," I told him.

"Have you not noticed," he said, "the appallingly small amount of food and drink you have been served?"

"It's true, we are always hungry, but I assumed this was the sailors' lot."

"Not true," said Charles. "Your Company provided adequately for your mess, but your governor is being miserably cheated by this charter captain. We have overheard a deal struck between your Accountant Althorp and Hurley. Before you came aboard, they filled the larbord midship's hold with victuals, beer, and brandy meant for your consumption on this voyage.''

''Why was this done?''

''For reasons of pure greed and profit,'' Davol answered. ''This ex-Navy swine plans to offload you Baymen and pick up the French governor and his men from Fort Bourbon. Then he will sell those extra rations to the French in exchange for fur or other treasure they may have acquired.''

''Why did you wait so long to tell me this?'' I asked Charles.

''Because I have only just discovered the plot, and I believe you should be the one to advise your governor. Do it soon, for all of you look painfully thin. Payment for this theft of rations has already been made to Althorp. I would be surprised if he had not made a plan to stow away and return to London with his profits.''

It did not take me long to pass that grim information on to Governor Knight.

Two mornings later, I heard a seaman shouting, ''Ahoy, sir! Something strange! Ahoy!''

I rushed up on deck, hoping that I might have the luck at last to see a mermaid. The man on watch was pointing to a swimming white sea bear. ''He can't be too far from land,'' he called, and we all peered westward into ice and fog.

Toward evening of that same day, the fog lifted and we heard the lookout in the crow's nest shouting, ''Lowlands lying to the west, Captain! Land ahoy!''

We crowded, cheering at the starboard rails, to see that welcome sight. Our period of passage from England to the western shore of Hudson Bay had been exactly eighty-nine and one-half days – so noted in the voyage journal – for on the evening of September 9, A.D. 1714, we were laying safe off the estuary of the Hayes River in calm though murky weather.

At dawn the frigate *Union* eased into the river's mouth, taking cautious lead-line soundings. Charles Davol showed me on the Navy chart the place marked Five Fathom Hole. When we reached it, Captain Hurley shouted at James Knight, ''Here we stay. I'll not risk my vessel further up that muddy, bloody river for the likes of you." He sent a jollyboat in with a copy of the Treaty of Utrecht, to inform the French they should not fire on us but prepare instead to leave aboard this vessel.

James Knight bellowed to the captain, "We are not in such a hurry that we do not intend to unload those rations you have stolen from us in the midship's larbord compartment."

Our men, already armed with muskets, went below and carried our foodstuffs up on deck. Althorp turned deadly pale and Hurley did not say a single word as we lowered the cargo nets of stolen food into the longboats.

When Accountant Althorp attempted to leave with us, two sailors came and roughly hauled him off to the captain. Money changed hands before the sailors returned to the side and thrust Mr. Althorp into one of the longboats.

"Your plans for sneaking back with us this voyage are null and void," the captain shouted. "I hope you die out here of winterkill."

Althorp shook his fragile little fist at Hurley.

After saying good-bye to my friend, Charles, I was among the Company men who rowed with small sail in four longboats five miles up the river, helped by tide and driving wind and icy rain. Whilst we were stroking hard and raising blisters on our hands, the spiteful Captain Hurley took advantage of the favoring wind and, raising his smallest jibs, sailed the *Union* slowly after us. I, like all the others in our longboat, weak from scurvy, sat slumped over the oars staring dejectedly at York Factory as the cold mists rose. The fort seemed to squat on the swampy muskeg of the riverbank like a wet brown toad. Its two flanker cannons eyed us coldly.

"Those French wretches," Henry Kelsey groaned, "have let our fort fall into rack and ruin."

The pointed wooden stockade walls were sagging, and streaked black and gray with rot and rain. In places the river waters lapped against the crumbling stone foundation. On the roof of the river flanker, I could see three Frenchmen standing nervously around the cannon. One of them had a long brass spy glass trained on us. Beyond the jagged stockade wall, I could see the crude shake roof of the central mess hall and the warehouse on its second floor. On top of that hung an enormous white flag, so rain-soaked that I could barely see its huge weathered fleurs-de-lis. James Knight had told us that the French taking York Factory from the English had been a comedy of errors. We Company men, he said, must correct all that the moment we set foot inside that fort.

"Bravo!" I heard Surgeon Carruthers and the oarsmen in the other boat shout as their bow touched land. "Bravo!" we answered as our longboat crowded in close beside them.

We climbed out weak and sodden wet, but glad to be ashore. We knelt in imitation of our surgeon and crammed our mouths like starving cows with fresh green English lime grass. Each mouthful, he assured us, was the best cure for our scurvy. Off to the right of the fort along the bank, I could see a loose horde of Indians who stood motionless, watching us in stunned or hostile silence.

Our governor had previously ordered our ironsmith, Phineas McAlpin, an amateur piper from the Isle of Skye, to don his kilt and feathered bonnet and to bring his pipes ashore with him. Now James Knight called McAlpin forward and ordered him to play a rousing march, as we twenty-nine officers, clerks, and bonded boys stepped ashore.

"Form fours," the governor shouted, as he pulled down his vest and made sure his sword was at the proper angle. "We're going to march up there very smartly and take our fort back from the French. Can you hear me, Accountant Althorp? You're just the man to bring up the rear."

While I was worrying our bonded boys all into line, I heard James Knight say to his surgeon, "That flag of ours is the first thing that's going up, you mark my words."

Anyone could see that both the governor and his best friend were flushed in the face, and the surgeon was very unsteady on his feet, for they had been drinking brandy and had lost their land legs and were hoarse from cursing Captain Hurley as he trailed them in the chartered frigate.

As we prepared our march on the fort, we looked up and could see a dozen Frenchmen and some painted Cree in blankets peering down on us from the stockade walls and cannon flankers.

"You carry this flag for queen and country," James Knight ordered Surgeon Carruthers. "Keep it folded neatly and don't dare drop it, with all those froggies looking on."

The good doctor clutched the Company's royal-red flag against his belly and stood there swaying on the landing, as though he still rode the *Union*'s deck in a tremendous swell. Governor Knight was, by comparison, as steady as a rock, splendid in his tricorn hat, scarlet Company coat, doeskin breeches, and freshly varnished high black boots, his dress sword wagging out behind him like a coach dog's eager tail. With a forward sweep of his hand, he ordered us to march. Had he said three abreast or four? It didn't matter! It had not been easy for us to form up, watched as we were by a hostile crew of English sailors at our rear, an unknown band of Indians at our flank, and Frenchmen skulking up above us, in our fort. McAlpin was out in front. Our surgeon staggered gamely just behind our governor, and the rest of us followed, trying to regain our land legs.

Have you ever tried to march behind a wretched inept piper while crossing over boggy ground? I was not at all surprised when Surgeon Carruthers stumbled and fell belly-down, getting the flag quite muddy. It took three young bondeds to help him to his feet.

We were accompanied by several hundred Cree – men, women, and children – and barking dogs, all trying to keep up with us on either flank. Except for Knight, Kelsey, and a few of the veteran Company journeymen, none of us had ever seen a red Indian before. These Northern Cree were tall, well-made men and women, many with handsome brown faces, wide cheekbones, and dark, piercing gypsy eyes. They wore a baffling mixture of French and Indian clothing. The men had elaborate feathered trade hats and wide bright bands of woven wool bound round their waists. Their women, young and old, were dressed in moccasins and skin leggings, topped off with colorful wool blanket shawls worn over deerskin shirts. They displayed string upon string of brightly colored beads and countless fluttering ribbons. Almost all the younger children were naked, even though the day was cold. Far off to our left, I could see thin wisps of smoke blowing from their skin-covered lodges and hear what sounded like a hundred dogs yapping and howling, returning their insults to the piper.

When we arrived at the entrance to Fort Bourbon, as the Frenchmen called it, the rotting wooden gate remained barred shut. We halted there and waited, so unsteady from our long sea voyage that some swayed from side to side. The French guard on the stockade cupped his hands against the wind and carefully lit his pipe before he shouted down to us, "*Qui êtes-vous?*"

James Knight answered, using the most awful French pronunciation, "*La Companie Royale du Grand Bretagne.*" His words were followed by an unkind burst of laughter from a bevy of Frenchmen staring down at us from the flanker roof. The governor may have heard wee Hamish snicker, too, for he quickly turned his head.

"All right, Stewart. Try your French on them. Tell those froggies up there to open up this gate!"

I called out the governor's order, and we heard more cackling from the Frenchmen in the *Companie du Nord*, but eventually they disappeared, and we heard them all together grunting and straining, as they forced open the near-collapsing main gate. McAlpin began skirling on his pipes again, playing some unrecognizable march that sounded more like a wild Irish lament.

So it was that on Tuesday, September 11th, 1714, we Scots and Englishmen went marching proudly through the gates and repossessed York Factory. Little did I dream of the joys and terrors that lay before us in that uncharted wilderness of North America.

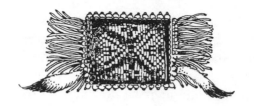

THANA

4

"Dingee!" I screamed when I felt Kunn's hand catch me by the hair. I turned my head and bit him with all the strength my jaws possessed. He bellowed in pain as my teeth tore into the muscle between the thumb and forefinger of his left hand. I rolled from beneath him, scrambled to my feet, and ran. He came racing after me in such a rage he would have caught me, but the big male dog, Cunwah, ran between us and sent him sprawling in the darkness. He cursed me as the sharp gravel cut his knees.

Now our four pack dogs came gamboling along beside Dingee and me, as though all of us were free.

"Catch them! Bite them! Kill those Copper bitches!" We could hear Kunn yelling to the dogs.

We were not afraid. We were far more friendly with his team than he was. Their excited barking urged us on.

Kunn was falling back now, running and limping far behind us. We two had grown lean and strong because of our hard summer's carrying, and that cruel brute had grown soft from overstuffing on rich caribou meat and yellow goose fat.

Finally, two of his dogs grew tired of the game and fell back, remaining with their master, but his two best pack dogs – the bitch, Suscan, and the male dog, Cunwah – stayed with us. When we stopped for breath, Dingee gave each of them a few scraps of the meat she had snatched out of the cooking basket. The two dogs stayed with us, and we were overjoyed to have them, for one needed only to sniff the night air and see the misty ring around the moon to know that snow was coming.

Now that Kunn was without us and his two best toboggan dogs, we had some hope that he would lose our trail and never find us. We ran and walked and ran again all through the night, until dawn spread itself across the eastern sky. We stopped and listened, crouching, staring south. Our mouths gaped open, better to hear every sound. Kunn must have been far behind us, for we had been careful to keep to the rocky eskers where we would leave no trail.

We drank some earthy-tasting water from a rain pool and ate a few cold scraps of caribou, then lay down exhausted, trusting that the dogs would warn us if he came. We knew they would not run away. Our dogs, unlike their cousin wolves, cannot hunt for themselves, cannot survive without human beings. We slept and woke in frightened starts, for neither of us could believe that we had escaped, that we were free!

"Those two dogs of his will find us," Dingee worried. She held Kunn's iron knife in her hand.

I had placed a pair of fire stones in the basket. Sometimes we could strike these, then light the tinder. I had hoped to find my mother's small yellow flenser, but there had not been time. We had only the pair of dogs with us, Kunn's knife, two copper needles, a hank of sinew, and the clothes we wore. I wished that one of us had taken a caribou sleeping-skin. It was going to be a torture trying to stay alive out on the land, without tent or cover and winter coming on.

Before dawn, we stood up, shivering, and took our direction from the fading Wolf Star. Thus we two began our journey back toward our homeland, hoping to reach the enormous lake and find some of our Dene people before starvation or the cold could lay us down. On the first days of our freedom, even the wind-bent dwarfed trees that edged the tundra looked like friends. But now, each morning, all the smaller lakes and ponds were edged with ice. We longed to build a fire each night, but we did not, for we feared that rising smoke would lead Kunn or the other Wood Cats to us. "How can we go on wandering like this, no food, no tent, no fire?'' Dingee asked on the fourth day. ''If we don't find food, we'll die like this pair of dogs we hug to try and keep us warm.''

''Don't talk like that,'' I told her. ''Keep moving. Sing inside yourself, sing to the animals. Ask them to come to us.''

As we walked, Dingee pulled the longest hairs from her head, as I did mine, and we each braided half a dozen long slip-noose snares. When we felt the cold of evening, we searched the low willow clumps for any signs of ptarmigan, those plump birds that were turning white, and the round black droppings that rabbits leave along their runs. When we saw signs of either, we bent willow saplings and tied to them our thin hair nooses and set them ready to be sprung by little wooden trip sticks we shaped with Kunn's knife. On those hungry nights, while we were waiting for the snowshoe rabbits to appear, we would cling together on the open ground and hold the two dogs close for warmth and shudder when we heard the distant singing of the wolves.

ptarmigan

Each morning, when we woke, we ran out to our sets. But day after day, our snares took nothing. We were traveling between the southern Wood Cat country and our northern lands, a place of desolate emptiness known by all to be a starving ground for animals and humans. On the ninth morning, when we woke, we found two long lean snowshoe rabbits hanging in our snares.

We crouched in the protection of a rock and devoured them like a pair of wolves, sharing the last parts with the dogs.

Two mornings later, we caught three furry-footed ptarmigan with their brown autumn plumage almost gone. We cut one in half for our two dogs, then ate the others slowly as we kept on walking to warm ourselves.

We had journeyed on the barren grounds for the same number of days that I have fingers on both hands and toes on my feet. When we looked at one another, we could see that we were scarcely staying alive. I, like Dingee, lost all track of time. We had gone beyond the country of the ptarmigan and rabbits. Our stomachs rumbled, and our hunger became so desperate that we were forced to suck at the clean-picked bones of the birds we'd taken days before. Sometimes the dogs dug up ground squirrels but ate them quickly, before we could snatch our share.

"Without you I would die of loneliness," I told Dingee.

"We'll find our way back," she said, then sang a song that we had learned as children.

We both felt better after singing. "It's hard out here, but at least we know that we are free. No Wood Cat is going to make us kneel for him tonight."

I laughed like a crazy woman when she told me that.

The wind blew against us and the walking got much worse, but in the end, the hunger and our endless nights with empty snares seemed to harm Dingee more than they did me. She grew silent and no more songs came out of her. She staggered behind, with me pulling at her wrist, and became so weak that one morning she could not rise or walk. I was forced to kill and share with her our much-loved bitch, Suscan. This set us both to weeping, as we flayed away her fur to use it as a sleeping skin.

While that poor dear bitch's meat lasted, our other dog, Cunwah, like ourselves, grew stronger, and we regained some hope. We tried chewing caribou-hide strips, cut from our leggings. But all too soon, we were starving once again. Our worn-out moccasins let our bare feet feel the dampness of the newly fallen autumn snow. Early each morning, I set my course by the Wolf Star, trusting it to lead us to our country.

"Do I look really old?" I asked Dingee, as I felt my face.

"No," said Dingee, "you look fine. Your eyes look big and your cheeks are just a little bit sunk in. But you still look good to me."

"You're saying that I look like a starved old woman. They are always skinny. I am never going to get a husband," I told her. "I am just going to wander through the snow, never lying with a good man, just waiting for myself to die."

"I had a husband. I wonder where he is," said Dingee, who then began to cry.

Night came down gray and heavy with the cold. I looked up sadly, as the Wolf Star appeared. He is the steady one that all the others swing round, the one that lay with the Big Woman and put us humans in the world. I could tell that we had been wandering that day, driven by the north wind, for we had circled slowly into the southwest.

We were excited when Cunwah dug up a large, sleeping, ground squirrel. We tried, but could not get it away from him before he gorged it down. We caught only one thin rabbit in our snares and ate all of it between the two of us. Our moccasins were worn beyond repair. Some nights we had to hack away the edges of our caribou shirts to bind around our feet. Most mornings the ponds and shallow lakes were frozen far beyond their edges, and on the horizon snow clouds scudded low.

"What does it feel like to have a baby?" I asked Dingee.

"Well, it's good, when it's growing inside you, and you can feel it kick. When it's coming out, it hurts," she said. "But when you've got hold of it and it's lying warm against you, it's the best thing in the world." Then she started to cry again, and I was sorry I had asked her. Still, it wasn't fair that I was going to die out here without ever knowing how it felt to suckle one, to have one for my own.

That night Dingee and I clung together, trying to catch any warmth from our dog, Cunwah. He shivered just as much as we did and whined from hunger and despair. In the morning, we were desperate and our stomachs clutched and sent sour juices to our mouths. Dingee wept as she held Cunwah's head between her knees, and picking up a heavy stone, I quickly killed him. I let out a wail, hoping somehow that his spirit would forgive me.

We made a small fire and ate as much of his meat as our cramped stomachs would hold, then rolled the two dog skins together as a sleeping mat. Poor Cunwah's flesh kept us going for eleven more days.

Our night snares gave us nothing until the moon was on the wane. Then, in the clouded darkness, we heard the whirr of wings, and in the morning Dingee's sets held four plump white ptarmigan. Mine held three. We ate a whole bird each and walked all day and slept curled close together with the skins of those two life-giving dogs beneath us.

When we awoke, the weather had turned warm. The north wind that had plagued us day and night had died and a silence lay over the whole land. The ice on the muskeg had a soft gray glint and every blade of lime grass was glistening with hoarfrost. How had we survived?

"This warmth means that it is going to snow," Dingee said. "A heavy snow will kill us. I don't care anymore. I've been thinking about my baby thrown away in the snow, not warm, not breathing . . . I don't mind. I'm ready to go and see him soon."

"Try to forget that," I pleaded. "We're going to keep on moving."

"Where?" she asked me. "We're not going into Dene country. So we must be looking for the Wood Cats. Maybe we can find Kunn again."

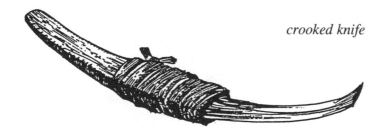

crooked knife

65

I didn't answer her.

Even as she spoke, the first big soft flakes came drifting lazily down and settled on the silent bogs, blocking out the distances. The snow fell slowly at first, but we could hear the wind moaning and sighing high above us. The flakes then grew small. Riding on the east wind, they came slanting at us sharp as sand.

I had to pull Dingee by the hand and make her hurry with me, hurry to reach a stand of willow that stood almost shoulder high. Dingee seemed to be in a dream. Using Kunn's knife, I cut some small trees and left others rooted in the ground. We bent short branches, weaving them into the crude form of a bird's nest, upside down. We heaped snow against this shelter from the wind before we crawled inside. We left the snow on the ground within our nest, for snow is soft and almost warm, whereas bare ground will freeze you far more quickly.

Lying wrapped in the two dog skins, I was almost asleep when Dingee asked me, "Would you have run from Kunn – if you had known it would be like this?"

"No, nothing could be worse than this."

Dingee hugged me tight and said, "I hope my husband is alive."

Sometime in the night the wind died, and a great snow fell in silence, burying us within our own crude shelter. When we awoke, the weight of snow above had pressed our willow shelter flat down against us. We had to raise the shelter with our backs and prop it, then dig with our hands. We jerked our two dog skins out from under the heavy blanket of whiteness. When I looked at Dingee, I laughed, and then I began to weep, for she stood waist-deep in soft clinging snow. When this kind of storm occurs in our country, neither the humans nor the animals go abroad until a cold wind comes and hardens the drifts.

"We can never walk in this," said Dingee.

The new snow lay like an endless trap, stretching to all horizons. I tried to stagger, then crawl, through it, but my arms disappeared in the deep soft covering. "We must have snowshoes," I told myself. "We can weave them. But how can we make frames?"

We shook off the load of snow and crawled back inside the hole where we had slept. Taking the knife, I cut four branches thicker than my thumb. I spread out one of the dog pelts and Dingee took the knife and carefully sheared the skin along the edge. Working together, we cut dozens of long thin strips of hide. Then, of the four willow sticks, I picked the one that bent most easily. I placed its center in my teeth and bent the two halves downward with my hands, until they formed a long crude oval. Dingee quickly bound their ends together with a dog-skin thong. We bent three more frames and tied them roughly into oval forms and stretched each one with a wooden cross piece.

Now came the woman's part that we knew far better than any man. Using the thin-cut dog-skin thongs in place of the usual caribou hide, we twisted and wove the mesh that turned the willow frames to snowshoes.

"Those dog-skin thongs," said Dingee, "they may not last too long."

We bound our makeshift snowshoes to our feet and were surprised at how light they were and how well they carried us across the snow.

"What is that?" said Dingee, pointing.

"Probably you are dreaming things again," I told her, but I shaded my eyes and soon I saw a small black speck hanging in the air. It did not move. "I have never seen anything like that in all my life," I told her.

We could not stop ourselves from walking toward that speck. There was no edge to the world that we could see.

We were so cold and stiff in the morning that we could scarcely rise. The only thing that drove us forward was that strange black speck, which still appeared to be motionless, in the sky. By nightfall it had grown much larger.

Next morning, Dingee woke me weeping. "It's gone, it's flown away."

"No, it is just hidden by the blowing snow," I told her.

About midday, we found a bloody patch where a snowy owl had swooped down and killed a rabbit. We carefully took up that red snow and ate it, then put our backs to the north wind and wandered aimlessly south.

In the morning, I woke Dingee. "There it is again."

We were much closer and could make it out more clearly. It was large and round, perched like a huge brown owl atop a straight stripped tree upon a hill, not too far off.

"What can it be?" asked Dingee.

"Perhaps some humans have put that strange thing there. Be careful," I told her as we wrapped the skin rags around our feet and limped toward it on our tattered snowshoes.

If we wished to reach it before darkness came, we would have to cross a very long narrow lake that barred our path. It was completely frozen and covered with newly fallen snow. We squatted on the shore and stared at the long expanse dejectedly.

"It will take a whole day's walking to go halfway around this lake," I said to Dingee. "Do you have the strength?"

She shook her head.

"We could go straight across," I admitted. "It would save us two whole days of walking around its shores. Do you think the ice will hold our weight?" I asked her.

Dingee started to weep again and chewed crazily at the tattered sleeve of her caribou shirt.

"Come on. We'll try it," I said, helping her stand again.

Taking Kunn's knife from our cooking basket, I bound it to the staff I carried.

"You walk behind in my footsteps, but don't come near me, even if the ice seems strong." I started probing the snow before her with the knife point.

"Walk with your feet spread wide apart," said Dingee. "You listen for cracks, and run if you feel the ice sagging."

The two of us tried to pad as softly as a pair of lynx across the windswept snowy surface of the lake. The image of the brown owl on its perch grew in size with every step we took.

Suddenly Dingee called to me, "Wait! The skin thong on my snowshoe has broken!"

I tried to force my mind to think of something helpful, as I saw Dingee take off both snowshoes and sling them across her back. "It's all right," she called to me. "The snow here is harder. I'll go ahead now, if you give me the knife and stick." Dingee started moving toward the edge of the lake, cautiously probing the ice.

As we approached the shore, I saw before us a small, not fully frozen stream. I could hear it softly gurgling. I remembered my grandfather's warning to be careful in winter of any place where moving water joined a lake. "Dingee!" I called to warn her, when suddenly I saw her freeze in terror, then leap back. Too late! She spread her arms wide as the ice collapsed beneath her. I saw her plunge straight down into the blackness of the lake.

I started to run toward her, but my grandfather's warning forced me to untie my snowshoes, then fall flat upon my belly. Cautiously, I crawled toward the deadly opening, calling, "Dingee, Dingee!" But my tongue had grown so thick with fear that her name came out only as a whisper. I heard a long cracking sound, and I imagined my own body dropping into the freezing water. I spread my arms and legs and started wriggling away from that black hole. I could see the water seeping toward me in a spreading gray stain. My weight was making the thin ice sag.

I rolled away from the hole in terror. A deadly silence hung above the lake.

I saw something black rise and float in the steaming patch of open water. Then I recognized the sodden remnant of Dingee's dog skin. I watched as the dark tips of hair turned hoary white with frost. I don't know how long I lay there weeping on the lake, but when I looked up, I believed that I could see the souls of Dingee and our two dogs moving silently toward me. I struggled to my knees, and when I looked again, all three of them had disappeared. I crawled away, too frightened and too weak to stand, for I could no longer trust the ice.

When I reached the safety of the land, I lay down and wept for Dingee and myself until a freezing wind came creeping underneath my tattered shirt and drove me shuddering to my feet. Without Dingee, without the dogs or knife or fire flints, I had nothing. I shambled forward hopelessly, hearing Dingee's gentle singing distorted by the wind.

———

I do not know how far I walked or how many times I fell before I found myself staring down at a wide jumble of dog and human tracks. The snow was pressed by the smooth weights of toboggans. I pulled off my mitts and fell down and caressed those human footprints with my bare hands and my cheek. Like an animal, I sniffed the tracks. Yes, they were sharp and fresh. Humans and dogs had passed this way not long ago! I admired their well-fed urine splashes as I staggered after them. Sobbing crazily, I ran forward, for I believed that I was saved. The tracks followed a narrow frozen river.

I stared in disbelief. There, on a hill, stood the strange thing in the sky, which I saw to be a wooden object on a post. Among a dwarfed grove of tamaracks nearby stood a camp. Three skin tents were huddled close together. Snowshoes were suspended from the little trees, and four toboggans stood upright in the snow. Among the tents were many more owl-shaped wooden baskets like that perched atop the post. I sniffed the sweet familiar smell of wood smoke in the air and the mouth-watering scent of goose fat as it drips into a fire. Oh, I knew by their shape that those tents were built by Cree. I didn't care. I stumbled forward. I would be anything for them – a slave or a toboggan dog – as long as I could have my mouth stuffed full of goose meat and be with humans once again.

When their toboggan dogs caught my scent, they rose in a pack and rushed at me. To protect myself, I screamed for help and threw my mitts – one right, the other left – pretending they were chunks of meat. The dogs turned and lunged at my skin mitts, fighting for them, tearing them to pieces.

My screaming, or the noise of the fighting dogs, caused all three tent flaps to be flung open. Several men leapt outside and ran toward me, shouting violently to warn away their dogs.

"*Ahwahena keya*? Who are you?" they called to me in the northern dialect of Cree, as they peered cautiously into the winter gloom behind me.

"*Coshake*, a friend," I answered in their language.

"Are you alone?" a man asked suspiciously.

"Yes, alone," I answered. "Everyone I know is dead."

70

Two of them came cautiously toward me.

"*Whit to co*? Are you a devil?" one demanded in Cree.

"*Pung ke petun en weweson*. I am a starving woman," I answered in his language.

"*Es tum*, come here," another said.

I tried to do as I was bid, but staggered shamefully and fell down, and had to crawl toward them like a dog. I had lost all feeling in my bare hands and trembling knees.

When they saw that I could not walk, they called to a tall man who wore a green coat. He came and picked me up quite tenderly. "You don't weight much," he said. He called other men to hold the tent flap wide, and they eased me in and laid me down beside their fire. He lifted up my half-eaten pointed shirt to feel my ribs and breasts.

"All of you keep off her," the green-coated man threatened them. "I'm going to take this woman in and show her to the guvnaar. Later, if he doesn't want her, you can have her, all of you. But don't touch her until I say so. Do you understand?"

They nodded.

"*Neya nipalia kustisow* . . . I'm starving," I whispered to them. I was not afraid of these strange men. I only thought of food.

I had been half-blinded by the snow, and it now seemed so dark inside their tent that I could see nothing but human shadows and feel the warm glow of their fire. My ears could clearly hear the steady drip, drip, drip of goose grease as it fell and sizzled in the flames. That rich smell was so overpowering that I cried out and clacked my teeth together.

Green Coat lifted my head and shoulders, and squatting, held a wooden food bowl to my mouth. He kept pulling it away from me, so I could not drink too fast. I begged for more, but he would not let me have it, knowing it would make me sick and I would lose it all.

The last thing I remember was the sight and smell and sound of those dozen hunters crowded close around me. I didn't care about them. I was alive. Alive! I could feel the spirit of life rising like a song inside me. The warm goose fat was spreading through my body, softly oiling my cracked lips and throat, filling my belly, soothing my raw red wrists, my elbows, all my limbs. I curled up small and drifted blissfully into the dreaming world.

Halfway through the night, I jerked awake, seeing in my dream the frightful image of poor Dingee's eyes staring at me from that icy hole. I must have cried out, for several of the Cree sat up and looked at me.

Instead of using me, these men fed me another bowl of thick goose soup.

"Now be quiet, woman," Green Coat said. "Go back to sleep."

I did not wake again until mid-morning, when they fed me once again. Then I slept for one whole day and half another. When I woke, the men were gone. But some dogs were lying just outside the tents, and I knew those hunters would come back. I could have run away, but I was afraid to be alone, and there was no place I could go.

On the third day, the Cree returned. Still, they did not bother me. I could stand by myself again, but only if I used a staff. That evening, I walked slowly along the snowy paths between their tents.

"Do you understand me, woman?" Green Coat asked me.

"A little," I answered.

"Tomorrow we are traveling. You should weave yourself a decent pair of snowshoes." He held out a handful of sinew thongs and a new-cut pair of frames. Eagerly, I wove them, using our Dene snowflake pattern, which was not at all like theirs.

Next day at dawn, the Cree were up and working hard, rolling the heavy round wooden baskets onto their toboggans and lashing them tightly into place. Then they caught and hitched their dogs and lashed on their snowshoes.

Snowshoeing in a line behind their trail maker and the four toboggans, the Cree pushed sometimes and urged their teams until we arrived at the place they called *Wawi Yepeyamatin*, Egg Hill. Here was the tall stripped tree Dingee and I had seen, with the wooden basket set on its top. The Cree unloaded half of all their heavy wooden baskets and, digging away the snow, they buried them in soft sand.

"*Sapomin* – smoked and stiffly salted goose flesh." Green Coat wrinkled his nose and pointed at the casks. "Disgusting! But that's the way those Ballahooly traders ruin their geese. You'll see. They live not far from here."

Just the thought that I might someday see a Ballahooly caused me to hide my face in fear.

I moved forward with the Cree, traveling behind their head man in a long line of humans, dogs, and toboggans. Sometime after midday, we crossed a low rise. Before me I could see a huge, dark, ugly-looking square that was squatting in the snow. It appeared to me like some enormous deadfall built to catch a giant bear. As we approached, I could see that it was made of an endless number of upright tree trunks sharpened and lashed together with all their limbs hacked off. It was far larger in size than forty or even eighty of our tents, if they were sewn together. I was afraid to look at the huge red skin tied to a tree post at its very top. It made an angry sound as it rippled in the wind. The Cree moved fearlessly toward this enormous Ballahooly trap made of rows of sharpened spears.

WILLIAM

5

I looked carefully around the inside of Fort York, which the French had renamed Fort Bourbon. It was the last place anyone would wish to call home. Even nature seemed ashamed of it and was turning the wet sleet into snow, trying to cover up the ugliness that man had made. Soggy, star-shaped flakes came spiraling in over the lead-roofed flankers, whitening the sagging rooftops and plugging the mouths of cannon, hiding the nasty litter strewn across the inner grounds.

The French commandant, a young man named Jérémie, stood before us, flanked by his officers and servants. He appeared to be not more than twenty-four or -five. Like his three officers, he was very grandly dressed in gartered pantaloons and multi-colored doublet. Snow-sodden ostrich plumes drooped from their hats. Handsome as their costumes were, I noticed that both officers and their men were shivering from the cold – or could it be from sheer excitement, since the first jollyboat brought ashore French orders to yield the fort to us and embark for home.

Beside them our governor, James Knight, looked as squat as an English bulldog. He took five paces forward and handed the young French commandant a red-sealed and beribboned parchment scroll, which stated our authority to reclaim York Factory. The three French officers huddled anxiously around this new document, reading it and eyeing us with a mixture of amusement and suspicion. James Knight asked me to explain to them in

French that their orders were to return to France aboard the chartered vessel *Union*. When they fully understood my words, every one of them began laughing and shouting, "*C'est formidable! Vive le Roi!* Take down zee flag *tout de suite! Bonjour, cochons anglaise!*"

The youngest of them ran and hauled down their limp white flag with its faded fleurs-de-lis. Fort Bourbon was no more. Our new and only slightly muddied Company flag was proudly hoisted. As it rose above the wet stockade, we heard two hundred Cree let out a mournful groan, which could only mean they were not pleased to have English traders return. Our coming was all part of the Treaty of Utrecht, a truce made between the English and the French. McAlpin, our so-called piper, began his vile caterwauling again. The Frenchmen responded by clapping their hands across their ears. We didn't care, for we had clearly won the day.

"*Au revoir, mes amis. Baissez mon derrière!*" the young officers shouted back as they and their men went running helter-skelter down toward the waiting longboats. They waved and made lewd gestures to young Cree girls who waved as they watched the French row out to board the *Union*. Its sailors carelessly flung our Company supplies ashore.

"What does '*baissez mon derrière*' mean?" James Knight asked me.

"Something about kissing, sir," I said, "anatomical and quite rude, I believe."

Our governor led us all inside the fort, and for the first time we had the chance to look inside the buildings. We soon discovered that the French, upon hearing the first news, had held one final orgy, no doubt a farewell celebration. The Indians had joined them in throwing rotten goose eggs and rancid seal oil everywhere. We could not believe the awful litter, or the overpowering stenches that hung in every hall and chamber.

"The sailors say the frigate's leaving on the morning's tide," McNulty whispered, "if they can get our food and trade goods all ashore."

In the darkness of the mess hall was a single candle sputtering near the end of the long table. "Stewart! Why are you always elsewhere when I need you? Stew-art!'' the governor shouted. ''Bring your inks and quills and writing box and sit here close to me.''

When I joined Governor Knight, he glanced around to see that Accountant Althorp was not listening. ''This is urgent, Stewart. I have got to pass a private letter back to London on that ship.'' He handed me a piece of crude brown wrapping paper with his own graphite scrawls upon it. I tried but could scarcely read a word.

''Fine penmanship,'' the governor said, ''has never been one of my ambitions.'' He snatched the paper from me. ''I'll read this out to you as written, then you can twist and turn my words about and give each one a fancy curlicue fit for those dandies in the London office. Dip your quill, lad. Let's get on with it. I want to sign that letter first thing in the morning.''

Before dawn I had his letter nicely reconstructed. Its proper grammar still contained his message, penned in my most elaborate style.

To the Board Members
at Hudson's Bay House, London.

Honourable Sirs:

This letter of 11 September, 1714, is to inform you that we have today accepted the formal surrender from the French commander of the Companie du Nord. *We arrived safely after a prolonged voyage of ninety-two days, much of that in ice. The* Union's *Captain Hurley, the miserable master of this vessel, will undoubtedly blame me for all our violent disagreements throughout this voyage. The fault, gentlemen, was entirely his, not mine. He stored the boxes belonging to me and your Company officers in an open deck space, causing them severe saltwater damage. Also, the food we received aboard this vessel was utterly disgusting – the salt beef mouldering, the cheese alive with weevils, and the bread all mildewed green. Surgeon Carruthers reports that most of our men are suffering from various degrees of scurvy. I earnestly recommend you never again charter Hur-*

ley or that filthy, leaking frigate Union, *and further, that you refuse to pay the other half of the charter sum originally agreed upon.*

I shall do all possible to restore your fur factory here at York which the French, during their occupation, have allowed to fall into utter rack and ruin.

In haste to place this letter aboard the outgoing vessel, I rest your Honours' most faithful and obedient servant to command,

> *James Knight*
> *Governor at York Factory*
> *West Coast Hudson Bay*

"Looks fine to me," said the governor, and he signed the letter in his usual rough-handed style. "Get a move on, Stewart," the governor warned me. "That hellish ship will soon be under sail." Then, snatching off his Company ring, the governor pressed its seal into the sealing wax he motioned me to drip onto the folded letter. "There, that's done right, *pro pelle cutem* – it's the Company motto," he said with satisfaction.

I tied the letter inside a fish-skin pouch. The governor sent four of our strongest oarsmen rowing a light French skiff out to deliver it, just as the *Union*'s crew was hauling up her anchors.

I climbed the ladder to the catwalk of our Company fort with the governor and all the others, to watch the *Union* as she set sail for France.

One of our bonded men was Terrance Orbs, an Irish gunner who had seen action with the Royal Navy. He had climbed up on the lead-sheathed forward flanker and just for old time's sake was busy sighting in the cannon and gauging with his instruments the correct degree of elevation.

"Is that gun in working order?" James Knight called to him.

"Indeed, sir, I believe she is," Gunner Orbs replied in his lilting Irish voice. "I should greatly like to test-fire her, sir." He stroked the cannon's pitted barrel. "Yonder ship is still in easy range, sir. Would you like me to send them all a farewell pair of balls?"

"No, no!" the governor shouted. "If you sunk 'em now, Captain Hurley might somehow make his way ashore and we'd have to put up with that sorry bastard through the winter."

Following our surgeon's orders, we made fires and gathered English lime grass to boil with river water, mixed with vinegar and strong dry mustard. He instructed us to vigorously rub our gums above our loosened teeth. "This is beastly," Mr. Althorp groaned on that first night, because the fort itself was such a mess that we were all twenty-nine of us forced to bed down out in the open, laying side by side beneath a pair of abandoned French short-rigged sails. These were pegged up by our shipwright, Smithers, against the inside stockade wall.

The bonded boys stood shivering in a miserable huddle, waiting for the porridge pot to boil. We put everything on, including our blankets, then drank a round of English apple brandy. Everyone felt much better after that.

Our governor, who had endured almost twenty years of trading in this same heathen country, took immediate precautions. "A lot of strange Northern Cree have come down here," he said, "and don't you dare to trust 'em." He ordered the main gate closed and barred and instructed me to be first sentry on guard. I was to set up a roster of regular sentry duty with each man standing a four-hour watch, day in, day out, around the clock.

Our governor, James Knight, was a very vigilant man. When I first met him in London, he seemed as uneasy as a tethered Highland bull. His face had the rough red color of a farmer, his short strong arms hung awkwardly from his shoulders in a coat that was too small for him. The great rounds of his buttocks seemed about to burst out through his breeches. He would clasp his hands behind his back and purse his lips, listening to others as though his thoughts were drifting far away. Now that James Knight was in command of this gloomy Company fort, I began to see the true man emerge.

He had the habit of staring every man directly in the eye. The home guard Cree and the Northern Cree he viewed quite separately. Yet each one of them, male or female, he considered essential to the Company. Only through these Indians, he believed, could we hope to succeed in trade and expand westward in this country. They were the ones who would help us or prevent us from finding gold, silver, copper, and the precious gems that James Knight was always seeking. He had an insatiable curiosity about the vast uplands that lay north and west of Hudson Bay. He was determined, against all odds, that we must explore them.

The Assiniboin seamstress named Owinipeg, whom the French had left behind, was the only native person James Knight allowed to sleep inside the fort. He did this out of compassion, we were told, because that proud Assiniboin woman would be terribly abused if he forced her to live among the Cree. Only our goose captain, Cheechoo, was allowed to come and go, but even he had never slept inside the fort unless, of course, among the French.

The governor and his deputy, Henry Kelsey, definitely did not like or trust each other, but they both shared many friends among the home guard Cree. Those grand beaver catchers had traded first with our Honourable Company, and later with the French, year after year. In spite of all their differences, on the second day we were at York the governor and Henry Kelsey went outside the fort and sat on some red trade blankets and smoked a pipe of peace with those same Cree and a horde of younger men. Captain Cheechoo, after his dozen years of dealing with the French, gave his allegiance once more to the Hudson's Bay Company. He had earlier possessed many useful words of English, but he had almost forgotten them, or got them all mixed up with the French. He now waved his hands and said, *"oui, oui,"* instead of "yes," and called James Knight *"mon cher commandant!"* which our governor found intolerable. Nevertheless, Captain Cheechoo was rehired as the Company's head goose hunter and our go-between with all the Cree.

James Knight and Kelsey were easily able to understand and speak many useful trading words in Cree. Together, on this day, these two seasoned Company men made gifts of tobacco, molasses, gunpowder, and cheap brandy, much coveted goods which the French had long since traded away. The Cree then presented them with three bark baskets full of reeking fish with sunken eyes, a score of soggy rabbits, and two dozen brace of limp gray geese long since past their prime. All of these James Knight ordered our cook to boil until they turned to broth or hardened into leather. Alas, all of it tasted dreadful. Still, Surgeon Carruthers assured us that such victuals would help cure our scurvy, clean out our nether regions, and fortify our innards for the coming winter.

Later I heard Mr. Althorp grumble, "The way Knight runs this fort, things can't get any worse!" But he was wrong. They could and did. Three days after the *Union* had departed, a pair of Cree paddlers found a crumpled object bobbing in the waters off the River Hayes. This curiosity they brought to us. It was the governor's parchment letter that he hoped was bound for London. Its seal had been torn open. Hurley must have read it, then flung it into the sea.

James Knight was in a rage that night. I heard him say to Surgeon Carruthers, "I was wrong! Dead wrong to miss the chance. I should have let that cocky Irish gunner sink the friggin' lot of them."

"It's too late now, Jimmy," the surgeon belched. "You must get another letter off to London next year."

My turn for sentry duty came at dawn. I climbed up the ladder to the catwalk that led around the inside of the rickety stockade. Smoke rose from the Cree lodges more than two gunshots away.

The last autumn moon that rose above York Factory marked a painful time for all of us. We had to burn six hundred rotted beaver pelts and endless bags of sodden, mildewed goose down. That was not surprising, for no ship had reached this fort for several years, and the French had sent out nothing. The main mess hall, the storeroom, and the cannon flankers and even the smaller buildings were supported by log props, to shore up the collapsing walls. "They didn't cut a bloody stick of winter firewood," James Knight complained. "Shipwright Smithers, I'll give you a work party of nine men, and you go upstream. Cut the wood and float it down, before the river freezes."

We clerks were left behind with hoes and shovels, to scrape the fort's filthy floors and walls.

When these chores were finished, the governor inspected everything. "Well done, lads," he said. "But remember, we have not yet traded a single pelt or earned a ha'penny for this Company, though winter's all but here. I want prime beaver. *Pro pelle cutem* – that's our motto, 'a skin for a skin.' You can read it on our Company's coat of arms. Down in James Bay, they'll tell you it means, 'We'll skin you like we skinned your fathers.'

"Don't worry, boys. We'll be trading with them soon enough." He paused and eyed us sharply. "You must trade fairly, especially when a fox-eyed troop of Cree is watching you.

stretched beaver pelt

"The Company wants beaver as well as otter, marten, fisher, mink, lynx, ermine, fox, wolf, white bear, black bear, seal, caribou skins, and musk-ox hides, and be always on the lookout for an Eskimo unicorn's horn and ivory sea-horse tusks. Good bonuses are paid for such strange things. Remember, we trade fresh caribou meat, swans, geese, fish, partridges, porcupines, rabbits, and birds' eggs in season for our table. Now, mind my words," he said, "if a Frenchman or a Chinaman reached this fort tomorrow, I would expect you to trade the hair right off his head. But be careful with these Cree. They are backward in some ways, but they have a memory sharper than a razor, and they are dead keen when it comes to trading. If they see you cheat them by a penny nail, the lot of them will not forget it, nor forgive you, 'til your dying day.

"Besides getting all their fur," the governor said, "I want every one of you to keep a lively eye for any metals – especially gold, silver, copper, maybe even diamonds, rubies, emeralds.

Who knows what strange wonders some Indian may bring in here to trade – tanned dwarfs' skins or giants' ears or heavy mammoth ivories from the distant lands of China. That's the great excitement of it, lads. We're all of us lucky to be living here in this great country. You'll see – I'll wager you'll be homesick for this dear place when you get back after spending only seven years upon these unknown shores.''

One of the cheeky bonded boys from London broke wind, and the rest of us groaned and rolled our eyes toward the ceiling.

The governor laughed and pointed north, then swung his finger west. "Before I leave this country, I plan to know a whole lot more about those uplands. Wild folk live out there." He sighed. "Which one of us will be the first to see them?"

By mid-morning of the following day, the sun was glaring weakly off the newly fallen snow. To protect those Cree who wished to trade, Shipwright Smithers and his carpenter had rigged a sailcloth lean-to against our outer stockade wall, and from its poles they hung bright pennants. Eagerly we unbarred and raised the trading opening in the outer wall of the fort. When the Cree saw the pennants, they came running, for as Cheechoo had told us, they believed that though we were not nearly so much fun to have around, our trade goods were superior to the French.

Deputy Kelsey advised us to display our longest muskets and fancy lace-trimmed hats, our brightest multi-colored strings of beads, gleaming copper tea buckets, and neat fan shapes of penny nails, stacks of red and blue wool blankets, plump brown twists of Brazilian tobacco, and squatty wooden casks of cheap English apple brandy, as well as little kegs of black molasses, shiny skinning knives and iron hatchets, brass thimbles and packets of needles, skeins of Irish thread, tinkling sheeps' bells, bundles of green parrot feathers, silverish mirrors, and a dazzling array of colored ribbons.

To further whet their appetites, we sent Captain Cheechoo magnificently dressed in a tri-cocked hat and a new-styled London coat of peacock green with huge gilt buttons. We encouraged him to stride boldly back and forth before the awestruck viewers, while I spoke to them loudly, using phrases such as, "Oh, what a lovely hat that brave man wears. That hat," I continued, "trades for only ten" – I help up ten fingers – "marten skins. Oh, see the strong captain," I cried, "he is wearing a beautiful coat. We will trade it to you for only twelve prime otter skins. Look, how he aims that splendid six-foot musket that will put balls on the moon – only twenty winter beaver skins, brave hunters, and such a firing piece belongs to you."

Captain Cheechoo, who had been teaching me, said I spoke wondrous Cree.

Kinnon McNulty, who had a friendly way with all Cree grandmothers, mothers, and their daughters, started dancing and singing Gaelic songs and wooing them with sugar tits, offering short bits of brightly colored ribbon and shorter strands of strong snare wire as gifts. They had no prime beaver pelts as yet, and we did not trade a single skin, but we wished to give them rosy hints of things to come.

"Do beaver really build houses?" Collinwood asked me.

"Oh, yes," I said. "Back in London, Mr. McGillvary told me the beavers build houses and keep them very neat inside. They arrange three separate rooms, he said – one to sleep in, one to eat in, and a little one they use especially for pooping."

"You are joking me," Collinwood laughed, as he crawled into his bed. "Did I hear you say the beavers make a special room for pooping?"

I awoke next morning to the screaming of McAlpin's bagpipes passing by our door. His ghastly din was the governor's way of forcing us to rise and do our early duties. I sat shivering in the blackness, flung on my outer clothes, and with the other clerks ran slipping and sliding across the icy inner yard toward the mess hall.

Inside the kitchen stood the cook, a mean-eyed man in the morning. I fished about inside the big iron pot until I found half a goose carcass that still had a leg attached, then I filled my wooden bowl with broth and took my place at the mess hall table.

I unrolled my sailcloth napkin from its ring and tucked it tight around my neck. The Company had issued me with a red woolen doublet, and I was determined to keep it clean.

At any time, Cook Matiloo was a slow-moving, pale-faced brute with a long hog belly. On this morning, his voice gave off that rasping sound of a meat saw hacking bones. "Who of you has ever laid your eyes on such a bloody awful place as this?"

Taking up a meat cleaver, he began angrily hacking at the dripping sheath of icicles on the inside of his kitchen wall. The wall, like much of our fur factory, had been quickly flung together of unseasoned hemlock logs. These had been crudely squared with axes and laid one atop the other. In the kitchen's heat, the logs had shrunk and spread apart, until in dozens of places you could look out between wide cracks at the snow in the inner fort yard.

"Time and again I have begged that bloody useless . . . shipwright, Smithers, to come in here . . . and caulk this bloody . . . wall." The cook stopped hacking at the ice and glared at me. "Will Mister Smithers help me? No, he will not! He's too tired from bedding that young Cree doxy of his. I've seen her sneaking through that little secret door he cut for her. She keeps him tuckered out. He hasn't got the strength to swing that caulking hammer . . . to weather-tight my kitchen. But you'll notice that he ain't too busy when it comes to stuffin' hisself with the goose meat that I cook for all of you. Well, if Smithers doesn't fix this windy wall, I'll put something nasty in his soup! You tell him that for me."

I must admit that the north wall of this kitchen was an awesome mass of dripping ice. To make the cook feel better, I took up his stove axe and helped him hack at the inside wall until ice was lying knee-deep on the floor.

"You deserves a drink," he said, "for helping me."

I sat down again at the mess hall table across from Kinnon McNulty and Little Harry. All three of them had the winter glums. Kinnon used his sleeve to wipe the goose grease off his mouth, then started grumbling about the future.

"Captain Ch-Ch-Cheechoo says that real winter hasn't nearly come." He shuddered, glancing toward the tight-closed shutters, as though he feared the howling winds would tear them open.

"The Honourable Gentlemen planned this fort all kicky-cocky," Collinwood said. "Looks like a little child had built it. It's supposed to be star-shaped, but the cannon flankers go this way and that, and the stockade walls just zigzag everywhere. Probably wasn't too bad until the French came here and ruined the bloody thing!"

At that moment, Shipwright Smithers came in carrying a wooden roofing mallet and a wedge, his leather apron sagging with its weight of nails. "I swear we shall choke to death in all this smoke," he coughed.

"Cook told us this fort is falling down," said Little Harry, "because you keep cutting little secret doors to let your doxy in at night."

"Don't you worry, lads, about my private doings," growled the shipwright. "You'll be going home yourselves in seven years, and nearly be old enough to jump aboard some little girls yourselves."

To change the subject, I nodded toward the shelf. "Boatwright Smithers, what do you think of those two lovely stuffed white swans the Frenchmen left behind?"

"They ain't lovely, and they ain't white at all," Smithers answered testily. "They're a very nasty-looking pair, if you ask me. Their feathers have turned yellow, and you can see some Frenchman's clumsy sewing up their breastbones and all along their necks."

"In England, swans are protected. They're Her Majesty's royal birds," said Collinwood. "I've heard she calls them all her privates. Any poacher who dares to touch Queen Anne's privates gets hanged right away. I wish we had a fresh swan here to eat."

On Monday, November 5th, after making an entry in the Company journal, my turn at sentry duty came around again. I piled on all my heaviest clothes and bandaged both my feet with fur before I stuffed them into an enormous knee-high pair of sealskin boots that the French had traded from the Eskimos. Four hours up there alone seemed like a lifetime. I went slithering back and forth along the catwalk, hating sentry duty. Twenty paces north, then ease about, and twenty paces south! The wind came moaning in across the sharpened pickets and made a horrid hooting sound inside my musket barrel. The icy rain turned to driving sleet that froze the moment it touched my hat, my musket, or my greatcoat. I soon forgot to look for any raiding Indians, for I had to set my mind against the marrow-freezing cold.

Down below, the whole enclosure of York Factory had become a star-shaped field of glinting ice. In its center, our massive mess hall squatted like a rude square oven. Through its tight-drawn shutters, I could see thin cracks of yellow light and I could hear the muffled sounds of mugs banging and clerks stamping, yelling, singing. And where was I? Staggering and shivering, back and forth, and back and forth.

"McNulty, what's keeping you?" I shouted. My unheard words went moaning out across the frozen marshes.

At long last, the mess hall door flew open, like a stove casting its hellish glow across the snow. A lumpish figure in a wolfskin hat came lumbering across the icy yard of the fort and lurched up the ladder to the catwalk, singing.

"What took you so bloody long?" I rasped, as I slapped the icy musket into his mittened hands.

McNulty giggled in my face. His breath was ripe with apple brandy. "They are having a grand time down there, Willie!" he cried as he shouldered the clumsy flintlock and went swaying along the catwalk's slippery path. "What are you complaining for? It's lovely up here. Aye, that cool sleet is very refres . . . !" He slipped and fell.

I did not wait to see him rise but climbed quickly down the trembling ladder and ran toward the cracks of light between the logs. I jerked open the heavy mess hall door and squinted my eyes against the blurry glare of torches through the choking wood smoke. My ears rebelled against the boisterous English singing and the hammering of pewter mugs against the messing table. I flung off my soggy coat and hat and dried my face and hands on the surgeon's woolen scarf. At first, I drew in my breath, enjoying the smell of Brazilian rope tobacco, overripened cheese, and the cook's green-spruce beer.

As I reached the middle of the hall, everyone was crowded around the mess table, and I observed that our tall goose captain, Cheechoo, had drunk his double ration of English apple brandy with wondrous effect. Suddenly, he rushed to the door and, snatching up a musket, ran out into the darkness. There was a blinding flash and roar and the clash of shattered icicles falling from the eaves. We all cheered together, for that explosive sound marked the true beginning of our Guy Fawkes celebrations.

When I heard McNulty shouting from the sentry's walk, I stuck my head outside the door. "What in hell is going on down there? Stewart, will you do me a wee favor? Tell the governor I'm fuggin' cold up here. It wouldn't spoil his Guy Fawkes Day to send me up a cup of brandy and a bit of suet pudding. Will you tell him that for me?"

James Knight was a generous man, and to celebrate on that bleak night of November 5th, he had ordered the cook to bake four huge laughing-goose pies and to brew not one, not two, but three large oaken casks of proper beer, brewed with hops. "A Guy Fawkes frolic," the governor had said, "might put a little spice into our lives."

The governor ordered another round of brandy for every man within the fort – except McNulty – and we toasted good Queen Anne. Soon after, the governor had cause to realize that he had been overly generous, not only with Cheechoo, but with all the rest of us. When the double brandy ration reached their heads, instead of eating their share of the laughing-goose pies, my clerks started tossing great wet slabs of it at their least favorite persons, who quickly scooped them up and threw the soggy pie chunks back again. Cook Matiloo, who was serving the pie, was struck squarely in the mouth. No one would have minded that, but suddenly they started pelting tight-lipped Accountant Althorp and poor old Surgeon Carruthers.

The Cree hunters and their families had certainly heard Cheechoo's gun discharge and, perhaps, our boisterous singing. I believe it was Sentry McNulty who let the women in. Suddenly our mess hall was alive with sprightly young Cree females, dancing, jiggling, giggling, hugging, shrieking all the French that they had learned, and snatching sips of brandy. Heaven alone knows the varieties of forbidden womanizing that went on that night before our Guy Fawkes feast was ended.

But chasing women wasn't everything. With my own eyes, I saw some of the youngest bondeds assault Accountant Althorp. Worst of all, someone accidentally stepped upon his eyeglasses. Mr. Althorp stood against the wall, aghast, as he watched our young bondeds pursuing partly naked girls around our mess hall table.

Next morning, the mess hall looked no better than the day the French had left it. The governor paraded all clerks and servants before him in a line. He ordered all of us to stand stiffly to attention.

As punishment, Governor Knight cut off our daily brandy ration and banned all conversation around the table for a fortnight. We were not even permitted to whisper "Pass the salt!" Those two weeks of mess hall silence taught us all a dreadful lesson.

From the beginning, it had been James Knight's custom to place himself at head of table every evening. Remembering our conduct at the Guy Fawkes feast, the governor would stare balefully down the table, shaking his head in deep despair. Slowly he would shift his gaze to each one of my apprentice clerks and all bonded boys, then his eyes would wither each of the indentured servants – first the Shipwright Smithers, then the ironsmith, the cooper, the stonemason, and the others, saving his most awful gaze for me, the cook, and last of all, Accountant Althorp. When the meal was ended, the governor would bow his head and say, "Thanks be to God for this good food we ate. Amen." Then he and Surgeon Carruthers would rise and take their leave, past Captain Kelsey's seat, which was empty as usual.

Two weeks after our Guy Fawkes frolic, I was able to make an entry in the Company journal declaring that Captain Cheechoo was on his feet again and well enough to lead a mission. We clerks gathered on the catwalk and watched with the long glass as Cheechoo mustered half a dozen of his better hunters from the Cree lodges, finally getting six of them, with their dogs and toboggans, all in line. The fresh air seemed to cheer Cheechoo. He turned and waved at us as they marched away in single file toward the high barrel beacon that the French had perched on top of Egg Hill.

toboggan

When our fortnight of silence ended, James Knight's cheerfulness returned. He clapped his hands together, and he spoke to all of us at mess: "There's a ring around the moon tonight, my hearties. You'll soon feel some boisterous weather. Not long after that, we'll be doing some real peltry trading. You can mark my words on that!''

That night, a heavy gale of winter winds put us in grand disorder and made our clerks' room intolerable. Next morning at breakfast, Shipwright Smithers issued me a good-sized square of weathered canvas which we pegged up inside our north wall. On windy nights, it used to billow like a topsail. I bribed that dreadful piper cum blacksmith, Phineas McAlpin, into fastening lengths of chain to three French cannonballs. McNulty, Neal, and Collinwood, who shared the room with me, would go clumping into the mess hall every evening like three prisoners and cast their iron balls into the mouth of the fiery stove. After eating, they would use the chains to haul these red balls out, then drag them back to our room, where they would hang them on iron hooks in front of our frost-split window shutters. Some nights that room became so warm that we did not even need to wear our fur caps or our outer woolen stockings underneath our bedcovers.

On Saturday, November 24th, near noon, exactly three days after the first heavy winter snow had fallen, we heard our sentry call out a warning, and Crees shouting and their dogs barking just outside the main gate. Robert Emmett, who was then on guard duty, hollered down, "Willie, Willie, come up here – quick! You won't hardly believe your ruddy eyes!"

I scaled the ladder to the catwalk, and squinting against the glare of the snow beyond the pointed stakes, I could see tall Captain Cheechoo snowshoeing vigorously toward us. Behind him came all six of his goosers, and their dogs dragging salted casks lashed onto their toboggans. Cheechoo was decked out in his peacock-green coat, bright sash, and wide three-cornered hat. With his left hand he held a gypsy-looking woman with wild hair. As she moved, she rolled her hips and drove her curious snowshoes forward in a style quite different from any of these Cree.

The strange woman wore a tattered long-tail parka, sharply pointed front and back, with only the remnants of a fringe. Although she appeared to be young, as they drew near I saw that her deeply tanned face was haggard, and her thick, black, unbraided hair streamed in the wind. As they reached the fort, I saw her try to break free, but Cheechoo hauled her back.

Below me, I could hear the main gate creaking open. Looking down, I saw the enormous round-domed beaver hat and the great cone-shaped beaver coat that covered Governor Knight from head to heel. I watched him stalking stiffly forward, holding his great beaver gauntlets wide, as though he wished to grasp that foreign female to his breast. He shouted out in English and in broken Cree, "Captain Cheechoo, do my eyes deceive me, or have you caught a Copper woman, alive?"

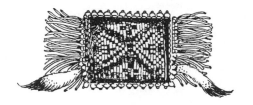

THANA

6

Careful, Thanadelthur, this could be the end for you, I told myself. What size of monster would be caught in a deadfall trap as large as that? Wait! Could this truly be where the Ballahooly dwell?

Weak as I was, I placed one snowshoe before the other, trying to keep pace with the tall Cree, Green Coat, who so tightly gripped my arm. The Cree toboggan dogs barked and whined in answer to many others that were tethered near some large winter dwelling places where the Cree had made three long, skin-covered lodges. Off to where the sun does rise, I could see the mouth of a frozen river and the cold salt waters of the inland sea.

The Cree dogs strained in their harnesses, eager to drag their heavily loaded toboggans toward that terrifying trap. High, near its top, I could see two mouse-sized human figures moving among the sharpened spear points. They peered down at us, then waved. The goose men all waved back. I watched in horror as a huge hole opened in the middle of the trap like a great mouth eager to devour me. I could hear its jaw muscles creaking, and I tried to run away, but the long-legged Cree took an even tighter hold on me. We halted and I stood there trembling, waiting for the other goose men to grab me and throw me in its mouth. Their leader, Green Coat, marched me forward, as I stared in horror at the strange fur-covered creature that appeared between the open jaws and moved toward me. At first, I thought it was a barren grizzly bear. but it was something far more strange and frightening, with its round furry head and a pelt that hung down like that of a musk ox with hair that trailed along the snow. The creature started grunting in a strange half-human voice. Its eyes flashed white beneath bushy eyebrows, straddling a red nose and a chin of blue. I was terrified when I realized that I was staring at a real live Ballahooly, with paws widespread ready to crush me to death.

Green Coat, who had saved me, seemed equally unable to understand the confused roaring of this creature. Then a flush-faced young human head appeared among the tall spear points. He called down some words in Cree which I understood to mean, "Inside here – bring her – quick – let not – that Copper woman – flee – from you."

Those words further frightened me, for I knew very well from Kunn those Cree words *quick*, *flee*, and *Copper woman*!

What could I do but stand trembling as I watched that huge bear of a man moving ponderously toward me, his pale eyes rolling as he studied me. Would he simply rape me, or devour me? We Dene children had been warned to be alert against every kind of evil, if we ever met a Ballahooly. For we were told that Ballahooly, though not as clever, were just as dangerous as the Eskimos, but they lacked the little people's magic killing power. Oh, yes, we Dene have had our troubles with the Eskimos, but not even the widest travelers among our hunters had ever seen a Ballahooly, though many hideous tales were told of them. In the south, they were said to ride astride the backs of huge, fast-running dogs and could split young girls like me in half, if we ever dared to lie with them.

Out of the sides of my eyes, I could see a horde of Cree men, women, and children surrounded by their dogs, racing across the snow toward us. I thought, oh, yes, they are hurrying here to see this Ballahooly split me apart before he eats me.

"Stay back!" Green Coat shouted to his people. "Stay back! She's mine, this Copper woman. I'm going to trade her to the Ballahooly guvnaar!" He pointed at the bearlike man who was coming toward me. The crowd stopped running and stared at the Ballahooly, then at me.

Green Coat let the bear man grab me, and between them they dragged me inside the jagged, gaping teeth. As the trap jaws closed behind me, I heard them squeal and groan. Now I stood staring at a frightening smaller horde of Ballahooly who came pressing around me – more of them than I had fingers and toes. They spoke together in strange whining voices, using their lips and teeth to form their words in a way that made me think of ground squirrels chewing seed. The clothing that they wore was so oddly shaped and very brightly colored that most of it must have come from where the Ballahooly dwell.

The flush-faced young man, whom at first I thought was Cree because he spoke their language, climbed down from the high spears. He stood lean and straight beside the squatty bearman. Green Coat told this young man how I, a foreign Copper woman, had come crawling like a starving dog into their camp. Then the young man quickly turned every word that Green Coat said into words the Ballahooly could understand. Green Coat took me under both my arms to show how he had dragged me away from his dogs into the safety of his tent. He pulled up my pointed shirt exposing my lower belly, ribs and breasts to show them all how thin I was. The Ballahooly seemed really interested and crowded close around me, to have a better look.

Bearman turned and shambled off ahead of everyone, waving his huge beaver mittens, signaling us to follow. That frightened me so much that Green Coat had to take me by both wrists and drag me after him.

Inside the outer wall of pointed wooden spears was a large, flat, snow-covered space, and at its center was the largest, strangest lodge that I had ever seen. It was not at all like our skin-covered tents, for it was made with long, thin tree trunks laid flat, one on top of the other, to form a huge square. Each log was notched at the corners, so it would stay in place. The top of this Ballahooly dwelling was pointed upward, like a tent. At the peak of this bloodthirsty cannibals' den hung the huge blood-red skin that I had seen from far away.

I listened to the Ballahooly talking and watched the way they moved their mouths to form the awkward guttural sounds they made. It was a curious language that they spoke, and at first I could not understand the smallest word of it. Bearman continued staring at me and pointing to my parts. It is very rare for them, I thought, to catch a Copper woman.

"Tell them I am very skinny," I said to Green Coat. "Tell them that they won't get much good eating off of me."

He snorted when he heard that and started talking to the lean young Ballahooly. Together they tried to explain their thoughts to me, in Cree. The young Ballahooly kept smiling at me in a kindly way, and I soon lost my fear of him.

"These Ballahooly don't eat humans," Green Coat told me. "They eat smoked goose meat, and they like fish and caribou and brandy. They like brandy, so do I. They say they're going to feed you until you get nice and fat, then they will give you a new shirt and leggings and some mitts and moccasins." He shook his head as he stared at the crude skin bindings on my feet. "This guvnaar says he will give you a blanket and a place to sleep." That made me feel better.

I looked once more at that pale young Ballahooly. He spoke Cree very clearly, not rough and mean like Kunn.

Green Coat pointed to Bearman and said, "Do you see that great chief standing there? He has been hoping to get hold of a young Copper woman."

"Why?" I asked suspiciously.

"I don't know why," Green Coat answered. "He says he wants to talk to you."

"I can't speak one word of that Bearman's language," I told Green Coat strongly. "Anyway," I whispered, "I'm scared to get too close to him."

"No need to be afraid," the young Ballahooly said, and smiled at me again.

"I am very afraid of that Bearman," I said, "but I'm not too much afraid of you."

The young Cree-talking Ballahooly laughed when he heard that, and I could see his teeth were white and even. His blue eyes looked straight at me. Too bad about the size of his ears, and, like me, he's far too skinny, but when the caribou come maybe we will both fatten up a bit.

The young Ballahooly said, "Copper Woman, come with us."

Bearman jerked open a square wooden hole in the logs and stamped the snow off his huge fur-swaddled feet before he ducked his head and entered. After we had unbound our snowshoes, Green Coat pushed me in ahead of him.

It was dark and gloomy as a cave inside, and filled with strange and awful stinks. There was a hot fire burning in a reddish box, but there was no hole in the roof to let out the choking smoke and fumes. Green Coat hauled me through the darkness into the center of this enormous lodge. Bearman went and stood beside another Ballahooly. He seemed old but kept smiling at me nicely. He made me open my mouth, while he tried to wiggle my teeth.

Both of these men eased themselves down onto a square wood sitting log. The young Ballahooly talker sat beside them. Green Coat hauled me around to the other side of a heavy deadfall trap big enough for bears. It was made of flat smooth-cut logs. He had to show me how to sit up high like all the others, not to squat or kneel. I slid in very carefully, hoping not to trip the deadfall trigger. I hated having my legs dangling beneath that dangerous-looking slab. Green Coat was wise, he stood behind me.

Bearman let out a growl, and a fat Ballahooly with a greasy leather skin tied around his belly came shuffling forward and gave each of us a bowl of broth. Mine had chunks of goose meat floating in it and was so hot it burned my lips. I blew it cool, then drank it down in one long gulp. He filled my bowl again.

I started to drink off the second bowl, but Green Coat grabbed my tattered sleeve and said, "Not so fast, wolf woman, don't you throw up in here."

To please him, I slowed down and took my broth in little birdlike sips.

Bearman growled, and the young Cree talker asked me, "What's your name?"

"Thanadelthur," I told him. "My name means stretcher for marten skins."

The young man scribbled black marks on some thin square animal skins. "Where have you come from, Tha-na-del?" He left off the rest.

Twice I tried to answer him in my own Da-Dene language, but no one understood me.

"You, speak Cree," said Green Coat angrily.

"How is it that you speak Cree?" the young Ballahooly asked me.

I frowned at all of them. "The Cree way of talking was forced on me and my cousin, Dingee, by a crazy man, a Wood Cat from the south."

"Never mind that. Answer his question," Green Coat ordered me. "The guvnaar wants to know where you come from."

"Very far north and west of this place," I told them.

"How did you arrive here?"

"I ran away with my cousin, Dingee. We were both stolen from our families, made slaves by a real bad bugger we named Kunn. He nearly killed us during the nine long moons he had us, before we got the chance to run away from him. My cousin, Dingee, fell through the ice, poor thing, and drowned. I was alone when I crawled into this man's camp," I said, nodding toward Green Coat. "He fed me goose broth and kept his men off me." I guessed he was saving me for this big Ballahooly.

The pink-faced young man smiled and shook his head at me. "No one's going to hurt you here," he said. Then slowly he repeated the words that I had said to Bearman. Of course, I could not understand their language, but I listened to that young man carefully and guessed that he, too, was just learning to speak Cree. His ears seemed smaller now, and I was starting not to mind the look of his blue eyes. But when he pulled off his hat, I was shocked to see that he had hair the color of a red fox. When he spoke, this tall Ballahooly boy moved his hands as though he wished to help his mouth curve around those long slithery singing sounds that good Cree talkers are so fond of making. I was getting used to his longer nose, and I liked the steady way he looked at

96

me. I wondered what name he would have that I could call him. Yes, he is just like me, I thought. He speaks two languages. I hope he doesn't go away.

"Are there – beaver – living in your – country?" he asked me, speaking very slowly for the other Ballahooly who knew not a word of Cree.

"Yes, we have some beavers," I answered him.

"Marten, too?"

"Oh, yes," I said. "We have so many minks and martens that sometimes they come stealing food inside our lodges."

"You have lynx, too?"

"Yes, sure! We have lots and lots of lynxes."

"And wolves and foxes? What else?"

"Yes, wolves and foxes," I said. "And we have musk ox, caribou, brown bears, black bears, lots of big fish, and swans, owls, and long-tailed ducks and geese, and loons with very handsome feathers."

"We don't want any feathers," the young Ballahooly told me. "We want only skins, and . . ." He used another word I did not know. Then he pointed at the little hammered copper bracelet on my wrist. "That is something that we want. Do you have any in your country?"

"Sure, we have lots of that," I said, and he leaned over and told that to Bearman, who took something off his middle finger and handed it to me. It was smooth and yellow. "Yes," I said, "in my mother's country we find two kinds of colored stones like that, the yellows are lying in the little river. Our men hammer both into flensers and needles and gifts for the women, and knives and arrow points for themselves to use."

Bearman stood up quickly when the young Ballahooly told him what I'd said. He walked fast twice around the table.

"How many moons does it take to walk back into your country? We want to trade for the furs and yellow stones."

"Are *you* two going to be doing the walking?" I asked Bearman and his friend who had looked in my mouth, for I could see that with their big bellies and wearing all those heavy beaver skins, they would not move very fast.

"No, no," he answered. "Someone younger, like this young man talking to you. He will go."

"Is he going to be the one to go with me?" I asked.

Bearman nodded, meaning yes.

"Do you want us to go now, or when the snow goes?"

The young Ballahooly talker shuddered and said to me, "I hope we go in summer."

I thought he must not know that summer is the worst time, a terrible time to travel. It rains and the land is soggy underneath your feet, and you have to walk around many lakes and ford the rivers. If the wind is down, hordes of black flies or mosquitoes can suck blood so fast they will sometimes kill dogs, caribou, and even children. But I didn't want to tell Bearman and his friend that. I didn't want to discourage them from sending that young Ballahooly to walk with me back to Dene country. "I would be glad to go with you anytime," I told that young red fox-haired man.

Sitting there among those Ballahooly, I started counting moons upon my fingers, nodding my head like my grandmother used to do. "You could walk into my country in three moons, maybe four, camp there with the Dene for the hardest winter. Then start snowshoeing toward thick tree country, before the snow is gone. That's the best time," I told them, "my people always go out hunting during those two caribou moons."

"Would you be able to find your family?" the young Ballahooly asked me.

"No," I said, "we won't find them. They were . . . killed. Dingee's family is dead as well. Our whole camp was . . . killed. But maybe not Dingee's husband, Kasba, or my brother, Keewatan. I hope those raiding Wood Cats didn't find our hunters sleeping, too."

"Her people are as bad as any Wood Cats," Green Coat warned the young Cree talker. "You tell the guvnaar not to try and send any Ballahooly out to find her Copper people," he said, pointing his big bony finger straight at me. "If you dare go into their Dene country, this slave woman's people will slaughter all of you. We Cree are not afraid to trade with her wild Copper people. But you traders should stay safe inside this fort. We Cree will go and trade for you. No guns, no knives, no brandy trading with her crazy people . . . do you understand? You give us Cree lots of tobacco, fish hooks, beads, ribbons, needles, mirrors, shiny buttons, everything light to carry. We will do the trading with them.''

When I heard Green Coat's words, I told the young Cree talker, ''You tell Bearman my Dene never hurt a Ballahooly. My people have never even seen one! It's the Wood Cats who sneak north and kill the Dene. Young women are the only ones they take alive, as slaves.''

I listened carefully as the tall young Ballahooly repeated in his tongue all the words that I had said. Of course, I could not understand his foreign speech, but his whole way of talking was slowing down for me. I could hear him repeating certain words like 'yeesss,' and often 'nooo.' I wondered what they meant. He had cut my name in half and only called me Thana, and used the words 'noorth' and 'weeest' and 'traade' every time he pointed toward me or my Dene country.

Bearman sat with his elbows on the food trap, steadying his heavy head between his hands. Then he, himself, spoke slowly to me using Cree. ''Bad winter coming – too cooold – for walking. You, Thanade – , you sleep here with Cree. They feed you. In spring – when geese come – some people – with this young man will go walking with you – back to your country.''

When Green Coat heard the guvnaar's words, he shook his head and pointed to me. ''Cree women here will want to kill that Copper woman. If they don't, our men will use her up,'' he laughed.

The guvnarr frowned. ''You tell this Copper woman – she is going to live with us – inside this fort.'' He had the young man tell, ''You be very wary of Cree women!'' Then Bearman said to Green Coat, ''This Company is going to trade with her Copper people – whether you Cree help us or not.''

Green Coat glared angrily at me and the other three men, then slammed on his black hat and strode out of the smoke-filled lodge.

The young Cree speaker said, ''The guvnaar wants you and me to sit and talk together every morning, so you can help me learn to speak your Copper language.''

99

"I will be very glad to do that. I hate speaking in the Wood Cat tongue. But I am glad I learned it, for it is almost the same as Cree," I said. "I will be glad to teach you my language. It is called Dene, or Da-Dene, which is the name of my people. I wish you could have heard my grandmother speaking. Her words came rising from her throat like the songs of birds. I would take you to her, if the Wood Cats had not killed her."

"That is too bad," the young man answered. "I would like to have heard her speak."

"I could teach you best if we lay together every night," I told him. "I will feel shy if we just sit talking in this big smoky place each morning."

He smiled and his face turned kind of sunburned when I said that to him. I noticed that he did not translate those words to Bearman or the other Ballahooly man who had looked inside my mouth.

"You know my name is Thanadelthur?" The young man nodded. "Do you also have a name?"

"Oh, yes," he laughed. "My name is William Stewart . . . Will-i-yum Stu-arrt," he said his name very slowly, then repeated it three times.

I closed my eyes and tried it. "Will-i-yumm Stu-Stu-Stu . . ." What an awful sounding name it was, almost impossible to say. I could say Will-i-yumm quite well, but I had a terrible time saying Staarit. "I'm just going to call you 'Williyumm,' and forget about the 'Staarit.' "

"Yes, Williyumm will do fine," he said smiling, showing me his good strong teeth. "You've got it right. I'm going to call you Thana."

"It's only half my name," I told him, "but Thana will do for me."

Bearman mumbled something to Williyumm, who said, "He wants to show you the place where you are going to sleep."

"Do I have to sleep with him?" I asked.

"No!" Williyumm laughed. "Not with any of us." He motioned me to follow them outside.

We trailed along a hard-packed snowy path until we reached another little wooden lodge leaning against a much larger one inside the wall of spears.

Bearman gently opened another wooden door that hung on leather hinges. I thought, there's a good idea! Inside the lean-to was a handsome-looking woman sitting on a bed of caribou skins piled upon the floor. She was sewing by a bright oil lamp. This woman, who had very wide cheekbones, crinkled her eyes at their corners and gave me a long suspicious look. She was not young anymore, but she was still beautiful, with blue-black hair brushed neat and clean and tightly braided, in a special way that I had never seen before. She had wise eyes and a well-shaped nose, generous lips, and strong, even teeth.

Williyumm told me this woman's name was Owinipeg. He said she was the only female living in the fort and that she did sewing for the guvnaar and some others. He explained that I was to share this little wooden lodge with her.

The woman, Owinipeg, nodded to me and said, "Come in." She used the Cree language, which she spoke in a soft ripply way, but I could tell by her accent, dress, and manners that she was not herself a Cree. I guessed that she, like me, was a foreign woman from some place far away.

After the two men left, Owinipeg told me that she had seen me come in through the gate and had understood how afraid I must have been. She rose from her sewing place and went to a large wooden box, which she opened. From it, she took blankets and two caribou sleeping skins, which she gave me to make my bed. The blankets were soft and thick and berry red, the most beautiful things that I had ever been given.

"Poor thing," she said, "tomorrow we will make new clothes for you."

Owinipeg hung a sooty little black iron pot over her lamp, and in a while she poured me something hot and brown. It was strong and bitter. She made it sweet by putting in pale sand. That was the first time I ever tasted what she and the Ballahooly call 'teeehh' and 'shoogar.' Then, as another welcoming present,

Owinipeg gave me a shiny iron needle. It was sharp and almost as thin as a mosquito's stinger, and would easily pierce the toughest hide. I pulled up my pointed shirt and showed this new friend of mine the colored porcupine quill designs on the hip string that my grandmother had given me.

It wasn't long before Owinipeg and I were laughing together and gladly getting to know each other. She told me that she had been brought here in her family's canoe by the curving river that flowed toward the Wolf Star from their lands beside a long lake, far away. She called that place Assiniboiya, buffalo country. I was interested in everything she had to say, but on that first night I could not keep my head from nodding.

The Assiniboin woman smiled at me and said, "You lay down and go to sleep."

I took off my worn clothes, and she gave me a warm wet cloth to wipe my body, then wrapped my new red blankets round me. I had the warm feeling that I was once again resting in my father's lodge with my family all around me. I even fancied I could hear Dingee's clear voice singing, as I closed my eyes.

In the morning when we woke, Owinipeg and I drank tea again and shared the soft boiled flesh of a snowshoe rabbit she had snared. Owinipeg told me we could both set snares at the riverbank on the off side of the fort, where the sentry would warn us if he saw Cree men approaching. After eating, the Assiniboin woman gave me six summer caribou skins that she said Captain Cheechoo had bartered for her from the Cree. That is when I first heard Green Coat's real name. These skins were just right for making women's garments.

She handed me a woman's knife. "Together we will start your clothing. Cut the pattern in your family style," said Owinipeg, "and I will help you sew them."

By evening, we had thick new moccasins sewn onto new skin leggings, and Owinipeg basted some of her own beautiful quill work across the yoke and down the arms of my shirt. That was to bring me luck in marriage, so she said. I thanked her and admitted that I should make another marriage veil. But Owinipeg reminded me that all the Ballahooly and the Cree had already seen my face. "It would do you no good at all," she said, "to hide yourself behind a veil." I did not disagree with her, for those marriage veils are very tiresome, dangling endlessly against your face. A Dene girl scarcely dares to eat when young men are near.

painted shirt

That evening, Owinipeg showed me a lovely ivory comb that had been given to her by the young French guvnaar. Then she helped me wash myself once more all over, using a slippery yellow lump that smelled like flowers. That, too, was a gift from him, she told me. When we were finished, she helped me dry myself beside her oil lamp. Owinipeg combed my hair out very smoothly and put some red ocher above my eyes and drew down both my cheeks three delicate black lines, which she said were almost as modest as a veil. She showed me my face in a little shining frozen pool; when I saw myself, I fell backwards in surprise. I felt like a truly different person, one who had never been a Wood Cat's slave.

While I was putting on my wonderful new clothes, I asked Owinipeg, "Did you ever lie down with a Ballahooly in the bed?"

"Sure, lots of times," she laughed. "They don't do it all that badly. They know how."

"Did the Frenchman get behind you every night when he was with you?"

"Sure, he did it that way sometimes. Oh, he tried it every different way." She laughed. "And usually in the mornings, too, they like to jump around in bed. My Frenchman and even a few of these English, they are just as good at doing it as most hunters . . . and much better at it than some Great Lakes people. It is what the Ballahooly prefer to do in every season. Not like our Assiniboin horsemen, who try to hold themselves back before and during all the buffalo-hunting seasons, then other times go kind of wild."

I felt excited listening to this foreign woman talking about the habits of strange men. I watched her start to sew a pair of winter moccasins for someone who had huge wide feet. I didn't say a word, but I could tell that they were for some Ballahooly living here inside this lodge!

"Sure," said Owinipeg. "You ask me anything you want. We have plenty of time. You and I are going to talk together all this winter. I like that," she said, "having a woman here to talk to. I have nothing much to do, except to eat and talk, and sew, and satisfy myself and the guv-naar."

It was morning when Williyumm came knocking at our little lodge, coming to get me, so I would start to teach him to speak Da-Dene. When he opened the door, I was all dressed up and kneeling on the bed skins, looking shyly up at him. When Williyumm first saw me, he sucked in his breath. "Who," he asked in Cree, "is this beautiful new woman?"

"It is only I. Thana – Thanadelthur," I told him. My cheeks began to burn and I turned and stared at Owinipeg, whose beautiful quill work was spread across my chest. I shook a little just to make the delicate new fringe on my skin shirt dance. I wished then that I had on my proper marrying veil, for I felt almost too shy and excited to look up at him again.

Williyumm laughed and so did Owinipeg. He took my wrist, pulled me up, and led me outside. In the daylight, I examined Owinipeg's small lean-to propped against the larger lodge. "That is where the governor sleeps," said Williyumm.

We walked along the narrow path toward the pointed, smelly wooden cave where I had first been taken. Once inside this eating place, Williyumm showed me where to sit on the flat log, quite close beside him. He kicked and wiggled the eating boards to prove that they would not fall down and trap us.

"Let us start," said Williyumm, speaking Cree as he spread the fingers of his left hand, "by you teaching me how to count in Dene." He held out his thumb.

"That is *el cloye*."

"Oh, one," he said, and squiggled on the white skins. Then he held up his scratching finger.

"*Naw gee.*"

"Yes, two," he made another mark.

"Then *toye.*"

"That's three." He marked it.

"*Dingee.*"

"Four, thank you."

"*Sees sooly.*"

"Five, yes, five," he said.

Perhaps Williyumm's ears were big to help him hear and remember every Dene word I taught him. He counted one to five in Dene. Then I said, "Oh one, yes two, that's three, four thank you, five yes. Five." Williyumm stared at me as though I were a ghost.

"I wrote down mine," he said, in Ballahooly, "but you just remembered everything I said. Try plain one, two, three, four, five, and six."

I said, "One, two, three, four, five, and six."

"You are most remarkable," he said.

As we continued counting, Williyumm kept opening the folded leather boards. To my surprise, he kept flipping quickly through dozens and dozens of thin, buff-colored skins. They had been beautifully cleaned by some very skillful woman and most neatly sewn together. Some of them had his gray squiggles on them, but most were clean as snow.

"What are you doing?" I asked Williyumm in Cree.

"Just making marks," he told me. "That last mark means *sees sooly* – five."

105

"I don't understand why you do this," I said, examining the book. "Was it women in your family who flensed and stretched these skins so smooth and clean for you?"

"No," he answered. "Men do that kind of work in my country."

"Williyumm," I said, "you make more marks for me. I am watching you most closely."

When he was finished marking, I took his sharpened stick and laboriously wrote HBCoy, Outfit 44, and drew a good-sized beaver all across one skin. "What does that mean?" I asked him.

"Oh, you're much too quick for me," he said. "You remembered that from one of the Company's dry-good bales. You teach me Dene first," he said in Cree, "then I'll teach you how to make the marks and what they mean."

I taught Williyumm all the Dene words he asked me, until we heard all the other Ballahooly come clumping in with their hard boots to sit down and eat. Darkness had come, yet we two had not noticed. Inside this dank, smoky, winter lodge, day was always just as dark as night.

It was the first time I had ever sat with twenty-seven men all bunched together. Owinipeg was amazed when I told her I had eaten food with them. She said that she had never once sat down at that long board with all the Ballahooly or the French.

"I did it because Bearman said I must," I said. "He is in a hurry to have Williyumm understand my Dene language. Williyumm wants me to learn the Ballahooly tongue. I still felt shy, but I was getting used to all those strange gruff voices, the foul food, and so many eyes upon me."

Six days later, using some Dene words slowly and Cree only when necessary, I said to Williyumm, "You tell Bearman to make a hole up there to let away the smoke – as we do in our tent tops."

Williyumm looked at his squiggles and answered mostly in Dene, "Heat fly out – we all – freeze – very dead."

"That's not good Dene," I told him, "but still I get your meaning. Do you understand wrong? Yes? Well, you are wrong!"

At each night meal, while sitting at the long boards, I had a good chance to study the blue chins and red noses of the older men and the baby-smooth faces of the Ballahooly boys. I tried to imagine the country they had come from and what their sisters and mothers must have looked like. Were many of their young girls afflicted with such strange hair colors and pale eyes, gray, green, and blue?

I liked best watching the four rough older men who, like my father, had deep lines on their faces. They always sat opposite us. They wore heavy leather aprons down their fronts, wiped their noses on their sleeves, and pounded on the table to tell the food man that they wanted more meat or spruce beer. Six other younger men about the age of Williyumm always sat in a long row beside the two of us. They were fond of whispering and jostling each other and slyly eyeing me. Then there were the six young boys who looked round-eyed and frightened when Bearman spoke to them. But when he wasn't looking, they twitched and giggled like a flock of nervous bum-tilt birds.

Bearman, always in his long coat of beavers and his hat, sat at the far end of the long board. Whenever he wanted all the others to listen to his words, he would growl and bang his heavy fist before him. Beside him sat his best friend, the tooth-peeker, with the purple jowls that wobbled, and next to him a thin man who wore ice-like chips beneath his eyes, one of them cracked across the middle. He was sly and watchful as a weasel.

On the log beside Bearman sat a tall, long-legged man of middling age who sometimes spoke to me in Cree. He used their language very well, almost as well as Captain Cheechoo. I noticed that he and Bearman almost never spoke together, and that they did not seem to like each other. Then, for more than one whole moon, that long-legged man's seat was empty. Williyumm told me that he was away snowshoeing with Cree hunters, seeking to find new Cree, Assiniboin, or Wood Cats who lived far along the rivers to the south and west. Both he and Bearman wanted them to come to this spear house, to trade their furs.

All these Ballahooly ate in curious ways that always interested me. They used iron knives and scoops instead of fingers. The fat soup stirrer never once sat down with us. At home, our Dene women prepared all food, be it meat or fish or birds or berries.

This man did all that woman's work behind his fire box, with sharp iron stickers and with choppers. Could that be because they had no women? I would ask Williyumm, why had they not brought any Ballahooly women here with them? How did they get their babies?

Captain Cheechoo was the only person besides Owinipeg and me allowed to come inside their fort. He often took broth and meat with us, but he never slept inside the fort. He always returned to the long Cree lodges.

I counted thirty-one humans who slept inside the house of spears that winter. Over in the lodges lived maybe three hundred Cree. Owinipeg told me she was afraid of them, and most especially their women. She, like Bearman, warned me never to go near their lodges. I told her I was not against all the Cree. I said that Cheechoo was a good man. It was those raiding Wood Cats that I hated, especially that devil, Kunn.

According to my way of counting, and sometimes by looking at the moon grow wide or narrow, I reckoned that eleven days had passed since I was brought here. Williyumm and I still used mostly Cree to speak together, but he was learning Dene, and I was learning lots of the Ballahooly language, because I heard it all day long. Yes, Owinipeg helped me speak it, too, and I was learning very fast. I had been eating rabbit meat, thick goose broth, and porridge every day, and in the icy little look-at-face, I could see that the hollows in my cheeks were gone. My ribs were not so plain to see, and I was feeling cheerful once again, if I didn't think of Dingee or my family.

Williyumm said that before dark each day we should walk around the inside of the house of spears and practice talking to each other. He would point first at one thing, then another, giving each its proper name in his language, then ask me each name in Dene. I warned him that there were many queer things here for which my Dene people did not yet have a name. I pointed to the big iron cannon. "Our people have never seen a thing like that," I told him, "or that blood-red skin which is your good-luck amulet. Or those round wooden baskets that hold musket powder, brandy, and molasses.

108

"For each of those things, I have to make new names. The cannon – I am going to call the 'one that spits iron baby heads at humans.' Your flag – I'm going to call it 'blood skin.' For molasses – I will say 'sweet mouth'." Almost every time I gave a name to something, Williyumm made some new squiggles on the thin skins he carried. He could say back to me each Dene word that I had given him. But I could remember inside of me every Ballahooly word that he or the others gave to me.

"If I could learn to make the squiggles that you do," I told Williyumm, "it would be very useful."

"You never forget words anyway," Williyumm laughed. "You can remember everything anyone tells you and hold it in your head."

"You have got that wrong," I told him, and rubbed my lower belly. "Heads are only for looking, listening, sniffing, talking, chewing food, and drinking water. Heads are too small to keep very much inside of them. All the things I learn, I swallow right down here." I lifted up my pointed shirt and showed Williyumm my bare belly.

He didn't say a word, but kept studying the fancy porcupine hip string that held up my two separate leggings. When I pulled my shirt down, he asked me to lift it up again. This time I don't think he was looking at my grandmother's quill work.

I was always interested in the big red flag they raised and lowered on top of their eating lodge and the high catwalks around the inside of their wall of spears. Williyumm said, "I'll help you climb this 'la-la,' " or some such word as that. It was a thing that I had never done before. The la-la was made of two long tree sticks bound together by short steps until it looked a lot like our winter sleds. A good idea, but very long and frightening to climb.

"It's easy," Williyumm said, and holding me around the waist, he helped me take the first few steps upward. I worried about the la-la trembling and I was trembling, too, I think, because of the feeling I got when Williyumm put his hand beneath my rear end to help me up.

After I got going higher, Williyumm took away his hand and I said, "Williyumm, I'm afraid I'm going to fall."

So he took another, even better, safer hold of me, this time lower, around my thighs. That felt a whole lot better. And in that way, we two made our way very slowly up the la-la to its top.

I rearranged my shirt, and we looked out between the high jagged spears. Never had I dreamed of being inside such a place. The whole snow country was spread out below us, reaching to the farthest edges of the world.

Cautiously, I crept around the high narrow walk, and Williyumm kept one mitt around my waist. Looking out to where the sun rises, we could see the huge saltwater sea that was now frozen all along its edges. Across the river lay endless groves of wind-blown tamarack trees looking blue-black as a woman's hair against the snow. From the sundown wall, we looked over a wide flat plain turned white with snow. Ice-blue shadows glinted between the still pebbly eskers. Dwarfed trees huddled like wandering ghosts along the frozen river courses dwindling to the far horizons. Narrowing our eyes against the Wolf Star wind, we could see far storm clouds scarcely moving, like dreams of musk oxen treading slowly across the windswept muskeg.

"These Cree are very lucky," I told Williyumm, speaking Scotlan'ish. "They, too, live in the Big Woman's country. See how beautiful – it is – out there. These Cree have seals and white bear and small whales swimming in the salt water, and swans and laughing geese come here when the moons call them. They have plenty of eggs and fish and caribou, and lots of fur to trade and wood to burn. It's a bloody good wee country! Don't you think it? B'oootiful!''

I believe Williyumm understood every word I said. Even so, he leaned against the wooden spears and started laughing until I could feel the whole wall shake and see tears coming into his eyes, then turn frost-white as they ran down his bright red cheeks. "Beautiful?" he gasped. "Everybody in this place believes that this is the worst frozen hell hole in the world!" I didn't know the meaning of some words like helll hooole, but I guessed it was the Ballahooly way of telling me that they loved this country just as much as I did.

WILLIAM

7

"Did you hear the story Thana just told me?" I shouted along to wee Fergus who was leaning against the upper stockade, looking more like a frozen corpse than any living sentry standing guard for The Honourable Company.

"Did you hear her, Fergus?" I called, to try and liven him up. "This girl says the whole country around here to the north, south, east, west – all of it – is beautiful. Did you get that, Fergus? Beautiful?"

Wee Fergus rolled his eyes and said, "Poor lass, she's lost her mind, and I am freezing to death."

I took Thana's hand and encouraged her to follow me along the shaky sentry walk. I was so delighted with the quickness of her mind and her amazing ways of viewing life that I, too, forgot the stinging cold.

"She gets mixed up sometimes and calls me Wee Willeee-yummm, too," I told Fergus whilst he was trying to part his frozen eyelashes. "She cannot seem to get her tongue wrapped around the 'Stewww-arrrit.' Ah, well, neither can the English."

Fergus laughed, for my west Highland burr always tickled him.

"I can tell you this about her Copper language," I explained. "It is full of glottalized consonants pronounced like . . . this . . . with delightful momentary halts of breathing. Listen when she speaks. You'll hear her natural pushing as those rich vowel sounds come rolling smoothly from her throat. I am enjoying her language even more than I did Latin, French, or Cree. Between the Northern and the Southern Cree, there seems only a small dialectic difference like that between high and low Dutch. But this girl, Thana, is speaking in a wholly different way. Imagine all the strange tales she will have to tell when she comes to better understand our language.''

Fergus, an ironmonger's son from Perth, cocked his head, raised one dangling earmuff, and stared open-mouthed at me. "Have I misheard you, Willie? How in God's name are you going to talk with that wee Copper lassie when I cannot understand a single word she saaays.''

"Oh, you can understand me a wee bit, laddie,'' Thana told him, speaking Scotlannish.

"Listen to her carefully,'' I said. "She's got her accent from the west Highlands; that's what's confusing you.''

Fergus shook his head in wonder and tried to stamp the numbness from his fur-wrapped feet.

"Ah, well,'' said I, "the Dene word *chawther* means 'beaver' and *hoochelth* means 'metal,' probably gold, silver, or copper, and *tawhoosnee*, I'm pretty sure, must mean 'I don't understand.' ''

"You have that right,'' said Thana.

"Oh, my lord,'' said Fergus, "in London you grasped the Cree way of speaking and now you've gone and taught her English. How did you ever get that way?''

"I cannot tell you how, but languages do come quite easily to me. But Thana learns her English ten times faster than I could ever learn her Dene. She doesn't keep any notes, for she cannot write a word. Not yet.''

"Let's climb down the la-la,'' Thana said.

When the Cree came to trade, I found it strangely exciting to stand near them, listening as they spoke freely to each other. I understood a good deal of what they said. I was overwhelmed by the soft singsong voices of the young Cree women, so beautifully different from the rough pronunciation of old McGillivary's Gaelic-sounding Cree. Still, I knew almost nothing of these people or how they lived. None of us have ever dared go near their lodges, though they were but three musket shots away. A fortnight later, I got the chance that I'd been waiting for.

"My people are going to give a feast," said Captain Cheechoo. "You can come with me, but don't bring that Copper woman."

"I'll be right with you," I said, and hurried to get the shoulder bag that held my word lists and drawing books, my quills and graphites. I was more than eager to see the Cree inside their lodges, but I would only dare to visit them under the strong protection of Captain Cheechoo.

"You be damned careful, Stewart," James Knight called after me as we two departed through the one and only gate at York, which McNulty forced open just enough, then barred behind us.

I hurried after Cheechoo, keeping close behind him in the Indian fashion, as we hurried along the narrow snowshoe trail that led from the fort to the home Cree encampment. When we arrived, the dogs set up a savage barking, and a small crowd gathered in front of all three lodges. The largest was made of dozens of smaller skin tents bound together, or pinned with wooden skewers. Along its top were five separate smoke holes. From inside, I could hear a high-pitched male chorus, accompanied by the steady pounding on a drum. The very sound made me tremble with excitement.

Cheechoo and I unbound our snowshoes and tossed them on top of the lodge, away from the hungry dogs. He pushed our way through the crowd of Cree, flung back the entrance flap and led me inside. The lodge was like a long dark tunnel faintly lighted by the flaming embers of five fires. The drummer's swaying body and the figures of seated people cast distorted shadows wavering along the whole length of the lodge. It was warm inside and filled with the fumes of wood smoke, tanned clothing, and the aromatic smell of fresh crushed spruce boughs that served as underbedding. Mixed with this was the powerful odor of a simmering sturgeon broth.

In the place of honor beyond the central fire sat an old man. He nodded sociably to Cheechoo and me, offering us a favored place to sit, on a caribou robe, across the fire from him. Cheechoo told me proudly that this old man of rank was his great uncle.

"Will they be angry if I make drawings?" I asked Cheechoo.

"Yes, they will not be angry if you make drawings," he answered in the negative-affirmative. Then he told a young boy to light a pine pitch and hold it near me, so that I could see my papers.

I started to make a drawing of the drummer, whose head was flung back, and eyes closed in ecstasy as he pounded on a tambourine-like drum suspended from a lodge pole near the central fire. Then I drew one of the women easing more hot stones into a rind basket that was already boiling near the fire. I was passed a ladle of a rich broth, which Cheechoo said was made from beaver hams and fatty tails. Before I could start my third drawing, the great uncle sent me a prime red-fox skin, two marten skins, and a small packet of bright, dyed porcupine quills. I was overcome with his generosity and the warm feeling that I felt around me in the lodge, as adults and children came and sat near me to watch.

The rhythmic drumming softened, but went on and on as we ate steaming chunks of caribou meat. When my drawing of Cheechoo's great uncle was finished, I showed it to him, and the old man then made a very good drawing of me. I lay back like Cheechoo, resting on one elbow, enjoying the food and the soft bed of furs and boughs beneath me. I smiled at some handsome young Cree men and women, and they openly smiled back at me.

I thought, this is the place for me to live with Thana. Why do we have to suffer that damned fort? Perhaps I could convince the governor to let me bring her over here and spend the winter, learning both their languages and customs. When I tried to speak to these young people about living here with them, they smiled and nodded. But when I spoke of bringing the Copper woman with me, they turned down the corners of their mouths and cursed her.

Captain Cheechoo leaned close and warned me to keep my mouth shut and enjoy the food and dancing, which I did while making some more drawings and writing down the meaning of Cree words I did not know. When it was time to go, the sweat was running down my back, and my stomach was filled to bursting. How could anyone, I thought, speak badly of these soft-singing, generous Cree?

Captain Cheechoo told me that the 'guvnaar' had warned him that I was not to sleep here, and that he must see me safely back inside the fort.

The darkest days of the year were now upon us, and the constant cold had settled everywhere. It was necessary for each man to wear all of the Company clothing issued to him and any odd squares of wool or fur robes he could find to keep from freezing. Naturally, all the officers, clerks, and journeymen at York were envious of the governor's costume, which had been fashioned for him by a London furrier and brought back here in a special cowhide trunk. Of course, he wore his beaver outfit indoors and out on those bitter weeks around the Yuletide. He readily admitted that his awesome floor-length coat was heavy as a suit of armor but underneath, he said, it felt as warm as summer.

Our governor had been a carpenter when he first joined the Company. He could barely read or write; perhaps for that reason, he had become an absolute fanatic about keeping up York Factory's daily journal. The London office had provided him with a dozen sturdy leather-bound books for that purpose. Each day's events, he said, must be gathered by him and recorded legibly by me. After that, I was charged to make a second handsome, faithful copy which would always remain locked in the governor's Company trunk until the next ship arrived, when the journal would be carefully wrapped, sealed, and shipped to The Honourable Company's London office.

Keeping up the journal was a task I greatly enjoyed, for it allowed me to practice penmanship and drawing. Besides that, I had a natural curiosity, and it gave me the opportunity to know everything that was going on inside the fort and what was planned. I had chosen the mess hall as the place to make my journal entries because it was the only room, except the governor's, that was kept stove-heated throughout the winter. This required a tremendous lot of firewood. When I say heated, I do not mean so hot that it would melt the sheath of ice that formed on the inside of the windward walls. Nor would it prevent my ink from congealing in its horn, unless I held it in between my legs. Even then my trembling forced me, some days, to keep the journal entries in graphite. That was only when the wind came howling underneath the door and blew fine drifts of snow across the floor.

Our shipwright, Hazekial Smithers, had built me a tall slant-topped desk and a sturdy high stool. Thana had made a thick fur cover for the seat. I could perch my feet on the high rungs and keep them well above the icy floor. In the warmest corner, near the stove, I had suspended two iron oil lamps that cast a fairly even glow across my pages.

I had a good pair of woolen clerk's gloves that had been supplied me by the Company. Like Accountant Althorp's the thumb and index finger from the right-hand glove were missing. If I blew on them quite often, those two fingers were sometimes warm enough for me to write with style. James Knight wanted very much to see his journal pages filled with flowing lines and fancy curlicues. I separated each daily entry from the next with a ruby-red ink line. I must say I, too, enjoyed the artful look it gave each page, especially those that had small drawings. I wore my Stewart hunting plaid bundled like a shawl across my back and shoulders, and on my head I wore Mr. McGillivary's gift of a thick wool Scot's bonnet, pulled well down below my ears. On the coldest days I wrapped a caribou skin round my legs and feet, for one writes very poorly when the trembles come.

Every morning, faithful to his duty, the good doctor would come staggering into the mess hall, carrying his worn leather medicine bag which, as I had seen, was full of saltpeter and sulfurous medicines and powders, along with frightful-looking tools in case, as he put it, things went from bad to worse. He had knives and bone saws of several different sizes – one for fingers and toes, and larger ones for arms and legs – also a variety of strange-shaped pincers and some awful-looking augers made for drilling through head bones, hip bones, etc. Surgeon Carruthers would plump down heavily at the dining table, sigh and stare at me, then rest his head upon his chins.

"Come along, lads, get in line for sick parade," he would say after a bit. "Bend your pretty head, my dear," I could hear him advise one of my clerks or some rough journeyman. Dr. Carruthers would hold up a candle and peer inside his patient's ear, trying not to drip in wax. "Now, open up your lovely little mouth." Then he would gasp and turn away his head. "Oh, Lord, how glad I'll be when cook runs out of those friggin' garlic cloves! Who's next?" he would call out in a dispirited voice to the sick line. When an ailing man approached, he would cheer up a bit and say, "Well, what's plaguing you, dear lad?"

Each morning there were usually five or six in the sick parade. No wonder! They were almost always the men or bonded boys assigned that month to the dreaded chore of cutting wood. It was a disheartening sight to see those poor indentured servants, mostly gathered from the streets of London, staggering out in work crews to face the murderous cold, trying to hack the twisted tamaraks with crude blunt axes. I didn't blame them for trying to avoid that thankless task, but still we needed firewood if we were going to stay alive.

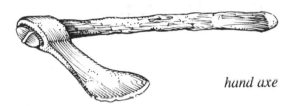

hand axe

Not a week had passed before Shipwright Smithers, who was then in charge of woodcutting detail upriver, sent down two of his men, dragging young Collinwood. He had one set of his toes frozen. Not frostbitten, mind you – frozen! Dr. Carruthers examined them. They had already turned blue-black.

"They've got to come off," the surgeon told him, and he spread a sheet of old sail canvas on the mess room table. "I'll go and get the necessaries."

I talked to Collinwood to keep him calm until Surgeon Carruthers returned with his bag of strange-shaped chisels, knives, and saws. The doctor was humming to himself and already smelled of brandy. He produced the bottle from his coat and recommended that his patient take a long strong drink and that I do so, too. Then Surgeon Carruthers took another good long swig as well.

"You take another one," he said to Collinwood, his patient. "On second thought, I would take two, if I were you."

Collinwood took another long gulp and so did I, and so did Dr. Carruthers, who, like his patient, now seemed greatly cheered.

"Let us have a look at this foot of yours. Stewart, will you hand me that scalpel and the saw? Are you any good at singing?" Carruthers asked his patient.

"Not much fuggin' good at all," laughed Collinwood.

"Neither are we; are we, Stewart? So what are we going to sing? 'Green grow the rushes, ohhh,' " croaked the surgeon. "Do you know that grand old song? Let's all finish off this wretched apple brandy, then we'll get to work. 'Green grow the rushes – Ohhhh!' " the doctor sang in his hoarse cracked voice, and Collinwood and I joined him singing, until all three of us were laughing, drunk as sailors playing ride-a-cock-horse in a Limehouse brothel.

I could hear the sawing. Collinwood shouted out once in a while, but mostly he didn't seem to mind too much.

When it was over, the surgeon wrapped some cloths around the poor lad's foot. Then he laid his head upon the table, and he and the patient went sound asleep. I somehow managed to make it back to my quarters, still singing "Green grow the rushes, ohhh." I've always liked that song.

My sacred task each Saturday morn was to be there early, sitting straight and alert, with fresh ink made and warming by the stove, and all quills nicely sharpened, ready to perform the governor's task. Even as he came toward me with the journal tightly tucked beneath his arm, I could see him rummaging through his beaver coat's enormous pockets, searching for little twisted scraps of paper that he would then interpret. I never learned to read them. I don't think any human could.

Thana was starting to look much better, but for a young woman she still moved slowly. She used to come into the mess and squat down in the warmth between my desk and the stove. Governor

Knight did not mind her being there at all, for he was very anxious that I learn the Dene language.

He would look at me as though I were a backward child, then leaning heavily against my desk, he would squint hard at his scribbled notes. "Oh, yes, thanks be to God, I recall it now! Mid-morning, January 17th, 1715, old Passiaks came in and traded two otters and six prime beavers and a lynx cat pelt. And our good doctor bled the stonemason, to see if that would cure his swellings. Oh, yes, and mark this down as well: Tuesday was a cold and blustery day and I bagged two white ptarmigan on that same morning, and Surgeon Carruthers finally shot a sitting hare." James Knight paused and stared into my face. "Are you by any chance a spy for Mr. Althorp? Has he offered you some reward to inform on me?"

"No, he has not, sir," I answered truthfully. "I mistrust Accountant Althorp, and these days he will not even speak to me."

"Good," the governor chuckled. "Remember, Stewart, I place my trust in you. Never allow that nasty worm of a man to get his bony fingers on my journal."

"I am very careful, sir," I said, "not to let anyone see anything, not even your deputy, Mr. Kelsey. If any person who knows how to read comes near this desk, I hide my work and turn the lock."

"That's the way to do it, Willie. I can't stand Kelsey or Althorp, that pair of nosy blighters, making their own peltry counts and reporting back to London. Them's my private affairs. By the way, where is that secretive devil, Kelsey? Is he out wandering as usual?"

"Yes, sir. They say he and Captain Cheechoo went upriver to the deer hedge yesterday."

James Knight shook his head and snorted. He enjoyed gossiping about his deputy. "If that wandering gypsy, Kelsey, had paid proper attention to the Company's business, which is aimed at increasing trade, he would have been the governor here, and I his deputy. Trouble with him is he's an Indian lover."

He sighed and stuffed his hands inside his beaver pockets. I was shuddering with the cold and envied him his giant coat. My oil lamps sputtered as the icy winds moaned through the cracks between the shrunken logs. I could hear the cook cursing the drafts that set his brick stove smoking and made waves across his greasy soup.

To cut down the winter's chill, I had nailed on the east wall a large French map. On it a low hill near the fort bore the name *Côte d'Oie*. Clearly that meant the French must have kept their salted geese buried in the sandy slopes to hide them from the animals. Following Governor Knight's instructions, I nailed a second piece of parchment over this map and traced a large new drawing of the country around the fort and renamed everything in English. On it I also drew our proper Company's crest. I changed the name Fort Bourbon back to Fort York, and marked in the Nelson and Hayes rivers. I drew one ship anchored at Five Fathom Hole and a hoy in the mouth of Ten Shilling Creek. But instead of changing *Côte d'Oie* back to Goose Hill, I carefully renamed it 'Knight's Hill,' using lots of elaborate curlicues. The governor only grunted when he saw what I had done, but still I knew it pleased him. Governor Knight was not a vain man, but like Henry Kelsey, who wished to win fame as an explorer, Knight was always interested in enhancing his fame as the governor in North America, while he improved the Company's fortune – or better still, his own. He was always eager to leave his name on any major river, plain, or mountain in the vastness of those mysterious broad lands running west of Hudson Bay that I had marked *Terra Incognita*.

ink quill and journal

Saturday morning early, as I was busy copying some of the governor's scribbled entries into the journal, I saw Thana's figure come drifting ghostlike through the smoke. She came and stood beside my stool, leaning innocently against me, warming her hands between my upper thighs.

"Williyumm," she whispered in English, "will you trade with me some words?"

"We are not supposed to teach each other languages until this is finished," I told her. Then I winked my eye and answered her request. I counted in English very slowly until I reached the number twenty.

"Oh, onward!" she said, nodding her head as though it helped her to remember every number.

So I counted clearly to one hundred.

"Good!" she said. "I like best the sound of eetee-eat."

I drew the figures 88 for her in the margin of the journal, and she brushed the numbers with her fingers. "They look like a little pair of bugs, about to mate."

Thana had been born a nomad with a wanderlust inside her. She seemed to have all but lost her fear of us, and certainly she was not bothered by the cold. Thana told me that except for me and Owinipeg, she hated living in this place. The Assiniboin woman was of a far more placid nature. Sleeping with both the English and French governors in that wide warm bed had gentled her nomadic ways. Owinipeg was now content to remain in her small room, quietly humming buffalo dream songs and sewing by her lamp, through every season of the year. Thana was not at all like that. She would bind on her snowshoes and make a fast tour near the fort, keeping well out of sight of the Cree village, eagerly setting her snares in the ptarmigan hollows and on the rabbit runs.

Thana borrowed a pair of Cheechoo's snowshoes for me and urged that I come out with her. She was determined to teach me how to snowshoe in the Dene style. Believe me, that's not an easy skill to master. I tried walking slowly, following her trail, but she moved faster and faster until I was forced to run after her. She looked back, then crouched down in a duck walk. Even with that awkward handicap, she easily kept ahead of me, until I tripped and fell, exhausted in the snow.

In the end, I was glad that I had practiced for a week with her. I wanted to learn to snowshoe well, to pitch a tent, to work the dogs and lash loads on the toboggans. I wanted to measure distances with my instruments and travel by the sun and stars. Being out and running in that clean snow country appealed to me. Like Thana, I hated being trapped inside that icy, smoke-filled fort.

The most bitter days of winter came to us on a howling February wind that swept in off Hudson Bay, as the days began to lengthen. Every man had long since set aside his leather boots and wore Cree moccasins that were stuffed with inner slippers lined with warm musk-ox hair. Still, I could hear the clerks and tradesmen pounding their feet beneath the table, trying to drive away their chills. If he had not ordered an issue of cheap brandy and spruce beer for each of us, the surgeon assured us, we would all long since have perished from the weather.

While I was making the journal entry for 27th February, A.D. 1715, Governor Knight said, "Stewart, I put a good deal of trust in you. Did you notice that last week?"

"Yes, sir," I answered. "Mr. Althorp was in a rage when you and Mr. Kelsey journeyed south and you left me, your clerk, in charge of this fort instead of him."

"Don't you worry about that London spy, Althorp," the governor growled. "I hold great expectations for you, Stewart. As a clerk, you've proved trustworthy, you speak Cree well, and I hope you're learning her language from that Copper woman. The only problem is that you know almost nothing of this country beyond these gates. Cheechoo tells me he has seen you using your strong legs for snowshoeing."

He paused and squinted narrowly at me. "Mr. Kelsey admitted to me last evening that he intends to journey south and west when the moon of early spring appears. On his return, he plans to circle inland in search of new savages that he will urge to bring their furs here to trade. Kelsey has a letter from the London office instructing him to explore that whole part of the country. But,"

122

he waved his stubby arms in a broad gesture, "the whole land running north and west of here is mine! Do you understand me, Stewart? Mine! I want *you*, not Kelsey, to explore those western broad lands."

"I'm ready, sir, to go," I told him.

"Oh, no, you're not," the governor snorted. "That's why I'm going to order Kelsey to take you south with him. He'll hate that and raise hell with me when I tell him. But he's the best man to teach you, give you the experience you'll need to carry out my plans."

Governor Knight was not what you would call a religious man. He rarely conducted Sunday morning prayers. But I always felt he meant to do it. On those rare occasions when he did, he demanded that his services be attended by every single person living in the fort, except Owinipeg and Thana and the cook, whom he considered some rare sort of European heathen. The Honourable Company, James Knight told me, steadfastly refused to hire a Church of England vicar, fearing that he would try to Christianize the Cree and teach them English, thus endangering their whole fur trade, which any Cree-speaking Company men could learn to control.

One Sabbath morn during prayers, James Knight frowned when he saw that I was dressed in my Scot's bonnet, Company doublet, and kilted in my Stewart plaid with my badger-headed sporan. True, that kilt of mine caused my naked knees and thighs to turn blue from the paralyzing cold, but it was worth it, for it gave me the grandest feelings of belonging to a famous clan.

On that same Sunday morning, our governor and Surgeon Carruthers were dressed in Cree style, prepared to go off shooting ptarmigan and hare. The pair of them, with Shipwright Smithers, were in a tearing hurry to be gone.

"Be sure to write in the journal that I conducted lots of prayers," the governor called to me, "and note as well that we three went off shooting and plan to spend the night at the Frenchmen's hut, up near the deer hedge. Have you got that, Stewart?"

"I shall record it, sir," I answered smartly.

"Good," the governor shouted, so Mr. Althrop could easily hear. "I leave this fort in your charge, Stewart, since Mr. Kelsey is away meandering as usual."

This was the second time that James Knight had left me in command of Fort York. I climbed up to inspect the man on sentry duty. Whilst there, I peered out over the stockade fence and watched those three bulky Englishmen grunting red-faced as they bent and tried to lash their snowshoes on. The young Cree orphan boy named Jako and his brother, whom the surgeon had purchased as his personal servants, set out, one ahead of them and one behind, snowshoeing along the frozen river.

The governor, heavy though he be, kept right behind Jako, strutting agile as a gamecock, for in his earlier days he had snowshoed endless distances. Behind him trailed poor Dr. Carruthers, staggering and stumbling, trying desperately to keep Shipwright Smithers's snowshoes off his heels.

I cannot say exactly why, but I began trembling with excitement when I watched those three men moving up the frozen river in single file. I waited until I was sure that they would not turn back. Then I skipped down the ladder, scarcely feeling the chilly breezes that had paralyzed my knees and numbed my backside. I hummed a Gaelic tune as I ran along the snowy path that led me straight to Owinipeg and Thana's dwelling. Oh, what a glorious Sabbath this would be for me.

I tapped lightly on their door, and without waiting, pulled it open and leapt inside because my scarlet kneecaps were spotted frosty white. Owinipeg was kneeling, adding seal oil to her small iron lamps. She smiled at me, making gentle crow's foot crinkles beside her eyes, and called, "Ahyoohah," which is a pleasant Assiniboin form of greeting. She reached over and shook Thana, who sat up, sleepily.

Seeing my plaid kilt and the uncle's badger-headed sporan, Thana laughed and pointed at my raw knees. She studied my strange costume with a look of pure astonishment.

"What's that?" she asked, pointing at Douglas Stewart's sporan.

"A place to keep my money," I told her, using English.

"What is money?" she asked.

I held up the ledger which James Knight had given me to keep my linguistic notes. "Forget money. Come over to the mess hall," I said, "teach me new Dene ways to speak."

"Go with him," Owinipeg told Thana, and with her fingers she made crisscross pattern signs and said to me, "I like your green dress. But your poor knees must be cold."

"They do not pain too much," I lied as I felt the stinging blood return to them.

Thana quickly dressed, then followed me across the stockade grounds into the mess hall. It was Sunday and just as I had hoped, it was deserted. I wrapped a caribou skin around my knees and feet.

Our language lesson started slowly. Thana stretched like a cat and yawned and rubbed her eyes. She was a person slow at waking, but when she did, I never saw a livelier, more intelligent human being. In no time, she was teaching me her language, but she was also busy absorbing all my English words and querying me about their meaning.

I opened up a blank leaf of my notebook and began to copy down the words and sounds that Thana taught me.

"I don't understand your marks," she said, examining my work with care. Then taking my quill pen, she made long squiggling lines in imitation of my writing. "Does that mean anything to you?" she asked.

"No," I answered.

"Nor to me," she sighed, then quickly drew a picture of a fish. "Do you understand that?" she asked.

"Yes, that's a fish."

"*Ramars*." She then drew a hook. "*Gith*," Thana said in Dene. "Now, how do you say fish in your two other languages?"

"*Piscis*, Latin," I said, "and *le poisson*, French – both words mean fish."

Thana smiled. "So I can make a mark and it is understood in all those languages. Our Dene way of writing is quite wise."

"Yes," I admitted. "That is a very old way and a useful way."

Thoughtfully, she waved my marker in the air, then quickly drew a bird, a beast with horns, and then a woman with an infant on her back. "That should be me," she said.

It was mid-afternoon when we were finished, and the cook was sound asleep behind his stove. So I went to his bake oven and took out a fresh unleavened bannock the size of a small pie. When I broke it in half, it steamed in the chill air and gave off that rich smell of new-made bread. I took up a small cask of molasses and I let it run out thick and brown in circles over Thana's half. I did it badly and got molasses on my hand. Thana held my wrist and slowly licked my palm with her hot wet tongue. Small trembles, then violent shivers, journeyed up my arm, then spread downward through my body. I closed my eyes and hoped that it would never end. When it did, Thana licked her lips and smiled at me.

"Williyumm, you taste very good," she whispered.

After that wonderful molasses licking, everything began to change for us.

Thana took a bite of the hot bannock with molasses, then savoring it, she sighed and closed her eyes with pleasure. I studied her thick, blue-black hair which was once more unruly and seemed to better match her frisky character. Thana's face was somewhat flat with a smooth sun-browned forehead, wide cheekbones, and a short narrow nose that contrasted with the sensuous fullness of her lips. She opened her dark eyes and stared at me.

Easing into the kitchen where the cook lay snoring near his stove, I filled a crock with warm thick goose broth, then took a large hot suet pudding. Thana carried the crock and, with the hot bread underneath my arm, I guided her by the hand. We ran together through the darkness, staying near the wall where my man on sentry duty would not see us.

When we reached the governor's quarters, I opened the door and drew Thana in toward the warm glow of his small fireplace. Using a twisted spill, I held it to the fire, then applied it to the four candles in the brass candelabra that stood on the table. I took

126

down a bottle of the governor's best French brandy and two fine crystal glasses and placed them on the table.

Then bowing as deeply as I would for Lady Islay, I drew out Thana's high-backed chair. She sat down very nicely and admired the thick-stemmed crystal as I filled our glasses. She said it was strange that they were not cold as ice. Thana took a cautious sip of the brandy, made a face, then gasped.

Staring through my glass, I drank off half, felt the brandy reach down inside, tickling me beneath my sporan. "The governor," I said in English, "will not mind us resting here tonight. He does not come back until the sun is high tomorrow."

"You speak bonny words," said Thana, answering me in the way she called "Scootlan'ish."

When we had finished eating and drinking the brandy, I felt Thana slide her softly moccasined foot between my knees. "Look! There is Bearman's sleeping place," I said in Dene.

"Oh, is that his place for sleeping?" she asked in English.

Together we rose and examined the governor's high bed. Clinging to me as we peeked inside the blankets that hung down as curtains, she gently stroked the beaver bedrobe. I parted the red woolen curtains and boosted Thana onto the bed.

"It is soft," she said, as she lay back upon the beaver covering and wove her fingers before her eyes, forming a kind of veil.

"We'll both be warm inside," I answered in Dene.

"Williyummm," she whispered, "use the English. I want to learn all the words for what we are going to do."

I took hold of the fringe of her fur-lined pointed shirt and lifted it. She smiled at me, then raised her arms. It came off very easily, leaving her naked. She ran her fingers through her hair and shook it, until it lay wildly spread across her shoulders.

"Och, lassie!" I gasped when I saw her softly rounded beauty.

"Feel me, if you want," she said. "I am getting plump again."

She untied her two separate leggings from her hip string. "It is cold with nothing on," she shivered, "and the beaver's hairs, they tickle me."

I hauled back the governor's heavy beaver cover, and Thana slipped inside. It took me only a moment to fling off my plaid,

Company doublet, and shirt, slide off my sealskin boots, hastily unbuckle the two straps and let my kilt fall to the floor, then squirm in close beside her.

"Ohhh, Williyumm," she sighed in English. "I been waiting for this."

I answered, "So have I."

"You're getting very hot all over," she whispered.

Trembling with excitement, I slipped my arms beneath her back and gently drew her to me.

At that very instant, I heard voices gruffly singing and the heavy thump of snowshoes on the hard snowpath just outside the governor's door. I could hear Surgeon Carruthers reciting his sacred Hippocratic oath in half-forgotten Greek.

"That's very fine, Doctor! Yes, very nice, indeed," I heard the governor bellowing. "You go, get some sleep."

He fumbled with the latch to open his outer door.

Thana raised her head and stared at me in fright, just as my cheeks felt a sudden draft of icy air.

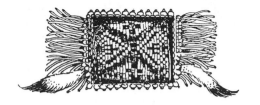

THANA

8

I jumped into Owinipeg's little house and slammed the door.

"Why are you running?" she asked me. "It's cold outside, but you look very, very hot."

"I am hot," I told her. "My body is hot all over because I've been lying naked in the bed with Williyumm."

Owinipeg widened her eyes in surprise. "Have you been lying in Williyumm's bed with all those young boys staring at you?"

"Oh, no," I told her. "We were not in Williyumm's bed. We were lying together in Bearman's bed. Have you ever seen that bed with the four tent poles holding up the blankets that keep it warm inside?"

"Yes, I have seen the guvnaar's bed," said Owinipeg. She pronounced *guv-naar* very carefully, because she didn't like me calling him Bearman.

"It was wonderful," I told her as I fanned my cheeks. "Williyumm put wood on the fire, and we shared some food and a throat-burning drink. I had to blow out my breath! We sat on two tall padded chairs and ate off a round deadfall on which were four fat candles burning. Right after eating, Williyumm took me to the guvnaar's bed, and to stay warm, he said we should climb inside, because I was naked, and the fire was getting low."

"Then what happened?" Owinipeg asked, biting her thread like a hungry woman.

"Williyumm got excited and flung his red coat and his dress onto the floor, then jumped inside the bed and beside me. That's when I started getting hot all over. Just look at my hair. It's sticking to my forehead. Lying beside Williyumm made me shiver first, as if I were freezing, then burning hot, like fire. Did you ever feel like that?" I asked her.

Owinipeg nodded. "I used to, before my French guvnaar went away. Tell me," she asked, "what did Williyumm do when you two were inside the bed?" Owinipeg's thimble clacked faster and faster against her thumbnail.

"Hard to explain," I told her. "I could feel that Williyumm was getting ready to do something different than the Cree."

"Yes, yes, I know," Owinipeg sighed. "The Frenchmen, they've got lots of different ways. Go on," she urged, "tell me then what happened."

"Just when Williyumm was starting to roll on top of me, he stopped and said, 'Do you hear singing?' I raised my head and listened. Yes, it was Bearman and the ear-peeker. They were coming back too soon. We could hear the two of them laughing and shouting, coming close to us when they were supposed to be far away.

"We heard them struggling to open the outside door. Bearman was giving orders to the ear-peeker's two boy helpers. 'Quick!' Williyumm warned, 'Get out! Get out!'

"Williyumm grabbed his clothes and I grabbed mine, but we had no time to put them on. Williyumm pulled me into the shadows behind a tall wood box."

"Did the guvnaar see you?" Owinipeg asked me.

"I think he would have seen us, but he was so tired from hunting rabbits that he was swaying back and forth, giggling and talking to himself."

"He does that sometimes," Owinipeg admitted.

"We watched him struggle out of his Cree clothing, so tired that he could hardly keep his eyes open. I watched him take a long drink from the bottle on the table, then turn his back on us and try to warm his *yeak*, not noticing that his fire was nearly out. Then he crossed over to his bed and crawled inside behind the hanging blankets. Williyumm and me, we put our clothes on very quietly. Soon we could hear Bearman breathing hard, then snoring louder than my grandfather used to snore. Williyumm crept across the room and blew out all four candles, then we sneaked out the door and ran in two directions. Oh, I wish those two Ballahooly had stayed out hunting overnight, or even stayed away a little longer. Why did they have to come back like that? Just when everything was going to happen!''

"You two be careful," Owinipeg warned. "If the guvnaar or that man with the broken glasses finds you and Williyumm lying together in this fort, there will be trouble."

As soon as the heat started going out of me, I laid down in my bed near Owinipeg. I asked many questions about Frenchmen, Ballahooly, and about Williyumm, too.

Owinipeg propped up on her elbow and looked me wisely in the face. "You're too anxious," she said. "Relax. You can't learn all the Ballahooly ways tonight."

"Not all of them," I answered. "Only some of Williyumm's ways I'd like to know, right now."

"I understand," said Owinipeg, "but it's going to take you time to learn about the Ballahooly. They are much harder to understand than Frenchmen, Assiniboin, or Cree. Frenchmen are easy. They're the best. When we first came here to trade beaver with the Ballahooly, I was very young. My family brought me north with many others in Assiniboin canoes. The guvnaar, whose bed you laid in, he was here at that time, a strong young boat-maker who had seen about as many winters as Williyumm."

"Six summers after that, some Frenchmen came here in a ship and fired their cannon and drove all the Ballahooly away. The Frenchmen took this fort and stayed here, trading. That first winter I got changed by their guvnaar into a woman. My father and my mother were both drowned during the next summer moon, leaving me alone inside this fort, with more than twenty Frenchmen," said Owinipeg. "I was afraid to go outside among the Cree. Although I missed my parents very much, the young

French guvnaar took good care of me. This fort was *très, très jolie* when he was here." Owinipeg smiled and sang the best French song that she remembered:

Le Fils du roi s'en va chassant
Avec son grand fusil d'argent,
Rouli, roulant, my boule roulant,
En roulant my boule roulant.

"Oh, yes! All those Frenchmen adored to dance, and my guvnaar wore very sweet perfume. Together we made a lovely little *enfant*. We named him *Oiseau Blanc* . . . he isn't living here with me, because my first French guvnaar took our son across the water, to live in his family's lodge with all of them.

"Oh, I felt very bad because my son was gone, and then when the ship came this last French guvnaar, Jérémie, told me that the Ballahooly were returning and for that reason he would have to leave with all his men. I was sad to say *bon voyage* to Jérémie, but I was truly glad to see the face of my Ballahooly boatmaker return. When he came marching through those gates, I wept for joy. He had grown much heavier, which suited him, for now he was the guvnaar, the chief. Anyone could see how proud he was to fly that big red Company flag. Now we are good close friends again," said Owinipeg.

As I laid down to sleep, I told her, "No wonder you know a lot about the Frenchmen and the Ballahooly."

On that same night, I had an animal dream so powerful that I woke before the dawn. I got dressed and climbed the la-la and stood searching the whole snow country that lay west beyond this house of spears.

There he was, the big red fox that I was looking for. His coat was ruffling in the wind, just like Williyumm's hair.

On that same day, using my own hair, I braided a fine new snare, singing my grandmother's song that I knew would bring the fox to me. Carefully, I set the snare that evening, and when I went out the next morning, there was that fox, hanging up so nicely on the pole, with his red tail fluttering in the breeze.

"I caught my dream," I called to Owinipeg, holding the fox up high. We thawed him out beside her lamp and carefully stretched his pelt. "When it is dry, I'm going to make the finest hat that anyone has ever seen."

Not too long later, when my needlework was finished, Owinipeg examined it with care. "That hat is not Assiniboin, French, nor Cree, and it is not a Ballahooly hat. It must be pure Dene, with the tail coming out of the top like that."

"No," I replied. "It is a new kind of hat, a marrying hat, the same one I saw in my dream of Scootlan'."

dream hat

Williyumm was delighted when he saw the red fox hat. He tried it on, then ran and got some green trade ribbon which Owinipeg tied in a special way, and Williyumm urged me to sew it on the top. That evening, he wore it when we went into the eating lodge and all the clerks and bonded boys began to shout and sing.

Next day, Williyumm came into our small house still wearing his fox hat and said he had to go to the trading room to help press some beaver pelts for baling. When he left, I said to Owinipeg, "Did you notice him kind of shivering from the cold?"

"It's true," she said. "He hasn't got good clothes."

"I wish I could make Williyumm a real Dene winter shirt of caribou skins," I told her. "They're just as warm as beaver, but not half so heavy, and besides, a caribou shirt won't make him look like Bearman."

Owinipeg gave me a warning glance for saying that about the guvnaar, but she agreed to help me sew a hunter's shirt and leggings just for Williyumm.

When we two asked him, Captain Cheechoo brought us seven of the finest caribou skins and some sheaths of well-dried sinews. I spread these carefully apart with Owinipeg's thin-toothed antler comb, then coiled them in my mouth until they softened into fine strong thread. I remembered the shape of Williyumm's body, as Owinipeg and I carefully cut the skins: front, back, hood, arms, and then the leggings. Lastly, we made him three pairs of moccasins and mittens.

"We have to make an extra fawnskin shirt with the hair turned in to wear beneath his thicker pointed shirt. During these winter moons," I told her, "he'll need double leggings, too. I don't want him to freeze his *yeak*."

Owinipeg was a very skillful sewer, much faster than I shall ever be. We got colors – ocher red and lamp-soot black – and we very carefully made the decorations, most of them Dene, but a bit of them Assiniboin, in honor of her buffalo people. Finally, when we were finished, Owinipeg held up the long shirt and leggings. It was the most beautiful winter costume either of us had ever seen.

That evening, after dinner, I ran back with Williyumm to Owinipeg's lean-to house. We had his caribou-skin clothing spread out on my bed. Owinipeg was just like me, excited. She could hardly wait to see Williyumm try on his new clothing, hoping that it would fit.

"Wait! Wait!" I said. "When a Dene woman gives you a present, you must give something back to her."

"I'm eager to give something back to you whenever I get the chance," said Williyumm.

"Not here! Not now!" said Owinipeg. "I don't want you two getting all of us in trouble."

"Then next Sunday," Williyumm said. "The guvnaar is going shooting again."

"We'll get started earlier this time," I told him. "Now you try on your clothing."

When Williyumm donned his shirt and leggings and put his fox hat on, he looked as grand as any Dene chieftain's son. He whirled around, making the thin-cut fringes of his shirt and leggings fly around him.

Next day, Williyumm went begging, as he said, to Bearman and became indebted for a good-sized bag of colored beads and two large silverish hair combs. Williyumm gave one to Owinipeg and one to me. Besides that, he gave her a large box of tea and me a little pool of bright-edged ice that would not melt in spring. Also he gave Owinipeg a pair of iron finger snippers that come together like a loon's beak and would clip threads almost as neatly as a woman's teeth. He calls them thithers, a Scootlanish word, very difficult for me to say.

I began to look at myself in my new mirror, and got interested in combing out my hair and arranging it in three very different ways: Dene, Assiniboin, and Cree.

Williyumm came to our lodge very often and admired the elaborate way that Owinipeg arranged my hair. He made a drawing of me from the front and side. After that, Owinipeg and I drew animals and birds and humans on those thin smooth skins of his. Once Williyumm came in and stared into the mirror he had given me. When he turned around, we could see that he had painted four thin black charcoal lines across his cheeks beneath each eye, which was our way of making Dene husbands and married women look most beautiful at feasts.

I said, "Williyumm, you look like a Dene hunter."

He answered me in Dene, which Owinipeg would not understand. "I found a secret place where we two could lie together."

"That is good," I said. "When will we get a chance to use it? I am . . . you know . . . kind of ready."

"Oh, so am I," sighed Williyumm.

But he never got the chance to show me the secret sleeping place that he had found. Longlegs, the good Cree speaker, announced that he would leave early in the morning, going southwest, on a walk-across into the broken lands. Later, Williyumm came running into our house very much excited. "I have to pack," he said. "I'm going on the walk-across with Captain Kelsey and the others."

"You get your snowshoes and come outside with me."

I tried very hard to teach him all the finer Dene tricks I knew.

Owinipeg and I rose early and went up the la-la to watch the six of them depart. I saw Williyumm try to speak with Longlegs and the four Cree, but none of them would answer him. I thought, that is a bad way to start a journey. Dene men would not do that.

I watched them move away in a single file. Longlegs was out in front, breaking trail for all of them along the frozen river. He was setting a killing pace that I knew would soon wear Williyumm down. I watched them go with such a feeling of despair that I did not even notice the sharp Arctic wind driving at me through the spears.

I worried about Williyumm, knowing he could not long keep up to a pace like that. Certainly Longlegs and the Cree must want to lose him. I believed that we would see Williyumm return along that same trail in a day or two, discouraged and alone.

WILLIAM

9

As we set off from the fort, I did not realize that the sixteenth of January, A.D. 1715, would be one of the hardest days in all my life. I didn't even notice the cold as I hurried right behind Captain Kelsey, followed by four Cree and two toboggans. From the beginning, I was shoeing as fast as my legs could carry me.

It became a little easier after we struggled down the riverbank and headed inland on the flatness of the frozen Hayes River. But when we turned south on what was called Ten Shilling Creek, almost beyond sight of the fort, Kelsey began to increase the pace, calling back to me that we two had been holding up the Cree because he had tried to make an easy start for me.

My shin muscles were already drawn tight as bowstrings and the muscles on my inner thighs were throbbing like two enormous toothaches. Still, I refused to give up, though I could see that Kelsey was drawing too far ahead of me.

Finally, he looked back and shouted in Cree so the others would understand him, "Get out of the line, Stewart. You've got to turn back, man. You're holding all the others up."

I was losing and my legs could not possibly keep the pace. Finally, I stepped sideways and stopped to watch the four Cree pass me with the two toboggans and six dogs. I gaped mindlessly at them, waiting for the pain in my legs and hips and thighs to fade away. It didn't. The line of men and dogs began to dwindle in the distance.

I reshifted my shoulder bag, which was troublesome, slung my musket across my back, and started after them at my own snail's pace. By now I felt worn out and stiff, cramped with aches and pains. The short winter light was fading fast. I had not felt the cold at all when I was racing, trying to keep up to Kelsey, but now that I had slowed down, I could feel the difference. First, the sweat that trickled down my spine seemed to freeze and turn to ice, then my cheeks and nostrils stiffened. The others were far along the snow-packed creek, disappearing in the gloom like a scurrying line of ants.

There were no stars that night, and an icy fog was forming all around me. Although I could still follow the course of the snow-covered creek between the small wind-twisted trees along its banks, I began to suffer from frightful pangs of loneliness and a fear that I had never known in all my life. Even while herding on the stormy Appin I always had a friendly collie and the gentle sheep nearby. But out here a man was utterly alone. I wanted desperately to stop and rest again, but knew the cold would stiffen me and slow me down again.

In the darkness I could hear wolves howling on the river. Were they following my trail? I tried to increase my pace, but my body refused, allowing me only to move like a bent old man. I did not worry about losing the trail even in the dark, for the loose top snow had been compacted almost knee-deep by their snowshoes, then smoothed by the toboggans.

Some time beyond midnight, I caught the faint smell of wood smoke growing slowly stronger. Their trail turned and left the river. Painfully, I followed it up the bank and into a grove of tamarack. There I saw the wide low tent, its sides half-buried in loose snow.

The work dogs barked and snarled at me until I swung my musket butt at the boldest one of them. After hanging my snowshoes in a tree, where they could not eat the thongs, I crawled through the low entrance, aching in every bone and muscle. The harsh smell of smoke, goose broth, human sweat, and untanned animals' skins filled the whole tent. Five humans lay wrapped in their blankets, feet toward the warming embers of the fire, each a red spoke in a wheel of exhausted sleepers, or those who pretended sleep.

skin tent

I sucked warmish water from the kettle spout and gnawed the remaining scraps of leathery goose flesh left in their pot. Spreading a sleeping skin between two bodies, I wrapped myself in my blanket. Two of the Cree were snoring violently, but that didn't bother me. I could feel the muscles in my legs and back twitching and uncoiling, until finally they allowed me sleep.

In the morning, when I woke, there was a robber jay perched on a needle branch close to my face. His gray feathers were fluffed out against the cold, his head cocked to one side as he watched me boldly with one eye. Dear God, thought I, did I dream about the tent? Where is the tent?

It was no longer about my head, and everything from within had been taken as well. I jumped up and looked around me. The sky was overcast, and I could not even guess the time of day. After arranging my bundled blanket and sleeping skins on my back, I was relieved to find my musket and snowshoes still hanging in the tree.

On legs as stiff as an old sheep dog's, I started out again along Kelsey's trail, and I confess my thoughts of him grew more murderous as I went. That whole day was so grim and numbing that I cannot remember even one detail except my hatred of them all. As night began to fall, terror gave me new resolve. It drove me forward faster.

I could not even guess the hour, but once more I smelled smoke. Beside the river's edge among some trees, I saw the tent, an orange cone of light softly glowing from within. I snowshoed fast toward it, not knowing what I would do.

The dogs seemed to have grown used to my late arrivals, for when I hung up my snowshoes, they made no complaint. I kept my musket with me as I crawled inside the tent. Kelsey was sitting eating, facing me directly across the fire.

At first, he did not speak, nor did any of the Cree. Then Kelsey said, "I thought we had lost you, Stewart. We judged that you'd be tired and sleep a good bit of the day, then wisely turn around and follow your own tracks back to the fort. You are a lucky man it did not storm and fill them in. That would have killed you."

Between clenched teeth, I answered Kelsey, "If you ever dare to fold up a tent from above my head and sneak away from me again, I'll challenge you. I'll fight you out here or back at the fort. I'll do my damnedest to kill you."

Kelsey rubbed the stubble on his long lean jaw and stared at me.

"Do you understand me, Mr. Kelsey? Do you take my full meaning?"

The Cree were looking at us, then at each other, not understanding any of our English words.

Kelsey stood up and pushed past me as he stepped outside to urinate. When he came in again, he was carrying a heavy clublike tree limb. He stood above me for a moment and could easily have brained me. But instead, he tossed the wood onto the fire and said, "I'm going to get some sleep."

After wolfing down everything I could find to eat and drinking all the broth that they had left, I made my place and slept with my musket by my side.

"Stewart!" I heard Kelsey's voice yell at dawn.

All the others sat up, stretched, then rose around me.

"If you love this tent so bloody much, you can help Wapasu take it down while we harness the dogs."

I hurried like a whirlwind as I helped Wapasu, for I was determined never to be left behind again by that inhuman devil, Kelsey.

I cannot tell you why, but I found the young Cree, Wapasu, a very sympathetic person, good to work with. He was neat in his person and eager to do more than his share in folding the tent and lashing it properly onto one of the toboggans, while I took down the poles. He took my sleeping robe and blanket and, rolling them carefully, loaded them as well, then showed me how to arrange my shoulder bag so that it would rest comfortably on my back as I was traveling, instead of bumping endlessly against my hip.

When camp was broken, I took my proper place in our line of file. Kelsey led us down to the river and continued southwest in silence all that day.

I fancied that he did not set such a fast pace now, or was it that I was perhaps becoming a stronger snowshoer? Kelsey ordered every man but Wapasu and me to take their turn breaking trail. On this day, I did not fall behind.

When we camped that night, Wapasu was the man to spread the spruce boughs and arrange the sleeping skins. I was amazed to see him unroll two blankets in a way that formed a double nest.

After we had finished our night meal, we all lay down with our feet toward the fire. Wapasu, the slim young hunter, and Captain Kelsey pulled off their outer moccasins and leggings and rolled them into pillows for their heads, then got into bed together, arranging themselves so they were hugging one another. The other three Cree hunters showed no surprise at this and quickly went to sleep. Some time later, when their passionate movements had ceased, I closed my eyes and slept.

In the morning, I raised my head and stared at Captain Kelsey's place. He had already gone outside the tent, but I could see his young bed partner, Wapasu, still sitting in their bedding, carefully repairing a hole in one of Kelsey's snowshoes.

Kelsey thrust his head inside the tent and said to Wapasu, "*Esqua'u-wippe' mawagan taonish.*"

I thought I must have misheard his words, for they had been something like, "Woman, bedfellow, *pursta o'nish*, put on your clothes."

Wapasu turned and smiled at him and then at me. I saw now that Wapasu had well-formed breasts and was a slender youngish woman disguised in hunter's dress.

Kelsey came in, smiling. "Knight's getting kind of old for the sporting life," he said, "but not me. I like to travel out here in the clear country air and enjoy the greater pleasures of this world."

Wapasu quickly rose, dressed, and set Kelsey's rewoven snowshoe outside the tent. She tightly rolled their sleeping skins and blankets, then went outside and lashed them onto the toboggan. Once again I helped her take down the tent, but this time I could not keep from staring at her in amazement. She was a strong, handsome young woman. None of us ever had to wait for her.

We continued our travels southwest along various lakes and rivers for eleven more days. We were held up by two violent winter storms that left soft new snow piled waist-deep in the forests, which grew ever denser. But it was hard and windswept along the lakes and river courses.

I often helped Wapasu when Kelsey and the others went out to track down the moose we needed to feed ourselves and the dogs. It was our job to set up or take down the tent, gather firewood, melt snow into water, set snares, and spread the sleeping boughs. All of these were useful travelers' skills that I would have to master.

One morning, I bent a brittle tent pole and it snapped, its sharp end tearing a rent in the center of my outer shirt. That evening, after we and our dogs had shared the rich meat of a yearling moose that our hunters had taken, Wapasu asked me for my shirt, and she sewed it by the firelight. In the morning I found it neatly folded beside me. Over the mend in the center of my chest she had stitched on a round Cree device. It was a handsome, palm-sized decoration, with colored rings within rings of flat-split porcupine quills, beautifully arranged.

I put the shirt on, proud that I had been given this true Cree symbol. Kelsey stared at it and then at me and Wapasu. She smiled at both of us. I noticed that he did not return her smile but looked bitterly at me.

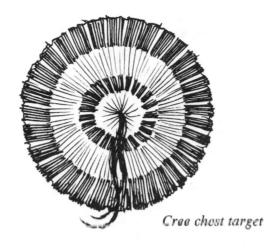
Cree chest target

By the time we had broken camp next morning, Kelsey was already some distance along the river, running by himself, breaking trail for the rest of us. It was almost noon before he allowed us to draw up to him. His bad humor of the morning had almost vanished, and he seemed his usual silent self again.

In my journal, I noted that we had slept out for twenty nights when we made camp on an island in the frozen river. The weather had cleared, but it became unbearably cold. We could hear the frozen tamaracks split with the sharp sound of a musket shot. Once I scooped up a horn of water from a fish hole in the river and flung it toward a thieving dog. The water froze in midair and struck the animal like a load of shot.

On the twenty-seventh morning out, I woke to find Kelsey and the others gone. Only Wapasu remained. She was outside gathering wood. I went to help her.

"They left early," she said. "They saw caribou some distance back along the river." Suddenly she stopped and pointed to a line of fresh lynx tracks. "Oh, he's a big one," she whispered. "Take your musket and track him. These men with us admire a hunter most of all."

I tightened the lashings on my snowshoes, primed my musket, and asked her if she would come with me.

Wapasu looked at me very seriously. "The captain would be very mad at you and me, if he saw my tracks following yours into some hiding place among the trees. You go,'' she said. ''I'll wait for the others here.''

I stalked carefully along the lynx trail, wanting desperately to prove to the others that I, too, could become a hunter.

Some time later, I saw a dozen ptarmigan burst into the air. The lynx leapt and caught one, then went bounding away with it still struggling in his mouth. His tufted ears were laid back like a huge, excited housecat. I kept on tracking him, moving farther and farther away from the camp. It began to snow, softly at first, with big spiraling flakes, which clung to the thickly needled arms of every tree.

As the falling snow increased, the lynx track almost disappeared. I looked in alarm, then started back along my trail. A sense of panic gripped me. I ran, then stumbled in the clogging snow. I stood up and called out, hoping someone would hear me. But there was only ominous silence.

Hours passed while I sought to retrace my own almost invisible tracks. At last I recognized our camping place and rushed forward, delighted that I had found it before dark.

There was no tent, no humans, nothing there. To prove to myself that I was in the right place, I dug beneath the snow and found the charred remains of our fire. Then, almost hidden by the laden branches, I saw my sleeping skin and blanket hung beside a not yet fully frozen chunk of meat. Where had Kelsey gone? Why had he left me a second time?

As the rising wind caused the tree to whisper and wave its ghostly arms, I rushed away down the bank and out along the river, impelled by terror. In the darkness, I could see that the snow-white river on which the others were travelling had split into two separate branches that formed a wide V. Which fork had Kelsey taken? I ran along the left branch, certain that the wrong decision would be the end of me.

My fear of being wrong drove me to retrace my tracks until I reached the river's fork again. What was I to do? Which fork should I choose? I squatted, trembling on my snowshoes, trying to calm myself. With my blanket tentlike over my head, I gnawed on the cold raw meat, watching the storm grow worse.

A strange sound caused me to raise my head, fling back the blanket, and listen. It came again, a dull sound carried on the blustering wind. A slow metallic clanking-banging that recalled the wretched, chained Scots and English prisoners outside of Newgate Prison, waiting to be branded, then transported to the colonies and sold as plantation slaves.

I rose and moved cautiously toward the sound. It came again, it was real. It was from the right fork of the river. Clang, clank-clang, clang, the noise increased, then died away.

"Kelsey! Wapasu! Keelsee!"

Clank. Clank, claaang! I rushed forward, then stumbled when my face was jabbed by sharp tree needles. Snow showered down on me. The sound was right beside me. Reaching out, I touched Wapasu's copper tea pail. Tied beside it was our largest pewter spoon.

I thanked God, believing that the clanging signal in the darkness had surely saved my life. I hung the spoon and tea pail on my shoulder bag, and moved confidently along the right fork of the river, cheered by the sound it made.

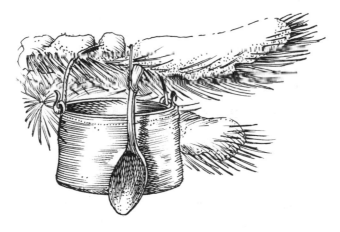

tea pail and spoon

Gradually, the storm moved eastward and in the moonlight their tracks were visible again. Much further on they turned and led up the riverbank. Among the trees I saw the dark form of a tent. I wondered if I should instantly challenge Kelsey to a duel and try to kill him for leaving me a second time.

When the dogs came near me, I was amazed to see that their mouths were all tied shut. I stuck my head inside the black interior of the tent. Unseen humans were huddled there in silence, awake and watchful.

"Kelsey, are you there?" I called. "Why have you no fire?"

"We crossed the trail of twenty men," he answered. "They cannot be far from here."

Wapasu's voice whispered, "It is well you found us. Make no noise. They may be very close and could attack if they discover we are here."

"Scratchers." A Cree hunter spoke. "We do not want to draw them with the sight or smell of smoke, or have them spy our firelight in the darkness."

I hung my snowshoes in a tree and took my musket, bedding, and shoulder bag inside and gently clanked the spoon and tea pail to let them know that that was how I'd found them. My belly was rumbling with hunger, and perhaps with my anger against Kelsey. I cut more meat and ate it in the darkness, overjoyed to be near humans again.

We rose cold and stiff at dawn next morning, ate snow and gnawed frozen meat, before setting out along the river. We soon picked up the fresh deep trail of many men and easily followed it to where they had camped the night before. The air was cold and still. Twice we heard the distant sound of howling; not wolves, the hunters said, but dogs. It was midday when we saw eight thin plumes of smoke rising arrow-straight into the sky.

Well before evening, we six turned a bend, and there on the riverbank we beheld their camp. Our six dogs yowled and their dogs answered. Two women who were outside turned and saw us, then darted down inside their snow-buried lodges. We could hear voices calling as they warned each other of our presence. I listened carefully, but could not understand a word.

"They're Scratchers all right! I've heard of their camps. Looks like a mess of badger holes. Listen to them," muttered the Cree behind me. "They are Scratchers, a bad lot, our elders say. I don't want to go near them.'' Then he called forward to Kelsey. ''You be careful of them, Captain. They are *wit-tico*,'' he said, using the Cree word for devils. He told me that they were savages who were said to kill their captives very slowly. I detested the sound of that.

''Who will come with me?'' asked Kelsey. ''I'm going up there to meet them before it grows too dark.''

There was a long silence.

None of the Cree answered him. Captain Kelsey started forward alone.

''Wait! Wait'' I called. ''I'm coming with you.''

''*Awahhh, gustach!*'' I heard Wapasu cry. ''I am so fearful for both of you.''

As we two started up the riverbank before their camp, we could see two dozen of these so-called Scratchers spreading out before us in a loose half-circle. When we approached these unknown wild men, their leader did not come forward and lie down on the snow, in the customary northern way of testing strangers. All of them stood stiff as dogs about to fight, their faces charcoal-blackened. The four Cree behind us slithered their two toboggans around, preparing to see us killed before they took flight.

Like us, the Scratchers were on snowshoes. Most were armed with two or three antler-pointed caribou spears. Their long tangled hair and their dark animal skins made them look like the wildest creatures on earth. As we moved cautiously forward, side by side, the Scratchers started chanting and yelling and closing to encircle us, moving steadily as they stamped a deep dance ring. We both cocked our muskets. Their excited dogs rushed in barking, snarling, showing their fangs. With our long guns held at the ready, nervously I now counted thirty-one of them closing in around us.

Suddenly, Kelsey shouted, ''Stop! Stop! Stop!'' in three separate dialects. Luckily, the last one they seemed to understand.

These wild-looking Scratchers stopped and stood like statues, pointing their spears at our middles. I slipped my hand out of my mitten and slid it beneath my shirt to cock the pistol in my waistband.

147

"Good Lord!" whispered Kelsey. "Have you noticed that everyone of these hostile maniacs is clothed with nothing but prime beaver skins? Dressed up fancy as the poor old governor, they are. This country must be swarming with beaver.

"Don't move," he added as he carefully slipped his bulky shoulder bag around, untied it, and removed a small double strand of colored beads. Looping these on his musket barrel just behind the front sight, he turned and held it pointing toward their most important-looking hunter.

This man came boldly forward, frowning at us, then reached out with the tip of his spear and took the precious gift from Kelsey.

I watched him repeat this distant giving of the beads to half a dozen others. Then Kelsey took out a small trade mirror and, catching the last rays of evening sunlight, flashed it in their eyes. We heard them gasp.

"Does anyone here speak Cree? Does anyone understand me?"

An older woman holding a child by the hand answered him, "Yes, I understand you." She came ploughing through the deep snow toward us. "These people," she said, "caught me when I was a girl. They are good hunters. I have children by them now. It is good with them."

"Do they know how to smoke tobacco?" Kelsey asked.

"Sure they do, but they haven't got any. Have you?" she asked him.

Kelsey took out a big twist of cheap Brazilian plug tobacco and pipe and showed it all around. The spear points went down when the woman told them we had come to talk of trading.

Their head man now came forward and smiled when he took the gifts from Kelsey's hand.

"These people never ever heard a gun," said the woman. "Why don't you make a bang for them? I heard one once before they caught me," she laughed. "It scared me half to death."

Kelsey warned me to uncock my pistol so I wouldn't blow my balls off, then told me to go along the stream a bit and stand up a slab of wood that we could see.

He gathered the Scratchers close around him before he aimed and fired. In the confusion of smoke and noise, nearly all of them fell down, but most of them saw the wood jump up and topple over, split in two.

The Cree woman who spoke one of Kelsey's southwest dialects told the Scratchers that we could easily make thunder and kill the lot of them. They were delighted and asked through her if we would like to come inside to smoke and feast, then rest in their lodges overnight.

Kelsey thanked them but said our people were already setting up camp and we, too, had lots of food and tobacco. But he assured them that we would meet again next day, to smoke peacefully and to talk about some beaver trading. They agreed.

Only after that was Kelsey convinced that these Scratchers were a trustworthy tribe who kept to themselves, wandering the wooded river valleys and ponds of what he hoped would prove to be the richest beaver country in the world. In our camp that night, Henry Kelsey kicked up his long legs, for he had found the beaver and the people to bring them in to trade.

When morning came, the captive woman helped Kelsey explain how they could trade their beaver pelts for tobacco, apple brandy, muskets, iron axes, knives, pots, brass thimbles, needles, fish hooks, brilliant blankets, beads, and cloth – if the Scratchers would visit Fort York every summer. In token of this promise, Kelsey traded the chief a musket for his best beaver dance costume and those of his two sons, then gave the chief's wife a present of a brass finger ring and cotton head scarf.

To make sure that our house of treasures was not a dream, the chief sent two strong snowshoers to break trail on our return. They stayed with us to the outlet of Ten Shilling Creek where they, themselves, could see the Company's blood-red flag floating above the fort. Those two shy Scratchers waved farewell to us, then ducked down and scurried back toward their own country. Kelsey assured me that the Scratchers would pack their bark canoes with beaver peltry and come to trade. Speaking Cree so the others would understand him, he explained that he was proud of me, a young clerk, for joining him, so we two could walk together into trouble. He further said that I would always be welcome on any walk-across with him, and that in time he would make a lively Company trader of me, or a dead man, if my luck ran out.

The Cree laughed and readily agreed with him on that!

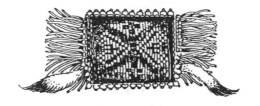

THANA

10

Williyumm had not come back. He had been gone for all of the eagle moon and the gray goose moon as well. It seemed like a hundred moons to me.

One midday, when the spring sun was glaring off the snow, I heard the sentry shouting and thought some Cree had been mischievous. I was wrong. Wee Fergus ran past our door, and I heard his high voice call out, "They're coming back! Guvnaar, you can see them marching in line along the river. Williyumm Staariit, Captain Keelsee, and four Cree. All of them are coming. They are all but here."

I ran up the la-la and looked out between the spears. My face started turning hot, then cold, as I saw Williyumm coming straight toward me. He was the one who was breaking trail! He was so lean and snowshoeing so strongly that he didn't even look like the Williyumm I had known. His face was burnt dark brown, and he was shoeing with the easy, steady hip roll of a Dene hunter. Right behind him came Longlegs.

I spoke only a few words to Williyumm that day he arrived, for he had to go with Longlegs and make squiggles on big skins to show their camps and trails and describe to Bearman everything that they had seen and done. I could quickly see that Williyumm and Captain Keelsee had become good friends.

Next morning, I went in the eating lodge and sat close by Williyumm. It was good to be with him again. I was not surprised that after traveling and speaking mostly Cree, Williyum had lost some of the Dene words that I had taught him. We spoke mostly in Scootlanish or Ballahooly.

On the second night, Bearman told Williyumm and me to follow him into his room with the big bed and the beaver robe where Williyumm and I had almost got our parts together.

Bearman spoke to Williyumm only Ballahooly, and so I missed words here and there. But by listening carefully, this is what I understood. First, Bearman said to Williyumm, "Keelsee admitted that you did well out in the country on your first journey. Keelsee said the Cree had to wait for you a lot because you were very slow and green at first."

"That's one way you could say it." Williyumm laughed.

Bearman then asked him, "Did you see anything strange about Keelsee? Did he do anything not usual?"

"No," said Williyumm. "Everything he did looked right to me."

Bearman asked him, "Was he always considerate and helpful to you?"

"Indeed, he was," said Williyumm, "very thoughtful."

"Did he try to bed down with any of those Scratcher women?" Bearman asked. "Such an act could turn the Scratchers dead against all trade with the Company."

"No, he never touched their women. He didn't seem to need to." Williyumm sighed and looked down at the colorful Cree target he was wearing on the Dene shirt that I had made for him.

Bearman's eyes narrowed when he said, "You seem now to like Keelsee very much. Is that true?"

"Oh, yes," said Williyumm. "He's a hard man, but a strong one on the trail. He taught me a lot of useful ways. I'd travel with him any time."

Bearman coughed and said, "Don't you get too cozy with that damn deputy of mine." Then he looked from Williyumm to me and said, "Remember, I've put my hopes in you two, not in Keelsee. I don't trust him and certainly I don't trust Accountant Althorp. He's a spy! It's you two I'll send running west, not Keelsee. If he ever found a piece of gold or silver, I'd be the last man on earth to ever get my share of it.

"Don't forget," he told Williyumm, "finding gold, silver, or copper could be of great benefit to you and me. I intend to bribe these Cree to help you and this young Copper woman go exploring. Next year, I am going to build a better fort on the Churchill River, further north so I can trade the western waterways used by her western people."

Speaking words of Dene and Cree, Williyumm turned and made Bearman's talk clear to me. Then Bearman moved quietly across his room and looked out into his porch to see if any ears were out there listening to his words before he whispered, "Take a whole year for your walk-across, if need be. Search carefully and see what you can find. I want her people to learn that they can trust us to treat them decently when it comes to trading furs or gold. When the weather turns fair," Bearman added, "I'll set you on your way."

To be sure, I asked Williyumm in Dene and some Cree, "Does Bearman want us to look for the yellow pebbles in my father's country?"

"Yes," said Williyumm. "Did you not know that?"

"Yes, I did not know that," said I. "If he wants us to find the yellow stones, we must go into my mother's country."

"Oh!" said Bearman, who was surprised at my Ballahooly talk.

"Oh!" said Williyumm. "Is that still more distant?"

"No, it is closer," I told them, "if you mean we must look for this kind of stone."

I pulled up my pointed shirt and undid my mother's little yellow scratcher from my hip string. Both of them stood back staring at me.

scratcher on hip string

"Cover yourself," said Williyumm. "The governor only wants to see that little scratcher."

"Speak for yourself," said Bearman, as he took the little gift that my mother had given me.

He held it close to the candle flame, then put the handle between his back teeth and bit very hard.

"Look at that!" he said to Williyumm, pointing at the dents. Then making it flash in the light, he gasped, "This is made of gold. Pure gold!"

I knew the scratcher was made only of yellow stone and did not care about that. I was interested in the bright Cree target sewn on the front of Williyumm's shirt. Where had he got that from? Who gave it to him? Who sewed it on for him? Williyumm could not sew! Only a skillful woman could make such a beautiful quill device. But Williyumm said they had seen no skillful women on this journey, except Scratchers, and everyone had told me they could never make a clever thing like that.

Because I was staring into the fire, Bearman seemed to forget about me, or that I understood a lot of Ballahooly.

I heard him say to Williyumm, "Think of her having a golden treasure like this dangling from her hip string." Bearman laughed. "And you, you simple booby, not knowing the least thing about it."

"It's against the Company rules to know that," Williyumm said. "You told us no one could have anything to do with native women whilst inside this fort."

"Indeed, I did, but I never dreamed that a smart young buck like you would take me seriously!"

Bearman held my mother's golden scratcher up for me to see and said, "It would never do to have others in this fort see this small yellow tool. I shall keep it safe for you." He then slipped it in his large side pocket. "I'll give you a sharper, brighter tool than this one," he told me. "Don't say a word of this," he warned, "not to a single person."

"We'll not say a word," Williyumm promised him.

"Good!" Bearman laughed. "This should be fair for all. The fur is something that should properly belong to this Company.

154

But any precious stones or metals . . . that's another matter. The way I see it, anything we find belongs to us.''

As we went out of Bearman's door, he closed it. I leaned against Williyumm in the darkness and said, "I been missing you most badly for those two long moons.''

"We have to get together right away,'' said Williyumm. "We have to find some secret place. Can't we go to Owinipeg's lean-to?''

I shook my head most sadly. "I already asked her. Owinipeg says Bearman can look right into her lodge through the little opening he had cut and see everything that happens there. That would not be good.''

"Keep thinking,'' he said, as I left him and went through Owinipeg's door.

Next night, when we were finished eating with all the others, Longlegs came and sat down beside me and Williyumm. He smiled at both of us. "I'm going overnight to sleep at the Cree lodge,'' he said. "Captain Cheechoo's going with me. If you two want a quiet place to . . . talk, you could use my room. The latch string is difficult to see. It's hanging high on the left side of the door.''

"Thank you,'' Williyum said to him. "You've already been much help to me.''

When we two got out of the eating lodge, we ran along the snowy path to Keelsee's sleeping place. Neither of us had ever been in there before. We didn't bother lighting a candle. There was enough glow from his small fire box to see a low bed made of wood against the wall. It was very narrow but soft with furs and blankets on it.

"Och, look at this,'' said Williyumm.

"Good place,'' I said, as he reset the latch bar inside the door.

We stepped across the room together and sat down on the side of Captain Keelsee's bed. First, Williyumm helped me off with my shirt, and then I helped him off with his. Then our leggings and moccasins seemed to go flying around the room.

Williyumm took me by the hair, but oh so gently, not rough and bad like Kunn. I hoped that Dingee was sitting somewhere in the shadows watching both of us, for she had told me that the greatest thing in all her life had been to lie with a real man. Oh my, how right she was!

I got to shivering and shaking just as hard as Williyumm, and I cried out and so did he. We put our hands across each other's mouth, not wishing Bearman or Althorp or Owinipeg or any others in the fort to hear us.

When it was sort of ended, we both lay back panting, sighing, still keeping hands on one another, glad to be alive, glad to know our coming together hadn't been a dream. I could never have imagined that the pleasure of jumping around the bed with Williyumm could cause such thrills in me.

Maybe we both went to sleep a little after the next time. When he woke, Williyumm said, "I always wondered how that was going to be," and we held each other very closely.

"Where did you get that small quill target you got sewn on the shirt I made you?"

He didn't answer for a wee bit. Then he laughed and told me about Wapasu, a young Cree woman, being with Keelsee and the others on the journey.

"She must have liked you to mend my shirt so nicely and give you that pretty target. It makes you look like a Cree."

"Wapasu is a wonderful girl," he told me, "very good at journeying."

"If you need any more sewing or mending," I told him, "you bring it straight to me."

Williyumm said he would.

"We shouldn't do this too much, it being the first time," I told Williyumm.

But we did.

When he awoke, I knew he would find me gone because the sun was rising earlier every morning, and I didn't want the man who looked over the spears to see me. I knew that Williyumm would miss the round quill target on his chest that had been made by that Cree woman. So I asked Owinipeg for a few well-colored quills to make him a small chest square in the Dene style, with two small dangling ermine tails, which are said to put lots of jump into any Dene woman's new or old bedfellow. That's what my grandmother told me; she knew a lot about all that.

I gave the round Cree target to Cheechoo and asked him to give it back to Keelsee's woman who pretended to be a man.

Later, when Keelsee talked again to us, he told Williyumm that the square Dene crest looked fine on his shirt front and that he was glad that I, Thana, had sent her Cree quill target back to Wapasu.

"What did she say?" Williyumm asked him.

But Longlegs only smiled and did not answer him about that. Not saying one way or the other. That's the way Misstaair Keelsee was.

WILLIAM

11

Winter died on Tuesday, April 25th, in the year A.D. 1715, and so I carefully noted in the Company's journal, for every man and the two women at York Factory were more than ready for a change. We flung open the thick wood shutters and let the sunshine and spring air come in. Lake-sized expanses of blue water appeared on top of the ice out on Hudson Bay and along the Hayes River, and mirages shimmered over the western uplands.

Governor Knight could be seen at almost any hour of day with his big woodworker's hands clasped tight behind his back wandering around the fort yard or pacing on the sentries' walk, looking out over the whole country that lay to the north and west of us. Clearly, he had his mind set on our journey. But he was not half so eager to have us go as we were. Food had been scarce that spring, and almost all our ship's supplies were gone.

First, the geese and ducks and swans returned. Then the home Cree hunters, with their sons, went out and came back with eighteen caribou. Their wives and daughters caught an abundance of river fish, which they lent us until our ship came in.

On the twelfth of June, the mosquitoes came to life, humming up from the shallow ponds to plague us when the wind was down.

James Knight announced that night at dinner, "It's getting time for you to go, Stewart. You should start to ready your kit and so should that young Copper woman."

He knew her name was Thanadelthur, or just Thana, but he seemed to enjoy calling her that young Copper woman. It wasn't that he didn't like her. I think more it was that he wished he was young and running west with her instead of sending her with me.

The governor waited until June 24th, when he judged the time to tell the Cree was right, then give us all a royal Company send-off. He called in Captain Cheechoo and told him to alert the home Cree and the Northern Cree to wear their best and gather tomorrow before the fort. Our officers, clerks, journeymen, and bonded boys shook out their Company costumes and polished up their pewter buttons. Of course, I, like our pitiful piper, wore my Scot's bonnet, my plaid and kilt and sporan.

The Company feast began near midday, with the weather holding fine. Governor Knight ordered the creaky main gate opened just a bit, enough to allow some of us outside. Only the sentries, the Irishman, and his powder monkey stood guard, our two cannons loaded with grape and smaller shot. Thana and Owinipeg, of course, remained inside. The governor told Accountant Althorp to stay with them, on alert for any troubles outside the gate.

Then the governor, his deputy governor, Captain Kelsey, Surgeon Carruthers, and myself and Captain Cheecho, in that order, marched boldly out, followed by McNulty and wee Fergus bearing muskets. Then came Shipwright Smithers, our blacksmith, carpenters, and cooper, all heavyset men wearing their thick leather aprons and small tricorn hats. We marched cautiously yet boldly forward to meet the oncoming horde of Northern Cree. It was comforting to know that the big red Company flag was blowing nicely right behind our heads.

The governor ordered the bonded boys to lay a circle of blue blankets on the ground and spread a scarlet one over the governor's high-backed chair. Our most important home Cree hunters in their finest costumes already stood waiting, and at the governor's signal they stepped forward and sat on the blankets. Deputy Kelsey sat on the governor's right side and Surgeon Carruthers on his left, and I stood close behind them. Captain

Cheechoo sat next to Kelsey and the Northern Cree, following in order of their varying rank, then took their places, forming a perfect ring. The Northern Cree had painted their hands and foreheads red or blue or pale ash white, with thin black stripes drawn down their cheeks.

Their highest chief, named Cawcawqua, The Raven, sat opposite the governor, staring at him. He was dressed much more impressively than all the other Cree, with a brilliantly beaded quill shirt and dozens of dangling necklaces, earrings, and fluttering fringes. Even his skin leggings were covered with elaborate quill designs. He was one of those scowling northerners whom Kelsey had warned me never to trust. I noticed that the fearless Captain Cheechoo edged away if Cawcawqua even seemed to lean toward him.

When the formal passing of the peace pipe and the coughing and the wheezing finally ended, both sides sat in silence, not wishing to miss a single word or take the slightest chance of losing out on any gifts. The Company was expected to be very generous at an important gethering such as this.

peacepipe

The governor looked around at the circle of faces and the crowd behind, then he spoke slowly, stopping at the end of every sentence. I did my very best to translate, though Mr. Kelsey was a far more able Cree interpreter. The governor told those gathered that the Company planned to send a party west, to find the Copper people and smoke a pipe of good will with them. I was relieved when Cheechoo nodded to me, meaning that all of them had understood my words.

As soon as Governor Knight was finished speaking, Caw-cawqua rose and made a great harangue, speaking violently against Thana's people and their neighboring Eskimos still farther north. He said that all of them were nothing but an evil horde of spirit snatchers and sly thieves. He called them demons, conjurors, and other words I did not even try to translate. He warned the governor against ever going near the Coppers, ever trading even the oldest rusted blunderbuss with them. He warned Deputy Kelsey and then me never to trade so much as a fish hook, needle, or a bead with any of the Copper people. He added that if the governor insisted on trying to trade with those miserable devils, that his Northern Cree must be the ones to do it for the Company.

Thana let out a scream when she heard Cawcawqua's words. "Bad-mouthed old bugger!" she yelled down to him in Dene, Ballahooly, then in Cree. "They'll kill you if you tell lies about my people."

Old Cawcawqua raised his head, giving her a murderous stare.

"Be quiet, woman," the governor warned her. Then he had me translate his words against all that Cawcawqua had said. I interpreted Knight's thoughts firmly, declaring that the Company was sending me and Thanadelthur west, to link up with her Copper people.

The governor said that our walk-across could be long and difficult. For this reason, he was prepared to offer gifts to those who would, with good heart, accompany us northwest, then help us to return safely to the fort.

Cawcawqua appeared more reasonable after hearing the governor's closing words.

Both the Northern and the home Cree then crowded round the brandy casks and porridge in the iron pots that the cook and his helper had dragged outside. There was ecstatic moaning from the Cree drinking the last of our cheap apple brandy, for it had that sharp rotted taste which took their breaths away.

A blanket covering was pulled from a long toboggan to reveal huge piles of steaming raisin bannocks. Each cake was thick as a woman's wrist and round as a Highlander's cap. These were divided, one to every hunter and his wives and children, with another pint of English apple brandy just to wash it down.

"Which of you strong walking men," the governor asked, "are willing to go? Who will join our Company for this brave man's walk-across?"

When I had finished translating that, there was a silence. Then he added, "We will give each hunter, carrier, who goes for us one new long musket, four full horns of powder, also one hat's measure of bird shot and another filled with lead ball."

The Cree still held their brandied breaths.

"Also," the governor called out loudly, "we will give each man who goes for us a length of red blanket."

Their women gasped, but their men still held their silence.

"Also, one half pint of colored beads, with four best iron needles."

Still no sound from the men, but a louder whispering of approval from their women.

"Also, six brass thimbles and two spools of strong linen thread, and that is definitely the end!"

Now a buzzing sound arose as from an excited hive of bees. The governor looked around him at the gathering of sun-bronzed faces.

"I don't want any of those crazy murderers coming into my country. You tell them that again!" Thana shouted down to me in Cree and more or less the same to the governor in English.

"Be quiet, woman!" Knight and Kelsey shouted up to her.

The Northern Cree screamed out, then rose, turning their backs on all of us.

"Wait! Wait!" Knight himself called out to them. "I will also give a long knife, a hatchet head, and a hatful of beads to each man who will go on the walk-across. And to each woman going shall be given a kerchief full of beads and a half sack of oatmeal porridge."

When I called that to them, they all turned around. That promise of the beads plus porridge did it. Captain Cheechoo told me afterwards it was what those wives had held out for.

Cawcawqua, still frowning, nodded to his son, Nishcock, who shouted, "I will go."

This Nishcock was the youngest of the Northern captains, fully six feet tall, straight and strong. He now stepped boldly forward.

"I, too! I will go!" A hundred others shouted scornfully.

Before long, almost every youthful hunter and a score of wives had volunteered.

Both Thana and Owinipeg were busy trying to count numbers on their fingers and toes.

"Too many! We cannot have so many," she screamed at me. "You tell Bearman that my people would think of that horde below me as a raiding party, pushing in to murder our families and make slaves of our younger women."

"Silence, Copper bitch!" Nishcock bellowed, for he hated every word that Thana said.

This seemed to me a dreadful way to begin any expedition, with the Company employers and Cree employees in wild disarray, sharing feelings of mistrust on either side. However, James Knight was a forceful man determined to send us forward. He was anxious that every day of our journey I keep careful notes and observations recording our exact line of march, the weather, the terrain we crossed, and the distance traveled. Above all, he wanted me to gather samples of any gems or metals that we saw. I was directed to make a map and mark each sizable lake, river, hill, or other noticeable landmark on it, and to locate exactly the position of any valuables we discovered. When we did, we were to erect a well-made stone cairn at that place.

The governor said that as we progressed, I should send two of my fleetest and most trusted carriers back to him, each bearing a written message and a map attesting to our position and our situation, as well as samples of any metals found, especially gold or silver. He warned me to send messages and specimens bound into a cloven stick, for these Cree have no knowledge of pockets or of written messages. James Knight reminded me that he had heard a rumor about an early Danish sea captain, Jens Munk, who had wintered on the Churchill River and described an inland long knife that he had seen. It was hammered out of perfect gold.

I worked feverishly for the next few days, gathering spare journals, compasses, navigational instruments, and other traveling gear, including a pistol and a hefty navy cutlass. In a sturdy iron-strapped trunk of oak, I carefully packed a Company telescope, sextant, an azimuth compass, parallel rulers, dividers, and a brass plumb bob, as well as all my shipboard notes from Charles Davol concerning the Royal Navy's latest rules for navigation.

double-barreled pistol

Just before our departure, I took a noonday observation of the sun with the sextant and azimuth compass, then computed our latitude and our meridian. I was overjoyed to have been chosen by James Knight to be the first Company man given the opportunity to enter this vast unmapped country, to go out searching across the broad lands. This honor should rightly have befallen the more experienced Mr. Kelsey, but the governor had disclosed his reasoning in this matter to me. To Kelsey, Knight argued that I was young and a sturdy walker who possessed a better working knowledge of the Dene language and of navigation than anyone he knew. Therefore, he had concluded, with the young Copper woman guiding me, we stood the best chance of success.

As I latched my heavy trunks of instruments, I thought of Thana and Owinipeg and wondered if they had finished sewing the clothing we would need. I left my quarters and walked through the early summer twilight to their lean-to, calling out a greeting to wee Fergus, who again had sentry duty on the wall.

When I went inside, I was surprised to see Thana sitting by herself in the candlelight, binding our spare mittens and moccasins into small tight bundles.

''Are you finished?'' I asked her in English.

She smiled and nodded.

brandy glasses on cask

"Where is Owini . . . ?"

She reached out and put her fingers across my lips to silence me. Then she pointed to a small wooden cask where Thana kept her sewing things. On top of it stood two large crystal goblets. Each bore the Company crest and was filled with the governor's best, golden yellow French cognac.

Thana widened her dark almond-shaped eyes as she handed me the candle and indicated that I should cup my hand around the flame. She then reached up and carefully took down from the wall Owinipeg's best dance shirt, draping it over her arm. With one finger she traced a fine line cut into the log wall. It was square and not much larger than a cannon port.

Cautiously, Thana pressed. It opened just a crack. She pushed a little more until I could see just inside the governor's room. There was a warm glow from his fireplace, and two candles sputtered in their stout brass holders. The rest of the room was in dark shadow, but I could clearly see James Knight's raised four-poster bed with its red blanket hangings closely drawn.

As we two peered into the room, we could hear faintly at first, then growing louder and faster, the heavy groaning of the bed ropes and the governor's singing in time with the bedstead creaking. "*Then . . . us will come and pick up ducks . . . pick up ducks . . . in Ilk-le-more-Bat-tannn.*"

Thana smiled at me again and cautiously closed the secret door. She lay back on her own soft bed of winter skins and reached out, signaling me to pass one of the cognac goblets to her. I took the other and lay propped up on my elbow by her side.

Could this really be, or was I dreaming? Was I alone with Thana again at last?

I reached out and touched her. Her body was as hot as mine. I raised my glass and together we drank a large draft of the aged cognac. It made us flush and gasp.

"Did Owinipeg put these glasses here for us?" I asked.

"No," she whispered. "It was Bearman who poured them full and left them here."

Thana put her ear to the crack in the secret door and listened. "No bed creaking now," she said. "Probably they have gone to sleep."

We set our empty goblets on the little cask beside the candle. I helped Thana sit up as I drew off her shirt. She untied each legging from her beaded hip string and slipped them off. In the wink of an eye, I was free of all my clothing.

Thana laughed and hid her face against my chest, saying, "Will-liyumm, I been waiting a long time for this to happen again."

The feeling of her wild black hair flung over me like a ticklish mantle set me giggling like a schoolboy. Then for the second time in my life the moon dipped, the stars blinked, and all the cannon in the world went off. When our trembling had subsided, I lay there trying to remember what life had been like before.

Thana woke me in the morning. I stretched, then pulled her to me, for I had the greatest feeling of well-being. Thana stared peacefully at me and I was gathering my passions to repeat our glorious rout again, when I heard a clatter on the ladder. The guard was changing. That reminded me that it was six o'clock in the very morning we planned to leave.

"We'll have other times to play," said Thana as she eased me out of her bed.

I struggled into my clothing and slipped out the door.

At first, I stood blinking in the bright morning sun. Then using my cap to cover my tousled hair, I climbed the ladder onto the lead roof of our flanker. I could hear my roommates rising noisily below. I leaned against the cannon since my legs had become weak, but it was a very pleasant feeling.

Looking eastward over Hudson Bay, I could see dawn spreading orange across the sky, over long blue-shadowed skeins of ice riding on the mirrored surface of that inland sea. When I looked down, I could see beneath me James Knight's cropped gray head. He was hatless, with his red woolen doublet spread across his massive shoulders, his fists clenched tight upon his hips. His face looked as relaxed as mine.

"Well, Mr. Stewart," he called up to me. "My pewter calendar tells me this day is the 27th of June, A.D. 1715, and I see we're blessed with fairest weather." He smiled. "I trust that you slept well last night and that you'll go now and wake that fiery young Copper woman."

"Aye, I'll do that, sir. I feel sure she slept as well as I."

"Good!" the governor nodded. "I was hoping that might be the case."

Still weak-kneed, I came down the ladder, trying to look quite perky, for I was starting to feel a different thrill run through me. This morning marked the first time that James Knight had ever honored me with the title "Mister" Stewart. Mister is a rank jealously reserved for junior officers in the military and rising members in our Company of Honourable Gentlemen.

I knocked lightly on the lean-to door and entered. Both Thana and Owinipeg sat smiling at me as they simmered a plump rabbit in a dried mustard broth. Both crystal goblets had disappeared and Owinipeg's dance shirt hung once more over the secret entranceway.

I squatted by them, enjoying the tender feast but at the same time trying to think of anything that I may have forgotten.

"I will miss both of you," Owinipeg said to us in Cree. "Come back here . . . " She paused. "Come back here if you can. And be very wary of that northern mass of savages the guvnaar is sending out with you."

"We'll be careful," I promised her. "You help get Thana ready. I'm off to take my boxes and my kit for loading."

When I reached the sleeping quarters, there was no one there, the others having gone to breakfast. I drew on my handsome new skin leggings, with all the fringes dangling, and my new moccasins. To show I was the leader, I wore my royal-red Company doublet. I pinned my Stewart hunting plaid across my shoulder and wore my badger-headed sporan to hold my gunflints, silver toothpick, and my sister Sheila's lock of hair.

The governor chuckled when he saw me. "I must say, Mr. Stewart, you do look the part with your small green blanket and those feathers in your bonnet. Though I rather miss that red fox hat of yours."

"Thanadelthur made that hat," I told him proudly. "I've got it and I'll wear it when the snow begins to fly."

"Oh, yes," James Knight chuckled. "I have no doubt that you and that strong young Copper woman will share a lively journey. God bless you both," he said as he shook hands with me. "Remember, I expect you to lead those cocky northerners, not follow them. Never allow Nishcock or any of the others to get the upper hand on you."

Surgeon Carruthers called to me, "Hold a moment, Willie. You know I purchased two young orphan lads. I need but one. Would you care to take the other along to help you?"

He pushed forward a young Cree boy who did not appear to be more than nine or ten years old.

"Yes," Thana whispered. "Say yes, quick! We'll take him."

"Do you want to come with us?" I asked the boy in Cree.

He hesitated, then smiled at me and Thana. "I will go with you," he said in English. "I being not afraid."

"I call him Jako. That's short for Jacob and his coat of many colors," said the surgeon. "I've taught him a little English." He pushed gently forward. "There, he's a present that I give to both of you."

"Thank you, sir. That's very thoughtful," I said.

The surgeon told the boy, "Run quickly, get your blanket and your warmest shirts, mittens, moccasins."

Thana stepped close to me and whispered, "Now's our last chance to tell Bearman to send all these slave-takers home. It will be a lot better if we two do the walk-across alone, or maybe with a few of

Captain Cheechoo's goose men and some dogs and that boy," she said, pointing to young Jako, who was running back to us.

"I'll ask the governor to keep the party small," I promised her.

Thana was wearing Owinipeg's gift to her of a handsome new deerskin overshirt with a wide beaded yoke and moccasins sewed to her leggings. She wore her hair loose in the Dene style. I noticed again that the top of her head did not quite reach my shoulder.

"Are you sure that you have everything you need inside that one small bag?" I asked her.

Thana nodded, then raised her overshirt and showed me that Owinipeg had made her a small sheath that she had attached to her hip string. This sheath held Owinipeg's delicate French steel dagger.

dagger on hip string

"Good," said I, "but pull down your shirt." My cheeks flushed with embarrassment at having the bonded boys see her lovely nakedness so early in the morning.

"Are you not worried that you'll catch cold, lass? Going around with those two separate leggings and nothing else between?" wee Fergus asked her.

"Summer's coming." Thana laughed. "And my legs are free for walking. I have that knife hiding there because I do not trust these northerners that Bearman wants to send with us."

By this time, Cheechoo's men had all our baggage stacked outside and stood guarding it. At least twenty dogs were hitched to their toboggans. Each had sealskin stretched beneath it to allow the wooden slats to slip smoothly over the rocks in summer. These toboggans, like the women and some men, were loaded with tents, bedding bundles, and thin lodge poles. The women were mostly carrying packs of food, bags of clothing, trade goods, and powder casks. Most important of all were the three heavy iron-bound trunks which held all our valuables as well as my navigational instruments.

I had slung the leather bag that held my hand compass and the small brass telescope and sketching book across my shoulder. Whatever happened, I planned to take sun shots each noonday, weather allowing, and plot our progress by observations of the stars. I was resolved to keep very careful route maps and make daily journal entries as the governor had bid me.

Thana stayed close behind me as we stepped outside the narrowly opened gate and for the first time saw the enormous herd of unruly northerners that had gathered for the walk-across. About one hundred men had chosen to accompany us. Each one was being issued a new trade musket. Most had their faces painted red or blue, with vertical black charcoal streaks. About twenty additional strong young wives would be the bearers of the heaviest packs. Both Thana and I were horrified. How could there be so many?

"I hate this!" Thana screamed.

I shook hands with all my fellow Company men. Then, followed by Thana and Jako, I strode out in front of the treacherous horde.

Captain Cheechoo came up to me, pulling two yelping dogs by their harness. Both dogs had skin packs tied across their backs and balanced on their sides. "These are my gift to you," he said. "They are filled with dried pemmican and some gifts of red ocher, seashells, and porcupine quills of many colors.

I thanked him, scarcely realizing what a splendid gift he had made to us.

As we moved off, I looked back at the rickety gray stockades of Fort York. Above the gate, the governor, Owinipeg, the surgeon, Kelsey, and almost all of our Company clerks and servants were gathered, waving us off. Thana, Jako, and I waved back. We saw the big red Company flag dip down and rise again, saluting us as we marched away. First one and then the other cannon roared, and two thick sulfur-yellow smoke rings came belching from the flankers just above our heads.

Thana clasped her hands across her ears and fell onto the ground, as did many of our carriers. It was the first time in her life that she had ever heard a cannon fired. She said it almost frightened her to death.

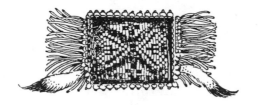

THANA

12

I thought I was blown to pieces when I heard those two big guns roar above my head. I fell down flat and so did little Jako and many of the others.

Williyumm only laughed and helped us to our feet. "Those guns were not loaded; they couldn't hurt you," he said, though, of course, we only understood their frightening roar. "It's just the governor's way of saying good-bye."

"That is a terrible way to say good-bye," I cried, still holding my hands over my ears, afraid that Bearman might try to say good-bye again. This thought kept from my mind the long, twisting line of Cree behind us.

The house of spears grew smaller as we walked away, and I breathed deeply, pulling the good clean air into my body. I was out on a walk-across at last, beneath the whole clear sky with my Williyumm walking just in front of me. I thought, if these wild northern wives have come for carrying, I will let them do it.

At noon, we passed through the old deer hedge and beyond the empty Frenchmen's hut. Mid-afternoon, we rested, drank water from the stream, and slapped mosquitoes. I was grateful for the light wind rising along the river, because it would drive away these tiny fliers who took blood.

"I'm feeling kind of weak-legged," I told Williyumm. "I'll be glad to get into bed again, with you."

"I can scarcely wait," he answered.

We all got going again, but not so fast this time. Jako trotted joyfully beside me, carrying a light sack of ground oats across his shoulders. He kept a watchful eye on the two pack dogs that dragged our toboggan, which had caribou-leg skins stretched beneath to make it slide over muskeg and stony ground. On it was tied our small tent, eight poles, food, and cooking things inside bags.

The endless line of carriers followed, like a caterpillar leaving its winter tent. Behind Nishcock the four leading men were carrying Williyumm's heavy trunks, then came the carriers with boxes of trade goods: tobacco, brandy, jackknives, lots of beads, fish hooks, thimbles, mirrors, hatchet heads, sugar tits, large and soft iron nails for pounding into spear points or arrow heads – all valuable, light things we would trade or give away to my Dene people when we found them.

When I shaded my eyes to look out over the land before us, I could see summer riding in on the lengthening light. I could feel it, smell it, hear it in the small bird sounds carried on the softening air. Yes, the Big Woman who made both summer and winter was truly close to us.

When I stopped, stood on my toes, and looked back, I could no longer see the house of spears. Williyumm smiled and pointed out the owl-shaped barrel perched on top of what he said was now Bearman's Hill. He said it was a beacon for the ship that would come this summer.

The little wind died as the evening settled all around us. The sun dulled into a huge red ball and sank beyond the flat edge of the world. Above our heads a pair of little sharp-winged hawks chirped and wheeled as they hunted insects through the darkening sky.

The evening star was flashing brightly, and I could see that Williyumm's knees were sagging after such a night followed by so much walking. I tugged at his green shoulder blanket and, when he turned his head, asked, "Are we going to walk all night?"

173

I pointed out a long, flat gravel esker, and when we reached it he shouted to the carriers, "*Pa cosh* – take time!"

Nishcock, the Cree captain, bellowed, "*Pa cosh*," repeating Williyumm's words, as though he were the boss shouting back his own orders to those behind him.

We watched the carriers drop their burdens to the ground.

"*Man kau* – make tents. *Pu naw* – make fires. *Atho me nuck* – cook oatmeal," Nichcock shouted.

"This soft moss here will make a good bed," said Williyumm.

"Yes." I answered, "but it will soak up water if it rains. I'm going to put our tent on that gravel, while Jako finds the firewood."

I blew into my little pipe-stone fire box until its glowing embers lighted up a tiny twist of dried grass, which I had rubbed in goose grease and sprinkled with a few flakes of gunpowder. It burst into flame. Jako was busy unhitching our dogs, then feeding them. It was not long before we two had the fire blazing and our poles up for the cone-shaped *ittsee*, a Dene word for tent that I taught Jako. We covered it with caribou skins, allowing an opening at the top. From a small grove of trees, we cut enough sweet-smelling spruce boughs to spread inside for a soft sleeping place.

While all of this was going on, Williyumm had his shiny brass toys out and he was peeking at the stars and the new moon in the sky and making squiggles quickly in his new book of skins.

When our tent was finished, I had a good idea. Taking our small hand axe and the new trade kettle, I hurried to the river and returned with fresh water and six slender alder poles, each one only a little thicker than my thumb. These Jako helped me arrange in a small half-cone shape, tight against our tent. We bound them together at the top, then I wrapped a spare piece of scraped skin around the poles and skewered it neatly into place, making a small separate dwelling.

"What is that?" said Williyumm.

It looked like an infant riding on its mother's back.

"Jako eats with us and lives with us," I told him, "but he sleeps in his own small tent."

That idea pleased Jako very much, and he quickly made his bed inside.

Of course, I would have liked to sink a bark basket in the gravel and boil the meat the way a Dene woman should, but I thought no. I am sort of getting to be like Williyumm's wife, and I will do the cooking like a Ballahooly woman, although I had yet to see one, and did not know if they cooked or not. I set three sticks over the fire and hung the small copper kettle on it. First, I made porridge with some water and goose fat and when we were finished eating that, I threw in half a handful of tea. Williyumm gave me a kind of funny look and blew the goose grease off the top of his cup before he drank it down. He said it tasted very good.

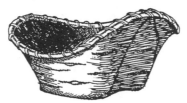

bark basket

When Jako crawled into his side tent, we two sat together, staring at the long row of Cree fires glowing in the twilight a little ways off. We listened to a male wolf howling and a female answering him from far away. Oh, it made me feel like singing to be free again, far from that smoky house of spears, moving west across the clear uplands toward my own people.

Both Williyumm and I had trouble rising from beside the fire, because our legs were stiff. I went into the tent and spread our skins and blankets, and he came in and let himself down beside me. He never even got his clothes off before he fell asleep and I did the same.

Jako had to wake us in the morning. He had nine fresh goose eggs in his coat of many colours, and I could hear the fire crackling outside. "You boil them just a little," I told him.

Williyumm stretched and rolled over on his belly and stared outside the tent. "I feel better," he said. "I don't remember going to bed."

I sat up and reached for my shirt. Williyumm reached for me.

"Do you think we should?" I asked him. "We've got a lot of walking to do again today."

"Just once," he said, and so we did.

Outside the tent, I took the goose eggs out of the boiling water and threw in some tea. These were the first eggs for us this season. They were hard-boiled by now, but they tasted fine.

"Look back at the carriers' tents," Williyumm said. "I think most of them must be asleep. We'll never get anywhere this way," he sighed, "if they're going to sleep late, then rise and slowly stuff themselves with food."

"Shout at Nishcock," I told him. "Tell him to get the carriers moving. Now!"

We did not get underway that day until the sun was high. Nishcock and his people looked sullen and their bellies bulged from eating eggs with porridge. They did not follow half so swiftly as they had the day before. We made our long, mushy summer march across the swampy ground, arriving at the second river only late that afternoon. A grumpy old home Cree lived at the river crossing with his wife and son. He refused to ferry any of us in either of his canoes.

Finally, I told Williyumm, "Trade him for them. Buy his two canoes."

Williyumm had to give him a dozen iron nails in trade to buy them. I thought that outrageous. Any decent Dene would have thought two iron nails a fair trade for a good canoe.

Crossing the river was painfully slow, because we could cram only five persons in each canoe at any one time. The water was cold, but a few of the hunters and all the women stripped off their clothes and, holding onto logs, swam the narrows of the river, yelling at their dogs to follow. Williyumm and I made the last crossing with Jako, Nishcock, and another hunter.

"You call that old man over here and tell him you'll trade him back his two canoes for only half a dozen nails," I said to Williyumm. "Or, tell him I will take this axe and hack his boats to pieces."

The old man quickly agreed, and Williyumm said, "Lassie, you're like those canny Scottish traders from Orkney Isles."

That evening, we camped on high ground on the other side of the river. I pointed to the northwest, where we could see the highlands rising, clear blue, in the distance. A light wind carried the gentle smells of new sweet grasses and budding berry bushes.

Williyumm and Jako brought up the iron trunk and carefully took out the shining tubes that slipped into one another. They were hollow as a swan's wing-bone, but inside at each end were rounded chips of never-melting ice. Williyumm set these on a rock and stared through the hole in one end, out over the land. Then, just as the first stars came out, he stood holding another shiny thing up to his eye and looked quickly at them and made his thin marks on the skins. After, by the firelight, he scratched still more before pointing toward a small notch in the distant hills and saying, "That's where we shall go tomorrow." Looking through his bring-near tube I could see the old moon's face as it began to rise.

I watched Williyumm as he wrapped each one of his shining treasures in thick, green blanket cloth, as carefully as a mother wraps her infant in the carrying sling.

That night, we three shared a big trout that Jako caught. It tasted delicious.

Early in the morning, Jako and I took down our tent, while Williyumm went to speak to Nishcock. He came back looking angry, but would not tell me why.

We traveled a long way on the third day. I watched the blue-gray haze that gathered on the distant hills, making them fade, each one softer than the next, until they disappeared at the flat edge of the world.

Our third night together was as wonderful as the night before we left the house of spears, but in a different way. We seemed to join together in some never-ending way.

My thigh muscles had stretched after our third day of walking, and so had Williyumm's. Here we were, running west together, free as animals, winging slowly like a long line of gray geese straight toward the place where I was born. Inside my bones, I started singing to the Big Woman, thanking her for Williyumm and for Jako, humming the bring-to-us-animals song and swinging Owinipeg's fish amulets in my hand as we started to enter the hungry lands.

When we woke next day, the skies were dark and sullen. It began to rain as the line of carriers came up behind us. After we had walked some distance, the rain stopped, and the muskeg shimmered like the water of a pond. Large flights of snipe and thin-beaked plovers came flashing in on sharp-cut wings across the marshes. Sometimes Williyumm would whistle aloud, trying to imitate the birds, making sounds which no human being should utter out here. Several times I tried to stop him, because I knew that whistling during a walk-across would call in evil creatures that would follow us. Williyumm laughed when I told him that. He was interested in every living thing, sometimes down at the edge of a pond or peering under a stone, staring through his little bring-near glass at some kind of creeping thing, then other times he would make drawings of the birds.

On that fourth evening, we pitched our tent near a pond, only a little off from the carriers. We three lay on our stomachs waiting for the water to boil, feeling close together. Resting our chins on our hands, we looked lazily back at the line of Cree fires and listened to the singsong of their voices. One of them blew a few long ghostly cries on the hollow wing bone of a crane. I basked between the warmth of Williyumm and Jako.

"We don't have to worry," I told them. "Big Woman, she's going to take good care of us."

"Who is Big Woman?" Williyumm asked me.

"Jako knows who she is," I said.

"I don't know her," Jako replied. "I know Winisks, not Big Woman."

"Well," I sighed. "You both listen and I'm going to tell you how we all got started.

"In the beginning, all around us were the broken lands, with stones so rough it was impossible to walk upright. Nothing at all lived here, until one day a big woman came wandering into the country. She was always lonely until a wolf dog appeared. He followed her.''

''Was that wolf dog the same size as these Cree dogs?'' Williyumm asked.

''No, much bigger, it is said. My grandmother told us that this dog used to enter Big Woman's cave each night and turn into a handsome man. He and Big Woman lay joyfully together, as we do. Each dawn, the handsome man became an animal again. Big Woman would stare at the wolf dog and say, 'Surely it was my dreaming that made such a fine man of you.'

''Four moons passed before that first woman in the world felt something stirring deep inside her. That was when another giant appeared, a man so tall that his head was often hidden in the clouds. This giant carried a heavy copper stick. Waving it this way and that, he smoothed the roughest places, making these uplands wide and beautiful. Then taking his stick, he dug holes for the lakes and drew long curving lines to form the rivers and the streams. He poked his stick into the air, making the thunder rumble and the lightning flash. Winter snows turned into summer rains. The rivers and lakes were filled with sweet clean water; moss and trees grew along their banks.

''When that was done, the giant strode to the mouth of Big Woman's cave and, grabbing Wolf Dog, jealously tore him into pieces. His slippery innards he tossed into the rivers and the lakes, to become all the various fishes. The red flesh of Wolf Dog he flung out over the uplands and the forest, and they became the caribou, musk ox, bear, beaver, fox, and hare, and all the other animals that live with us. Lastly, he tore the skin of the wolf and flung it into the air. It changed into flights of laughing geese, swans, loons, owls, ptarmigan, and all the smaller birds. The giant called out to all those creatures, 'Increase, dear ones. Increase.' And then he went away.

''On the tenth moon after the coming of Wolf Dog, Big Woman gave birth to a fine litter. Thereafter, humans were able to live on the earth, because the giant had given animals and humans the right to survive on each other's flesh. Although Big Woman disappeared and has not yet returned to this country, Wolf Star still watches over us and guides us with his bright eye.''

''Do you believe that's true?'' asked Williyumm.

''Certainly!'' I told him. ''My grandmother would never have lied to us.''

That night when Williyumm and I lay together, I could not believe that any two could have such pleasure in this world.

Williyumm awoke in the middle of the night. This stirring roused me and I handed him our small birch-rind urine basket.

''I don't need that,'' he said.

I watched him rise and push back the tent flap. He strode out naked into the summer night.

In a few moments, he came leaping back inside and jumped into our bed. ''*Suckemaw* – mosquitoes! There are millions and millions out there! Listen! You can hear them humming.''

''The air is still and warm, the way they love it,'' I told him. ''You have a lot to learn about this country.''

I used the little basket, then set it back in place. I tightened the tent flap, killed the few mosquitoes that had come in on him, and curled myself close to Williyumm's long smooth back. He was already traveling in that other world of sleep.

On the fifth morning when we woke, I looked and saw that a dozen of our carriers had already set off, but were hurrying east. Williyumm was furious. Not me.

Jako and I returned from our snares with two lean snowshoe rabbits and five plump ptarmigan whose feathers were no longer white but summer brown.

''I snared the rabbits,'' I told Williyiumm, ''but Jako got the birds.''

''How did you do that?'' asked Williyumm.

Jako reached underneath his shirt and produced a well-worn leather slingshot. It had an arm-long thong that widened in the middle to hold a stone.

''Show Williyumm what you can do with that,'' I said.

Jako searched the pond's edge carefully until he found three smooth flat stones. I pointed to a narrow yellow willow leaf drifting on the water's surface near the center of the pond. Jako whirled the slingshot until it made a sound like an old squaw duck's wings, then released the stone. It drove the leaf beneath the water's surface.

"Hit something else," Williyumm asked him.

"I don't want to do it," Jako whispered. "Bad luck to throw smooth sling stones at nothing."

Next day when we were walking, I told Williyumm, "If we can get ourselves across this stretch of hungry country, we can probably hunt and snare enough food to help us until we meet the caribou herds. They will soon be moving south to winter in the forest. Soon after that, we should enter Dene country. There you will see endless game trails crisscrossing one another. Great heavy trout swim in the rivers and lakes." I sang to the Big Woman when I remembered how grand those big fish tasted.

That night after Jako went into his small tent and we went into ours, I lay down very close to Williyumm and was soon lost in a dream. When Williyumm woke at dawn, he drew a long line with his finger in the fur sleeping robe beneath us. "We could cut this bed right down the middle and throw that other half away – we would never miss it."

"Listen!" I said to Williyumm.

We could hear the new rain falling softly, sounding like mice trotting quietly over the east curve of our tent.

"I love to lie and listen to the rain," said Williyumm.

"Rain makes me want to go to sleep," I replied. "It also makes the muskeg squishy and the walking very bad."

"Nishcock has been good," said Williyumm. "And the worst of the Cree have gone. I think the others deserve a day of rest."

"They are only staying with us until all that Company porridge is finished. Then you'll see what happens."

We did rest throughout that rainy day. I didn't want to tell Williyumm, but I knew that before us lay the low, flat, boggy country now hidden by the rains and mists. Kunn had called that place the starving land. It was said there were no fish in the waters and few animals could survive. It is true that countless geese and ducks and swans stop down to rest and feed in that bleak country, but usually they took off quickly, flying north to their summer nesting grounds. Later they flock south again, to escape the grip of winter. In such country, a Dene woman of much experience might set out two dozen snares and perhaps catch a skinny hare or two, or maybe a few lean ptarmigan. Caribou only hurry through that country, and the musk ox usually remain much further north.

"Oh, we'll survive," said Williyumm cheerfully. "You are able to catch birds and rabbits in your snares when those carrier women are taking almost nothing."

"That's because my grandmother taught me to respect the animals," I told Williyumm. "When I was small, she taught me to braid fine snares, using my own hair. As I went out walking with her, I heard her singing the magic songs that she possessed. Those songs made the rabbits and the ptarmigan come near her. My grandmother taught me the songs and showed me how to tie her secret knot that slips the snare. That knot belongs only to a few good Dene women. I wish I could show it to you, even to those Cree women," I said, "but I must not. There is nothing wrong if you hear me singing to a bird or hare, but don't you try to remember all the words. When I have a daughter and later a granddaughter, I will teach them. Yes. I must do so! For that is how this slip knot and our sacred songs are known forever to the women of our Dene families."

We walked very far the next day. When we had made camp that night, I closed the tent flap and covered Williyumm, for he had fallen asleep with his cheek upon his writing skins. Jako and I stayed outside and shared a large lean hare, leaving a plumper one for Williyumm when he woke. To chase off the mosquitoes, Jako and I sat so that the smoke from our small fire drifted over us.

The next evening, I said to Williyumm, "The carriers are not bothering to catch any fish or meat. They are just stuffing themselves on that dried pemmican and porridge Bearman gave them. Soon that will all be gone, and so will they. But I don't care."

In the morning, Misstaar Staarit went with Jako along the line of carriers, stopping to speak to each of them. I carefully watched him while he spoke to Nishcock, but instead of listening, that

Cree captain rudely turned his back on Williyumm, and all of them went on gobbling down their starvation rations. I thought, this will surely turn from bad to worse. As if to show that I was right, soon after our slow departure, a pair of our greatest tricksters, the ravens, called down to me, "carrrok, caaa-carook," as they flew above us, twisting and turning, pretending to chase each other through the air as they slyly examined our long slow march.

By mid-afternoon, heavy clouds had gathered overhead and the air grew still and warm. It began to rain. My skin shirt clung to my back beneath the small pack. The mosquitoes came humming up from the muskeg with every step we took, eager to suck the blood of any living creature. We drew our shirt hoods forward and put on our mitts.

When I looked back, I could tell that Nishcock's carriers were soaking wet and growing surly. They waved faded rags of trade cloth before their faces and argued among themselves. Men tried to pile their loads onto their already overburdened women or their staggering pack dogs.

Flocks of gulls winged over our heads, flying inland from the salt-marsh ponds. Suddenly, the carriers began firing their muskets in the air at them. Not one bird fell, and yet they reloaded and fired again. Williyumm had to order them to stop.

Nishcock laughed at him and many of the others rudely shouted, "*Wemustakushu nemaweder!* White man, I will not!"

I became very angry with Nishcock. He was the captain of the carriers and supposed to be a help to Williyumm, but now he gave only trouble.

The three strongest men who walked behind Nishcock, carrying Williyumm's iron-bound trunks upon their shoulders, pretended to stumble in the willow roots. Williyumm watched in horror as they slammed the heavy trunks down on the rocks. They split wide open. Williyumm's which-way-to-walk box, the sun-catcher, his star-gazer, and his bring-near glass all flew out of the trunks and I could see them break like icicles as they rolled away in pieces.

Williyumm's face turned red, and he went running back to the place where his trunks lay broken. He knelt down and looked at

183

all his precious treasures scattered on the stones, staring at each one sadly. Nishcock and the big brutes who had thrown the trunks and lots of the other carriers started sneering and laughing at Williyumm as he tried to gather up the shiny broken bits. I, myself, was afraid that Williyumm was going to show them too much weakness.

I cast off my load and ran back to help him. With every step I took, I was getting madder and madder. "Quick!" I said to Williyumm using Ballahooly. "You jump up! Don't let them see you sitting sad upon the ground while they are standing tall above you."

As Nishcock and the others turned their backs on Williyumm, he got up, but I could see that he was feeling sick at losing all his treasures. The needle-pointer which told the way and the star-gazer were both lying smashed to pieces on the rocks. Then Williyumm shouted angrily at Nishcock, demanding that he and the strong men turn and stand before him.

Nishcock came walking back loose-jointed, trying to make a fool of Williyumm, crudely joking about the two of us with every man or woman who could hear him. The strong man who had broken the box was laughing and boasting as he followed Nishcock.

"Nishcock, you take the blanket, powder, shot, oatmeal, and new knife away from that man," Williyumm demanded.

When he failed to do it, I screamed at Nishcock, "You tell those clumsy brutes behind you to go back to the fort. Mistaar Staarit doesn't need them anymore." I was so mad I had to wipe the spittle off of my chin.

"I didn't hear red hair tell you to say that," Nishcock shouted angrily at me.

"You tell those brutes to go now," I screamed at Nishcock, "or this Miss-taar Staaarit will tell the guvnaar NEVER EVER to trade with you again. Do you hear me? NEVER!"

Those words alarmed Nishcock greatly, for such Company trading bans on chiefs were well known and could easily ruin a man. Nishcock cursed the three strong men who angrily kicked the broken boxes. Then snatching up their blanket rolls, small packs, and muskets, they started walking fast toward the east. Four other carriers and two of their woman swore mightily at us as they followed them away.

"Good riddance, dog people!" I shrieked, and did a little dance when I saw twelve more carriers turn their backs on us and hurry after the others. I didn't care what they shouted back at me or Williyumm, I was so glad to see the last of them go.

"I didn't tell you to say all those things to them," said Williyumm. "Here we are only nine days walking from the fort and already more than twenty men and some of their women and dogs have gone back, mad at us. When he sees them returning, the governor will know he sent the wrong man out exploring."

Williyumm felt so awful that he would not eat at all that night. Instead, he just sat staring at the few broken twisted pieces he had saved. Finally, he dropped them on the ground and said, "It's no use to go farther. We might as well turn around and start back to the fort tomorrow."

"Why?"

"All the things I need to know the way are broken. How can I mark the places where we camp? Or know how far we walk each day?"

He sighed and got up sadly, then went and lay down in our tent, staring up at the cold smoke hole. I left for a wee while until I saw the first star he called Jipider flashing in the western sky.

I went in and put my arms around Williyumm and made him rise up off our bed. Then I pushed him outside our tent. I tipped his chin so his eyes looked up at the stars that were coming out above our heads. "Williyumm," I said, "you don't need all the heavy how-to-get-there things that were in those boxes. See up there?" I pointed to the Wolf Star, growing brighter in the north. "My father showed me and my brothers how to use that star and how to travel. We don't need all those broken things of yours to find our way. I'll show you."

We went inside together and lay down. The clothing we took off filled the tent with a wet dank smell. Williyumm scarcely raised his hand to brush away the mosquitoes that always bothered him so much. He made a few marks on the skins, then looked at me. "I've failed," he said, and started talking again about our going back to the fort.

"Oh, no," I told him. "You have brought us far, and we move farther every day. All we have to do is keep on going."

Jako and I laughed and sang a bit to try and cheer him up.

"I'm glad the worst of those troublemakers have gone," I whispered in Williyumm's ear. "We didn't need them anyway. They cheated the Company, finished all their oatmeal porridge, and now they're running home again. I hope they all go, and that on the day we cross the last river before my mother's country you and I and Jako and our two dogs will be walking strongly, all alone."

But my cheerful words were not good enough for Williyumm. He still felt very badly. When I crawled in between the blankets and wiggled close to him, I could tell that he was worrying hard.

"Whatever is going to happen is going to happen," I said.

"How am I going to know how far we've come each day?" he asked again.

"That is not difficult. Before we enter my mother's country, we will have to cross thirteen large rivers, and we will have seen a lake so big you cannot see across, even when the sky is clear."

"How do you know that?"

"I know because other Dene travelers told my grandfather who told my father who told me," I said. "Later, when the sky grows truly dark, we can look up there together and watch the other stars go swinging slowly around the wolf's eye. If we obey that one star, we will find our way into my mother's country. Later, if we decide to leave, that same star will stare steady at our backs and help us find the house of spears again."

Poor Williyumm, he was just starting to learn the hardships of the walk-across while traveling with such treacherous people. I knew that both Jako and I would have to be very watchful for him, and help him in every way, for in this lonely, hungry country, things can easily go from bad to worse to very worst.

186

I was only staying awake waiting for Williyumm to get wild ideas or fall asleep, when I heard the sound of a pebble scraping. Using Owinipeg's thin dagger, I made a tiny slit in the tent. When I peeked out, I saw four big carriers. They were making signs to each other and worrying about the pebble sound.

I carefully put my hand over Williyumm's mouth, then whispered, "You cock the musket and give me the scatter gun!"

WILLIAM

13

Thana silently signaled me to put my eye to the slit she had cut.

I saw the four Cree waiting, listening, as they prepared to come against us.

Thana cocked the hammer of our heavy blunderbuss, and I did the same with my long musket. Then with my pistol I flung our tent flap open.

Seeing our array of weapons pointed at them, the four carriers froze in alarm. They dropped their bayonets onto the gravel and retreated slowly, their hands spread out before them to show they were unarmed.

"We will surely kill you," Thana yelled at them, "if you ever dare come sneaking around our tent again."

Jako eased out of his small tent carrying his slingshot and my sword, which he had grabbed from underneath our tent. The four Cree turned very slowly, then walked away fast. We three stayed awake and watchful for the remainder of the night.

Next morning, Nishcock came to Williyumm and told him that he had heard of the trouble . . . saying he had cursed those four crazy men and forced them to leave. He pointed to four men, two women, and a pack dog walking east across the uplands, already far away.

Before we started west again, Thana insisted that Jako set up a target and I teach them both exactly how to load, prime, and fire the deadly blunderbuss, the long musket, and my twin-barreled pistol. She made a great show of this, talking loudly all the while in Cree. She wanted them to know that we were carefully preparing ourselves against any future attack. She warned both of us to be forever on our guard.

We moved on that day and the next uneasily, our minds burdened with hatred and mistrust.

On the third evening after this incident when we stopped, Thana raised the tent with Jako, then went out to set her snares. Jako and I relaxed beside the fire, using two sticks to lift the hot stones from the coals and place them in the cooking basket to make the water boil.

We both heard a sudden sound and, turning around, I saw five big carriers squatting in front of our tent, pawing through our packs and bags, taking anything they fancied.

When I shouted, they continued, paying no attention to me. I rushed back to the tent, remembering as I went that all our weapons were inside. I looked around in desperation and saw Thana running hard toward us. She flung down her snares and snatched up the blunderbuss that she had hidden.

When she reached the tent and they heard her cock the heavy hammer, the Cree leapt up and started backing away. She shoved her foot inside the tent and snagged my long musket. Jako darted in and snatched up my pistol and my sword.

"Now, you be the one to tell those sneaking thieves to keep away from our tent or we'll kill them," Thana called to me in Ballahooly.

Jako placed my sword between his legs, then whirled his sling until it began to make that angry chattering sound. We all kept on shouting and cursing the five of them.

Suddenly, Jako released the stone, which struck one of the thieves on the bridge of the nose, causing it to spurt blood.

"Get away from here," Thana yelled, raising the blunderbuss and taking aim, "or I am going to bloody all of you."

The five carriers stood still as statues, watching Thana's ugly weapon, afraid to move. Oh, I was proud of Thana and Jako.

I bellowed at them, "*Witteko*! Devils! *Kemutau*! Stealers, thieves – go back to where you came from!"

Those pillagers laid our possessions carefully on the ground and held their open hands out.

"Not stealing. Only looking," said the tall gaunt man as they backed cautiously out of range, then turned and hurried off toward their tents.

Many eyes were watching, but there was only silence among the Cree.

Very early next morning, we heard shouting among Nishcock and the carriers as more than a dozen carriers departed with their women, heading toward York Factory.

Thana laughed. "Poor Bearman, what's he to think when so many of those useless northerners come staggering back to him? I feel very glad to see the last of them." She opened the small slit between our tents and peeked in at Jako, who was sleeping soundly. "Did you notice how quick he was to use his sling, to help us fight? We must care for him," she whispered. "Let's get ready. I'll take down the tent while you ask Nishcock about the trouble."

Later, I told Thana that Nishcock admitted the carriers were mad at him, at all of us.

We marched northwest, guided only by the Wolf Star. I noted the five main rivers that we crossed. Nishcock, like the others, remained sulky and scarcely spoke to me or Thana. Still, sixty men and a dozen of their women followed us.

It was overcast and raining again. I tried to keep a kind of running map and panorama in my daily journal. During rests, I tried to draw and describe the shape and nature of lakes and rivers that we passed and kept a crude estimate of the distance that we traveled. I was getting used to walking. I had lost weight, and my leg muscles were hard. It was boring doing the same thing every day, until, without warning, everthing was changed for us.

I heard Nishcock call out to the carriers, then point to a man who sat on the brow of a distant hill. I stopped, speechless with surprise, for we had been on the march for more than a month without seeing a single human soul who was not one of us.

I lay prone on the lip of a shallow ravine and was examining this solitary figure through the cracked lens of my telescope when I heard Thana gasp.

"Look over there," she said. "That man is not alone. there are many more of them."

I moved my spyglass along the unfamiliar line of humans coming toward us over the muskeg. As was our way, they moved in a long single file, following their head man. I counted almost forty of them, including their women, children, and old folk, with their dogs loping beside them. When they saw us, they, too, stopped dead still and gaped in disbelief. Only fog and foul weather had kept both parties from seeing or smelling the other's smoke before this.

After a while, their head man made a motion and they continued cautiously toward us. They, like ourselves, looked soaking wet and weary.

Seeing them so close did not give Thana any peace of mind. Instead, it seemed to increase her nervousness, as it did Nishcock's and our remaining carriers'. It was not long until their fear reached out and touched me. Once more, the strangers stopped, waiting like ghosts in the drifting fog.

"Who are they?" I whispered.

Thana narrowed her eyes, peering across the russet-colored autumn glen. "This fog makes it hard to tell," she said. "Just wait. Do nothing. Let them come to us."

I did that, wishing they would turn away and go. I could hear a low murmuring from our Cree when the strangers started forward again and entered the ravine, disappearing briefly behind some rocks. We waited in watchful silence until half a dozen of their men reappeared, climbing toward us, then paused in plain sight just beyond musket range. Their head man was carrying an old-fashioned musket, its lock wrapped in fish skin. The other five each carried bows or a handful of hunting spears.

Although they were not far off, the fog-spreading wind now distorted every sound. When Nishcock called to them, they seemed not to understand his words. I wondered if they could even understand his language, for they wore strange costumes not at all like Northern Cree.

I watched the head man of this tribe of wanderers hand his musket to another and stride boldly halfway to the point where we were standing. There, to my astonishment, he lay down and rolled partly over, with hands and feet up slightly in the air, like a male toboggan dog that wishes to avoid a fight.

"That's a good sign," Thana whispered.

After our Cree had observed the stranger carefully, Nishcock handed his musket and his bayonet to another and walked out unarmed. When he was a dozen paces from the prostrate man, he, too, lay full-length down and rolled over. First one and then the other began calling out their greetings.

Thana grasped my sleeve and looked at me in horror. "I tell you these wanderers are Wood Cats. See their lynx-skin head-dresses with the tufted ears? Look at their leggings. They are Wood Cats. I would know them anywhere."

"Can they understand Nishcock?"

"A little. They speak a different kind of Southern Cree."

"Why is Nishcock being so careful?" I asked.

"Because it is the custom," she said. "These northerners with us have never met these Wood Cats. They are wise to be so cautious."

"What are these people doing this far north?"

"I don't know," Thana answered. "Hunting and raiding, if they get the chance. Look how strangely they are split. Some here and others there. Look at that man, far off on the hill. Nishcock is wise to be so careful of these tricksters."

We watched both prone men wriggle forward slowly on elbows and bellies, then rise to kneeling positions and move together, cautious as a pair of foxes, their knuckles on the ground like animals' forepaws. Finally, they straightened and stood facing each other, sleeves drawn back with open palms extended, each proving that he bore no weapons.

It was not long until Nishcock waved to us, and we went toward him. The other head man summoned his people. Of course, their pack dogs started fighting viciously with ours. But so intent were we humans in studying one another that only a few of their youngers bothered to kick the dogs apart. Their head man was short and broad-shouldered, with quick eyes set in a solemn, watchful face.

"Listen to their awful whiny voices," said Thana, imitating the nasal Wood Cats' accent. "Our carriers will understand only half the words those southern Wood Cats speak at first, and they won't know these people's names or clans. Perhaps the animals and the fish both failed them in the south. These wanderers may be hungry. No wonder," she continued. "These wretches drive out the animals by setting fire to the forest. It is not surprising that the caribou would run north to our Dene hunters, who respect them, and let these Wood Cats starve."

The Wood Cats' faces looked like ours. They, too, were dark from a summer's wandering. Their cheekbones were wide, their teeth looked strong and white. But their skin clothing was shabby and worn, cut in a different style. They possessed few trade goods, and almost half of their carriers were young women who put up their tents not far from the ones our carriers were erecting. With the rain persisting, I was glad enough to call a halt.

Our few remaining carrier women quickly went about their other chores, as did the Wood Cat women, gathering water and fuel for fires. By early evening, we had caribou parts boiling in our sunken birch-rind baskets and haunches slowly turning on twisted thongs suspended above the fires. We shared everything with them, not caring about tomorrow, only thinking of the pleasures that this night might bring.

During the feasting, we squatted on our haunches, our buttocks just clear of the soggy muskeg moss, or sat on the smoke-washed stones where our fires had dried them. I could feel a sense of excitement spreading between our two camps.

"I don't understand that," I said to Thana, pointing to the hill where the lonely man still watched us. "Why do you think that man has put up his tent so far away?"

"He must have been cast out by these Wood Cats for doing something bad," said Thana. "I knew a man as tall as that. But I hope he's far away or dead now." She shaded her eyes against the smoke and frowned. "I don't believe that could be the same man."

The rain had stopped at last, and both our carriers and the Wood Cats were warming flat tambourine-like drums over the fires, waiting for the heat to tighten the dampened caribou skins. While they warmed, I could hear the drummers tapping restlessly against the wooden rims. Finally, when all were gathered, the drummers began their beating, and the dancing started. Both our dancers and theirs had already painted their faces, and most had unpacked and put on their best dance finery.

First, the Wood Cats circled between their fires and ours, to the steady rhythm of their drum. Our carriers, like the Wood Cats, joined the dancing. Although the accent and the words were arranged quite differently, it was a song they all knew well.

The Wood Cats started singing, and our Cree supplied the answering chorus, "Ay yah, yah, yah, aah, aah, yah."

Hearing that, Captain Nishcock leapt into the air and started whirling, stamping like a rutting caribou. In a moment, Wood Cat hunters came toward him nodding, dancing among our people, trying to join them spiritually, like long lost relatives surprised to have found each other. A thick fog was settling as daylight slowly faded into darkness. Our women and theirs joined in, dragging in more damp wood which they flung onto fires that flared with pitch-filled logs. Sparks showered upwards into the blackness. Then dancing began in earnest, and the steady beat, like that of a military snare drum, took hold of me, pulsing in my blood. The rhythm already seemed to have control of Thana and of Jako. It captured everyone who heard it. The excited drumming and the repetitious singing cast a spell. As I sat watching them, all barriers dissolved, and Wood Cats and Cree, all of us, melted together. Thana told me that she hated the Wood Cats, yet she could not help swaying to their songs and rhythms. She seemed entranced, as though she were no longer a part of me, but had returned to the mist-hung wilderness that surrounded us.

Only when sheer exhaustion overcame the drummers and dancers, and the singers' throats were raw, did the intoxicating sound and rhythm cease. The fires had faded and the first long streaks of dawn appeared in the eastern sky. We, like all the others, stumbled inside our tent and fell into bed.

"Meeting them was a wonderful surprise," I said to Thana.

"I'm still thinking of that lone man," she answered. "Could he be such a bad and dangerous Wood Cat that they would not allow him to come and join the feast?"

I awoke in mid-morning to the harsh sounds of a violent argument between two Wood Cats. I could understand only some words. Thana already stood outside our tent. Through the flap, I could see the Wood Cat head man threatening someone who stood off by himself, a spear's throw from our tent.

This towering stranger, who wore a lynx mask on his head and an eagle-claw necklace at his throat, pointed at Thana and yelled, "That's her. She's mine! My *uwacan*, my slave! I took her in a raid up north. She has the name of Thanadelthur. I own her, she's mine!" He emphasized the meaning of his words with savage gestures.

I stepped out and stared at Thana in amazement. She hung her head in shame, then whispered, "Yes, that is him. Kunn. The one who stole me."

Nishcock stepped forward and called out to the head man of the Wood Cats. "Who is that man?"

"He's not one of us," their head man snorted. "He's gone out of his senses. In summer, he trails along not with us but never far away. He is bad. Crazy. Don't go near him."

"Who thinks they own that woman?" Kunn growled. "You?" He shot a murderous glance toward me.

"She is a foreigner," Nishcock answered, "not one of us. She is . . ."

"She is my *uwacan*!" Kunn yelled back, interrupting Nishcock's words. "What is that strange thing standing close beside her?"

"She calls him a Ballahooly," Nishcock laughed.

"A Ballahooly?" Kunn yelled crazily. "Oh, yes, I saw one of them once south of here. A trader, with long gray hair covering his face."

"Well, this one's young with red fox hair," Nishcock shouted. "This one is something very strange."

Kunn strode closer, menacing me. I was surprised to see the usually fearless Thana take a quick backstep and stand behind me. The big Wood Cat stepped sideways so that he could better see her.

"You get over here by me," he grunted at her, "or I'll take the dog whip to you. Remember how I made you bitches scream?"

"You touch her and I'll cut you into pieces," I warned him, for a flame of Highland anger was rising up in me. I watched his cold dark eyes and brutal face. I wanted more than anything to run a sword through this man.

"What are you going to do, Miss . . . staar Starrit?" Nishcock called sneeringly to me in Cree. "You want us to make war for you against these good dancers, these cousins of ours? We won't do that. You give him back his Copper slave, or you will have to fight him for her."

"I want no war between all of us," Kunn called out so all could hear. "But I will fight this Ballahooly and take my *uwacan* from him. You watch me." He boasted grandly, "I'm going to break his back."

"*Ayaahaa! Ahahaah!*" shouted the Wood Cats, for they, too, would enjoy this fight, and they probably didn't care who won.

"*Neaphaaha! Neapahaa!*" laughed our carriers. For was this not the solution to all their woes? If I were killed or maimed and left to die, and Thana humbled and beaten before their eyes, they would trade Jako to the Wood Cats, then return to the fort and truthfully tell the governor how their long and fruitless march to find the Coppers had ended in my cruel death and Thana's disappearance.

"Build up the fires," Nishcock shouted. "Get ready. No weapons. This is going to be a real hand fight. The man who wins can keep the Copper bitch."

"Do you call her your woman?" Kunn shouted, pointing straight at Thana.

The big vein was pulsing in my neck when I answered, "Aye, you're bloody right I do!"

196

"Get ready," the big Wood Cat sneered at me. "I am going to fight you for her." Then picking up a stout green tent pole, he fractured it slowly across his knee. "See that," he shouted, "that's the way I am going to break your spine. Don't worry," he laughed, "I won't leave you lying here all broken for the ravens to pick at you alive." He pointed to Thana. "I'll have my *uwacan* slowly cut your throat before she starts slaving for me again." He laughed and I could hear our carriers chuckling with him.

I could feel the sands in my hourglass begin to drain away. Thana and young Jako stared at me as though I were already dead.

The Wood Cats started bellowing in chorus, "Yaah! Fight! Yaah, fight, yaah, yaah, yaaah!" And our carriers answered, "Yaah, fight, yaah, fight. Now, now, now!"

That great brute in front of me stripped off his pointed shirt. His chest and arms were huge.

"Oh, Williyumm," Thana said in terror. "You must be very careful with that monster. He is strong. If Kunn kills you in the fight, I will surely kill him, or myself."

I could see that she had her hand on Owinipeg's French dagger.

"Don't say that," Jako cried, then turned to me. "Fight him. Fight him hard!"

For my part, I stood limp with shock. How could I win without a weapon? Wrestling against a giant like that! I could hear many cheering the big Wood Cat on. No felon standing before the gallow tree ever felt more miserable than I. All this while, Kunn continued marching slowly back and forth, shouting and showing off his formidable body, the necklace of eagle claws still around his neck.

"He stole that necklace from my father, after he had killed him," Thana said, her voice choking.

"What am I going to do?" I asked.

"I wish you had brought your hard-nailed company boots," she muttered. "You might have broken his feet. That could have given you a chance against him.

"This game of fighting for a woman," Thana said, "is not just Wood Cat custom. My Copper people do it, too. We know how it goes."

197

"Listen carefully," she whispered as she saw the Cree women rolling up clumps of the driest tundra they could find, with which to make the fires burn brightly. "It is a disgrace for either wrestler to snatch up weapons, but everything else is fair. Knee him in the tender stones, or gouge his eyes. Try not to let him catch you by the neck, or trip you. Now, come inside."

With her sharp dagger blade, she hacked away my queue. "Oh, Williyumm, even if you are lost in this fight, I'll carry you inside my body," she whispered as she knelt staring at me, her eyes filling with tears. "Why did that crazy brute have to come back and spoil all this for us?"

"Fight! Fight! Fight!" I heard the Wood Cats yelling.

"Yah, fight. Yaha, fight," our carriers answered them.

The pounding of the drums had begun and grew faster, louder, and made my blood race.

"Misstaar Staarit," I heard Nishcock calling. "Don't be afraid. This big man here, he's waiting to hug you, Misstaar Staarit. If he does not kill you, maybe he'll hitch you into his dog team."

I could hear the hunters laughing and the women screaming with excitement.

"You hit at his eyes," said Thana. "Gouge them, try to blind him. Move fast! Duck! Jump! Do anything! But don't let him get ahold of you."

Thana helped me pull off my leather shirt. "Keep on your leggings," she warned me. "I don't want him grabbing you down there."

Choking gray smoke was blowing across the fighting ground as the men from both camps began to form a circle. Kunn raised his arms high above his head; his body, like his shaved head, was aglaze with goose grease so I could not grip him. His necklace of big eagle claws glittered against his brown neck.

"Come, fox-hair," he shouted. "Come to me!"

Kunn came lurching into the circle of watchers, his legs held stiff as those of a dog about to fight. I had no choice but to step toward him.

He lunged low at me, then straightened up and kicked out hard with his right foot. I dodged aside and noticed that he nearly lost his balance. Bending, he held his arms out wide and came more watchfully at me. This time when he lunged, his elbow struck me as I narrowly escaped his grasp. When I turned, I could barely see him crouching in the billowing smoke.

He came hurtling at me suddenly and caught me. I could feel his powerful fingers meet and clasp together in the center of my lower back. I drove my right knee upwards with all my strength. He grunted and let go, doubling over. If I had been an experienced knuckle fighter, I would have taken this advantage. But I was not quick enough. Without warning, his right fist struck out and hit me a hammer blow across the chest. I reeled away into the smoke, stunned, gasping for breath. When he came after me, I kicked out low, catching his right shin, felling him.

The Crees and Wood Cats circled around us sent up a howling sound, and all the work dogs joined them. My heart gave a leap as I realized for the first time that they were cheering not for him, but ME!

When Kunn came up of the ground, his teeth were bared, his face contorted. I could see he now held two blackened fire stones in his hands. The drums were beating faster now, and louder, louder!

Kunn swung at me, hoping to land a blow on either side of my head. I ducked, but in my mortal fear reached out and caught him by both wrists. He laughed at me and stretched his immense arms out, easily forcing me to stretch mine to their limit. The strain was unbearable, but I clung on in terror, eyeing the stones he held, feeling his hot breath, and staring at the look of triumph on his face. I was transfixed by the thick veins bulging from his throat above the necklace.

Remembering Mad Duncan Campbell, I drew back my head, then drove the top of it as hard as I could against his neck. He screamed as the eight sharp eagle's claws pierced him deeply. The hot blood spouted from his torn throat over both of us. Savagely, I lunged my head against him again and again, driving the terrible talons tearing into his throat. I felt him stagger sideways. Then, with the last vestige of my strength, I fell on top of him and held on. At last, his arms relaxed. I looked at him and saw his eyes roll upward in his head. A great scream went up from the throng.

Now Thana was on top of both of us, her dagger in her hand. I thought she was going to drive it into Kunn, but instead she cut her father's blood-soaked necklace from his neck before she and Jako helped me to my feet.

As I stood trembling above Kunn's body, the drumming stopped, the shrieking ceased, and there was silence all around me.

Nishcock came forward and kicked the two heavy fire stones out of Kunn's big hands and stared down at him. "He's dead," he said. "I didn't think that you could do that, Misstaar Staaritt."

Thana held out the gory eagle necklace for Nishcock and me to see. It was made with large hammered yellow beads between each of the eight claws. "Kunn stole this from my father when he murdered him," she wailed. "Now it is back in our family again."

eagle claws

My knees were trembling as I walked down and scrubbed and cleansed myself in the ice-cold stream.

"Come to the tent," I called to Thana. "It's over now. It's over."

Thana ran to the bag that Kunn had flung to the ground before the fight. She began to rummage through it, then held up her hand in triumph. "This is it," she cried. "This is my mother's flensing knife, the one he stole from me."

Many Wood Cat men and women nodded and smiled at us as we moved toward our tent. Och! What a wonderful feeling! For the second time in my life, I had survived a fight against all odds.

When we sat down inside our tent, my hands and knees were shaking worse than ever.

"Can Jako sleep in here with us tonight?" asked Thana.

"Aye." I nodded at him and said, "Fetch your sleeping robe here, laddie."

Early next morning, Jako appeared with three brown hares, and we ate one apiece. It was going to be a bonny day for us.

"May I see your father's necklace?" I asked Thana, for I had seen her carefully wash it in the stream.

Beside our bed, she found it, unwrapped it, and passed it to me.

All eight claws were big ones from a white-headed eagle. I held the beautiful, deadly necklace near the light of our small fire, examining the yellow gleam of the pea-sized beads that held each claw apart. I took my wee knife from my sporan and made a slight scratch on the largest bead. The cut produced a brilliant yellow line. I weighed the necklace in my hand again and said in English, "I think these beads are solid gold!"

"We call them *u saw-wa-suthean*, soft yellow stones."

"That sounds right," I told her. "This is what the governor is looking for. Do you know where we might find some more?"

"Let's keep on running west," she pointed, "toward my mother's country. For there is a stream with many yellow pebbles like those lying in it. You can see them shining in the ripples." She handed me her mother's yellow flenser. It, too, had been hammered out of gold.

"We could let Nishcock take bags of yellow pebbles back to Bearman," said Thana, watching me carefully. "Then we three would be free to live in my mother's country. We could camp and travel with some of my relatives when we find them. There's no end to the caribou and birds and fishes where she lived. And you should see the berries, big as small birds' eggs some of them. Up there we could lie together every night and talk and dance and laugh and make lots of children, while we enjoyed every changing season."

I fell back exhausted in our bed, feeling more a man than I had ever felt in all my life. With Thana on my right side and Jako on my left, we three went sound asleep again, though it was almost noonday. There was not a single sound from our two camps, except the cheeping of some snowbirds. I woke in the night and heard the soft pattering of snow against our tent wall and wondered if we could survive a journey such as this.

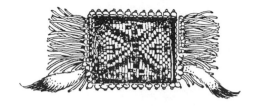

THANA

14

Today we parted from the Wood Cats, and I told a very bad lie to Williyumm when I said, "I am not afraid of those Cree men who skulk around this tent at night."

The truth was that I was very, very scared of them. I knew the sound of tent poles breaking as raiders with bayonets came crashing down to kill my family. Nishcock hated me, as did the other Cree. But I could not go on letting fear become my master. I told Williyumm, "Just double-load your musket and your scatter gun. Keep your sword and pistol ready, and always have them all at hand about our bed."

We slept close together. Almost always one of us was awake, ears cocked, listening for a strange sound. Jako had the senses and the hearing of a fox. One morning, in the darkness, he woke us so that we could watch another score of carriers leaving us, taking with them their women and four dogs. Now, besides me, we had only two other women with us: the wife of Nishcock and the wife of Nishcock's cousin.

"All together we are only twenty-seven," I said.

"Damn!" said Williyumm. "Double damn!"

"They're going, just the way I wanted them to go," I told him, not holding back a giggle. "I hope only we three, with our two dogs and toboggan, will reach my mother's country."

Imperceptibly, as we trudged onward, summer had drifted into fall, and occasionally snow fell. Then, as days on the trail became weeks, winter crept upon us and was here. Whirling blizzards sometimes hid the sun and stars. But one evening, when we could see the faint image of the bow-bent moon as it hunted through the clouds, the Wolf Star told us that we were still marching west, and we snowshoed along the flatness of a frozen river, struggling against a mean sharp wind.

"I hate this kind of noisy storm," I told Jako that night as we tried to pitch our flapping, billowing tent. By morning, the wind was down and the sky had blown clear blue. I was first out, snow-shoeing to the top of a low hill, where I could look over the whole snow country. The sight sent me bounding back toward our tent.

"Williyumm, get up," I gasped, pulling off all his covers. "I saw fresh tracks, seven caribou, they can't be far away."

Williyumm leapt up, pulled on his double-thick hair shirt and leggings, and snatching up his powder horn and long-barreled musket, he lashed on his snowshoes and hurried after me with Jako close behind. I led them up the hill, then crouching and motioning them down, pointed across a narrow ravine.

Less than a hundred paces from us stood two caribou. They had their heads down and were digging with sharp forehooves, revealing the gray-green mosses. A third animal moved into sight and then another, until we could count seven.

"It makes my mouth water just to look at them," Williyumm whispered.

Bending, with my mittens touching the snow to look like fore-legs, I showed Williyumm how to move toward them, like caribou edging east, until the wind was behind them, blowing toward us. He and Jako slowly followed me, until the two nearest animals were in easy range, a large bull and one not fully grown. The bull caribou raised his head and eyed us with suspicion. I lowered my head, pretending to graze, and saw that he was no longer fearful.

Cautiously, I urged Williyumm toward a good-sized rock and signaled him to kneel down slowly. The bull caribou must have heard him cock his musket and watched him sneak the long barrel out across the rock.

"Wait!" I whispered to him. "Wait!"

Williyumm looked confused and frowned at me, for the big bull was standing head up, watching the black eye of the musket that was pointed straight at him.

Wait!'' I whispered, for I could see other caribou moving up behind the bull.

When the near-grown caribou paused to feed, he was almost behind the larger bull.

"Shoot through both of them," I whispered.

Williyumm snorted in disbelief, but he waited. Then aiming carefully at the nearest animal, he fired. There was a flash in the pan. The musket bucked back in a cloud of sulfurous smoke. I saw the big bull caribou hunch its shoulders and stagger sideways.

"You hit, you hit!" I whispered.

The two-year-old caribou behind bounded away in fright when it heard the musket's thunder and saw the first caribou go down.

"Good!" I called.

"Aye, I got one!" Williyumm said excitedly, jumping up and running toward it.

"You go look," I called to Jako. "The other should be lying just behind the hill."

"How could you know that?" laughed Williyumm, but he hurried after Jako and whistled with surprise when he saw the two-year-old lying dead, with its nose buried in the snow. "Just imagine," Williyumm gasped, "killing two stags with a single ball. They would scarce believe that story if I told it in the western Highlands.

Williyumm was so excited that instead of reloading his musket, he stood it upright in the snow and started rummaging through his shoulder bag until he found his marking stick and thin white skins.

"Never mind making those marks now," I told him. "You reload. Five more caribou should be somewhere just beyond our sight."

I signaled Jako to go with Williyumm and to hurry. I stayed behind and skinned, gutted, and quartered this pair of fallen caribou, singing thankful songs to them. In a little while I heard a musket boom once, then a second boom. Jako ran back and signaled to me that Williyumm had taken a third caribou. The other four had run away.

While I waited for the two of them to tow back a toboggan, I skinned and cut up the third caribou and sang another Dene song of thanks. After rolling up the hides of all three animals and lashing them with the stiffening meat on the toboggan, I arranged harnesses for the three of us. In this way, Williyumm, Jako, and I skidded our treasure of food back into camp.

Nishcock was delighted when he saw the meat, and tried to perform some feats of magic to appease the nearby spirits of those three caribou as we readied ourselves to eat their flesh. Nishcock's wife and the remaining young Cree woman gladly helped me to prepare a feast.

Long strips of caribou loin crackled and dripped over the open fire as we stood together, letting the warm smoke and mouth-watering smell of cooking meat wash over us. We and the carriers fell upon the flesh of those three good providers, the caribou, and wolfed down as much as we could eat. Then we boiled and split the bones with little antler chisels and drew out the rich sweet marrow. Williyumm swore that he had never tasted anything half so fine in all his life.

That night when we crawled into our bed, Williyumm said, "It was wrong of us to eat up so much meat. We should have saved some for the coming days."

"Why would you want to save meat?" I asked him. "If we live right, more caribou, more fish, more birds, and snowshoe hare will come to us. Don't worry, Williyumm, the Big Woman will take care of us."

He did not seem to feel much better after hearing that. All men are eager to believe that they are clever hunters. Yet except for nine fish and six lean hare taken by Jako and the younger Cree woman, and about sixty ptarmigan snared by me, not a bite of food was taken by our men for eighteen days.

One night during the rising of the coldest winter moon, Williyumm lay wrapped in our covers looking at his marks carefully. He told me we had been walking from the fort for one hundred

---

sixty-one days. *Metar-tutme-tenawne-a'nun-'u-metenaw-piuc-coshop* was the quick way he expressed that number in Cree, so Jako could easily understand it. We didn't want him to grow up knowing only how to count on his fingers.

Jako and I continued our daily head count of the carriers. This morning we discovered that the last two women were gone. Of one hundred twenty who had left the house of spears with us more than five moons ago, only ten carriers and seven pack dogs remained, two of which were ours. Williyumm, myself, and our son, Jako – well, he wasn't really our son, but we thought of him as ours – brought that number to thirteen.

It began to snow again, softly at first, but that soon turned into a blinding blizzard that went howling and screaming across the whole world. Williyumm and I were not quick risers because we liked to lie together in our warm bed. We both enjoyed very much the different ways that we were made. Finally, when we had to rise, we were not idle. With winter lying heavy all around us, Williyumm would sit with a second small tent over his head that he made with our red blanket. Only his right hand and the steam from his breath could be seen as he made little gray pictures on his pack of skins.

While he was doing that, I began making the three of us each a fine new pair of snowshoes. Jako had helped do the whittling of the frames, which he did very nicely, with a crooked knife, even though that is always a father's or a husband's work. We didn't make those strange snowshoes that the Wood Cats use for running in the forest. No. Jako and I made the larger, more graceful kind of *akibaw* snowshoes, good for crossing deep snow in the open tundra country. When the frames were done, I cut thin strong caribou thongs and wove them into the Dene star pattern, then dried them very carefully. To bring luck to the three of us, I pulled some strands of wool from my own red blanket and threaded these through the webs, in the shapes of fireweed flowers. It is well known by our people that shin muscles do not become so tired when you have those lucky reds to quicken your pace.

On the third night of the storm, we could still hear it sighing high above us, but by morning it went moaning off toward the sunrise. The world outside was deadly silent. Our double-clad skin tent sagged with the great weight of snow. We had to force the entrance open; it was as though the whole world had been born again, for it had become a magic glittering place, a world that sent us into ecstasy. The very look of this soft, white, shining country that bordered on my homeland gave me new courage, new excitement. It made me want to leap and dance as my brother and I had done as children. The uplands behind us lay buried by the storm. My heart sang, for a clean, white Dene world was waiting, not very far from me.

As we shoed forward, I urged Williyumm to study every track. "Who made those?" I would ask him.

"Caribou?"

"Good. How many?"

"Six?"

"More, maybe thirteen," I would tell him. "Have they eaten yet, and how long since they passed?"

"How would I know that?" Williyumm would ask.

"Study their small round droppings. Feel them. Are they still warm and soft, or frozen hard? Taste one, see if it is fresh."

Williyumm gave me an awful look when I said that.

Once we found a large hare's running track. Suddenly, it started zigzagging this way and that. Then after one last long jump, its imprints disappeared.

"That's impossible," said Williyumm, "unless that snow hopper sprouted wings."

"You and those Cree carriers are not the only hunters here," I told him. "A big owl must have flown low over that hare and caught her in its claws and lifted her away."

"How do you know that?" he snorted.

"Didn't you see the owl's wing marks where they lightly brushed the snow?"

That made him kind of mad, and he said, "Well, how do you know that hare was a female?"

"Oh, Williyumm," I said, shaking my head at him, "when are you going to learn to read the urine signs?"

"What about us? Should we not be heading south to find those caribou?" Williyumm asked me. "There we might at least survive until spring comes."

"We can't start turning, running west, then turning north and south," I answered. "The Dene people will be hunting in the upland country taking musk oxen as well as fish from the frozen lakes. It won't take me long to find them."

After five more days of walking without taking game or fish, our starving carriers were forced to kill and eat two of their dogs. They shared some of the meat and broth with us. Later, my snares caught eleven ptarmigan and three hares, but a fox took one of them and, of course, we had to share our catch with all the others. For three days, the weather and the snow were good and we went far, though on lean bellies without another bite to eat. I said to Williyumm, "Those Northern Cree who stayed are hardy travelers. Even when they are truly starving, they still have it in them to laugh and joke a bit."

We saw no tracks, and the Cree decided to kill another of their three remaining dogs. Again they shared the stringy meat and soup with us. Everyone awoke next morning craving more.

On the following night, we camped near a long narrow lake which appeared to be quite deep, and Nishcock came to borrow our iron chisel. Jako and I went with them, and we made four holes in the ice. We started fishing, each of us using new Company hooks. I don't know if it was because of my magic Dene songs, or theirs, or the sharp Company hooks, but we took nineteen shining lake trout, each one nearly as long as my arm.

Jako ran back to Williyumm to tell of our success, and the carriers made a long lodge by loosely lapping all of our tents together. Using Williyumm's hand axe, they chopped down a small, long-dead juniper tree and built two crackling fires. Together, we feasted on rich fish broth, thick with floating chunks of lake trout. Even while we were eating, they brought more and more fish for the cooking baskets. Nothing ever tasted so good as those dear trout.

Later, when we all lay together with the carriers like brothers, basking in the warm glow of the fires, our full bellies made us feel as one. It seemed good, too, that we were growing friendly with these last and bravest of the Cree. I wondered as I nodded off to sleep how I could ever have felt such bitterness toward them all.

Fish, like hare, do not really fill you, and Williyumm longed for our Scootlanish porridge ration, which was long since gone. When Williyumm pulled off his shirt in the firelight, I could see each of his ribs caught in light and shadow. He and I and Jako would need more than hare or a few fish to get us through this endless walk-across.

"Are you not afraid that we might starve to death out here?" asked Williyumm.

"Not me. I'm not afraid," I said. "You and I and Jako are survivors."

After we went to sleep, I woke screaming, and Williyumm put his hand across my mouth, for in a horrid dream I had seen that bloodied devil, Kunn, attack me, then poor Dingee plunging through the ice again.

I went outside in the early morning, whispering magic words. But my snares held only one lean hare.

The icy winds swept down and painted white patches on our faces, and still we saw no tracks except our own. Now, we were truly starving. When I found a ground squirrel's den one day, I knelt and dug three of the sleepy winter creatures from their lodge, and we three shared them, sucking the thin juices as we shuffled forward. Ground squirrels are small creatures not much larger than a man's outstretched hand, but to a starving woman, I can tell you that even the memory of its flavor made my stomach clutch and beg for more.

On the following night, I cut most of the caribou-skin edging off my outer shirt and boiled it for us to share. It tasted smoky and was tough and chewy, but made juices one was very glad to swallow. Nothing in this world is worse than hunger. I examined the close-webbed sinews on our snowshoes and told Williyumm that the only reason we did not boil and eat them was that we could not do without them. If we stopped moving, we would surely die. That night, I had vivid dreams again, this time of large, silver-sided trout, sweet caribou haunches, and plump geese that dripped with yellow fat. Williyumm and Jako shared this great plenty with me, in my dreams.

Day followed day of our ongoing hunger. My snares snatched a pair of plump white ptarmigan, and Jako's sling killed one. I gave one of ours away and made a savory meal for Williyumm and Jako with the others. I took only the innards for myself, which has always been the woman's lot in our Dene families in times of hunger. When those two had finished eating, I rubbed my hands around inside the empty pot and smiled at them, then I licked their fingers and my own. On the following night, we killed and shared our weakest dog with all the rest of the Cree.

The next day on the trail was terrible, and that evening when everything was at its worst, all the remaining carriers came and stood behind Nishcock. In a commanding voice, he called out, "Mistaar Starrit, I have told our carriers here to get ready to go south. We will leave tomorrow, and so will you, unless you are crazy. The Wood Cats told us of a deer hedge. We believe that it is not more than five days' shoeing south of here."

Without giving Williyumm a chance to reply, they turned and made their way wearily to their tents, looking as thin as skeletons.

"We must never give in to Nishcock," I told Williyumm. "We must keep on running west. We are so close to my people now, we can't give up."

Williyumm did not answer me.

Using a snowshoe, I dug beneath the snow and gathered some gray-green caribou moss and made a bitter, gritty soup. Though it was sandy and tasted awful, it eased our hunger. My grandmother had told me that was what to find and eat before the final beastliness that starving humans would do.

To appease Nishcock and the others, we were forced to kill and share our last dog, as they had done earlier with their final two dogs. After that, we felt a little stronger.

Next day, the northwest wind and stinging cold struck us. The icy blasts seemed bent on turning us away from the Dene lands and driving us toward the deer hedge, where I did not wish to go.

Slowly, Williyumm and Jako began veering east, then south, with all the others. I stopped and screamed at them, first demanding, then begging them to turn west again. Even Williyumm would not do it. The Cree snarled and walked away from me. I stood and wept. Williyumm and Jako turned and called and waved to me as I watched their figures growing smaller.

Williyumm came hobbling back to me. "They say," he gasped, "there should be caribou south of here. We've got to try and find them. We can come back here later. We can try again!"

Williyumm took me by the hand and almost dragged me along in Nishcock's trail. I moved like an aged woman, led by an old man, staring at my shadow, which looked like a musk ox, with my pack being the great hump on its back.

At nightfall, it was Nishcock who led the others and now ordered everyone to halt and make camp. We three put up our tent in silence and crawled inside, too tired to make a fire.

"Don't be sad," Williyumm said when he heard me weeping.

I flared when I heard his words. "Have we come walking, starving days and nights, to give up now? When we are so close? You gave up so quickly. Now, look at Nishcock. He is our leader. Can you admit that to me?"

"I haven't given up," Williyumm told me angrily. "But if we don't find food, we'll die out here. It will matter little to the governor whether we almost reached your people, or missed them by a continent."

I was too weak to answer him, but I knew that he was right. I sat and licked my hands again to see if I could find some last taste of food between my fingers. I saw Williyumm licking round his reddish beard, but I guessed that he found nothing worthwhile either. Jako had fallen sound asleep.

I did not say another word that night, for I was mad at Mistaar Starrit. He rubbed my back a little as we listened to our stomachs growling and fell miserably into that other world of dreams.

We three followed Nishcock's carriers south in drooping silence until the sun was on its downward path, when suddenly we came across snowshoe tracks. These prints told us they were those of the twelve Cree who had last deserted us. They, too, were heading south. Just at sundown, we saw another set of snowshoe tracks that had come curving in from the northwest. They, too, were heading south. I, like Nishcock and his Cree, knelt down and carefully examined these new tracks.

"Different snowshoes," Nishcock said. "Not shaped like ours. Not Wood Cats either."

I blew the loose dry snow away and peered carefully at the woven webbed marks. Then I looked up at Williyumm and I let out a gasp of joy. "There they are!" I cried, pointing at the new tracks. "Those star patterns are like yours, like mine. These tracks were made by Dene hunters."

Nishcock and his Cree looked nervously behind themselves. They plucked the feathers, which keep out snow, from the ends of their musket barrels, and shook fresh powder into their priming pans.

We followed as the Cree moved forward, along the line of Dene tracks. I reached out to Williyumm and touched his back. "Keep going. Hurry. Stay close behind them," I urged him. "Those tracks are fresh. Keep looking ahead. You'll see my people. They'll have meat!"

Williyumm nodded, but I didn't like the look of him. His cheekbones stood out gauntly, and his lips were cracked and drawn too tightly across his teeth. Beneath his red fox hat, his whole face, like Jako's, had a grim, haunted look.

Traveling in single file, we crossed a long esker that the wind had blown clear of snow, and as we did we saw a sudden flurry of black wings as half a dozen ravens hopped away, then rose

raven

heavily and circled us in insolent silence. Williyumm turned and stared at me.

"They have found meat," I said.

Ahead of us, I saw Nishcock stop and whisper to the others. I urged Williyumm forward until we stood beside him. Before us lay nine fresh-killed human bodies grotesquely scattered on the snow beside their tent.

I caught my breath in horror as I recognized the clothing of the dead. Throwing off my bulky pack, I ran forward, knelt, and with a wail of anguish turned over one body and then another, peering carefully into each man's distorted frozen face.

"Who killed these Dene Hunters?" I demanded. "Who killed them? These men had no guns, but look at the round holes torn in their bodies. Yes, these men were killed by guns, by your runaway carriers with guns!"

"You don't know that," Nishcock shouted at me.

"Look there!" I screamed. "Whose web marks are those? They show us where your men came from behind those rocks over there, where they hid and fired their muskets at my people."
"Look at this poor man," I cried, rolling his frozen corpse over so it faced them. "He was my uncle. And that man lying there, he was my dearest cousin."

I began to wail, to scream, which is any woman's duty when her relatives have been killed. I, Thanadelthur, howled for these dead Dene men and tore my hair and beat my breasts until Williyumm and Jako caught my hands and stopped me.

"Beware!" I warned the Cree. "These dead men of mine have powerful spirits, frightening ghosts. They will be standing near you now . . . watching you . . . ready to follow you. Listen. Do you not hear their voices moaning on the wind? Oh, yes, you will hear them come inside your tents tonight."

All northerners hate any talk of ghosts. They held up their weapons to protect themselves from the horrors that I heaped on them.

"Let us leave that Dene woman here," said Nishcock's cousin, Kaswah. "Let us help her to fall down among these bloody relatives of hers."

I heard him cock his musket. Then Williyumm cocked the blunderbuss and stepped in front of me.

Nishcock yelled at Kaswah, "You shut your crazy mouth! I am the captain here."

Williyumm led me away from the ghastly place of murder. Jako and all the others followed. I saw some of the ravens swoop in again, landing heavily on the snow to resume their feast. I shuddered and looked away.

"Shall we not bury them?" asked Williyumm.

"No," I answered. "It is not our custom. Their bodies should lie where they have fallen and feed the animals who have long fed them. Their spirits have already gone out to seek revenge against their killers." I said this to Williyumm loudly, speaking Cree so the others could hear and understand my words.

They surely did, for our carriers set off in a great hurry southward, staggering on their snowshoes, even after the old moon rose to light the east edge of the world. We traveled slowly in single file until Nishcock judged that we had placed enough distance between ourselves and the ghosts of those who had been murdered. We made camp and slept until early morning when we heard the others taking down their tents. Even I knew now that we had no choice but to plod southward after them, or die.

Toward evening, we began to see a few and then increasing numbers of caribou tracks, places where they'd dug for moss, and their droppings scattered across the snow like berries. As the mists faded in the sharpening cold of evening, a distant streak of forest appeared along the southern horizon. We cut and chewed our skin shirttails before dropping into a fitful sleep. Moving out in the early dawn, we were driven like mad wolves in search of food. I could hear nothing but the hollow sucking sounds within my belly. I ate snow grinding my teeth together, trying to swallow the bitter juices that kept rising in my mouth as I staggered after the struggling line of men.

Nishcock made a sign for us to halt, then kicking off his snowshoes, he climbed painfully up onto a high round boulder. The Cree, with Williyumm and Jako, crowded around him.

"Mistaar Staariit," Nishcock said, "give me your bring-near glass."

Williyumm unslung the leather case and handed it up to him.

Using his musket barrel to steady the yellow tube, Nishcock adjusted it with greatest care, then carefully examined the distant edges of the ragged trees.

"I see no caribou," he said.

My knees grew weak when I heard that.

"I do see the deer hedge," he added, drawing out the bring-near tubes. "but that . . . is not what . . . I am looking at."

His voice rose with excitement. "Yes, I see one . . . two . . . three log platforms built high, to protect meat. On the first platform there is nothing." He paused. "On the second platform . . . nothing. But on the third platform . . . there is something. I believe . . . I see . . . a great pile of red meat."

When he said meat, Williyumm and Jako and I, with many others, started weeping, hobbling painfully forward. None of us could help ourselves. Nishcock tossed down Williyumm's bring-near glass, fell off the rock, and almost fainted when he bent to retie his snowshoes. Nishcock tried to run, to lead us. But I was already up in front with Williyumm. We shambled dizzily, trying to stay ahead of all the others in the winter gloom. The bulky tent weight on my back now seemed as light as air.

"There it is, the cache!" cried Williyumm. "Can you see? It's fully loaded."

We lurched forward like a horde of loose-jointed animals. Nishcock climbed the crude log ladder to the rough platform just above our heads. We saw him reach in among the quartered caribou carcasses which were piled higher than his waist. He hacked out a chunk of mostly frozen meat and jammed it in his mouth. Who could blame him? I heard him laughing, growling, chewing like a hungry dog. Excited by the sight of all that meat, his strength had come flowing back to him. Nishcock started flinging frozen quarters down to those crowded anxiously below.

"More! More!" we yelled.

As each haunch, neck, or rib cage reached us, we knelt, trying with knives and trembling hands to hack off bite-sized pieces.

216

I was so thrilled by the sight of all that meat that I don't remember putting up the tent or lighting a fire to make the snow-water boil, but suddenly I knew I was alive. Like Williyumm and Jako, I had a chunk of boiled meat in my mouth and could feel the hot, life-giving juices trickling down my throat. I ate as much as my stomach could hold, then went out, like the others, threw up, returned, and ate some more. We all slept well until into the following morning. I awoke to the delicious smell of caribou broth simmering in the basket. Jako was stirring it with Williyumm's sword and smiling at the two of us. Once more we ate our fill and slept again.

When I went outside, the sky above my head was a clear, blue dome. Winter was turning into spring. Before us stood the meat cache that had saved our lives. The snow around us was criss-crossed with countless caribou tracks. Off to the east and the west, I could see a few small herds, already far away, moving north again.

When Nishcock came to our tent, he was smiling, grinning like some other person. Our mistrust and hatred for each other, like our hunger, had gone away once more. "I believe," he said, "those hunters of ours who left us came here and were able to drive more caribou inside the hedge than they could eat or carry. They killed as many as they needed, then left the cache for us."

Williyumm said to Nishcock, "Now that we are no longer starving and have meat, we must turn north again and find the Copper people."

"*Never!*" grunted Nishcock. "Do you want to have us murdered, just when we've been saved? The killing of those Copper hunters was not done by us. Who knows who did it? Maybe those Wood Cat men. We have guns and powder, but we are only me and my men, you, Misstar Staariit, one boy, and that trouble-making Copper woman. We will eat and gather strength for a few days here, then we will turn back toward the house of spears."

He scowled at Williyumm. "It has been not so bad for you, Mistaar Staariit, carrying nothing, and laying in your tent playing night games with that Copper bitch of yours. Our men have been away from their wives for nearly eight new moons. Who knows what has happened since they left? Soon as we feel strong enough, we will begin our journey home. Do not try to say it any other way, Mistaar Staariit. That's how it's going to be with us."

Nishcock kicked his snowshoes around and gave me a terrible look before he turned and marched back toward his tent.

"That is exactly as I have always wished it," I told Williyumm gleefully. "I never wanted all those brutes trailing north with us. Now we have lots of meat. We three can easily go there by ourselves."

"No. We're not going to lose Nishcock and his men," said Williyumm. "They are going to stay with us while we go and find your people."

I got mad when he said that, but Williyumm could be a very determined man sometimes. "We three are going to find them," I told Mistaar Staariit, getting even madder. "I am not going back without seeing my people. Is my brother alive or dead? I have to know!"

"You are too headstrong, woman!" Williyumm shouted back at me.

Jako said, "Maybe the Cree will wait here until your Copper people come."

"They won't come here, unless I go and get them. This is too far south for Dene families to lodge. But they may be only a few days north of here."

"I don't want Nishcock and his men to leave," said Williyumm. "If we find lots of fur and yellow pebbles in your country, how will we carry it all back to the fort?"

"They won't go away from you," I told him. "Come, I'll show you something."

Inside our tent, Thana pulled back our blankets and the soft fur bedding, pulled back the evergreens, and dug into the snow. There lay the last keg of the Cree's gunpowder.

"Where did you get that?" Williyumm asked me.

"Young Jako, he went to Nishcock's tent for me when all of us were busy eating. He carried that barrel over here and buried it for us. How can Nishcock and the carriers leave without powder for their guns?" I asked him. "They will be haunted by the fear that my Dene people will be out tracking them, hunting for them. Those Cree know that they would be killed by my people if they can't use their guns to fight them off."

That same evening, Nishcock came with three of his strongest men and, squatting, drew back the entrance flap of our tent. We looked at them.

"Where is our powder for the guns?" His lips were drawn back in an unsmiling grimace that showed his lower teeth.

"That powder belongs to the Company," Williyumm said.

"We're going to keep it safe for the Bearman," I told Nishcock. "Bearman sent you here to find the Dene. You have not done that."

"We have traveled very far together, Mistaar Staariit," Nishcock said, ignoring me. "We Northern Cree have grown used to your ways. We no longer wish to harm you. But you are wrong to be driven by this crazy Copper woman."

I let out a nasty hiss at him.

"If you walk north with us for five days," said Williyumm, "I promise to give every one of you an even share of powder. Then we will all return together to the fort."

Nishcock snarled at Williyumm, then pushed me back so hard I tumbled over.

"Don't touch her again," said Williyumm as he cocked the double pistol.

Nishcock spoke more carefully. "It is this Copper bitch who causes all the trouble. We are only a few here now. If we meet her Copper people, who knows what she will say to them, or how they will avenge themselves against us."

"Run away, if you are afraid," I said to Nishcock. "But you will go without the guvnaar's gunpowder."

"Remember," Williyumm added, "if you reach the house of spears without us, you will do so in disgrace. None of you will receive the gifts the governor promised."

This was the worst threat Williyumm could have made. Nishcock mumbled some words to the others, words that Williyumm did not understand. But I understood them. I snatched up the scatter gun and cocked it, pointing it at Nishcock's head. That quickly changed his way of thinking.

Nishcock spread the fingers of his hands before its gaping barrel. "Be careful, woman! Wait! So, Mistaar Staariit . . . we agree. We will walk north with you for five days. Only five! If she has not found her Copper people, Mistaar Staariit, do you give me your word that we will share the powder evenly among each man, then start walking east together?"

Williyumm nodded and I carefully repeated Nishcock's words, to be certain that everyone could hear and understand: "Five days' fast walking to the Wolf Star, then if we have not found my people, you and your carriers will share the powder and go back with Mistaar Staariit."

Nishcock rose angrily, and he and his men stamped back to their tents while we watched.

"Don't worry," I told Williyumm. "I can feel the Dene, they're not far from us."

When we had regained some strength, we started north. Without dogs, we humans joined in pulling the two toboggans, one loaded with our pots, tents, poles, and bedding, the other with fresh meat. The northwest wind had died. Once again our bellies and the hollows beneath our cheeks were filled. As we marched, Nishcock's men triumphantly held up their fingers, and counted off the second, third, and fourth days. We saw no human signs. The Cree were gleeful. Tomorrow they would have their gunpowder back and begin the journey home to their families.

Many times during our fifth day trudging north, I ran forward and climbed any rise of ground to peer over the familiar landscape of my mother's country, hoping to see rising smoke, or some of their meat caches, or a line of snowshoe tracks – anything that might lead me to my people.

On the fifth night, I was silent. The weather was warming as we made camp. Even before the tents were up, it started to snow. Big wet flakes came spiraling down to us as we raised the tent and spread the boughs. We didn't bury the keg of powder.

Williyumm sat long-legged near the firelight, making his writing on the skins. We three ate our meat and drank the broth, then lay in silence in the bed.

"We should have found some sign of them by now," I said to Williyumm.

He slowly shook his head. "You've got to give up now," he said. "I gave my word. Nishcock and his men have come a long way with us."

"My people can't be far from here." I took Williyumm's hand in mine. "Will you try to hold these men here with you for four more days?" I begged him "Only four?"

"I can't do that," he replied. "They would have the right to kill us if I tried."

"Then three days," I pleaded, pressing his hand up under my shirt between my breasts.

Williyumm sadly shook his head. "Go to sleep," he said. "Nishcock will start early in the morning."

I could not even close my eyes that night as I listened to a storm come whispering, then wailing, outside our sagging tent. Long before light, I slipped out of our bed, being oh so careful not to wake Williyumm and Jako. Dressing quickly, I made a bundle of a few of my snares, my blanket and sleeping skin, and one small package of the meat. Quietly, I forced back the weight of new snow against the tent flap and crept outside. It was still snowing, but the wind was down, and I could feel that the worst of the storm had passed.

I was bending forward, binding on my snowshoes, when someone reached out and touched me, brushing hands across my back. I whirled around in fright, but saw no one there. Had that been Dingee, or one of the spirits of those nine slain men? Or was it only some dwarfed snow-laden tree pointing its long white fingers at me? I started running through the deep snow, followed by some ghostly presence I could not see.

WILLIAM

15

I reached over and felt for Thana. Her side of our bed was almost cold. Her clothes were gone. I leapt up naked and peered outside the tent. Her snowshoes had been pulled down from the tree. It was still snowing heavily, and there was no sign of her trail. I pulled on my leggings and both my caribou shirts, my fox hat and heavy mittens, and went outside where an overwhelming feeling came to me, a feeling of such hopelessness that I slumped to my knees. Thana had gone running, searching, into her own country! Would I ever see her face again?

Jako came outside and stared at the place where Thana's snowshoes should have been, and then at me. He did not speak.

I went back into our cold, deserted tent. Thana had taken so little with her. I tried to imagine her breaking trail somewhere out there in those vast spaces, alone. I sat on our bed and tried to make some kind of entry in my journal, but it was too dark. Both Jako and I tried to relight Thana's small fire, but without her, it seemed to have lost the capacity to burn. Thana had reached up and stuffed one of my inner mittens into the smoke hole, to try and keep in the warmth. As I stood up to remove it, my breath turned into icy fog.

I couldn't remain inside that tent without her. I pushed back the flap and crawled outside again. After more than eight months of wandering across this unknown land, surely we must be close to reaching Thana's people. But now, even she was gone.

Putting on my snowshoes, I made my way to Nishcock's tent. He shook his head when I woke him and said that Thana was gone. I begged him to wake his men and help me track her.

"Forget about that crazy Copper slut," he answered sourly. "I'll find you a good young Cree woman as soon as we return." Nishcock turned and shook his cousin, Raven. "The Copper woman's gone," he sniffed. "We won't see her again."

Raven sneered at me. "I hope that crazy-mouth keeps running, searching, until she falls off the edge of the world."

Seeing that I could expect no help from them, I went out with Jako to see if we could find any trace of Thana. The snowstorm had almost passed. By night, with a clear sky, I knew Thana would be guided by the Wolf Star, hurrying as quickly as she could into the northwest, searching for familiar Dene signs. But we could not find a single mark or broken branch that would give us the direction of her trail. It had vanished beneath the heavy snow. I climbed a ridge and found myself exhausted. Faint veils of icy fog drifted along the river course and across an enormous lake, one that I could not see across. It shone like silver in the morning light, filling our whole view. We two stood together in the immense blue bowl of silence, staring north, then west. Where was she? Three times I hollered out her name, and so did Jako.

We circled back in a different way, still hoping for some sign. When we reached the camp, Nishcock and the others were collapsing their tents and tightly bundling their bed rolls. "Load everything on the toboggans," Nishcock called so I could hear him. "We're leaving now."

"Wait!" I pleaded. "Will none of you stay and help us look for her?"

"No!" Nishcock answered. "We have the powder you've been hiding and we're leaving now!"

Raven shouted, "If that Copper bitch of yours ever finds her vengeful relatives, she will stay with them or bring them back to hunt us down and kill us."

"You and that boy can come with us, or stay," said Nishcock. "We are leaving now."

"I am going to find the Copper woman," I called to him.

"Fool!" Nishcock called. "You know nothing of this country. You and that boy will die out here alone."

When I did not answer, another voice called out to me in Cree, "Come with us, Mistaar Staarit. We shall reach the fort together. The guvnaar and all your friends will be glad to see you and this boy come safely back with us." He came toward me with a cheerful look upon his face. "Come with us," he said again. "When this eagle moon has passed, the river ice will break and the caribou will begin to move across our trail. Together we shall have all the meat we wish to eat."

"Yes, come with us," some of the others urged. "Look at this heavy snow. It is too deep for one man and a boy to break trail, but shoeing all together we will take turns leading and move swiftly home."

"It's true," said Nishcock. "Only two moons, shoeing fast, and we will reach the house of spears."

Nishcock's cousin, Raven, came up to me. "I know a beautiful young Cree woman who lives in the long lodge next to me. She will share your blanket with you. She is a calm young woman, not at all like that sly crazy runner who has left you. She seeks to find our enemy and guide them here for blood revenge. Join us." He nodded eastward. "We are going. Now!"

"You have guns," I said. "You told me her people have no guns. Are you afraid they will throw stones at you?"

"We are not afraid of them," yelled Nishcock angrily.

"Then wait here just a while." I snatched off my mitts and spread the fingers of both hands. "Remain here with me for only ten more days. If she has not returned by that tenth day," I wiggled my small finger, "then I will return to the fort with you and tell the governor that you are truly brave men who deserve the greatest respect and many splendid gifts."

Nishcock flung his mittens on the snow and stamped his snowshoes like a willful child. Then he began whispering and making signs to the others. Many of the Cree kicked their bundled tents and wailed in anguish. Others made wild gestures toward our dwelling. Kaswah grimaced and spat onto the snow.

I squatted in the entrance to our tent, holding the loaded blunderbuss ready in my hand. Jako nudged me in relief when we saw Nishcock ordering his men to set up their tents again. They built an outdoor fire, whilst throwing filthy looks at us. Crouching around it, they ate, heads close together, grumbling, glancing often at our tent. Some of them had rubbed charcoal on their faces, a sure sign that they expected trouble and were preparing to fight.

Clouds gathered in the afternoon, and snow fell again, wrapping the world around us in a gray silence that seemed to frighten the Cree. The sky hung down like Scottish goose-down bedding that some chambermaid had pegged above our heads. Nishcock and the nine remaining carriers stood outside their tents in two small groups, listening and sometimes pointing at the low rolling hills, whence they believed the Dene hunters would attack.

I watched Nishcock as he sent Wapuss shuffling over to borrow my wood axe. Reluctantly, I tossed it to him. I could soon hear him sharpening it, along with the two other hatchets they possessed. We watched six of the Cree set off, armed with muskets, for a grove of stunted tamaracks.

From the entrance of our tent, Jako and I could hear the muffled sound of chopping. By midday, three dozen arm-thick trees had been hacked down and their branches sheared off. All the Cree went out to drag back the wood on the toboggans. Working swiftly, the men split each log in two – quite easily, for the sap was frozen – then they sharpened each end into a spearlike point.

We watched them stamping out a circle in the snow, just large enough to accommodate a dozen men. Around the perimeter of this circle, the Cree fixed a palisade of the sharpened stakes, some eight feet high, binding them together with long willow roots and lengths of thong. I was amazed to realize that they, in imitation of Fort York, had partly built themselves a smaller house of spears. After such a long day's work, the Cree did not trouble us that night.

When we arose, they were all off, felling still more trees, which they brought in, split, and added to reinforce their palisade. Well before evening, their little fortress was completed and they prepared to move inside, using one of their collapsed tents as a covering. Soon I saw a column of smoke rising from the center of their stronghold. When they set out Raven as a sentry, I was much impressed.

Nishcock came hurrying along the snowshoe path and stood before my tent. "Mistaar Staarit," he grunted as he squatted down to talk. "You are a stubborn man and never generous with us. But we Cree are decent human beings who do not wish to see you lose your life. So you and that boy, bring your kit and move inside with us. Those Copper devils will surely murder you if they catch you sleeping here alone."

I watched his eyes, aware that Nishcock knew he must guide me safely back to York Factory to have any chance of a generous reward.

"Tomorrow that Copper woman will have used three days," he said. "We believe she may have found her people. If that is so, she will return with them to seek revenge for those nine men we found dead. So bring the boy and come inside our house of spears. We will need your guns and your sword to help us fight."

When I heard that, I said, "We two will stay here in this tent and wait for her return. She will be back very soon."

Nishcock pointed his trigger finger at me. "Mistaar Staarit, you are as much a fool as that woman you used to lay with. When those Copper hunters come in stabbing through this tent with their sharp bone spears, it will be too late for you to join us. Hear this, Mistaar Staarit," he warned. "The guvnaar smoked the pipe with me and made me swear to care for you. He said he would give wonderful gifts to me and all others who helped take you safely here and bring you back again."

"He also told you to take care of that Copper woman."

"He did not," yelled Nishcock. "He only said to me, 'Don't let your men abuse her.' I have allowed not one of them to pull up her shirt or throw her to the ground. And now she has run away. A few more sunrises, Mistaar Staarit. Then we are leaving. Soon almost all our food will be gone, and we will set out together, searching for animals on our way home."

That night I slept very badly, several times waking in fright, believing that I heard the creak of steps outside the tent. Next morning, when the sun rose like a bleary yellow eye, watching us through drifting scud, Nishcock came out of the little fortress and paced a wide circle round it. He called out to the others inside, saying, "If she brings the Coppers to us, do not fire your muskets until they have stepped inside this circle, do you understand?"

"We do," I heard the other carriers answer.

Nishcock shouted angrily across to me. "Mistaar Staarit, we have only enough powder to reload six times each. When they attack, you must swear to bring your powder horns and try to run inside the fort and help us with your weapons. Do you agree to that?"

"Yes, yes," I said, "if Thanadelthur comes back with many men who wish to fight you, I will come inside and help." Jako was as nervous as I was when that trickster, Raven, came shuffling toward our tent. We watched him carefully when he squatted near the entrance. He stared at me cruelly as he slowly cocked and uncocked his long-barreled musket. He did not point its barrel directly at me, but still the black eye of its muzzle was wavering close enough to worry me.

His mitted finger must have slipped, for suddenly his musket discharged with a frightening crash and a thick puff of smoke. I saw the ball kick up snow beside my tent. Jako yelled in fright and Raven leapt up when he saw me grab my pistol.

"I didn't mean to do that," he cried. "Don't shoot me. This crazy gun went off by itself."

I could hear a great commotion in the little house of spears.

"They're here! Get ready to fight!" I heard Nishcock shouting. "The Coppers are attacking! Get ready. Prime your muskets. Raven's seen them, they're attacking!"

Raven turned and ran toward the fort, yelling, "Don't shoot! Don't shoot me! My musket went off by itself."

"What a fool you are," I heard Nishcock shout at him. "Wasting powder and ball. Scaring all of us for nothing."

227

After that event, we remained in a state of high alert, suspicious of every move the other made. The worst of it was that I had sworn that the ninth day would be the last day we would remain here. Oh, how I prayed that Thana would return, for how could I bring myself to leave without her.

Wearing my powder horns crisscrossed around my neck, and a pistol hidden in my waistband, I set off one day for the little fort. Jako walked beside me, carrying my sword. I intended to beg a day or two's extension.

The Cree sentry, Kaswah, eyed our approach with mistrust. When we were admitted, we saw that each man had been at work constructing a thick, split-wood shield that was tightly sewn with sinew. With charcoal and red ocher paint, each shield was marked with a Cree clan device. All nine men now had their faces decorated with white ash from their fire pit; each had black charcoal streaks beneath his eyes. Only Nishcock, as their captain, had the privilege of painting his face a red and a startling indigo blue, which he had brought with him in case of battle.

shield and spears

"Those dog men, when she attacks with them, will never have heard a musket fired," said Nishcock. "They will be terrified. Then we will scream and howl like devils. In that way, we should drive them off."

"In case we have to fight them, we have made these thick shields," he explained, "because those Copper men are known to be strong archers and can fling their spears with deadly force. If you are wise, you and the boy will come inside this little house of spears with us.

228

"Mistaar Staarit," he spoke gravely, "we must all leave together in the morning if we are not attacked tonight. We do not wish to leave you to be killed."

When we returned, we found a fresh set of snowshoe tracks leading to our tent. Inside, we found it had been ransacked. Everything was tossed about, and my musket, shot pouch, and, worst of all, the scatter gun, were gone.

Jako rushed outside the tent and studied the trail. "Kaswah was here. He's the one who stole everything."

"What can we do?" I asked him. "We've got nothing but this axe and sword and a pistol."

"And this slingshot," said Jako, untying it from around his waist.

"You be careful," I told him, then, clutching the axe, I put on my snowshoes again and started along Kaswah's trail with Jako close behind me.

I felt an enormous sense of anger and outrage rising within me. I held the axe and sword behind my legs, for I had every intention of trying to surprise Kaswah, then cut him down with a single blow. My swordmaster, Captain von Cranach, had often warned me that it was foolhardy to fight when one was half-blind with anger. Yet that was exactly what I was bent on doing. Even Thana's advice would not have altered my plan.

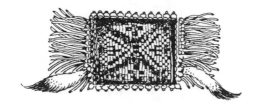

THANA

16

Setting out in the dark of night alone terrified me, and yet I knew that I must place enough distance between myself and Williyumm so that he could not find my trail. Of course, he would urge the Cree to track me. But they would probably refuse and dance with delight to see me gone. They would never help him find me. I kept up a rolling, running shuffle through softly drifting snow, for I, too, greatly feared our Dene ghosts like the dwarfs, the screamers, the whipping man, and all the others who hide themselves in falling snow. The light of the moon cast an eerie glow, but when I looked up to find the Wolf Star, I saw only the softly falling feathers of snow.

I broke off two green branches of a spruce and drew them on a thong behind me to wipe away my snowshoe tracks. The snow would cover every trace. I had to lean forward and vigorously swing my arms and thrust with my hips to break a trail. It was hard traveling, but now I had to find my people, out there somewhere. I thought of Williyumm and Jako sleeping peacefully in our bed. Could they outwit Nishcock and those nine cruel Cree while I was gone?

I journeyed all day along a frozen river that I knew, without seeing the rising or the setting sun, my body hot from hurrying. The whole world had become a silent, edgeless whiteness. At night, I found a tree which I could bend to make a miserable lean-to. Within, I lit a fire and ate, hoping the smoke would lead the Dene to me.

Next day, everything I saw looked red, a warning of snow blindness. Cutting a piece from my sleeping skin, I made an eye mask with two narrow slits. My burning eyes felt better. I could feel the sinew webbing springing underneath my feet, packing the soft snow down against the river ice. Sometimes I moved through strange and fearful snow-hung dens of trees. Oh, how I longed to see some familiar Dene sign, a tenting place, a deadfall built for bears, a meat cache, any man-made thing. But I saw nothing. Nothing.

On the third evening, it was snowing when darkness overcame me, but I went on until I found a tree so thickly laden with snow that there was a small white cave beneath the boughs. Gratefully, I crawled inside, bundled myself in my sleeping skin, and slept the night.

I rose while it was still dark, but the sky was clearing. Singing my thanks to the Wolf Star and the morning star, I started snow-shoeing fast to try and warm myself. After a while, still moving along the river, I ate a little of the dried meat I had brought. The powdery flesh melted in my mouth, and I felt a warmth spreading like tiny fluttering moths through every part of my body. Above my head, I could see long ghostly fingers of pale light flickering as they reached nervously down toward the edges of the world. These strange lights are known to be sure signs that caribou are grazing near our hunters. Did that mean my Dene relatives were near?

That evening, the eagle moon rose in the eastern sky spreading moonbeams with his wings through the blackness of the spruce trees along the edge of a lake. Off to the west, I heard a lone wolf howling and soon enough a female answered him. Then other wolves sent up their lonely chorus to the stars. I could tell that they were gathering to hunt their prey. Far across the whiteness of the lake, I saw a smudge of gray shadows moving in the moonlight, a small heard of caribou running fast. Behind them I could see wolves chasing them.

Just before falling into an exhausted sleep, I propped a small stick in the snow, pointing at the never-moving Wolf Star.

When I woke, the stars were gone and the sky was clouded again. I ate too much of my small food supply. If Williyumm had been with me, he would have tried to make me be more frugal, for he is a man who believes in saving food until death stares you in the eye. My Dene, like the Cree, say eat now, enjoy life today; stay strong, for who knows what will come to you tomorrow, if you live to see tomorrow come. As I crossed the lake, I remembered explaining to Williyumm how our people think.

He asked me if the Dene ever starved to death. "Aye!" I answered. "That they have." He told me his countrymen in Scootlan' had rarely starved to death for years and years. They much preferred to kill each other fighting. "Is that a better way to die?" I had asked. And I imagined now that I could hear his voice saying, "Ahh, nooo, but that's the way it is, lass."

All that day, I had the sun's course to guide me. I sang small songs to keep the lonely spirits from humming bad thoughts in my ears. In the deep shadows of a tamarack, I was certain that I saw a poor dead woman hanging by the neck, but it was just a trick of light. It is not easy to move alone across these vast and silent spaces day after day. If you talk to yourself out loud or sing too much, it's frightening, for you fear that madness could be creeping up on you. If you neither speak nor sing, the silence becomes unbearable; you start to scream inside yourself.

That night, I made a bed of boughs again and rolled tightly in my bedding. I held my empty food bag in my arms and dreamed it was my newborn child.

When I awoke, I knew that I was not alone. I raised my head and looked north along the river. Against the glow of dawn, I could see a small herd of caribou. Two of them were females with their backs humped upward, straining to give birth.

They were not far away from me, and I wondered what a hunter would do. My snares would not help me; Owinipeg's steel dagger was my only weapon. My hunger told me that I must do something. I rose as cautiously as a wolf, rolled my sleeping skin upon my back and crouching, stepped into my snowshoes. At that moment, I saw one female caribou arch and strain until a newborn calf came falling from her womb. Wait, wait, I told myself as I saw the other female strain to drop her fawn. They are very small, I thought. You will need the pair of them.

It was not long until the second fawn was born and both mothers had turned to lick away the birth sacks and dry their young. Immediately, the mothers began to nudge them with their noses until the fawns stood up on wobbly legs. I'll catch that first one, I thought, and then I'll catch the second, before it has a chance to learn to run.

I moved confidently toward the first fawn, expecting the female to raise her head, then run from me. When she did not, I ran toward her. The mother snorted, bunting the fawn with her snout, which sent it skittering across the hard lake snow. I lunged forward on my snowshoes, and I almost had the young one in my grasp, when it gave another nervous twitch and broke into a zigzag run again.

It took all my strength to chase and catch that newborn fawn. Finally, when I had it in my grasp, it struggled only for a moment, then relaxed. It was not at all afraid of me. It laid its head against my breast and its long soft legs hung dangling from my arms. It looked up at me with dark and trusting eyes. I knelt down intending to kill it. Could I kill it? I needed it so badly. Any real hunter would certainly have killed it. But instead, I just knelt there on the place where the wind had partly swept the clear ice free of snow, and I hugged the soft newborn calf to me and I heard the mother bleating. She was standing waiting only half a stone's throw from me.

"I won't hurt it," I called out to its mother, but still I held her young fawn in my arms, feeling its heartbeat and its warmth. Then I carefully stood it on the snow and gave its rump a gentle push. It wobbled off toward its mother.

My head whirled around in dizzy circles when I bent to retie my snowshoes while saying to myself, "You stupid woman. It's almost spring and you're going crazy. When I catch that second fawn, I will surely kill it. Oh, yes, I will kill it without holding it against my belly or looking at its eyes."

I chased that second fawn as hard as I could run, but it was new and light and able to zigzag over the thin snow crust while my snowshoes broke through with every step. I never caught that second fawn and finally, when the small herd was far from me, I lay exhausted, hungry and sobbing on the great frozen, desolate lake.

Men are born to be the hunters. They know well that they must not look at a newborn animal's eyes. I was glad there were no men, no hunters near, for they would certainly have laughed at me.

I scraped spruce gum from a tree and chewed it. As the day wore on, I grew so lonely and so hungry that I was singing and talking to myself and yelling and sometimes dancing sideways on my snowshoes. I crouched down and slapped my face and said, "Silence, mad woman, you are walking in your own land now, Do you want good Dene people to hear you?

"No," I answered, and once more started marching very straight, though I was sure that only the pale Moon Man was watching me.

Suddenly, I stopped and shut my eyes in disbelief. But when I looked again in the slanting light, there were the telltale shadows in the snow. I ran toward them. Yes, they were true snowshoe tracks – packed hard – not made by one but maybe by six or eight men pulling two toboggans.

Here a man had stopped and stepped aside to urinate. Not far from his frozen yellow splash, I knelt and examined the web print of his snowshoes, and then I laid my cheek against the sharp fresh-cut impression of the weave. I wept, for the pattern of those snowshoe sinews could have been woven only by a skillful Dene woman. Best of all, those tracks had been made not yesterday, but since this morning's sun had risen.

I shouted, "Relatives of mine, do you hear me? Answer, please!" Pushing back my hood, I opened my mouth and listened carefully, turning my head.

But I heard no reply.

"Dene relatives! Do you hear me?"

Still no answer.

I ran along their track until my thighs and shinbones ached. I stumbled in a drift and fell upon my hands and knees. "Stop acting like a mink in heat," I told myself. "Those are strong, well-fed Dene hunters. They will be moving fast. You can follow their tracks, but probably you will not catch them until long after they have stopped to sleep." I pressed on, following the tracks as they left the river and crossed a high ridge. At its top, I stopped and let out a gasp of joy, for not far away I could see three, four, five, yes, five pale thin columns of smoke rising arrow-straight from among some trees. "There they are! I've found them!" I cried.

It was late afternoon when I crossed the last low hill, and there it was – the camp. I could see two women and their daughters unloading a toboggan, piling rich red meat onto two high food platforms. Nearby, a dozen skins were stretched on round drying frames.

When I was near enough but not too near to the camp, I knelt down in the proper way of a friendly stranger and called out in a meek and humble voice, "It is I, Thanadelthur, returning after being stolen – a Chipewyan woman alone, coming back to her own people."

The women at the meat cache turned, shading their eyes, and stared at the snow ridge where I knelt. The young girls ran in fear toward the tents. The camp dogs raised their heads and sniffed the air. They seemed to recognize me, even though I had been gone so very long.

As soon as I saw my people pushing back their tent flaps, I stood up and called to them, "I am Thanadelthur, daughter of Sossisi!"

That made them know that I was one of them. Many came running toward me. I dropped down on my knees again, showing the Dene that I possessed the proper humbleness of an enslaved woman, free to return to her own people.

Slowly I rose and walked into camp with them. At first, only the oldest man had the courage to reach out and touch me. Then he felt me all over. "Yes, she is a real person," he told the others. "She is Sossisi's daughter."

"Yes, I am real, and I am starving," I told them with tears running down my cheeks.

They led me inside their largest lodge and fed me thick broth and boiled musk-ox meat and had me rest close by the fire.

"Is my brother, Keewatan, here with you?" I asked.

"Yes," a woman answered. "That is his new wife, Sidhaw, sitting there near you. He and the other hunters came in yesterday with meat, but they went south again at dawn to bring in more."

That evening, after I had slept and been given food again, I told my people about Dingee and me being taken and enslaved, of our escape from Kunn and poor Dingee's death, and how I finally crawled into the goose hunters' camp and was taken by their tall Cree captain to the Ballahooly's house of spears.

"The Ballahooly's house of spears!" The oldest Dene woman laughed when she heard those words. "How far away is that?"

"Very far," I told her. "Six moons walking. It stands on the shore beside a wide river's mouth that flows into big water that you cannot drink. The house of spears is much bigger than all our winter tents if they were tied together."

"Did you go inside?" Sidhaw, the new wife of my brother, asked me.

I thought a while before I answered, for I did not like the sly, mistrustful look upon her face.

"Oh, yes, I lived inside with the Ballahooly for all last winter's seven moons."

"You spent seven moons with the Ballahooly?" my brother's new wife gasped. "What kind of men are they? Is it true they have enormous penises?"

"Some big, they say, some small," I answered her with caution. "Ballahooly are not all bad or good," I added. "But it is true that they are not at all like us. Most of them know nothing of the animals or fish or birds or any kind of hunting – except that some of them bring geese down when they are flying high."

Both men and women gasped and shook their heads in disbelief.

"Still, the Ballahooly have many wonderful possessions, shining beads of every color," I said, pointing to my chest. "They have thin iron sewing needles, and huge weapons that shoot iron balls as big as babies' heads and make a thunder that knocks you down. They have sharp iron knives like this one.'' Everyone stood up when I showed them Owinipeg's knife. Then I described their axes, good for cutting wood, or ice, or frozen meat.

While they were examining my few treasures, I ate tender chunks of meat and lay back sobbing, so glad was I to be among my people again.

''I want some hunters to come with me and meet with one Ballahooly, ten Cree, and a very good boy who traveled with us,'' I told them.

''Where are they?'' asked the oldest woman.

''Not far. Only four days from this camp.''

''So close,'' she murmured, looking fearfully outside the lodge. ''Go,'' she said to a young girl, ''tell your grandfather we need him here.''

The old man limped into the tent, leaning on a stick. He wore an extra caribou-skin shawl across his shoulders, his hair was gray, and his eyes were rimmed red from wood smoke. He squatted near me, for his hearing was poor.

''How many saltwater Cree did you say you brought into our country?''

''Only ten,'' I answered, ''not counting Juko. Their head man is a Ballahooly named Mistaar Staarit.''

''Have they got the thunder guns?''

''Yes, they have the guns,'' I told him. ''Mistaar Staarit and I won't let them kill you with the guns. There used to be more than a hundred Cree with us and twenty of their women and lots of dogs, but they are all gone now, except these ten. The others have returned to the house of spears.''

''A hundred men with thunder guns!'' the women gasped and held up their fingers and fluttered them to indicate that enormous number.

''Are you sure they went back?'' the oldest woman asked in a quivering voice. ''We know of that enemy trick – to pretend that they have gone away, then come sneaking up on us at night, pushing tents down and stabbing through them before we have the chance to rise and fight them off."

I held up my ten fingers. "Only ten are here now, with one captain, a Ballahooly. He's starting to speak Dene pretty well. He taught me a lot of the Ballahooly language, too. The chief at the house of spears, Bearman, doesn't want any killing or taking of young women for slaves," I told them. "He sent Mistaar Staarit here with me to meet you Dene folk and to ask if you will come and trade fur for all the wonderful Company things. Bearman wants to trade for beaver, mink, marten, fisher, otter, lynx, ermine, and fox skins. Oh, yes, and he would like to trade for the yellow stones that you hammer into arrowheads and knives and flensers."

Certainly, I should then have told the head man about the nine Dene hunters we found murdered, but I could not bring myself to speak of them just yet.

"If you brought those terrible people into our country," said my new sister-in-law, "they must have forced you to guide them because you are their slave."

"I am not their slave," I answered, stung by her words. "I am here because the Ballahooly head man sent me to ask you if you wish to trade with him."

"Well, that's the same," Sidhaw answered in a whining voice. "You are the one who has led those killers here to us."

When she said that, the old head man narrowed his eyes and peered at me as though I, Thanadelthur, might have become an enemy of my own people. "When the Wood Cats attacked your camp and you and Dingee were stolen and so many Dene were killed, we did not know what to do because those enemies had guns. We have no guns," the old man said and spat into the fire. "It is horrible to think that there is not a single soul left alive from your father's camp except you and Dingee's husband and your brother, Keewatan."

"I long to see my brother," I told them. "After our men trade fur for guns, the Wood Cats will be afraid of us."

When I said that, my new sister-in-law and most of the younger women stood up, giving me bad looks as they drew back the tent flap and looked south and east to see if the enemy I had brought with me were creeping in upon them.

"What worries me," said one old woman, "is that our hunters are out there." She nodded to the south. "They do not know that those Cree are skulking somewhere near them with their guns. If those saltwater Cree see our hunters' tracks, they will kill all of them with their thunder guns."

"That won't happen," I said quickly. "The Ballahooly is with them. Even if they meet, he won't allow any killing."

"Is this Ballahooly an old and powerful chief?" the head man asked me.

"No," I admitted. "He is a very young man. I want to take our Dene hunters out to meet him. When will they return?"

"Soon. Tonight or maybe tomorrow, if they are not ambushed," one woman answered me.

My new sister-in-law started simpering, "I don't want you taking our men near any young Ballahooly, with his Crees pointing their thunder guns at them."

I could see that all these women were very much against me. I would have to wait for my brother and the other hunters to return.

"I must go to sleep again," I told them, for I felt truly sick at heart. Here I was, just back among my own people, and everything was going wrong.

Later, a young girl woke me, saying, "All our men are back. They brought in six caribou, and they've got more cached farther south."

"That's good," I said, as I watched her take her baby from its carrying strap and suckle it. "You're lucky," I told her. "How I want to rest in this country and have a baby with Williyumm, instead of having to walk ourselves skinny back through that dangerous Wood Cat country."

When I went outside the tent, the first hunter I saw was my only living brother, Keewatan. I ran straight to him, and we two just stood there with our fingers touching, staring at each other. There were tears in both our eyes when he touched my face and said, "I believed that you were gone forever."

239

"So many nights before I went to sleep, I've wondered whether you were still alive."

"You look thin," he said, "as if you have been doing too much walking, too little eating."

"That is true," I said, "but that doesn't matter now that we're together."

We couldn't stop looking at each other, remembering all the talking and running and the laughing we had done while we were growing up together. Then it was time to give my brother something precious, and I reached beneath my shirt for my father's eagle-claw necklace. I had kept it safely hidden, for such a head man's decoration should not be worn by a woman. I was eager to pass it on to him, my only brother, Keewatan, who had the right to inherit it and wear it.

Keewatan was overwhelmed to hold once more this treasured object, for it was his link with our father and our clan. I proudly told my brother that I had cut the necklace from the throat of the Wood Cat who had enslaved Dingee and me after the Ballahooly, Williyumm, had killed him in a fight.

I waited until our hunters had finished eating near the evening fire before I asked them, "Do you men want long guns? Good guns that make a lot of noise and will frighten any enemy away?"

"Uunuuh!" they answered strongly. "We want very noisy guns."

Of course, I knew our men did not need guns for hunting – their noise scared animals away. If they lived as the Big Woman desired, our people would respectfully take all the fish, birds, and animals they needed with their own spears and arrows, hooks, snares, and deadfalls.

"Yes," my brother said, "we need the muskets. How can we get them?"

"I'll tell you how," I said. "That Ballahooly, Williyumm, is waiting for us four days south of here. There are only ten Cree and one boy with him. They are all half-starved and weak from walking, and the Cree are nervous of being here in our country. They are nearly crazy, thinking only of going home."

240

"They will have to be fast snowshoe runners to get away from us," said Dingee's husband. "I want to put a spear through more than one of them."

"Don't be too greedy," said my brother. "Do all of them have guns?"

"Yes, every one of them," I said. "But they are only ten."

"Then we shall gather maybe twenty or more hunters," said my brother. "We will move up on them quietly, in the darkness, spear them, then take the guns."

"No, you won't!" I said. "I promised the Ballahooly that I would bring you to them only peacefully, to talk of trade together and smoke a pipe in friendship. I don't want any more killing." Still I did not tell them of the murdered Dene hunters.

"What do we care what you want?" the old chief's wife called out. "The Wood Cats have been killing us and stealing our young women since long before your great-grandmother was born. I want to see our men come back here with bloody spears and all ten of those thunder guns."

"Be quiet, old woman," her husband warned. "We have wise hunters here to decide what shall be done."

"Good," said I. "Remember, the Ballahooly winged canoe will return this summer, packed full of long guns, tobacco, knives, and axes, beads, blankets – everything that you desire. You can have these for a few baskets of yellow pebbles, beaver, otter, pelts, and marten. You need noisy guns to scare away raiders."

I paused and sipped a bowl of broth because my voice was raw from arguing with my stubborn kinsmen, especially my new sister-in-law, who could not imagine anything she had not seen.

"I will go to trade for guns, iron knives, and fish hooks with them," my brother finally said, and most men nodded.

"Many will go with you," Dingee's husband added, for I had told him through my brother how his dear wife and child had died.

Soon every Dene hunter was speaking up: "I will go to have a gun" . . . "We will gather other hunters from the fish lakes" . . . "They will want the long guns, too."

"Not too many men," I warned my brother. "We will leave early in the morning, and we will be traveling far."

"So, has it come to this?" Sidhaw, my sister-in-law, demanded. "An unmarried slave girl who runs with the Cree and Ballahooly now tells our hunters what do do?" Her own mother agreed with her.

"I am a slave no longer," I rasped. "I broke loose. I am a free Dene woman!"

The head man thumped the fire log and growled, "Be silent, all you women. Our men will go after them in the morning. Every one should carry his own dried meat, shields, bows, arrows, extra spears."

I did not sleep at all that night, but spent it in my brother's tent mending my torn clothing and making moccasins for myself. His wife was so angry that she would scarcely speak to me and neither would her widowed mother. When I asked for sinew thread, those two just turned their heads. Sidhaw said, "You are taking my

cooking basket

husband and all our best young men away . . . You don't care if they get killed."

Her words wounded and inflamed me. I spent the last part of the night in a rage, pounding dry meat into pemmican. As dawn was breaking, I lay back utterly weary and fell asleep.

I was awakened by my brother, who came rushing in and out of the tent, searching for extra moccasins and mittens. I fished in the stew basket for some boiled meat and ate it. Then I went

242

outside and bound on my snowshoes. The wind was down and the sky was dawning clear. I did not even say good-bye to my new sister-in-law or her mother.

When we reached the fish-lake camp, my brother talked to the hunters there, while their wives took their anger out on me. When my brother, Keewatan, told them of the long guns, we were joined by sixteen Dene. They all looked strong and well fed and carried heavy fighting shields and spears.

I counted on my fingers. "We now have twenty-four men," I told Dingee's husband. "When those Cree see you carrying shields, they are going to be afraid and will fire their long guns at you."

"Hear her!" shrieked a hunter's wife from the tent where she stood listening. "Is she trying to get all of you massacred?"

"Let us go!" I whispered to my brother. "These women make me crazy."

I stood humbly aside and waited until all twenty-four of our Dene hunters passed before I joined at the end of their well-beaten snow trail. I drew up my hood, trying to cover my ears from the bad things that their women were screaming at me. A few of the children ran behind, flinging frozen dog turds at me.

I didn't care. My brother and our strongest hunters were moving on the river now toward my Williyumm. Together we would lead them to Bearman, who sat waiting for us in his house of spears. I would do everything I could to prevent a fight and find a way to have these Dene hunters smoke a pipe of peace with Williyumm and the Cree so we could travel eastward to trade at the house of spears.

My hopes kept me hurrying after our strong shoeing men all that day and the next. When we made camp on the third evening, I went forward to help my brother arrange his tent. "Tomorrow," I begged him, "don't let these men smear fighting paint upon their faces."

He looked at me fiercely and then laughed.

Next morning when I woke, my brother was already up and spreading war paint on his face and so was Dingee's husband. I

243

pleaded with them to wipe it off, for I knew it meant that they were bent on killing and that all my plans were going awry.

They snorted at me, saying, "Do you really think that we would miss this chance to bloody these invaders who dare to come and steal our women?"

Fearful though I was that these Dene men were eager to attack, I was just as worried that the Cree might have devised a deadly ambush, counting on the awful power of their long guns. I warned my brother and the others that exactly such might happen.

The day turned warm and foggy, and it passed miserably for me, slogging dead tired after that long line of men. That evening, it turned killing cold, and yet our hunters built no fires in camp, for I had told them that we were now close to the Cree. I, like the others, sniffed the air, believing we could smell their wood smoke. My heart trembled as we stood together, peering south.

We blew out our breaths, when suddenly we heard a heavy musket boom. Its sound came echoing like thunder along the frozen river. My brother raised his hand for silence. We all stood motionless, listening in the gathering gloom.

WILLIAM

17

I surely thought my time had come. There in the shadows just beyond the entrance to their little fort stood Kaswah. He leered crazily at me as he cocked my scatter gun and pointed it directly at my head.

I ducked low and lunged at him before he had the chance to fire, knocking the wind out of him with my head, slamming him back against the upright logs. I snatched the heavy gun as he drew his bayonet and sprang to me. I had no choice except to shoot him, which I did. As he slumped forward, the noise went booming along the river.

Nishcock and Ta'Sam came rushing out, then stopped. Looking down, they said, "You killed him?"

I stood saying nothing, fearful of the pair of them.

"The thunder from that gun," said Ta'Sam, "will tell every Copper in this country exactly where we are."

"Come, Mistaar Staarit," Nishcock smiled at me, "we are not your enemies. Only that fool, Kaswah, was a thief. You did right to lay him down. Come inside and talk with us before our real enemies arrive."

I looked at Jako and he shrugged. What else could we do?

I bent down, following the two of them, squeezing through the narrow entrance to their fort. It was hot and dank inside and it took my eyes a while to grow accustomed to the smoke. These last carriers of ours had their muskets, spears, and painted shields spaced evenly around the walls beneath the weapon slits they had made between the stakes.

"This is a damn good fort that you have built."

"Your words give us pleasure," Nishcock answered.

The Cree looked proudly at each other. I was surprised that they seemed to mind so little my shooting Kaswah.

"My brother-in-law turned into a crazy man, a robber," Nishcock exclaimed. "We had talked of killing him not long before you did it.

"You and the boy, take all the broth and meat you want," said Nishcock, pointing at the cooking basket. "Maybe we will all be busy killing, or being killed, before we have another meal."

Jako squatted close by my side. I raised the bowl to my mouth and drank off half the savory broth, then gave the rest to him. After drinking, he fished inside the steaming basket for two meaty caribou shoulders, which we found delicious.

Jako went and got our bedrolls. We had to squeeze together with the Cree in the crowded enclosure, but I didn't care. I felt completely drained in body and spirit. It wasn't every day that I killed a man. In spite of that, I sank into an uneasy sleep.

At dawn, I awakened but remained dead still, watching the beams of bright spring sunlight probing like fingers between the crudely sharpened logs. I must have slept again and dreamed, for suddenly I sat up in high excitement, knowing that I had heard Thana calling, "Williyumm! Williyumm!"

I knew the sound was real when I saw the nine remaining Cree scrambling wildly to their feet. Nishcock held up his hand for silence, and we listened. We all heard Thana's voice again, calling first in Cree and then in English, "Williyumm, are you in there?"

Every Cree inside the fort leapt to his position and peered out through the narrow weapon slits.

"We two will go out and speak to her," I told Nishcock.

At first, he did not answer me. Then, finally, he said, "Yes, go out, Mistaar Staarit, but leave the boy inside with us, and you speak only in our Cree language. Do not ask her to come near, unless I tell you."

"You wait in here," I said to Jako sadly.

I stepped outside the little fort and looked around me. A light blanket of snow covered Kaswah's back. My eyes squinted in the glaring whiteness. Cupping my hands around my mouth, I shouted, "Thana! Thanadelthur! Halooo! Halooo!"

As if by magic, she appeared between the trees, no more than a stone's throw from me. "Have all the carriers gone?" she called to me in the Dene language.

"No, ten of them are still here. No, sorry, only nine of them," I answered in Cree. "They have the gunpowder now and my musket, sword, and pistol. Jako is inside with them. They are all listening, and want you to speak only in Cree."

Nishcock and his cousin, Raven, and Ta'Sam, who were always the most fearless among these Cree, came out then, faces painted, carrying their muskets and holding their thick war shields against their chests. They stood on either side of me.

I saw Thana sit, then lay down upon the snow traditionally. She started calling out her woes to me in Northern Cree.

"I was delayed by storms and clogging snows," she called, "and weak from hunger. I am so glad that you all had the courage to remain here." She lay motionless, waiting for some answer from the Cree.

Nishcock did not bother to return Thana's formal greeting. Instead, he stood his spears upright in the snow, and holding his shield across his chest and his musket high, he took several paces forward.

"Copper woman, we are surprised to see that you have returned on the very day that we are leaving." He turned and smirked at me, then said, "A pity you couldn't find your people."

Thana rose to her knees and called back, "Oh, I was grateful to find my brother alive. His name is Keewatan."

"Where is he?" Nishcock shouted.

"He is here with me," said Thana.

To our amazement, a powerful-looking young man rose from a snowbank. He had lain concealed, much closer to us than Thana. I was relieved to see that although his face was painted, he held nothing in his hands.

247

It was the first time I had ever seen a Dene hunter. He was handsome and broad-shouldered and towered over Thana. His hair was styled in a curious way. The lower half of his face and throat were dyed ocher red. We could see his fighting shield slung across his back. Now he, too, lay down upon the snow, calling welcoming words which Nishcock and the other Cree could not understand.

Nishcock ordered only Ta'Sam to stand his musket in the snow and to go with him so that those two would meet two.

"Do not fear. Come forward," Nishcock called to them.

Thana and her brother rose and snowshoed cautiously toward the little fort, knowing that the eyes behind hidden muskets watched them.

When there were scarcely eight paces between Nishcock and Ta'Sam and Thana and her brother, all four halted and squatted down, their mitts against the snow.

"You two are not alone?" I heard Nishcock ask.

"You are right," said Thana. "We two are not alone."

She called out, and to Nishcock's right a dozen Dene warriors with shields, spears, and painted faces rose along the riverbank.

A belch of yellow smoke, then a musket boomed through the wall of the small fort. The nearest Dene on the riverbank fell, blood spurting from beneath his jaw.

Nishcock, Raven, and Ta'Sam turned and ran almost into the arms of another seven Dene who stood up among the rocks to the left of them. Then still more appeared from inside the grove of tamaracks, each man armed with bow, shield, and a clutch of spears with sharpened antler points.

Nishcock realized his great mistake, allowing himself within spear range of this multitude of Copper warriors. Raven and Ta'Sam jump-turned on their snowshoes and lunged toward the safety of their fort. I saw Ta'Sam take one spear, then another lodged between his shoulder blades, and he dropped. Raven narrowly escaped three spears flung at him.

Being suddenly confronted by this band of ferocious-looking warriors quite undid my nerves and set me trembling. Had Thana lost control, I wondered, or had she no choice but to allow her

248

people to avenge themselves against the Cree? Was I about to see a massacre?

"Captain Nishcock," Thana shouted in his language. "Don't be afraid. We are even in this killing. These relatives of mine will now hold back their spears. They will come not one step closer, unless I tell them to." She called back in the Dene language to their hunters, "Crouch down, stay out of sight. Remember, they have guns."

"What did she say to them?" Nishcock gasped as he rushed past me into the protection of the fort.

"She warned them to stay hidden. She reminded them that you have long guns pointing at them from inside this fort."

"I would gladly shoot one for you," Raven grunted. "Look at my poor cousin, Ta'Sam, lying out there murdered, with two of their spears standing in his back."

"Do nothing now," Nishcock commanded. "But be ready if they do attack. I will never trust that Copper bitch. Especially when she has that horde of Copper warriors standing behind her."

Thana held up her hands and cried, "You, Cree, listen to me! Blood has been spilled on both sides. I have not brought my people here to fight, but to smoke a pipe of peace with all of you.

"Nishcock," she called, "my brother has brought you all a gift of meat. Let all of us, and all of you, lay aside our weapons. Let us sit down as friends and smoke and talk and feast together."

"We have no choice," Nishcock whispered. "That many men could easily overpower us when it grows dark."

Nishcock stepped outside the fort with me again. He held up eight fingers. "Only eight Copper men can come forward," he said. "Perhaps then we will smoke with them and share meat, here, before this fort."

Thana translated those words to her brother. He turned and gave a birdlike whistle, then called three words. Seven Copper hunters stood their spears upright in the snow and, joining Keewatan, came toward the fort, their snowshoes kicking up silver showers in the brilliant sunshine.

Thana's brother broke the trail as their men drew close to us. Like Nishcock, they each still held their wooden shields before their chests. I held out my hands in the native fashion to show I bore no weapons. The other Cree came out with their shields. They set aside their long guns and lined up beside the fort. Eight of them: Raven, Rumpbone, Wapuss, Agawan, then the others, and finally Jako. The two war parties stood as stiff as dogs about to fight.

"At last we have come together," Thana called to Nishcock and to me in Cree. "Now we can smoke a pipe at this peaceful meeting place."

I rolled my eyes when she said that, for there between us lay those two dead men.

The eight Dene and our eight Cree and Jako and I stood staring at each other with mistrust, for each side had shown violence to the other. Thana trotted quickly in a large circle, packing the surface flat with her snowshoes, smiling and nodding at both the Dene and the Cree. I tried to help her, as did her brother, Keewatan. Nishcock's men soon joined us, as did the other seven Dene hunters. What a sight it was to see arch enemies performing a peaceful snowshoe dance together. It was not long before we had a large round space trampled flat, just large enough for about eighteen humans to squat down in a circle. Every man removed his snowshoes and stood them upright just behind him. I could see the fear and anger seeping out of everyone. As a further sign of trust, each man placed his shield upright in the snow beside his snowshoes.

At Nishcock's order, Raven went inside the fort and brought out a burning stick to light the pipe. It was then passed round the circle. Each man took one deep puff of our tobacco and held it in his lungs until his head reeled and he almost fainted. I could see every Dene hunter eyeing the long Company muskets of the Cree, and our carriers glancing over their shoulders nervously at the other Dene hunters who now squatted some way off, watching us from a little forest of their upright spears.

Thana squatted humbly in silence behind us, for in both the Cree and Dene minds, silence in public becomes a woman. I knew, as did they all, that Thana was only pretending to be modest. In truth, she was master of this dangerous meeting between two bitter enemies. When I looked at her, she rolled her eyes and gave me a welcome smile.

Even after the smoking of the pipe and sharing of the meat, a cold reserve separated the Dene and the Cree. The formal meeting had gone on too long and everyone squatting on the packed snow was growing stiff. Thana gave me a look to signal me to speak.

I nodded at Nishcock, then faced Thana's brother. "We have walked for seven moons," I began in Cree, then quickly translated that to Dene. "We have suffered storms and cold and hunger, because we wished to come and speak with you. Our head man demanded that these Northern Cree accompany me and return your young woman, Thanadelthur, who was stolen by the Wood Cats. Our head man told us we should try to make a lasting peace with you, so you might come and trade with him."

Nishcock gave me a dirty look, but he once more filled the pipe and lit it, then passed it around again. For the Dene, tobacco was the rarest kind of treat, not to be wastefully blown away. I was the only one who offered to pass the pipe to Thana. She properly refused.

Nishcock said to Thana's brother, "We promise not to raise our muskets against you if you, the Dene seated here with us, and those others squatting near the riverbank, will give us your word that you will not turn your weapons against us."

I leaned forward and translated Nishcock's words, then interpreted the answer from Thana's brother, saying, "Yes, we Dene men agree. None of our hunters will come against you unless you Cree begin the trouble."

Keewatan beckoned all the Dene to come close, so they could hear him repeat those words in their own language.

I resumed: "Our head man told me to ask some of you Copper men to return to the house of spears with us, to receive muskets that thunder and other gifts." Translating this into Cree, I then asked Nishcock, "Is that not so?"

"Yes," he said, making a sour face.

"How many Copper men do you wish me to take with you?" asked Keewatan.

Although he could not understand Keewatan's words, Nishcock anticipated the question. "Only as many Dene as we Cree may come," he said. "Only you who have smoked the pipe with us."

"Are there more of you here whom we do not see?" asked Thana's brother.

"No, there are only eleven," said Nishcock, using me and Jako to swell their numbers. "Oh, one dead, that makes us . . . ten, with me, that boy, and Mistaar Staarit."

Keewatan smiled at his sister. "Then only nine Dene hunters will go with me," he said.

"And also I," Thana called out, smiling warmly. "I look forward to a friendly journey toward the morning sun, all of us traveling together."

Nishcock scowled at that, but being so close to all the Dene, he dared not say a word against her.

I gave Thana's brother the tight-sewn packet and the box containing all the good but light trinkets that we had carried here, as gifts for the Dene. In the packet and box were dozens of large and small fish hooks, shiny thimbles, beads, thin brass wire for snares, good-sized tuppenny nails that could be pounded into arrowheads or sharpened into knife blades, along with some brightly colored trade cloth with which men could bind their hair or give to favored females.

"These are only small, light gifts," I told the Dene, "for we had to carry them a long way. You men who are coming with us should give them away to others. Our chief will give you much larger and finer gifts when we reach the house of spears."

Keewatan thanked me and said, "We shall take these to our families and tell them that ten of us will run toward the rising sun with you and will return to them when winter traveling is good again."

"Oh, wait!" I called to Keewatan as he was leaving. "Where is that river with the yellow pebbles? We need to know that very surely."

"You mean yellow pebbles like the ones that separate my father's eagle claws?" He pointed to his necklace.

I nodded.

"These little things are nothing," he replied. "Our children gather them in summer, and it is not yet summer. Mistaar Staarit, when did you last see an open lake or river?"

"Five moons ago," I told him, "maybe six."

"You will not see open water in our country for one or two more moons." He paused, then asked me, "Do you wish to wait?"

"No!" I said emphatically as I watched the unhappy Cree returning from the task of suspending the bodies of Kaswah and Ta'Sam in trees, then preparing to pack and leave.

"That river of yellow pebbles is just like all the other little rivers here. It has good fish in it to catch and eat, and plenty of water to drink," said Keewatan. "I will bring you back any of those yellow pebbles that I find around our camp.

"I must go back with our other hunters now," he went on. "We must distribute your gifts and lie with our wives as many times as we would have done if we had stayed with them for the twelve coming moons. That's a lot!" He gasped at the thought, then smiling broadly, he turned and hurried away after the retreating line of Dene hunters.

"Tell them also," Thana called after her brother, "that the Ballahooly wish to trade many fine things for furs with all of them, twelve moons from now, at the mouth of the Pocothacoaoaw River."

When Keewatan departed from us, he led almost thirty men away. I groaned and said to Thana, "I wonder if we shall see any of them again."

She got mad at me for saying that.

Thana's brother had left us one long toboggan. The Dene men also had left us four half-toboggan-sized packages of dried and pounded caribou, for our journey.

Thana, Jako, and I sat with the Cree inside the fort that night, watching the broth simmering in two birch-rind baskets crammed with delicious meat. We groaned with pleasure as we ate. The very act of sharing food seemed to draw us close together.

"I wish to start our journey in the morning," Nishcock said.

"That is well with us," said Thana. "I shall leave a well-marked trail for my brother to follow."

After a sound night's sleep inside the fort, Thana and Jako and I rolled our tent and sleeping robes as all of us prepared to leave. I took my journal from my bag and tried to calculate the proper date. I judged it to be almost midday on the 11th of March, 1716, when we began our journey eastward.

As I passed, I could see Ta'Sam and Kaswah frozen in their blankets, tied into sturdy trees. The snow had hardened into a crust, covered with light new snow, perfect for fast shoeing. Nishcock was breaking trail. I followed, with Thana and Jako just behind me.

"Don't you worry, Williyumm," Thana laughed. "My brother and his men will soon catch up to us."

Six days passed, then seven, and still we did not see them, though there had been no bad weather, nothing to hide our snowshoe trail. On the eighth evening, I raised our tent flap and saw Thana standing in the star-filled dark alone.

"Where are they?" she asked me. "They should have come up to us days ago."

"I heard Raven say that they took all the gifts, but they will not come."

"That's a lie," said Thana. "But if they do not come, it will be because of that awful wife of his."

That night, Thana was so upset she could not even lie close to me. In the morning, I heard her go out early, then come rushing back inside our tent.

"They're all out there. My brother and seven others," she gasped with a look of joy. "They're just squatting, resting in the early morning sun and chewing spruce gum. I've talked to Keewatan. He says he gave your presents from the Company mostly to the women and they liked them. But even so, it took him three nights more to get his men away from their young wives."

I laughed when I heard that.

"Don't laugh," she said, and pushed me. "Think how we would hate to be left without each other for twelve whole moons."

Jako started laughing when she said that, and I did, too. Keewatan and his seven men each had large light packs of fur to trade when we arrived at York.

We did not march together in one long single file, as was the custom. Instead, we went side by side some distance from each other, Cree in one line, Dene in the other. I, like Jako, stayed mostly with Nishcock and the Cree to show that we were still friends. Thana usually followed behind the line of Dene men. Our men and theirs had wiped their war paint off but still carried their wooden shields across their backs, and both lines held their weapons in their hands, proving that in spite of all the smoking of the pipe and promises, we did not trust each other.

The most troublesome part for me was that the Cree and these new Dene competed endlessly, determined to outrun each other. I estimate that we made twenty miles and more some days. That left me puffing with exhaustion, and my legs ached. I was amazed at Thana and at Jako. They didn't seem to mind the pace at all.

I noted each day's events and every river that we crossed on our journey eastward in my journal. We suffered one last violent storm, which perhaps caused the Dene and the Cree to throw away their heavy shields. One bitter night when some went through the river ice, we all helped each other. That was the first sign of the good will that was slowly spreading among us. First, we learned each other's names; Thana made sure of that. She tried in every way to make the Dene and the Cree forget their ancient hatreds.

Thana and I were again relaxed and pleased with life, the way we had been in our early days before the starving times on the trail, and the killings. One night, in English, she asked me, "Is that a way to lie with women that you learned in Scootlan'?"

"I never lay with girls in Scootlan'. None before I lay with you," I whispered.

"I wish I could say the same," she sighed. "I should have been wearing my veil when I met you."

Thana reached up and tucked a damp strand of my hair behind my ear. Then she trailed her fingers like a feather down the inside of my thigh. "My grandmother and Dingee told me lots of ways to do things," she purred. "I'm only going to show you how to do them . . . one by one."

I lay clasping that wild girl weakly in my arms, sure that our small tent was the best place in the whole world to be. I had not made my entries in the journal, but I didn't care. I heard an owl hoot somewhere just across the river. I waited to hear an answer, but if one came, I missed it, for I was already entering that place of dreams.

Finally, the blustery month of March gave up and the slender, turned-up horns of the April moon appeared. Now we saw endless herds of caribou moving north. No longer did we carry meat with us, but simply took what we needed day by day. Strange to say, we had no use for the cask of gunpowder that had caused so much trouble. I would watch with wonder the subtle skills of the Cree and Dene hunters as they moved silently upon a herd with bows and spears. Their genius was to deceive the caribou into some place of no escape, by driving them through a narrow defile or herding them to a river crossing and spearing them. There was no need to fire a musket shot. Because when there was no foreign noise, the caribou herds remained calm and unafraid.

"It seems a shame," I wrote in my daily journal, "to trade these northerners our lethal muskets which will encourage hunters to forget their ancient hunting skills. Once the Dene possess guns," I wrote, "they will be forever fettered to us, forced to become trappers of fur, to trade for powder, flints, and ball. These splendid-looking Cree and Copper hunters whom I now lead toward the fort know nothing of the taste of cheap English brandy or Brazilian plug tobacco. But in no time at all, they will learn to crave them."

I tried to express my deep concerns to Thana, but she said, "My people are very strong. The Ballahooly will not be able to change them."

On the 27th of May, we beheld great rafts of snow geese flocking overhead on their way north. Thana called out, "Williyumm, show our hunters how you shoot geese in the air."

When the big birds were thick above my head, I cocked the scatter gun.

Thana called out to the Dene, "Look up! Look up! See Williyumm's trick!"

I aimed just ahead of a crowded flight about to land and fired. All eight Dene hunters jumped when they heard the heavy discharge, then stared in disbelief as five of the big birds came tumbling out of the sky.

From the first moment when he heard one fired, Thana's brother, like men everywhere, was overwhelmed by the power of a firearm.

"Oh, I would give anything to have a thunder stick like that," said Keewatan, his face beaming with amazement and delight as Jako and Thana came toward us carrying the five fallen geese.

I handed him the scatter gun and said, "It is yours, Keewatan. I give it to you now. But you have to carry it. When we next rest, I'll show you how to load it, aim it, fire it."

Nishcock was very angry with me for giving Keewatan that splendid blunderbuss, and his cousin, Raven, cursed me for a fool. "We never wanted them to have guns. We do not trust those northerners with guns."

"Why not?" I asked him. "Every one of you have guns. Would you say the Coppers must forever hunt with spears and arrows?"

"Why not?" Nishcock demanded. "Even you can see that they are clever in that way. None of them need guns for hunting animals."

"Nor do you Cree."

"Those Coppers only want guns for fighting," he answered hotly. "If they have guns, they will have no fear of us."

On the rest day, which may or may not have been the Sabbath – I had long ago lost count – I showed Keewatan how to load and aim and fire the scatter gun. He was delighted, as were all the other Dene who crowded round to watch us. Thana's brother took my hands and declared to all that I, Mistaar Staarit, was now his hunting companion, which Thana said made me his closest friend. I was more than pleased with such an honor.

On that same evening, Keewatan came to our tent and sat between me and his sister. "I have a gift for you," he said. "It is not at all as good as the magic goose-downer that you gave me, but it is the best thing I possess." He reached into his caribou shirt and withdrew a quill-decorated scabbard and knife, which he had suspended around his neck. "Take this," he said, "it's yours."

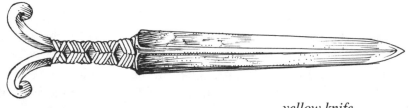

yellow knife

The scabbard was unremarkable, but the dagger's color took my breath away.

"I made it," Keewatan told me. "It is not at all as sharp as your iron knives, but it is useful."

The yellow knife was long and beautifully proportioned, with a raised rib running down its blade. Its hilt was bound with leather, and the pommel was elegantly split and curled back upon itself in two shell-like curves.

From my sporan, I drew my small knife and made a thin scratch on the blade of Keewatan's gift.

"Be careful, don't hurt it," Thana told me. "Knives like that have feelings. My brother could have told you that it is made from one of the largest of those yellow pebbles, the same as my small flenser."

I scarcely listened to Thana as I weighed in my hands the heavy knife, which I knew to be fashioned of solid gold.

"Do you like it?" Thana's brother asked.

"Oh, yes," I said. "It's beautiful. The finest thing I ever owned."

"Good," said Keewatan. "I give it to you gladly."

"Bearman will be pleased to see that yellow knife," Thana said.

"Perhaps I shall not show this knife to Bearman," I warned Thana. "And don't show him your flenser."

"Why?"

"I have something else in mind," I told her. Then I asked Keewatan if any of his companions had brought knives or other objects, such as arrowheads, made from yellow pebbles.

"Probably," he answered. "I will ask them."

I am sorry to say that Keewatan's inquiries of the other Dene turned up only a few more pieces of gold; the largest was another knife like his but smaller, and there was a tiny scratcher. Cawther, the thin man, had eleven good-sized golden beads in a necklace that he wore underneath his shirt to bring him luck. The fourth find was five hammered yellow arrowheads. The owners happily exchanged their gold possessions for three clay pipes and twists of coarse Dutch tobacco.

That night when Thana was asleep, I slipped the flenser and scratcher from her hip string, took the heavy knife Keewatan had given me, Agawan's smaller knife, the necklace, and three gold nuggets, and hefted them thoughtfully. I judged their combined weight to be well above three pounds. That amount of gold in Scotland would support a man in kingly style for years.

Thana made a new sheath for my golden knife, decorating it handsomely with many trade beads and long hollow dentalia shells. She said they had been traded by the Dene from the Tlingit people, distant relatives who lived on the ocean where the sun sets, beyond some mountains far away. The new sheath was a wonder and had a long, beaded leather strap by which to wear it hidden beneath my shirt or across my shoulder so, as she said, "All could see it and beware."

As I lay back thinking about that little river with the yellow pebbles that Keewatan had described, I began to imagine a map that I would draw. Despite the loss of my navigating instruments, I was reasonably sure that I could make one, showing the route from Fort York to the Dene country and the gold-filled stream, from my notes and Thana's keen memory, indicating all of the wide plains, lakes, and rivers that we had crossed and – always – where the Wolf Star was. I considered how I might pay my small indenture to the Company, then set out with my remaining portion of gold, as well as my map, for London. There I would sell the map and trade my gold, then take a fine house in Edinburgh. I would have tailored the finest Highland dress and, in full regalia, set off with spirited horses and a liveried groom to ride grandly through the Stewart lands by Loch Linnhe. If need be, I would bribe the laird of Stalker's Keep to reinstate me to my clan.

My head was spinning with such notions that I scarcely slept that night. I looked up at the smoke hole in our shabby tent and asked myself, are you, William Stewart, a cartographer possessing pounds of gold and knowledge of how to gain much more, going to continue forever lying on this hairy bed with nothing but coarse trade blankets and raw animal skins to cover your own hide? I turned my head and stared at Thana's sleeping face. She opened her eyes and looked at me in a sad way that made me feel certain that she somehow understood my thoughts.

By noon the next day, the weather warmed and the snow clogged our snowshoe webbings miserably. The ptarmigan were turning brown again and calling for their mates. The males groaned, "Coom heere, coom heere!" And the females answered, "Get- a-bible, get-a-bible," the same song ptarmigan sing each spring on our northern Highlands. Anyone could tell that warmer weather was about to spread its wings across the land.

Thana walked at the end of the Dene column sometimes, or up with me, Jako, and the Cree. She implored me not to tell her brother or the Dene any details of Fort York. She wanted everything about that place to remain a great surprise to them.

One clear, windless night when Thana came into our bed, she said, "Williyumm, I was afraid at first that there would be some kind of fight between my people and these Cree. But now I believe that they could learn to live in peace together."

"I believe that, too," I said. Then I remembered the awful troubles between the Scots, the English, and the Irish and, my God, the French! I told Thana, "It's much more difficult to stay friendly with other clans and people from other countries when they have grown more civilized.''

"I don't understand that word *ceeveeliz*."

"Perhaps you never should," I said.

For five days the snow melted as the sun shone, and we had to leave the rivers and travel on the higher ridges. Then, just as Nishcock and Keewatan had predicted, one last miserable blizzard struck us – on the 22nd of April, A.D. 1716, as I noted in my journal. It pinned us down and our tents bellied-in beneath several feet of soggy snow. We did not try to travel but slept and relaxed, eating quantities of goose meat and drinking gallons of rich yellow broth. When the storm passed, we used our snowshoes like shovels to dig our way out of the tents. Then, after two more warm days with wind and sun, the snow began to disappear.

Unlike the Scottish Highlands or the English Lowlands, this vast northern country does not have a proper autumn or spring. One day all is caught in the grip of winter, then, almost on the next day, the snow fades and the first star flowers appear, sometimes forcing their way up through the last snow. Small teeterarse birds arrive in skimming flocks, the ice melts from the shallow ponds, the mosquitoes rise in stinging hordes, and instantly it's summer.

To celebrate this astonishing change of season, the Dene and the Cree chose a shadowed north side of a valley still possessing snow. There they prepared for a celebration. They made camp early, lit more fires than usual, and heated their tambourine-style drums. When the frames were struck, they gave off exciting booming sounds and rhythms. Nishcock and Raven both performed a wonderful last snowshoe dance and the Copper men called out in admiration. Then Keewatan danced and sang. The men waved their horn-tipped spears and shot imaginary arrows into the air as they stamped round and round in an ever-narrowing ring, packing down the last snow and singing in two languages, far off-key. The sound reminded me of a lament badly played by our Fort York piper. But it also made me long to see Loch Linnhe and flocks of sheep grazing on the heathery hills of home. Around

261

the fires, the Dene and Cree dipped their hands into each other's cooking baskets as they celebrated this exciting change of season.

During the next three days of traveling, our whole world changed. The air grew mild, and the sun glared blindingly off the last snowbanks until everything looked red to us inside the tent. Now our hunters' snowshoes clattered on bare stony ridges. When we crossed a high esker, we saw the country beyond stretching gray-green before us, speckled with stone. Here and there, a few patches of snow clung to the north sides of hills.

"Throw them away! Throw them away!" shouted Nishcock and Keewatan, and we all unlashed our snowshoes and began to fling them into one great pile.

"That's a wasteful thing to do," I said to Thana.

"Why?" asked Thana. "We can easily make new ones. You'll not need them for the next five moons." She flung hers after all the others. She and Jako clapped their hands when I threw mine.

Without snowshoes, it felt strange to walk beside Nishcock and Keewatan, as we three now found ourselves competing as leaders on this quickening journey south and east to Hudson Bay. What Thana said was true. I had become a much stronger walker. Most mornings early, our eight Cree could be heard moving off, urging one another to go faster, so eager were they to see their young wives and families. They tried to gain distance on the Dene by using that powerful toed-in stride of theirs, which they could keep up until long after sunset. The Dene would often break into a trot to catch up with them, for they were much too proud to fall behind. All our packs were bulky with tents and bedding, but with little weight.

A few days later we forded a wide, shallow lake and continued along a curving gravel ridge. Before us a square unnatural shape came into view. It was set up atop four stones.

"What is that?" Keewatan called to me.

"You'll see," I shouted, with anger rising up in me.

When we came up to that strange object, Nishcock turned and glanced at me. Kneeling, I pulled away the weathered wooden sides and rusted strappings of my broken trunks. I withdrew the sextant that the big man had smashed against the rocks – its once bright brass fittings, like my ruined compass, had turned green.

"What are these?" Keewatan asked me, picking up two broken shards of glass.

Thana, who stood beside me, answered, "Those are part of a Ballahooly way of finding how to go from one place to another." She touched my shoulder. "I'm sorry they were broken, Williyumm. Still, we did go out and find my people and returned exactly to this box, traveling only by the Wolf Star."

"That is true," I told her, "but how far did we go exactly, and just where is that river with the yellow pebbles? That is what the governor wants to know."

"Together we will tell the guvnaar," Thana said with utter confidence. "We went into my mother's and my father's country, counting the rivers and lakes. We've brought Bearman back my brother and these others. What more could he wish from us?"

"I am sorry, yet also glad, to see that broken box again," Nishcock told me. "It means our lodges are . . . " He held up five fingers on one hand and folded in his thumb on the other. "Long ago, with so many, it took us nine days to reach this place. We will easily return in seven."

Nishcock was right. Not long after dawn of the 7th of May, A.D. 1716, we paused on a rocky elevation. Sharp-eyed young Jako let out a shout as he pointed eastward. Then all of us saw the loaflike mound of ground with the barrel perched high on it, the site that I had renamed Knight's Hill. In the distance, a line of silver clouds was moving, making dark blue shadows upon Hudson Bay. Inland from the mouth of the Hayes River I could see that familiar, toad-like fort. My heart leapt with joy, for at its center I could see the Company's blood-red flag floating southward on the breeze.

Seeing Fort York now, after nine months of hardship, deaths, and endless wandering, I could not keep myself from singing as my callused feet did a Highland sword dance on that stony place.

I flung my tattered fox hat into the air. "We're home!" I called to Thana. "We are home at last!"

263

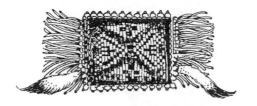

THANA

18

How can I express my feelings of excitement as we nineteen marched in one long line together toward the house of spears? I turned my eyes away when I saw a hundred home Cree running hard toward us. I heard the hoarse shouts of men, the screaming of women and children, and the barking of dogs as they all rushed from their lodges to greet the last of their returning men and stare in awe or disdain at me, Thana, my tall brother, Keewatan, and our other Dene hunters.

When I did turn my eyes back to the fort, that big blood-red skin was flying high, and the huge wooden jaws were slowly opening. Along the top of the stockade, I could recognize green-coated Captain Cheechoo and the ear-peeker, wee Angoos, and Mcnoooltee, who were Williyumm's closest friends, and Little Harry, and cracked-eye. But best of all, Owinipeg, screaming and waving, calling out my name. As we drew closer, they all began shouting down to us. Just inside the jaws, I saw Bearman dressed grandly in his high leather boots and best coat. It hung slack over the place where his vast belly once had been. Suddenly, that awful wailing started, and the man who squeezes the bag appeared. The Cree and, of course, the Dene clapped their hands across their ears, but I did not, for it was Williyumm's favorite sound, and I was trying to learn to like it.

When those crazy loonlike sounds were ended and we stood before the house of spears, Captain Cheechoo stepped forward with Bearman. He, too, looked lean and gaunt, with shadows underneath his cheekbones. He was wearing, as I hoped he would, his most beautiful coat, his lightning sash, and his three-cornered hat with feathers. I could hear my brother and the other Dene gasp with envy.

"When are they going to fire the cannons?" I whispered to Captain Cheechoo, speaking Cree.

"They cannot fire them," he whispered back to me. "We had to trade the last of our gunpowder for fur. The Company ship did not come into shore last year."

My Williyumm, who was busy shaking hands with the guvnaar, had heard this and asked, "What happened to the ship?"

"Come inside." The guvnaar tugged Williyumm's sleeve. "We'll talk about that later."

Williyumm followed him inside the gate and I, like all our Cree and Dene party, started to follow.

"Wait! Halt there!" the guvnaar bellowed, holding up his hand. He said to Captain Cheechoo, "Tell them only that one high Copper man," he pointed at Keewatan, "and the Copper woman, Thana-detour, can come inside. No others."

There was a grumbling sound from Nishcock and his seven men. They had been out walking for the Company for almost ten moons and now, when they returned in triumph, there was no welcome booming of the cannons, no brandy, no sugar tits, no tobacco, no gifts as had been promised, not even a bowl of oatmeal porridge, and they still had to remain outside.

As I interpreted Bearman's words, I felt worried about our Dene men. Somewhat angrily, I told Bearman that the Dene should be allowed, for safety's sake, to pitch their tents right beside the entrance to the fort, so the sentry on the wall could warn them of attack. Bearman agreed to that.

I took Jako's hand as we stepped away from our companions of the walk-across and disappeared inside the gate. My brother, Keewatan, declared loudly that he didn't want to be inside. He leapt around in fright when those awful wooden jaws came groaning closed behind him.

Owinipeg came running to me, her two beautiful hair braids bouncing off her shoulders. We touched fingertips and wept with each other.

Williyumm was surrounded by the whole crowd of Ballahooly, who were laughing and talking all at once. I was distressed by the gaunt thinness of their faces. Williyumm was so overjoyed to see them that he struck some on the shoulders, and they in turn pounded him on the back. I could see my brother eyeing this savage Scootlanish practice with alarm. Indeed, it did look like they were fighting, but I had seen it all before. It was just one more of the weird Ballahooly customs to show real friends they were glad to see them home again. The ear-peeker smiled at us and told Bearman that we looked a good deal plumper than anyone who had wintered in this fort.

Finally, Bearman ordered his working men and bonded boys back to work repairing the fort. He led Williyumm and Keewatan, Owinipeg and me into the dark and dingy eating lodge. It smelled stale and really bad in there, far worse than I had remembered. The one named Little Harry, who used to help the cook, now wore that big Ballahooly's white hat and leather apron. But even he looked starved to me. He brought us four bowls of thin fish soup, all sculpin heads and bones and tails it was, with the odd eye staring up at you. It had a thin, mean taste.

The guvnaar pointed down the table at Keewatan and then at me. He held up three fingers. Speaking swampy Cree, he said, "You, slave woman, tell your brother that . . ."

"You call me Thana," I told him in his language. "Don't call me 'slave woman.' I'm not an *uwacan*. You understand?"

Bearman looked surprised when he heard me speaking Ballahooly. He puckered up his lips and said, "Yes, well then . . . Tha-na is it? Yes, I understand. You tell your brother," he continued, "that in two . . . more likely three . . . moons our ship will come again. It will bring us all we want." He counted off the treasures that they wanted most. "Tobacco, brandy, long guns, knives, axes, needles, beads, enough to fill this hall! Enough for all you Copper hunters who come to trade!" He spread his arms toward the walls. "After the ship comes, you tell your brother, we are going to rebuild this fort. Then we will build another like it, but made of stone, farther north, so that you Copper people can paddle east along the Pocothacoacaw River to trade directly with us. Not with the Cree."

"Good," my brother answered when I told him. "We know the beginnings of that river very well."

Here in the feasting room, Keewatan mostly kept his eyes shaded with one hand, and held his nose with the other, telling me he hated the glare of the French iron torches and all the dreadful stinks around him. At first, my brother was as much against sitting at the Ballahooly table as I had been, believing it to be a dangerous deadfall. He tried squatting by the table, but it wasn't right. Finally, I urged him to relax and sit beside me, it was safe.

Keewatan sat up straight, looking along the table with great dignity. My brother was so tall and proud and handsome. Now that I had Williyumm and young Jako and my brother with me, I lost all my shyness and for the first time felt at home inside the house of spears. I didn't care about the smells.

We ate those pale-fleshed sculpin and dogfish that the Cree women had netted from the river, and some leathery goose flesh that had been in the salt brine casks for one whole year. I noticed that all the molasses, the oatmeal porridge, the China tea, sugar, and every drop of brandy had long since disappeared. Everything these Ballahooly had brought with them from across the world was gone, eaten up by them or traded for countless beaver pelts, lynx, marten, mink, ermine skins. These once proud Ballahooly were now poor beggars, alive only because of the fish and birds and animals the home Cree caught for them. Without the Cree, the Ballahooly might long since have become a pile of bones.

Until that first meal that we shared with them, we did not know how very poor they had become. Seeing their thin fish soup and leathery salt goose, Williyumm and my brother ordered in haunches of caribou that we had brought with us. When it was cooked, the Ballahooly gobbled the meat like hungry wolves.

After all the eaters had gone away, my brother cut open several of the fur packets our Dene had carried here, spilling out the beautiful pelts of marten, fisher, otter, and ermine. Bearman shook each skin with bright excitement in his eyes.

I was surprised to see Williyumm reach inside his shirt for the knife Keewatan had given him. Williyumm started to draw that dagger from its porcupine quill sheath.

Bearman saw it flash and must have guessed it was a yellow knife. He whispered, "You hide that away for now." He looked around suspiciously to see if the cracked-eye man or any other Ballahooly had seen the knife. Bearman then called Little Harry, saying, "You go out and bring back Cheechoo."

Becoming so skinny and being out of brandy seemed to make Bearman kind of crazy. When we began our walk-across, he had begged us to bring him yellow pebbles and anything my people made from them. Now, when Williyumm kindly tried to show him what he had brought, Bearman acted mad and wouldn't even look.

Oh, well, Owinipeg and I didn't care. We just sat close together, looking at each other and touching each other's hands. It seemed to me like a hundred moons since we had been together.

"You must have walked a lot of ground and crossed a lot of rivers," said Owinipeg. "But you look very good."

"We had lots of troubles going out, but it was easier coming back," I answered. "I've got a feeling of happiness inside me now!"

"I'm not surprised at that," she said, reaching under my long shirt, feeling my belly. "Not much there yet, but still I'm sure you're growing a baby."

"Oh, I'm fattening up now," I said. "You should have seen Jako and Williyumm and me and those poor Cree when we were starving. Almost dead. That was between the end of the horn-shedding moon and the coming of the old moon. We all looked very skinny then. But the animals, you know the way they are.

They must have heard our singing and felt sorry for us, so they provided us with a whole cache of their meat. That saved our lives."

"That's the way they've always been," said Owinipeg. "The buffalo have saved my people from starving many, many times."

"About the baby," I whispered to Owinipeg. "I am pretty sure I've got one coming to me."

When Little Harry returned with Captain Cheechoo, Bearman said, "Take Than-na's brother to the place where Mistaar Staarit used to sleep." Then Bearman told Williyumm that he could use Longlegs' room. "Mistaar Keelsee is away running around who knows where. You . . . " he said, pointing at me instead of giving me my name, "you can sleep with Owinipeg – but only for tonight. After that you and your brother will sleep just outside, with your own Copper people. I'm not having another woman besides that seamstress sleeping inside this fort while I suffer the spying eyes of that damned accoon-tant snooping around. He'll be sending letters back to Loondoon on this summer's ship, declaring that I am running the greatest whoor hoose on Hudson Bay."

Well, I didn't mind him calling me "you." It was better than his saying *uwacan*. I didn't understand the meaning of his words like snooooping or whooor hooose. Both words seemed to make Bearman very nervous, but Williyumm threw back his head and laughed out loud.

With my brother gone to find his sleeping place, Owinipeg took Jako and hurried away to make a bed for us. That left Bearman and Williyumm and me alone at the table in the eating lodge. Right away, the old guvnaar smiled, then said to Williyumm, "Now's the chance to show me that big knife."

He didn't even look at the beautiful porcupine-quill design that I had made to decorate Williyumm's sheath. He just hauled out that yellow knife and held it in his hands beneath the torch light, examining the shining blade. He took a tiny iron knife from his pocket, the one he used to pick his teeth, and I winced when he made a scratch along the blade. Bearman looked up at Williyumm, "It's *cold*!" he gasped with a wild look in his eyes. It wasn't cold at all. It was warm, hanging so close to Williyumm's body. But I didn't say a word. I just thought, yes, he has gone crazy, poor old Bear.

"Where did you get this?" the guvnaar asked.

Williyumm answered, saying, "Thana's brother gave it to me as a gift. He told me that he found one yellow pebble as big as a swan's egg lying in a river. He heated it and pounded it into a rough knife shape, then rubbed the blade against a stone until it was smooth. Then he polished it with spit and sand and ashes. Its hilt is bound with musk-ox leather."

"A cold stone as big as a swan's egg!" Bearman's eyes grew even rounder, and his stubby nose turned purple. "Did he see any other stones like that?"

"Oh, yes," said Williyumm. "Thana's brother says he knows of a river with lots of yellow pebbles, but most are smaller, not so big as the one that made this knife."

"Well," said Bearman, "I suppose we could make do, if the two of us had lots and lots of the smaller ones." He started breathing through his mouth as he felt the weight of my brother's gift to Williyumm. "You certainly found exactly what I sent you for." He leaned his head very close to Williyumm and to me. "Now, you two must help me further. The first thing is . . . do not say a single word to anyone about this yellow knife or the yellow pebbles lying in that river. Do you understand?" He whispered, "At least one of Loondoon's Company spies is within this fort. The other, Keelsee, will be back here before shiptime."

"I will not speak about the yellow knife or about the little river eggs," I promised. "But if the big canoe does come this summer, I hope you will give some good presents to my brother and the Dene with him, and to Nishcock and those Cree who stayed with us and did not kill us, even though they might have done so many times."

"Can I borrow this yellow knife?" Bearman asked Williyumm. "Just to keep it safe and out of sight?"

I could see Williyumm getting up his courage. When he had it, he said, "No, sir, not now."

"Why?"

"You say Thana cannot live inside this fort," replied Williyumm. "Well, where is she going to live? Not alone, out there, with so many womanless men."

"I don't know," said the guvnaar, looking worried. "One thing certain – she cannot live inside this fort with shiptime coming up."

"Well, for now," said Williyumm, "before I draw any map of that river for you, I will keep the knife, until I know where Thana sleeps."

Oh, my heart thumped with joy when I heard Williyumm say those bold words, for among my people it is bad luck to twice give away a knife, even if it has only a soft yellow blade that will not cut nearly so sharp as a Company knife. Bearman looked kind of mad at both of us as we two left. I went to sleep in Owinipeg's lean-to, while Williyumm took his bedding to Longlegs' room. It was not so hard to be apart for now as we were truly tired.

I found Williyumm in the eating lodge next morning, talking and laughing with his friends. McNoolty sent wee Fergoos for another plateful of the rich caribou meat that we travelers had brought with us. Beside it lay a bundle of English lime grass that the ear-peeker said we must eat, or have our teeth fall out.

Bearman came in and stared at the bonded boys and clerks. "Be off with you about your work, you lazy scuts!"

Williyumm told me the guvnaar was worried, for the first spring floods had almost brought down the walls of the house of spears.

As the clerks were hurrying out, the cracked-eye man came creeping ghostlike through the door. Oh, he was deadly thin.

"Hear this, Accoon-tant All-poop!" the guvnaar bellowed at him. "I am ordering Misstaar Staarit to go and make his quarters in the Frenchmen's hut up near the deer hedge. There is good light there, and he will be able to work well, copying his maps and rough observations from his travels, transferring them properly with ink and quill into my private Company journal. While there, he must not be visited by you! Do you get my meaning, Mistaar All-pooop? Do not disturb him. Stay away!"

271

"Yes, yes," answered that wretched man. "And what about this slave woman?"

"You call me Dene woman," I yelled at him in Ballahooly, for I, Thanadelthur, was tired of hearing these Loondoon men call me *uwacan!*

Bearman sneered at the cracked-eye man and smiled at me. "This young woman, Tha-na, who is in the Company service," he said, "is going to tent up near the French hut, with the Cree boy. She is going to help Mistaar Staarit translate many Copper words for this Company and prepare a good map for the Loondoon office, showing all the lakes and rivers and the route that followed through that unknown country which the Company map now shows as *Terra Incognita*."

Accoon-tant All-pooop blew his long thin nose into a rag of trade cloth. Then, without a word to anyone, he marched out and slammed the door.

"You two leave the fort today," said Bearman. "Your brother, Keewatan, will stay close by us, safe with his other countrymen. I don't want any of them killed or maimed by these jealous Northern Cree. I trust that living up there should make a better life for you. I will give you, Tha-na, enough twine to weave a fishnet, and Mistaar Staarit, you shall have almost our last horn of powder, some flint and ball. I am sorry that I cannot give you anything else . . . until this year's ship arrives."

"Thank you," said Williyumm.

"Now, what about the map and that yellow knife?"

"Sir, I would like to talk to you about that," said Williyumm, "sometime when we are alone."

"You can come to my room now," said Bearman, motioning Williyumm to follow.

I ran to be with Owinipeg, to tell her about my new and awful sister-in-law, but how lucky I was that the guvnaar would let Williyumm and I be off together.

With Jako's help, we were ready to leave before evening. He had loaded our sleeping skins, an old iron cooking pot, the fishnet cord, Williyumm's musket, sword, and pistol, and some meat into the small canoe which Captain Cheechoo had kindly given to me. Keewatan and Owinipeg both promised to come and visit us. Just as we were about to leave, they came down to see us off with Bearman. Williyumm reached inside his shirt and took out the yellow-beaded necklace, the three yellow arrowheads and the smaller yellow knife. He handed all of them to Bearman, who quickly slipped them into the deep side pocket of his Company coat.

As we pushed off, many Ballahooly friends of ours waved and called down to us "Gooobyyy, good fuggin," from among the high spears. Williyumm and Jako took the front strap and I took the back pole, and we three went walking up the river path, drawing our loaded canoe against the current. It was a clear summer evening with a little breeze, just enough to drive away the flies, and I never felt so pleased or contented in my life. Just Williyumm and I and Jako – and another tiny one growing inside of me. But as we walked toward the deer hedge, Williyumm seemed nervous. When I asked him why, he would not tell me what he and Bearman had agreed upon. Williyumm still had his gift knife and I had my mother's yellow flenser. That set my mind at rest.

When we arrived at the landing near the Frenchmen's hut, it was almost dark. I had never really seen this place. Williyumm said Frenchmen had built the hut some years before they had sailed away forever. He said they had used it sometimes when they came hunting or fishing or just card-playing up here, near the deer hedge. We unloaded the canoe and turned it over. The frog moon was rising in the sky as we three carried our possessions along a path until we reached the Frenchmen's hut.

Up close, our new lodge was like nothing I had ever seen before. It had stones piled square at the back of the hut until they stood high above the roof peak. The one door was cut in half so you could keep the bottom closed and swing the upper part wide open. A very good idea. Williyumm opened this entrance gently, for one of the leather hinges had broken. I will fix that, I thought, as we three stepped inside.

The place had a slightly musty smell, but nothing like the stink of the house of spears. And this house would be ours. There were only a few spots where we could see moonlight coming through the steep roof, where the wooden pieces nailed on like fish scales had blown aside. There were three looking-out places, each with zigzags of lead as soft as musket balls that held hand-sized bits of the ice that never melts.

Williyumm lost his nervousness when he saw this good old lodge that was to be ours. He showed me where he was going to make a high place to sit, so the light would come in over his left shoulder, and he could better see to make his markings on the white skins.

"Forget the tent," said Williyumm, "we will all sleep in here together." He grabbed me tight around the waist and bit my ear, a sure sign that he wanted to have me right there on the rough wood floor.

"Get away, you Ballahooly" I laughed and pushed him, and I ran outside the Frenchmen's hut, with Williyumm right after me until I fell down on the tundra moss, and he did, too. "Can't you wait until Jako goes to sleep?" I asked him.

"No, lass," he said. "I'd perish if I had to wait a moment longer."

"Go and see if there are any fish in the river," I thought to call to Jako as Williyumm breathed too hotly in my ear.

When we two finally came back to the house, Williyumm said, "Oh lord, I'm hungry."

There was already dry pitch wood set for a fire inside the stone box. Williyumm struck sparks with his gunflint, and soon the flames were flicking shadows all around our lodge. I hung my pot from a thin iron arm that cleverly moved in or out, then I cut some fresh meat and set it boiling. In the room were a small table, a bench, and two high-backed chairs. Stretching all along one wall, there was a colored painting of two strange birds sitting back to back. The walls, like the roof and floor, were made of axe-flattened wood.

Over one of the larger round logs that held up the roof, there was a huge covering filled with goose down. Williyumm pulled it down and I helped him shake it and dry it before the fire, then we laid it on the raised wooden square that had been made for sleeping. Across the room I made a smaller sleeping place for Jako. He lay down quickly and soon was breathing heavily. Williyumm and I took off our moccasins, leggings, and our shirts, spread out our sleeping skins, crawled into that soft wide bed, pulled our new cover up to our necks, and stared up at the tall peaked roof.

"Is this like the lodge where you were born?" I asked him.

"Yes," he said, "but I like this one better because it belongs to us."

I hugged Williyumm very hard when he said that. "I'm sure we've got a baby coming," I whispered.

Williyumm ran his hand over my belly, which wasn't getting big as yet. He held me tight. "Oohhh, lassie, I'm so very glad of that."

Moonlight crept across the Frenchmen's floor as we two traveled together into the dream country, thinking of all the wonderful days and nights that were to come.

Williyumm rose early next morning, and woke Jako. I heard him tell him to come look as he swung open the upper half of the door. There in the distance, beside the river's mouth, stood the house of spears, the blood-red flag of the Company waving above it. "We'll have good times here," said Williyumm. "I hope that ship doesn't come too soon. We will live life together as much as we can."

Before the sun was high, we three put our canoe into the water, We paddled across the river to a small cove where a painted canoe, much longer and fatter than any Dene had made, was cradled on logs above the waterline. It had a tall straight stick rising upwards from its middle, as tall as the rooftop of our lodge.

"This is a hoy," said Williyumm. "The Frenchmen used it for sailing on salt water out beyond the river."

"Why is it up here on the beach?" I asked him.

"Because the two boatwrights came up here and fixed it in the spring."

Williyumm showed me where they had hammered dark hairy ropes into every seam. "I used to sail a hoy like this near the place where I was born," he said, patting the side of the big

275

canoe the way a loving mother pats her child. "I wish she were mine. In this boat with a fair wind, I could sail us . . . somewhere south."

Quick as mink, Jako leapt up onto the flat deck of the hoy. "I'll go. We'll all go together."

I stood squinting in the morning sun, trying to look as though I cared about that awkward-looking big canoe which made Williyumm and Jako so excited. Truthfully, all I wanted was to get our fishnet woven, set my snares, and gather some dry wood. I planned to make a fire and put fresh water in my pot and sit with Williyumm admiring our soft feather bed and the scrubbed-clean table and our two chairs and Jako's sleeping bench and our see-through ices that never melt, and the painting of the two birds that looked like my familiar spirits. I had never had a lodge before. It would be a very good place, I thought, to raise a baby. Of course, I wouldn't dare give birth inside that place and make it foul for hunting men. When my time came, I would set up the small tent, Owinipeg would come, and I would go inside alone and let the child out of me, with Owinipeg not far away to sing some birthing songs to me. She had had a baby and would advise me how to do it, since I knew of no women relatives that I had left alive.

When we returned to our house, I fixed the fire and set the water boiling. I sat there humming to myself, planning how everything should go. Williyumm went poking around and found two wide, smooth wooden boards. I watched him and Jako as they iron-nailed them together, making a flat smooth place for Williyumm to make his markings. While he was looking for two wooden legs to hold this table up against the wall, Williyumm found a secret hiding place with plenty of strange things inside. Jako and I examined everything. First, there was a round green bottle that looked like black spring ice. It didn't leak a drop and was the best water holder I had ever known. Then there was one brass buckle, which I shined and wore around my neck, and sometimes I twinkled it in the sun. There was also a large roll of thin, rolled-up white skin, the Ballahooly kind that tears so easily. On the skin were many marks. Williyumm unrolled it carefully and took it inside where he could better see and understand their meanings.

"This is something I wish most of all to have," said Williyumm. "This is like finding food when you are starving."

"You can't eat that old dried skin," I told him. "It wouldn't even make a broth."

"No, no," said Williyumm. "I mean the marks on this skin show me what I want to know."

"What is that?" I asked.

"It shows the way far north of here, then this long river running west." He stopped and said, "It takes difficult words, words too hard to explain now."

I watched him carefully reroll the white skin and hide it safe inside the wall.

During almost every day of the egg-gathering moon we had fine weather. On those evenings when there was no wind blowing, I made a green smudge fire not far beyond our door, and so we were not much bothered by the stinging flies. Most mornings when I woke I would see Williyumm sitting near the good light from the window, staring at the rough gray marks that he had made when we were running west toward my country. Now he had a new red cover wrapped around lots of clean white skins. Williyumm began once more to do his curling marks, but this time with wet soot and a goose quill, carefully sharpened. Now the lines he made were hair-thin black, but some had grand thick loops and turns that made me think of fish scales. On each skin, Williyumm would carefully mark a red line that he said separated one sunset from the next sunrise. Sometimes he would take part of one skin to make images of the different objects we had seen. The simplest things interested Williyumm. He liked to draw the different shapes and weaves of Cree and Dene snowshoes, the shape of Cree crooked knives, and even their toboggans. He made a clever drawing of our lodge, showing the openings and the door. He drew my old bark-rind cooking basket and my moccasins, leggings, and pointed shirt. Then he would make a new red sunset line and next morning start making his curling, winglike lines again.

Sometimes in the afternoon when it was warm, Williyumm would lie on our goosedown bed and go to sleep. It was then that I would take his white skins and make marks of my own. I made drawings of the things that interested me. I drew the inside of our house with we three sitting round our small table and another picture of me and Williyumm jumping up and down in bed. I drew a picture of Williyumm dressed up half in the moccasins and leggings that I had made for him, and half in his red Company doublet, with his dog-tail sword stuck out behind him, and my dream hat with the foxtail waving from its top.

Sometimes when Williyumm woke and found me drawing on the Company skins, he would get mad and take the quill from me. But when he looked at the nicest pictures I had made, he would start to laugh and ask me, "What's this?" . . . "What's that?" . . . "Who's this?" . . . "Who's that?" I'd say, "You tell me," and he would almost always guess the people and the animals right and ask me to draw more.

I was feeling happy every day, with only a little bit of sickness in the mornings. As the new moons turned to full, I, too, was getting a little rounder, and once in a while the child inside would kick, to let me know that it was alive and getting stronger, getting ready to come out and see the sun and moon and stars and all the other wonders of this world.

The midsummer moon, the flying moon as the Cree call it, rose above our lodge pole. We watched it grow its old man's face as it ran through clouds. My brother, Keewatan, twice came up to visit me and hunt with Williyumm, who was glad to fling aside his goose quill. Together they went off to hunt the far end of the deer hedge.

The second time they set off, I heard the thick-mouthed boom of my brother's scatter gun and twice the sharper long-barreled crack of Williyumm's musket. I watched the caribou herd run down and swim the river, for they greatly feared the thunder of the guns.

I took my yellow flensing knife and went with Jako to skin and carry in the meat after Williyumm and Keewatan killed five caribou. My brother admitted that he had speared four of them.

"He's a wily hunter," Williyumm told me. "He didn't get them with the gun. He only used it for the pleasure of the kick it gives his shoulder and the sound of its echoing boom."

Keewatan laughed when I translated Williyumm's words. Anyone could see they were the best of friends.

My brother borrowed my canoe to carry the meat of three-and-a-half caribou down to the fort. I kept all the skins for tanning. I told Williyumm I was going to make him all new winter clothing, but he said no, I should only make new things for me and Jako.

"What are you going to wear when winter comes again?" I asked him.

"Oh, these things I have will do," he answered.

Each morning when we woke, Williyumm would go and steady his bring-near glass against a stone and stare carefully at the fort and out beyond the river's mouth. I knew that he was searching for the Ballahooly's big canoe. I wondered what it would be like. Owinipeg had told me ships were huge, with wings spread wide and white, like giant swans.

"Do ships have eyes and a beak and a tail?" I asked Williyumm. "Do they have webbed feet to paddle them through the water?"

"You will see. You won't be disappointed."

I could scarcely wait. I looked in his folded skins. His drawing of a ship was poor, I thought, for though it had wide wings, it did not look like any bird or canoe that I had ever seen.

With the coming of the autumn moon, it grew cold at night and a thin sheet of ice formed on the ponds, then melted in the morning sun. Now all the flies were dead and gone.

On the third evening of the goose-going moon, Williyumm aimed his quill and sent it flying out the open door.

"That Company ship of theirs is late! Bloody late! But there! I've got the whole damned journal finished!" he cried, slamming the red folded covers together and tying a green ribbon round them. "Now all we have left to do is make the map."

We lay close together that night, and I could feel the baby kneeing me. Williyumm didn't want to talk about him. He was thinking only of the map that we would make together.

***

In the morning, he nailed a long rolled-up skin flat upon his two boards. On it he made a tiny drawing of the house of spears, with its red flag flying, and then he marked the two biggest rivers flowing into the salt sea. Beside one he marked our little house, smaller than a slapped mosquito. Then he made a star shape near the top of this drawing he called a map.

"That's the Wolf Star," he told me.

"Move it a little toward the land where the sun goes each night," I said, and he did.

Carefully, we marked our tracks as we once more remembered each day of our walk-across. I told him where the rivers lay, and Williyumm drew small quarter, half, or full moons, to mark the time we had crossed them. Together we recalled our starving and our turning south until we found the meat cache. We drew in every lake and river across the Wood Cat country until we reached the huge river and the lake, so wide no human could see across it. Williyumm marked the place where we judged our last carriers built their fort, then my own march alone to find my brother and the fishing people.

The last question Williyumm asked me was, "Where is that small river where your brother found the yellow pebbles?"

"I don't know," I said. "You will have to ask him."

"Some day soon," said Williyumm, "I must go down to the fort and do so."

Each day not long after dawn, Williyumm would rise and stare down at the river's mouth with his bring-near glass. Most often there was morning fog, and he would pace back and forth until it lifted or was blown away before midday. Something was bothering Williyumm, had truly changed him, made him jumpy as a fox.

The snow geese and the gray geese came to us in countless numbers, and Williyumm loaded his long musket with small shot and brought down as many of the big birds as the three of us could eat. But even hunting did not cause Williyumm to enjoy our life as he had before.

On the very morning when the first thin curve of the goose-going moon came into the sky, Williyumm let out a great whoop of joy. "There she is! Thana! Jako! There's the Company ship. She's arrived! She's standing off the river's mouth."

Hudson's Bay III

I rose naked from our bed and hurried to the door. The ship looked like Williyumm's drawing, nothing like a bird. He rushed in and dressed in his best Scootlanish clothes and, laying down his sword, he did a skipping dance before our lodge. His face was red with excitement and he looked to me like a man who had drunk far too much brandy, though he had not had a drop.

"You and Jako stay here," he told me as he slipped his two red-covered journals and the folded map skin into his shoulder bag. "I'll ask your brother to mark in the little river where they find the yellow pebbles. Oh, I forgot," he said, "would you lend me that flensing knife of yours?"

I untied my hip string and handed him my mother's yellow knife. I sort of laughed and said, "I don't know why you want that flensing knife. If you get a caribou between here and the fort, I'll hear your musket and I'll come with Jako and skin it for you, and we'll carry back the meat."

"I'm going down with him," said Jako.

"I'll be all right here," I said.

Williyumm did not seem to hear our words, so busy was he packing all his things and rolling up his extra coat.

"I only remember seeing one ship," Jako said to him. "You came here on that one."

So eager was Williyumm to take even the little scratcher that he scarcely seemed to hear me. They went walking fast together, and when they reached the deer hedge they both began to run toward the ship, which now rested well inside the river with its wings neatly folded.

I dressed and wandered out to check my snares. I found that I had two plump rabbits and a ptarmigan with a few new white feathers, meaning it was getting ready for the snow.

When I straightened up, I looked down along the river path where I had last seen Williyumm and Jako. Coming along it was Owinipeg. She was not hurrying but wandering slowly, as though she were searching for small berries hidden in the moss.

I called out an Assiniboin greeting that she had taught me. She smiled and answered me in Dene. I proudly showed her all the treasures in our wooden lodge. She examined every one of them in wonder, saying, "I was never allowed to come up to this place. Only my Frenchman and his captains came up here to drink, play cards, and hunt the hedge.

"I've missed you," Owinipeg said. "Your brother and Chee-choo are still the only true men allowed inside the fort. The rest are Ballahooly who have been worrying endlessly about that grand *merde* of a ship." She nodded her head angrily toward it. "They've been betting each other on the hour and the day it would arrive, wasting their thoughts on nothing else. The guvnaar and the ear-peeker are the only ones I care about. The rest of them dream of nothing but leaving."

"Williyumm's not going," I said. "He and Jako are coming back to this lodge." I pulled up my pointed shirt and showed her the tight skin over my rounded belly.

"Well, that looks like something's got to happen," Owinipeg smiled. "You are going to have one sometime soon." Then she looked at me quite sorrowfully.

"The only thing wrong," I said, "is that I haven't got my marrying veil. Can't get married to Williyumm without a marrying veil."

Owinipeg held out her hands, but instead of looking at me, she looked at the ground. "He's gone down there to get on that ship. He's leaving," she said. "Two different Frenchmen and one Ballahooly have done that to me before. They never say good-bye. One of them took my only son with him, but none of them ever came back. Except the guvnaar. He came back. But he was away so long that my mother died. So instead of having her to warm his bed, he took up with me."

"It is not going to be like that with Williyumm," I told Owinipeg. "He would have married me already, but I never had a proper before-wedding veil."

"I remember you told me that a long time ago, before you and Williyumm went on the walk-across. Look," said Owinipeg as she opened her shoulder bag, "I brought you a gift of some brass thimbles and some very nice trade beads. They were the first things off that ship. Oh, yes, and kegs of brandy."

I stared at the wonderful gifts that Owinipeg had brought me.

"I also have dentalia and some small round shells to end each strand," she added, showing me twenty shells, clean white, the size of my little fingernail. "I had each one nicely drilled for you by Captain Cheechoo."

I took out a long strand of caribou-leg sinew, drew it through my teeth, and rolled it between my thumb and forefinger before threading it easily through the smooth iron eye of a Ballahooly needle.

We two worked together on that clear autumn afternoon, listening to the calling of the great waves of geese flying high above on their long journey south. Owinipeg and I began by knotting each line of sinew to a small shell, then added six blue beads, then a white quill, then four red beads, then a dark quill. Each of these were sewed tightly to well-scraped, caribou-skin cross-pieces. Each line of beads and quills hung from my beaded cap, just touching my collarbones, and they were set so close together that when I put on that veil, no one could see my face. When I looked at my dark reflection in my iron pot full of water, wishing I still had my mirror, I was very pleased.

"I like this veil better," I told Owinipeg, "than the one I used to have before."

She smiled when I told her that. "I prefer to see your face," she said. "I'm glad that veiling young women was not our Buffalo people's custom."

I didn't mind her saying that. But my grandmother once told me that for a Dene hunter to look one of our young women in the eyes would spoil his archer's aim forever.

"Oh, I know it makes you seem mysterious," said Owinipeg. "It makes men wonder what kind of face is waiting for them behind that veil."

I laughed. "Men always want to see what women hide."

I removed my new cap and veil and rolled it very carefully. "I will wait to put it on for Williyumm when I see him coming back along the path."

Owinipeg didn't answer me, but glanced away. "Could I stay up here with you for a few days? The guvnaar says he doesn't want any woman near the fort while the shipmen are still here. He says the captain might say rotten things about him to higher Company men across the water if they see a native woman hanging around his fort."

Next morning, Owinipeg got out of our bed just as the mists began to rise. She went outside. When she came back in the hut, she said, "The ship is spreading some of its small wings. It's getting ready to move down to the river's mouth. Tomorrow morning it will be gone."

"Who cares about that?" I said. "Williyumm and Jako will be back here very soon."

"Perhaps Jako will be back. But your Williyumm . . . he'll be gone."

"Williyumm would never do that," I laughed. "Do you mean leave, without telling me? Not him, he will not go away."

Owinipeg put her finger ends to mine. "I'll go down early in the morning. Will you be all right . . . up here . . . alone?"

WILLIAM

19

Jako and I gave a loud haloo as we approached the fort. McNulty, who was doing midday duty as a sentry on the wall, shouted, "Halt! Who goes there?"

"It's me, you daft fool," I shouted up to him.

"Well, how could I be sure? Ye're only half-dressed like a Stewart wi' your plaid and your sporan wagging o'er your Indian shirt and leggings. It's good to see you, Willie, and you, too, Jako," he added. "Willie, are you getting much out there? Because in here we're living on wet dreams."

In answer, I made an old familiar Scottish hand sign that set McNulty laughing. "Come on, slip in here, Willie. Wee Fergus," he shouted, "jerk that gate ajar. Most everybody's out having their last dram aboard the ship. They're done unloading, and she'll be moving down to Five Fathom Hole when the morning tide turns. She's called the *Hudson's Bay III* and there's a decent captain aboard her this year. He's generous with the grog. Nothing like that nasty Navy brute who left us here two years ago."

"I'm dying to go aboard her, laddie," said I. "Just seeing her out there makes me long for home."

I watched a long line of home Cree backpacking heavy bales and chests up from the river's edge to dump through the trade opening in the fort wall. There Accountant Althorp was in charge. He stood by the stockade, marking off each packet's outfit and

285

number. He was assisted by two bonded boys, who struggled with each case and bale and tried to stack them in some kind of order. Althorp looked out at me and Jako, then made a nasty face without giving the slightest nod. I did the same for him and so did Jako, who mimicked Mr. Althorp so perfectly that the two bonded boys reeled in laughter. When I saw James Knight and Surgeon Carruthers coming out of the fort yard, I hurried toward them.

"There is a Highland Indian creeping up behind us," the doctor warned the governor.

James Knight turned and said, "Oh . . . haaallo, Stewaart." Both their breaths were ripe with rum.

James Knight stared at me unsteadily with a look of utter disapproval. "I do not fancy you wearing such a mix of costumes – part Scot, part Dene, and part Company. Stewart," James Knight howled, "what a bloody sight you are. It's easy to see you've grown two parts wild and less than one part civilized."

"Jako!" called the surgeon, trying to change the subject. "You grow a whole head taller every time I see you."

"Stewaaart," the governor growled, "I want to have some private words with you. Come along . . . my quarters."

Inside, he closed the door and reached into his side pocket and hauled out a large flattened pewter flask. He took a long swig, then passed it on to me. "A splendid gift from the master of that Company vessel," he sighed. "He'll be leaving on the morning tide. This rum will brighten up our days." Governor Knight chuckled. "He left me three barrels, bless his heart. Now, Mr. Stewart, at last I can carry out my plans. Did you see on shore that great pile of musket boxes, cases of iron hatchets, fathoms of red blanketing, gunflints, casks of gunpowder, lead, ball, and shot, knives, molasses, a hundred casks of cheap English brandy – everything we've needed for a year and more? This time London's sent me two full years of trade goods and plenty of mess supplies."

James Knight took another hearty pull and handed the flask to me. I watched him wipe his mouth against his best coat cuff, cleverly weaving his lips between the sharp-edged pewter buttons. I only pretended to take a swallow, for I wanted all my wits about me.

keg

"Wait! Say not a word," the governor cautioned as he looked behind the stove and in his tall cloak box against the wall. "I don't trust that damned Althorp," he said, "nor Kelsey either, if he's about. Those two would gladly have the Company drive me out and hang me. Don't talk above a whisper," he warned, shoving his ear close to my mouth.

I handed him my rough graphite journal and the two new inked copies I had made – one to be sent to London, the other to remain safe in his locked chest, here at York.

"Good work, Mister Stewart," he said admiringly. "You do write such a lovely hand."

He held a thin pine spill inside his stove, drew it out aflame, and touched this to three new fat candles clustered on his table-stand.

"Spread out your map," he said, "and let me see what you've been up to."

When that had been done, I pointed at my wee drawing of the fort. "We begin here, governor. And follow this line west along the river and then cross on a northward heading, then west again. These small circles mark the places where we camped and slept. Each moon quarter and the numbers indicate the dates.

"This marks our ninth day from the fort," I showed him. "And the place where those damned carriers of ours flung down the iron-bound trunk containing all my navigational instruments. My last observation of position, taken the 3rd of July, 1715, had been latitude 59°.2 north, 19°.55 westerly. After that, I was without any instruments. I felt discouraged and sent a letter back to you, outlining all my troubles. But I had no answer back.''

"Not surprising," said James Knight, leaning heavily upon the table. "I received no message from you. Nothing came back here except about a hundred starving carriers who arrived in dribs and drabs for more than half a year, saying you had sent them back and that the progress of your party was going from bad to worse.''

"The worst of those idlers left first," I told him, "as soon as they had devoured all the porridge. I was cheered to see them depart, and so was Thana. I kept on going only because of her. She showed me how to find our way, in Dene style, relying on the Pole Star, which her people call the Wolf Star.''

"Interesting," said Governor Knight, "but let's get on to the gold and fur.''

I continued to trace with my dry quill along our entire route of march, giving the governor all the most important facts. "Only when we reached that vast inland lake on the edge of the barren grounds did Thana assure me that we were entering her mother's country. I judged it to be about 62° north.''

On my map, I showed him where we found the nine slaughtered Copper hunters near their tent, and the position of the meat cache that saved our lives, the place where Thana had set off alone to find her people, and the location where the Cree had built their own small replica of Fort York.

"Well, that's all clear enough." The governor grunted and took another drink. "But where did these come from?" He drew out the golden Dene necklace I had given him and the smaller yellow knife.

"The Yellow Pebble Stream," I told him. "That's what Keewatan calls it. He says it's a fast, shallow river. On bright days, one can see the yellow stones a-shining.''

"Show me on this map," said the governor. "Where is it?''

"Sorry, that cannot be done, sir.''

"Why not?" he roared.

"Your Cree carriers were in such a wretched hurry to get back here that they left me no time to seek that river. But Keewatan, who is here, can show us exactly where it lies.''

"Good," said James Knight. "Have you anything else to show me?"

"These," I said, wistfully, as I shook from my sporan the last two golden arrowheads.

"God bless you, Mr. Stewart," the governor gasped as he reached for the precious metal and made it twinkle in the candle-light. He scratched the gold ones with his knife point, then set each one on his delicate horn scales and added weights. "Did you see many more of these?"

"No, sir," I answered honestly, "but Thana says these copper and gold points are commonly used by Dene hunters in her country."

"You have been very fair with me, Mr. Stewart, and you will find me equally fair with you," he said as he tipped the gold and copper into the wide pocket of his doublet. "Tell me, is there anything you need? Is there any useful thing that I might give to you?"

He held out his rum flask for me to take another drink. I stuck my tongue into its neck and only swallowed a drop or two. "Sir," I asked, "do I have to stay here in this fort now that the journal and map are done?"

"Absolutely. Yes, you do!" he answered sternly. "You're not going anywhere!" He shook his head so hard his blue jowls trembled. "Absolutely nowhere! I need you here with me. Just look at this mess." He reached into his records chest and withdrew a Company journal. On the cover was written *IIB Coy 1716*. "Cast your eyes on that unholy mess," he said, flopping the journal open before me in disgust.

I laughed, never having seen a sight like that before. It was written in ink, in a mean scrunched hand, with blots and flattened dead mosquitoes, dirty thumb marks, and ugly doodles every-where. I could scarcely read the writing, and the spelling was atrocious.

"That lanky Yorkshire fool made such a botch of the job that I had to take it on myself. I hate keeping up that journal. See here!"

I could scarcely tell the difference in their scrawls. Knight's own handwriting was so disastrous that I could decipher only a word here and there that he had written.

"You could have Accountant Althorp keep the journal," I said slyly.

"You must be joking," he snorted. "Imagine me trusting that sneaking wretch." James Knight made a horrid face, then took another drink. "Soon as we get this new outfit sorted out and the trade goods stored away, you are coming back inside this fort." He thumped the table. "Did you hear me, Stewart? I shall allow you to keep that Copper woman and the boy up in the Frenchmen's hut. But I must have you here each day to make two clean copies of my Company journal, just the way you've done it in the past. In five more years, you can make your own choice to stay here or go back home.

"I've decided to send you north next summer, to the Churchill River. I'll be sending that Copper woman, Tha-na, with you, so she can greet her own people when they arrive. You two can sail north with a pile of trade goods. Take Boatwright Smithers and half a dozen crew to man that old French hoy and trade the Dene for their gold and copper and peltry. Everything you fetch back here we shall throw up to the ceiling. What sticks up there will belong to the Company. All the rest that falls back down will belong to me and you." He laughed. "Don't argue with me, Stewart. That's exactly how it's going to be!

"You have proved there is gold and copper to be gained in the northwest; together we are going to take it. All we can. Remember, Mr. Stewart, you keep your mouth tight shut about this yellow knife and necklace waiting for us when we go northwest along that Churchill River."

"Wait!" I said. "None of what you're planning suits me well at all. There are others who would like to have this." I reached into my sporan and drew out Thana's moon-shaped flensing knife, the one I had that morning asked her for.

"Well, look at that," James Knight clucked, his eyes wide with surprise. "You are made of gold!"

"How much would that be worth?" I asked.

"It's much too heavy for my small scales," he said, "but I would judge it to weigh seven or eight troy ounces. That's three-quarters of a twelve-troy-ounce pound of gold. It's probably worth forty guineas.''

I took it back from him. "And how much was my indenture, sir?''

"You were bound for seven years, is that correct? Then with two years done, you probably still owe the Company roughly 15 guineas.''

"I could pay that off with less than half this one piece of gold,'' I told him.

The governor frowned. "Hold on that thought for a minute, Stewart. If I allowed you to return to London with your pockets stuffed with gold, it would tip off the Company straightaway to what we've found. No, lad, I'm afraid you'll have to stay right here with me for five more years. When your full indenture has been paid off in wages, then we'll both go back to London and live like a pair of grand, rich men.''

He helped me carefully fold my map, then concealed it in one of his vast pockets. "Here, Willie,'' he whispered in my ear, "you take one candle holder and I'll take the other. We'll go and find Keewatan and have him mark out on this map the river where they find those golden pebbles.''

It did not take us long to find Keewatan or his new friend, Captain Cheechoo. We could hear them singing loudly in the mess hall. Cheechoo was sitting in the governor's chair at the high end of the table and Keewatan was beside him, busy passing a small cask of raw trade brandy back and forth between themselves and three comely young Cree doxies. I thought the governor might die of apoplexy when he saw this sight, but instead, he walked up amiably enough and gave them all a warm Cree greeting. We sat down among the five of them, Knight saying that he wished to speak with Keewatan.

Even in the poor light of the sputtering iron torches, I was surprised to see that Captain Cheechoo, who had had far more experience with drink than any Dene, could still sit up at such a dangerous angle. It was not at all the same with Keewatan. His singing had slowed down, his eyes were drooping closed, and his head had nodded down until his chin first rested on his chest and then on the table beside the empty brandy cask.

"Here, you, Dene man! Wake up!" Cheechoo demanded.

The young girls on either side of Thana's brother began to shake him. "The guvnaar wants to talk to you," they screamed into his ears.

The governor pushed the girls aside and started shaking Keewatan himself, trying all the while with his other hand to unfold my map.

"It's no use, sir," I told James Knight. "This man, Keewatan, is not going to be able to locate that river tonight. Maybe he'll do it sometime late tomorrow or the next day."

"Yes, I can see you're right, Willie. But you be back in here promptly in the morning. Nobody but you and this man's sister knows how to understand his Copper tongue. And I want this man – what is his name – to mark that river for me on this map. You understand me, Willie?"

To Captain Cheechoo he shouted, "Now you take these three damned doxies and get out of here, or you won't be my goose captain anymore."

They all four scampered, Cheechoo quite unsteadily. The governor tried to slap the prettiest girl across the rump but missed by a goodly margin.

"I hate Althorp and that bloody London office with their spying ways and stupid regulations. Imagine them forbidding decent working men like us the sweetest human fruits that life can offer. Yes, Mr. Stewart, I've decided you can stay up at the Frenchmen's hut and live with that young woman, Thana-detour. But certainly not until her brother marks the golden river on my map. You may make up a list of the two months' rations you require and give it to the Accountant Althorp. He'll doubtless go berserk when he sees I've signed it. But you may assure him those are my personal orders. Remember, do not dare to go near that ship tonight and do not dawdle in the morning, Mr. Stewart. I expect you to sober up this drunken man and get this map of mine marked exactly right."

As we two left the mess hall, the governor called up to the sentry on the wall. "Hear me, Dinwoodie. See that William Stewart does not leave this fort tonight."

"I shall do that, sir," Dinwoodie answered loudly.

I waited only a few minutes in the shadow of the wall before I slipped unnoticed through Boatwright Smithers's doxie entrance. There before me in the moonlight, I could see a small work boat on the landing and beyond it the Company frigate waiting for the morning tide. And me. Yes, it seemed that they were waiting just for me to come aboard, pay off the vessel's master, then set sail with them to England.

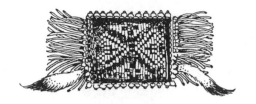

THANA

20

Williyumm and Jako had been gone for two whole days. The ship, too, had disappeared into the autumm fog. Owinipeg had warned me that Williyumm would go with the ship. She had set my snares and shared the bed with me that night. Then, early next morning, she had walked back down to the house of spears, saying that she would return, bringing some amulets and charms to protect me. She had said that she would talk to Bearman about my coming to live with her again.

I tried to be calm and peaceful, as I rested in Williyumm's chair, not wishing to stare endlessly along the river path. There was only a small glow from the fireplace, giving almost no heat. I didn't care. The iron pot that hung above the drying embers cast a dark shadow, like a flying raven. That was known to be a woman's most unlucky sign. I feared that if I turned to look along the path again, I would still see no one. So I closed my eyes and just sat waiting, listening, with my hands across my belly. Listening for what? For Williyumm to return? Owinipeg had assured me that he and the ship would go together, back to his homeland, maybe even taking Jako with him. Perhaps I was not waiting for them. Perhaps I was only waiting for our child to kick his way outside of me. I didn't know. I was not thinking straight. Not on a moonlight night like this, with that trickster raven, flying all around our Frenchmen's hut. Suddenly, the walls creaked and I could feel the spirits of those nine murdered Dene hunters moving stiffly, whispering around the hut. I rose quietly and put some branches on the fire. How would I greet those restless phantoms if they came inside?

I do not know how long I stood there waiting for the flames to rise and chase the frightening shadows, but I almost died when I heard the sound of running feet. The door flew open and there stood Jako. He looked behind, for he, too, feared spirits in the dark. After slamming the door, he darted across the room and pressed himself against me.

"Jako, are you alone?" I asked him.

"No," he said. "He, too, is coming. He wanted me to run ahead and tell you we were almost here."

"Oh, Jako, I'm so glad you're both back here. I wasn't ready for you or Williyumm tonight."

I hurried across the room and reaching into my carrying basket, pulled out my before-marriage veil. I set it on my head and tried to straighten all the strings of beads and shells and small brass thimbles that dangled down to hide my face.

bridal veil

"Is it on straight?" I asked Jako.

"I don't know," he answered. "I've never seen anything like that before. Can you see through it?"

"Oh, yes," I told him, but my hands were shaking, wondering what Williyumm would think when he saw it. I opened the half-door and looked through my veil along the path toward the river. But the truth was that between the darkness outside and the veil, I could see very little.

"He's got your canoe packed full of flour and molasses and other presents for us. New things that came off the ship," said Jako. "Red blankets, needles, thimbles, long knives, snare line, new fishnets, red sugar tits, oatmeal, sweet perfume, he says, to put under the arms and legs. He said he is tired, and it is too late to unpack it all tonight. He is going to leave the canoe tied up hidden in the cove."

"I hope he ties it tight," I told him.

"Oh, yes," said Jako. "He knows good knots. Don't worry. I tied the stern to that big stone as well."

"I can hear him coming now," I said, still trying to make sure my veil was right. "You put some of those pitch knots on the fire to make it flare."

He stared at me. "Thana, is that you hiding in there? Your face has disappeared. What is that damned thing dangling down from your head to your chest? Take it off, for God's sakes." He and Jako started laughing.

They weren't meant to see my face, but it was growing red as I got mad at both of them for joking about my veil.

"Stop that," I said to Williyumm. "Don't women ever wear a marrying veil in Scootlan?"

"Aye, indeed, they do," he told me, letting himself through the door. "But their veils are not near so thick or beady-looking. Scootlan's girls wear veils woven white and thin, like a *hawpetch*."

He used our word for fishnet.

"A smelly fishnet hanging in front of a Scootlan' girl's face?" I snickered through my elegant Dene veil. "A *hawpetch* doesn't sound too good to me."

"You don't look your best wearing that damned beady veil. You could be anybody." Williyumm shook his head. "You don't look like my wild Thana. I can't see your face."

"You're not supposed to see my face," I told him. "My face is to be hidden . . . it's to be a big surprise. You'll only get a chance to see me after I become your wife."

"Well. It's a wee bit late for that, lass," said Williyumm, "after we've been bedding down together for a winter, spring, and fall."

"No, it's not too late," I told him. "not for me. You've got to wait."

"I always liked your real face, just the way it was," said Williyumm, laughing.

Jako nodded in agreement.

How could I explain to them the troubles Owinipeg and I had taken, she having Captain Cheechoo drill all these shells and begging Bearman for the new brass thimbles, and I using up her best blue beads? And now, after all of that, the two of them just stood there howling.

"Stop that noise," I told them sharply. "I look the way a Dene maiden has to look before she marries."

Williyumm eased off his shoulder bag and stretched, saying, "I can't wait to get into that bed."

Jako went and curled up on his sleeping bench, drew a caribou skin up to his chin, and, still chuckling, fell asleep.

I turned back the goose-down cover of our bed, and we took off all our clothes and got in, one on either side, then rolled very close together. Williyumm ran his hand through my hair in the way he knows I love the best.

"Can you guess what's going to happen?" he asked.

"No," I answered, "I don't know, and I'm dead afraid to have you tell me."

"Don't be scared," said Williyumm, and he put his arms around me. "I don't know what's going to happen to either of us, but I do want you to know that you are the best woman I have ever known."

Williyumm had not known a lot of women, I knew that, but still I hugged him tight, and I could feel the child inside me give a double kick when he heard his father say that, one for him and one for me.

"Don't you think that you could take all those beads, shells, and thimbles off your face now that it's dark and we are alone in bed?"

"You are supposed to take this veil off for me. That will mean that we are husband and wife."

"That is fine with me," said Williyumm.

297

He took off my before-marrying veil and let it rattle down onto the floor.

"*Sidhaw*, husband," I said, using that title for the first time.

"*Sakosee*, wife," he answered.

We raised our heads and looked at each other in the faint glow from the fire.

I lay as close as I could to Williyumm on our bed of blankets and caribou skins with the Frenchmen's goose-down cover over us. I could feel the whole earth stretching around me, and the rivers curving to the sea, and the dancing stars over our heads. The whole world was peaceful. I could tell that Dingee and the ghosts of those two dogs of ours were resting quietly somewhere not too far away, and those nine slain Dene hunters were talking and warming themselves around their fire.

"Wife, do you want me to tell you what is going to happen tomorrow?"

"Ooh, nooo. Wait until the morrow, if it comes," I answered my new husband in Scootlanish. "I din'na wish to know. Let us just enjoy being a new wife and a new husband tonight." And that's exactly what we did, but very carefully so as not to poke the child that grew inside of me.

When that joy was over, I heard Williyumm sigh and twitch the way he always does before going to sleep. I was glad to follow him into that other world, where both the humans and the animals sleep and dream together.

The sky was still dark when I heard Williyumm creep out of our bed. The stars looked blurry through the bits of ice that never melt. He went outside to feel the weather and make yellow splashes on the stones. I sat up sweating, feeling strange, and gasping for my breath. Outside I could see the quarter moon running through bright-edged gray clouds, and I could feel the child inside me kicking wildly, wanting to be out. "It's too early for that," I told him. "Bide your time."

"You lay abed, wife," my new husband ordered me, using his slurry Scootlanish way of speaking, which he knows pleases me the best.

"I am your wife now," I told him. "I am going to rise and make your oatmeal porridge. Don't try forcing me around."

Williyumm spent the day at the fort with Jako. It had been sleeting hard since midday, and it lasted until the wintry-looking sun sank down.

When I heard them running, I called, "Get yourself in here laddies," for I could hear Williyumm puffing from his hurry up the long, wet, icy path beside the riverbank.

Jako Staarit helped strip off Williyumm's soaking moccasins and leggings and his pointed shirt, then hung them up to dry, for I was no longer good at bending. When Williyumm was naked before the fire but shivering, I rubbed him hard with my best warm shawl, then pulled him into the goose-down bed with me and covered both of us. He was still trembling badly. I tried to sort of wrap myself around him and that helped, for soon his shuddering stopped.

After a while I asked him, speaking Scootlanish, "Do you feel a wee bit better nooo, laddie?"

"I can scarcely tell," he groaned. "That sleet was wicked cold."

"Your *yeak* is warming up," I told him. "My grandmother told me that is the surest way to tell whether a near-frozen man intends to stay alive or leave you for the spirit world."

Jako kindly brought his new father a bowl of hot thick broth. Williyumm supped it, then went straight to sleep. I lay awake and listened for a while to the sharp sleet as it came tapping, like little children's fingers, against our lodge. After that I heard the icy pellets soften and turn into a whispering snow.

In the morning, the wind was gone, and the ground was covered with a thin new whiteness. I was feeling different than I ever had in all my life.

I woke Williyumm and told him, "I want a good plump ptarmigan. Could you and Jako go and find me one or two or three?"

"That's a strange thing to be longing for," moaned Williyumm.

"You, husband, load your musket with small shot and, Jako, take your sling and flat stones and go find a ptarmigan to feed me whilst I am in my bed."

299

"You're looking kind of pale," said Williyumm. "Are you not feeling right?"

"No, I am feeling all right, but I'll feel even better after you two bring me a ptarmigan. That's what I am longing for."

"Sometimes even a strong-minded woman like your mother can go a little crazy," I heard Williyumm telling Jako as they went outside the Frenchmen's door. "You be damned careful when it comes time for you to get married, do you hear me? Try hard to pick a really good one."

I peeked out through the never-melting ice, watching them go along the riverbank together where the thin snow had been blown away by the wind. I knew that was a place where ptarmigan rarely feed. I didn't care too much. I was still feeling strange and short of breath. I hoped the two of them would stay away all day, because I was starting to feel very bad.

I dressed and went outside and got busy setting up the small tent ready for my birthing. Three moons would pass soon, and I was trying to remember everything older women had said I'd have to do. First, I sewed two green sprigs of tamarack on the small tent top to shelter both the child and me, and then I tied a caribou thong around my back and crisscrossed it above my belly to help me in case I had to press down hard. I got our oldest, worn-out sleeping skin and I made a shallow hollow not much bigger than an owl's nest, then I placed the caribou fawn skin inside my nest with the soft hairs up. I undid my hip string, took off my leggings, then lastly I took my mother's little yellow flensing knife, and I placed it underneath my sleeping skin, knowing it would help to cut the pain. I could remember hearing of several other ways to ease a girl's first birthing, but I would need a raven's beak and a ground squirrel's claws and those speckled back feathers from a loon. None of those things did I have with me just then, so I would just have to make do the best I could.

I tried to drink a little broth, but it would not stay down. I put a few more broken sticks of driftwood on the small fire and as I was doing that, I could feel a rush of hot water flooding down my legs.

A little later, the first pain came tearing at me. I lay down on my side and called out, "Mother!" Then I called. "Owinipeg!" and "Dingee!" But there was no one near to hear me.

When the pain came again, it was not so bad. Then three more pains came, each one growing worse, and I could feel the child inside me, maybe trying hard to turn around or wriggling to get out. It's a boy, I thought, a strong one! He'll be like Williyumm, he'll be a long-legged walker and a good child-maker.

I got up on my knees over the nest and put my arms across my belly and pushed down hard. I must have gone into a dream again, for when I woke, I was lying on my face. I thought I could hear Dingee's voice singing the birthing song, but maybe that was only in my mind. I got up on my knees and strained again, pushing down hard, using the cord. I fainted. When I woke up, I thought, I'm going to die. Yes, this baby and I are going to die together. The fire had gone out, but my breath was still coming out of me like hot kettle steam. My hair was sticking to my face and my whole body was soaked with sweat. I didn't care. I hurt too much to care. First, I thought how lucky I was that Williyumm and Jako were away. Then I began wondering if those two were ever coming back to see me. I wanted to see them once more, in case I had to go away. Then I thought, maybe this one wasn't going to be a boy. Maybe it was going to be a girl. I didn't care which it would be. I liked girls. I'm a girl myself. Maybe that was Dingee singing, maybe she is coming back to me. I hoped this one would be as beautiful as Dingee. "Come out," I told her or him. "Williyumm and I will take good care of you."

I tried to make the fire go again, but I couldn't do it. I pulled the sleeping skin over my back, for I was cold and shivering a lot. I slept again or fainted. Anyway, I woke with a jump when I heard Williyumm and Jako calling me as they came hurrying toward my tent.

"Keep away!" I screamed at them. "Don't come near. This whole tent is unclean. Turn quickly, run away!"

"What's wrong with her?" I heard Williyumm say to Jako.

"I guess the baby is still inside her," Jako said. "Men should stay far from women when they are dropping new ones."

301

"Williyumm, Jako, you two get away from here!" I cried, ashamed that my voice was shaking.

"We will go . . . if you say so," Williyumm promised, "but when can we come back? There's no smoke coming out of your tent. Can we not build a fire for you?"

"No," I answered. "Go away until I get this baby out."

Then I lost the real sounds of their voices and went back to do my dreaming. After a while, I seemed to be awake and all the pain had gone away.

the birthing tent

Through the open door, I could see Williyumm and Jako running toward me, and somehow I was back in our warm Frenchmen's hut. When they were near enough, Williyumm shouted, "Oh, good to see you safe in here. How are you feeling?"

"Fine," I laughed. "I got a good one for you. A real baby. You'll soon see."

"Where is it?" they asked together.

"Right here on my chest," I told them. "It's not an it . . . it's a she."

"A girl?" Williyumm gasped. "I want to see her."

With my finger, I made very carefully in the caribou hair the lucky shape of deer horns, which is always done by women in our clan. The new fire I had built was going fine, and the tamarack needles were snapping, filling our lodge with their clean green smell. I told Jako to light a pine bough and go outside. I didn't have to tell him how. He knew just what to do.

He ran around our lodge four times, trailing the purifying smoke, weaving patterns behind him, making the Frenchmen's hut a safe dwelling place once more, for all of us.

When Jako came inside again, the two of them crawled into bed, one on either side of me. I carefully drew back my new blanket and the baby's fawn-skin cover. I could feel the new child turning her head against my breast, probably trying to get a better look at both of them.

"It's true," said Jako. "She did get a baby while we were away hunting."

"Did you get a ptarmigan?" I asked them.

"No," said Jako. "We tried hard but could not find none."

The fire was making our lodge warm. "I don't mind," I said to Jako. "Now that she is here, I don't need a ptarmigan. Do you want to see some more of her?"

They both nodded their heads.

I held the new child up, turning her proudly this way and that way for her father and brother to have a good close look at her.

"Strange," said Williyumm, "she has no hair."

"Yes, she has got hair," I told him. "Look close. Red hair. And look at her eyes, not real dark, like Dene eyes. Her eyes are going to be blue. Looks to me like she sailed over here from Scootlan."

"Can I hold her?" Williyumm asked.

"Sure," I said. "She is half yours and half mine." I felt Jako leaning against me kind of hard and I said, "She belongs to Jako, too. He's her brother."

The two of them held onto her together, one by the legs, the other underneath the arms. She must have liked it. She never cried. I could tell she was glad to be out of me at last and in the middle of our family.

"What name is she going to have?" asked Williyumm.

"It's up to her grandparents to name her," I told him, "but yours are far away, and mine are . . . "

"Well, we cannot just go about calling her 'her' or 'she' or 'it,' " said Williyumm kind of proudly. "It is up to us to find a name for her."

"I like the name they gave your sister – Sheelaah – that sounds to me like a Dene song word."

"You could call her Dingee," Williyumm said.

"Those will be her names. Sheelaah . . . Dingee . . . Starrit." I pronounced them very carefully.

Sheelaah started whimpering and I took her back from them and laid her on my breast. I had to help her find the milk, but then she started feeding on me right away.

I laid back on the thick winter caribou skins and Williyumm spread the Frenchmen's goose-down covering over all of us. Instead of going to his own bed, Jako stayed with us and put his arms around me, so all four of us were very close together. My thought was that after today, there is nothing more in the world that I will ever need, expect maybe another baby. Later, I heard myself screaming again, and I didn't really know if I had been dreaming, or if I had truly had this child of ours.

WILLIAM

21

Thana was not in the Frenchmen's hut when we returned, but Jako quickly darted out and found her. She was lying in her meager bark-rind shelter some distance from the lodge. This strange Dene-shaped tent of hers had outlandish charcoal markings of humans, birds, fish, and animals. Tufts of new green tamarack had been bound beneath its peak, but there was no smoke rising from the opening.

"Thana! Thana!" I called to her, but she did not answer, Jako seemed afraid of the tent and would not at first go near it.

I forced back the stiff bark flap that covered its entrance and thrust inside the burning knot of pine pitch. Thana lay sprawled hips up, face down, beside her small dead fire.

"What's wrong?" I shouted in English, then in her Dene language.

She did not move or answer.

"Run, put wood on our lodge fire," I called to Jako, "then rush back here with blankets and the toboggan. We've got to get her warm."

I crawled inside the shelter and rolled Thana over on her back. She was shuddering with cold and gasping very slowly, fighting for every breath that she drew into her body. I held her tight inside my arms and rocked her, trying to give her warmth. I talked to her in all the languages we knew, even a few words of Gaelic that she liked. But she never opened her eyes or answered me a word.

Jako came racing to us, dragging the toboggan. Together we lifted Thana onto it, wrapping the blanket and a caribou hide close around her.

The Frenchmen's lodge was warming when we got inside. I squatted down and held Thana before the open fire, while Jako fed her rabbit broth.

I startled when Thana's eyes opened wide. She looked all around, then turned her head and smiled at both of us. "Was I outside?" she asked.

"Yes, we found you in that wee bark tent," I said. "The fire was dead."

"Where is Sheelaah? I want the baby," she said to us, looking all around her.

"You must have been dreaming, wife. There is no baby. It's far too soon for you to have it yet. You and Owinpeg both told me that."

"Oh, I wish it had not been a dream," said Thana, and she looked carefully beneath her blanket, then struggled to see her feet. "I'm not sick anymore," she said, then squatted between us in front of the fire, her cold hands reaching in until they almost touched the flames.

We led her to the bed and helped her pull off her pointed shirt, leggings, and wet moccasins. I quickly got in beside her. We lay close together, listening to the crackling of the fire as we watched the shadows dance around the rough walls.

"I saw the baby," Thana whispered. "I held her in my arms. She's going to be a fine girl. Oh, you'll love her. She's got red hair, like you." She laughed. "Did you go to visit the ship?"

"No," I said. "I thought of doing that. I even went and pushed the small boat from the shore and sat and thought a bit. Then I came back."

Thana was growing warm again and feeling better. In a little while, she was asleep.

Next morning, Thana got up well before me, stirring the porridge as though nothing at all had happened to her. When I called, "Good day to you, lass," she turned and smiled at me.

"You and Jako have been running up and down to that river so much, you must be worn down. Go back and dream some more. I'm going to leave that small tent up," she told me. "But don't worry. I won't need it – not for two moons, even three."

When I finally did arise from our bed, I could see that the frigate *Hudson's Bay* was gone. The thin snow near the shore was melting, exposing all the stones and patches of gray-green muskeg in the morning sun. I could hear great flights of laughing geese passing just above our Frenchmen's hut. I stretched with pleasure, knowing everything had turned around and would be good again with us.

Early each Friday morning, I presented myself at the fort to carry out my duty of keeping the governor's journal. I took down notes, in graphite, of his conversations and gleaned what I could from his own unholy scrawls. Each Monday, I returned to the fort and carefully transcribed these records into the Company journal, using quill and ink. With red ink I drew a line to separate the entry for each day.

The hewers of firewood who labored in the timber stands upriver rolled off a share for us as they rafted past each Saturday returning to the fort. October was notable for icy sleets and snows, which grew much worse in November. December brought winter down hard upon us. We didn't care. The Frenchmen's hut was warm and dry, and we three lay happily together like bears in hibernation. In the mornings, we would find snow dry as sand blown in curious wind patterns, across our floor until it lay in small drifts piled against the opposite wall. Thana, clucking like a marsh hen, would quickly sweep it all outside, using her goose-wing brush.

Her pointed shirt was riding very high now and when we went down to the fort to join their Yuletide celebrations, it was easy for even the youngest bonded boys to guess that she was soon to bear our child.

All through January – which the Cree call *obesum*, the cold moon – Thana and Jako continued to set out her dozens of clever snares, and they brought in great numbers of pure white ptarmigan and snowshoe hares. Thus, with a good supply of her carefully smoked geese, frozen trout, dried caribou, English flour, Scottish oatmeal porridge, tea, and Bahamian molasses, we had all the good food anyone would ever wish to eat. Thana seemed fully recovered from the delusions of childbirth and the strange fainting spell that she had suffered in the little tent almost four months earlier.

Those concerns had been forgotten when Jako and I entered the lodge on the evening of the 26th of January, 1717, and found Thana in a faint again, poor thing, lying half in, half out the bed. The fire was dead, and the Frenchmen's hut was freezing cold.

We eased her back onto the sleeping skins and packed the blankets and the goose-down covering around her. Her hands and arms were icy cold. Her lips drawn tight, and her face was deathly pale. Jako made the fire roar as he loaded it with pitch pine starters and our driest split wood. Then he heated up the broth while I carried Thana to the hearth.

But this fainting spell was not at all like the last time. Chafe them as I would, her hands and arms and feet stayed cold, and her eyes did not suddenly open as they had before. When we tried to feed her broth, we could not get it down her throat. It ran out of her lips and into her fawn-skin undershirt.

Jako and I did not lie down that night, not for a single moment. When Thana seemed no better in the early morning, we decided to bundle her in skins, blankets, and goose down, then tie her to the long toboggan and haul her quickly to the fort. The ear-peeker, I told Jako, would know what had caused her spell of sickness and how to make her well again. I felt sick with fear that Thana's illness might be caused by our child which she was carrying.

It was perishing cold when we went out. The wind was driving hard, coming straight at us from the northeast. Thinking of nothing except Thana, lying bound and cold behind us, we harnessed ourselves like dogs, ran onto the frozen river, and rushed her toward the fort. My hands and face were freezing cold, but I could feel drops of sweat form and trickle, like a wandering louse, between my shoulder blades, then down my back. When we paused to rest, we both stiffened, then began to shudder. We were glad to rise and throw our weight into the traces again, stumbling east toward help.

A dozen times my mind retraced our long journey west when we three were running into Thana's country. How could anyone forget a killing winter such as that? My life in the Highlands seemed a thousand miles, a thousand years away. Now my life with Thana and with Jako seemed the only thing that mattered to me.

Probably they had seen us racing with our burden through the long glass from the high walk of the fort, for Captain Cheechoo came running upriver, with two of his strong dogs. As soon as he had them hitched, we three ran beside the toboggan until we reached the main gate, which had been opened just enough to let us enter. Owinipeg was there. She arranged the covers around Thana's face.

We pulled her to the doorway of Dr. Carruthers's sick room and quickly carried her inside. It was hot and evil-smelling in that airless place where he treated so many men with unwashed bodies. Here he gave them turpentine vapors for the flu and bled them when they seemed too flushed, or clapped on leeches for sundry ailments. I stared at his shelves, groaning under ranked jars of salves, ointment, and heavy volumes he had brought with him from London. The bluff but kindly healer also stocked and employed beaver castor, dried insects' wings, chopped goose spleens, and other rarities gathered by a medicine man who practiced only magic. For in the north, it was believed that curses were the only source of human sickness.

Perhaps it was the oppressive airlessness of that small sick room that made Thana start to gasp for breath, then open her eyes wide.

"I'm going to try sulfur and molasses on you first, my dear," said Surgeon Carruthers, taking down a yellow bottle of the powder. "Don't you two fret away your time worrying about this strong girl. But still, William," he added, "you might just give a good prayer for her every night and in the morning, too. Ask the Lord to help us all see her through these pains and troubles."

"She does not know who the Lord is," I told him. "She will tell us she is in the hands of the Big Woman now. That is how she thinks."

"Maybe there is no real difference," the surgeon said. "Now, you and Jako hurry over to the messing hall and break bread with all your friends. Owinipeg will stay here with Thana, and I shall join you over there in just a while."

I sat between McNulty and wee Fergus at the lower table, but I had not a thought of food.

I went to see Thana again that evening and once more at dawn the following morning. She smiled at me and seemed considerably improved, but there was a darkness around her eyes, and the flesh had sunk underneath her cheekbones. When I asked about the baby, Thana said that all was going well, that the child had not kicked her for some days.

And so it went with us. One day Thana felt better, then the next day would go hard for her. There was nothing Jako or Owinipeg or I could do to help. Governor Knight urged us to move her into Kelsey's room, for he was journeying south again among the Cree. His was a much smaller, cleaner smelling room. Jako, Owinipeg, and I took turns telling Thana stories, I in Scootlanish or Dene, and they in Assiniboin or Cree. As well, I told her every Ballahooly rumor I had heard inside the fort, and Jako told her what was happening in the home Cree lodges.

When the Company journal was finished on the last day of January, 1717, I drew a sharp red line beneath. I noticed that my hand was shaking and my penmanship was bad. The governor said it was the cold that caused it, but I know now that it was my fear for Thana.

In the middle of the night of February 15th, 1717, Owinipeg came for me and Jako, and we three hurried into Henry Kelsey's room. Thana's eyes were closed, but she opened them a little when we came near the bed.

I sat down beside her and suddenly I knew that everything was wrong. Thana didn't speak at all, but she was staring straight at me. I saw tears begin to fill her eyes. How could this be happening when she was so young and healthy, only some twenty years of age?

I said to her, "You've got to get better, lassie. Come on, where is that child you are getting ready to give us?"

Jako stood beside me, saying nothing, biting his lips to keep them from trembling.

Thana opened her mouth several times as though to speak, but only made a gasping sound. She looked desperately at Owinipeg and Jako, and then back at me, before she sighed once more and partly closed her eyes.

Surgeon Carruthers came up behind us, although I had not realized that he was in the room. He placed his hand against Thana's wrist and neck vein and then he held up a small mirror before her pale and parted lips. He waited for a while, then carefully examined it and showed us that there was no cloud, no sign of breath upon the mirror. He gently closed her eyes, then crossed her arms upon her chest, and raising the blanket covered her face. He put his arm around each one of us, then sadly left the room.

Owinipeg gently drew the blanket down, once more revealing Thana's face. Then she uncrossed her arms and began singing her a going-away song in Assiniboin. I sang to Thana at the same time, some in Scootlanish and some in her Dene. Jako, he sang, too, in Cree, all of us trying our best to help her on her way.

After that, I drew my plaid around me and went outside and walked around the inside of the fort wall several times while Johnny Wateridge, who was up on guard, watched me and sometimes called to me, asking what I was doing down there in the cold. I didn't answer him. I kept on walking.

Just as night was ending, I remembered again that little secret entrance hole that Shipwright Smithers had cut in the fort wall to let his Cree girl in and out. I decided to go out that way, not taking anything at all with me but snowshoes and the clothes I wore.

It was almost noonday when I reached the Frenchmen's hut, and it was deadly cold inside. I didn't bother to make a fire, but scratched the frost from the little leaded window and stood staring down at the fort where Thana lay. Afterwards, I lay down, too. Later, I saw Cheechoo, Jako, and McNulty coming through the door. They pulled away the skins that I had wrapped around myself. I could see their white breaths rising in the cold beside the bed.

"You can't stay here alone," McNulty told me.

Captain Cheechoo said, "You come with us."

I saw tears in Jako's eyes.

When I tried to stand, my legs buckled under me. I was like a man near death, who had lost all desire to move.

"Help me get him out onto the toboggan," Captain Cheechoo ordered. Jako translated those words to McNulty.

As soon as they had me wrapped and bound firmly into place, those three and the dogs pulled the toboggan onto the flat, frozen river to speed me to the fort.

At dinnertime that night, I was urged to the table. James Knight and Surgeon Carruthers joined me, one sitting on either side. They offered me a cup of hot apple brandy. I watched them drink theirs down. But I could not touch a drop. Nor did I eat the food that had been set before me.

"Willie, this is an unhealthy thing for you," the surgeon warned. "You must take food and drink to fortify your strength."

"I do not want my health or strength," I told those two good men. Then I shouted the same words to all others at the dining board: Dilks, Althorp, Jamie Gallant, Hicks, Downs, wee Fergus, McNulty, and the rest.

They all sat back and stared at me in silence.

I rose nervously and knelt down by the table and started singing a Dene death song, the one that Thana, herself, had taught me. I kept time to the words by beating my head against the table. Not too hard at first, but getting stronger. It didn't hurt me much but must have alarmed my companions, for James Knight and the surgeon grabbed me, and with others helped me to stand. I remember twisting hard against them while singing, screaming louder and louder, until I mistook myself for a howling wolf.

I heard Captain Knight order wee Fergus to quickly pull the shelves out of the tankard cupboard. When that was done, they forced me in and pegged the door tight shut. Finally, I fell silent in the narrow blackness. Where was Thana?

I heard Dr. Carruthers say, "He cannot hurt himself in there."

I started singing again, but this time I chose an ancient Highland lament. I was standing resting on my left side, watching the narrow crack of light around the door. When my throat grew raw, I stopped my singing and fell asleep.

When I woke, it was to a knocking on the cupboard door. "Are you all right in there, Willie?" It was James Knight's voice.

At first, I did not answer him. But when he called, Mister Stewart, I answered him quite smartly, saying, "Sir, I'm in much need of a chamber pot and then I would enjoy a mug of tea."

"He sounds greatly improved," I heard the surgeon say.

They knocked out the pegs that held the cupboard door and helped me to the bench beside the table.

After I had used the pot and drunk some tea, I felt strangely like another person. Something had gone numb inside my head, blocking off my memory of the past. A young Cree boy stood not far from me, someone whom I knew well and yet I could not recall his name.

I tried to eat a sea biscuit with sliced goose on top, but I could not manage half of it.

"You're going to live down here inside this fort, among all your friends," I heard James Knight say.

"I judge you shall feel much better in a week or so," the doctor added. "Just relax and try to think of gentle, pleasant pastimes."

I didn't answer either of them, for I was intent on watching Thana. She came walking quietly out of the shadows. She didn't speak, but smiled at me and sat down at the table very close to Jako and just across from me.

I called her name, quietly at first, saying, "So glad to see you here again. I thought perhaps I'd lost you."

But when she didn't answer me, I panicked and called loudly to her many times as I tried to crawl across the table.

Next thing I knew, there was a rumpus all around me and I found myself once more inside that tankard cupboard and heard them driving in the pegs that held fast the door.

When I awoke, I was tied into Mr. Kelsey's bed. Jako and Surgeon Carruthers were sitting one on either side of me.

313

"Did you see her?" I asked Jako.

He looked sad and shook his head.

"You only imagined that," said the doctor, and he unfolded a small square of paper and asked me to open my mouth. When I did, he poured in its powdered contents, then gave me water.

It didn't taste too bad at all.

"That should calm you, make you rest and sleep," he said. "It grows in India. The East India Company trades it to the Chinamen in Canton, who smoke it very gladly. The fumes, they say, make them feel quite calm, and they enjoy the pleasantest of dreams."

They told me that it was storming hard outside today, but that true spring should soon be on its way. I began to feel drowsy and my eyes kept closing. I don't remember them going away.

When I woke, I was alone. I thought, Thana used to be here, here in this same narrow bed. Where was she now? I easily untied my bonds and got up very quietly. I had no trouble finding all my clothing, which someone had hidden beneath the bed.

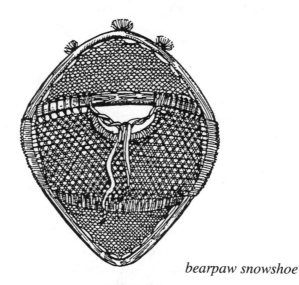

bearpaw snowshoe

I was cautious opening the door, but had no need to be because it was dark, and the parade ground inside the fort was filled with swirling snow. I went outside and found myself a pair of bearpaw snowshoes. It's well they're not my own, I thought, for I did not wish to mark my path with their distinctive Dene imprint, which a tracker like Keewatan or Cheechoo could so easily read and follow.

I carried the snowshoes until I let myself out through our shipwright's little secret door. It was blowing far harder outside the fort than I had imagined.

I planned to go and look for Thana in the Frenchmen's hut again, for it was the place that she loved best. I lashed my snowshoe bindings over the thick Dene moccasins that she had made for me. I stood up and turned several times around, then set off. If I did not find her there, she would surely come and find me as she had done before.

I started running west again, breaking trail as I veered into the north, propelled by the power of the storm. I kept my head down and my eyes closed mostly and listened to the wind's song as it hissed and whistled along the edges of the new-formed drifts.

As time went on, I grew immensely tired, though I now felt warm as though I were standing before a fire. Seating myself comfortably in a long drift, I watched as the snow slowly covered my legs. I tried to move them, but they were resting very peacefully. I tried to move one arm and then the other, but they just lay contentedly across my lap. Even my hood was filling up with snow. I did not care. I was warm and at peace at last.

I closed my eyes and when I opened them, everything in the world had changed. The snow had gone, and before me now I saw pale green caribou moss and bright fireweed blowing gently in the summer wind. Faintly at first, then growing clearer, I saw Thana. She was laughing and running toward me. In her arms she carried our child, Sheelaah. Before she reached me, she bent down and stood the child upon the ground. Sheelaah ran toward me, and I gathered her into my arms. Thana put her arms around the two of us. I thought, here we are, together again. Yes, I chose the right way this time, the only way that we could find each other.

EPILOGUE

William Stewart, or Stuart as he sometimes spelled it, Thana-delthur, the young Chipewyan woman, James Knight, and his deputy Henry Kelsey, Surgeon Carruthers, Accountant Althorp, as well as almost all the other characters in this book were real persons. From 1714 to 1717, they lived exciting and sometimes miserable lives in the vast uncharted wilderness beyond Fort York, or York Factory, running west of Hudson Bay.

This story attempts to illuminate the extensive record preserved in the letters and Hudson's Bay Company journals, to portray the human characters involved and the personal conflicts that threat-ened an existence so hazardous that bare survival was high achievement.

Governor Knight recorded in letters and his journal: "Thana-delthur, the Copper woman, rendered invaluable service to the Company by expanding trade northwest into unknown country." Besides the exploring party's quest "in search of beaver, mar-ten," they searched as well "to ye Westward of them, where the Indians did get Yellow Mettle."

William Stewart, after endless hardships and great personal joys, returned with Thanadelthur and the nine remaining Cree to Fort York on the 7th of May, 1716, accompanied by ten unknown Dene Indians.

Stewart's journal of that adventure has long since disappeared and was probably never sent to the Company's London committee. It may never be known exactly how far northwest Stewart's party journeyed. From his verbal report to Governor Knight, he reckoned it had been "700 miles into wooded country plentifull for beasts." He had apparently seen Great Slave Lake. "There we found ye tent with nine murdered Indians nearbye," and ventured no farther west. After their return, Knight wrote of Thanadelthur:

> *Wm. Stewart tells me he never See one of Such a Spirit in his Life. She kept all the . . . Cree . . . in Awe as she went with and never spared in Telling them of their Cowardly way of Killing her Country Men that he was Often Afraid that they would have killed her had I not given them such a Strict charge not to Abuse her and when she came with her Country Men to them She made them all Stand in fear of her she Scolded at Some and pushing of others that they all stood in fear and forced them to ye peace. Indeed She has a Divellish Spirit and I believe that if thare were but 50 of her Country Men of the Same Carriage and Resolution they would drive all the Northern Indians in America out of there Country.*

When she died, Stewart and Knight were left in deep despair. In his journal, the governor's entry read:

> *5th Febuary, 1717, York Factory. I am almost ready to break my heart. On this morning at the parting death of that good woman who was of the greatest courage and forecast that ever I see in all my days. This is the finest weather we have had any day this season, but the most melancholys't by the loss of her.*

Henry Kelsey's log informed the Company:

> *Wm. Stewart, poor man, had been lunatick three or four times and had to be locked in a cupboard or tied into bed before he died.*

Kelsey termed James Knight and William Stewart the gold and copper seekers, accusing them in his letters to London of having spoiled the Company's fur trade.

In 1720, James Knight set out in command of three smallish vessels, adventuring north and west. The *Albany* and *Discovery* were both shipwrecked in the autumn of that year near Marble Island, north of Fort Churchill. According to Eskimos, the men had got ashore and made shelters of clay and moss, but later died for want of proper food.

It is believed that William Stewart and the Copper woman, Thanadelthur, did return with articles of gold and copper and that James Knight was in search of a northwest passage to find more "Yellow Mettle" when he, too, met with death.

James Houston
Walrus Island
Hudson Bay, N.W.T.
September, 1988

ABOUT THE AUTHOR

James Houston, a Canadian author-artist, served with the Toronto Scottish Regiment in World War II, 1940–45, then lived among the Inuit of the Canadian Arctic for twelve years, nine as the first Civil Administrator of West Baffin Island, a territory of 65,000 square miles. He is widely acknowledged as the prime force in the development of Eskimo Art. He is past chairman of both the American Indian Arts Center and the Canadian Eskimo Arts Council and a director of the Association on American Indian Affairs. He had been honored with the American Indian and Eskimo Cultural Foundation Award, the 1979 Inuit Kuavati Award of Merit, and is an Officer of the Order of Canada.

He has lived and traveled throughout the Da-Dene linguistic world, one of the largest on earth, stretching from Chippewayan country on western Hudson's Bay to Tlingit-Haida areas on the Pacific Northwest Coast, to related tribal groups of Navaho and Apache.

Among his writings, *The White Dawn* has been published in thirty-one editions worldwide. That novel and *Ghost Fox, Spirit Wrestler* and *Eagle Song* have been selections of major book clubs. Author of more than a dozen children's books, he is the only person to have won the Canadian Library Association Book of The Year Award three times. He has also written screenplays for feature films, created numerous documentaries, and lectures widely.

319

Mr. Houston's drawings, engravings and paintings are internationally represented in many museums and private collections and appear in numerous books. He is Master Designer for Steuben Glass. He created the 70-foot-high central sculpture in the Glenbow-Alberta Art Museum.

He and his wife, Alice, divide the year between a colonial privateer's house in New England and a writing retreat on the bank of a salmon river on the Queen Charlotte Islands in northern British Columbia.